FROST FALLS AT THE POTTING SHED

FROST FALLS AT THE POTTING SHED

Jenny Kane

An Aria Book

First published in the UK in 2022 by Head of Zeus Ltd,
part of Bloomsbury Publishing Plc

9 7 5 3 1 2 4 6 8

A catalogue record for this book is available from the British Library.

ISBN (PB): 9781801102001
ISBN (E): 9781801101998

Cover design: Lindsey Spink

Typeset by Siliconchips Services Ltd UK

Printed and bound in Great Britain by
CPI Group (UK) Ltd, Croydon CR0 4YY

Head of Zeus Ltd
First Floor East
5–8 Hardwick Street
London EC1R 4RG

WWW.HEADOFZEUS.COM

To the good folk of The Old Well Garden Centre in Willand, Devon.

Thank you for the smiles, coffee and toast.

Prologue

'That's settled then.' Tony smiled as his younger daughter poured a fountain of tea into a row of mismatched china cups. 'You'll get the house and nursery Maddie, and Sabi, you'll inherit your mum's antique furniture and a portion of the profits from this place.'

Lifting their teacups as one, the Willand family clinked them together.

'How about a custard cream to seal the deal?' Maddie waved the regularly refilled biscuit tin towards her father. 'One or two?'

'Three.' Tony laughed as he took a handful of biscuits before passing the tin on to his son-in-law. 'Grab plenty Henry, or the girls will demolish the lot. I learnt that lesson a long time ago. I once witnessed them consume a packet of chocolate chip cookies in less than two minutes.'

'A slight exaggeration.' Maddie grinned at her brother-in-law. 'We were helping clear The Potting Shed's far polytunnel. Dad needed it done that day, I can't remember why now, but there was no time for a lunch break and biscuits were the easiest option.'

'*And* we were famished.' Sabi put her palm up, refusing the offer of a biscuit as the tin continued around the table.

'Are you sure you want to inherit all that hard work, Mads? I can't help thinking I got the better deal with Mum's furniture.'

'Only because you've gone off gardening. Anyway, Mum's things will look fabulous in your house.' Maddie gave her sister a hug. 'I can't wait to help Dad upgrade The Potting Shed from a nursery to a garden centre.'

'And I'm delighted to think the place will continue to flourish – or should I say blossom – long after I've gone.' Tony's habitual smile faded as he stared into his tea. 'I can't say discussing changes to my will is a fun way to spend a late Sunday afternoon, but once it's done we can forget all about it and get on with living.'

'When do you intend to start upgrading this place?' Henry flicked through a pile of scrap paper and old envelopes on which Tony and Maddie had scribbled their plans for changing their business – which currently provided seedlings, vegetables, potted bulbs, flowers and herbs to the local shopkeepers and hotels, as well as, at weekends, the general public – into a small garden centre.

'As soon as possible.' Tony refilled his teacup. 'It will take time to build up of course. But, if we are careful not to neglect our current customers, while expanding our range for sale on site, then I know we can do it. Might even have a café eventually.'

'Sounds fabulous.' Henry fished another biscuit from the tin.

Quiet for a moment, Tony turned to his daughters. 'You are both *completely* sure you're happy with these arrangements?'

'Totally.' Maddie looked at her sister.

'Absolutely,' Sabi agreed.

There was a clatter of china against china as Tony dropped his cup back into its saucer. 'Then tomorrow, I'll call our solicitor and set the wheels in motion. Then you and I, Maddie, can make a start on our plans.'

I

November: two years later

Pulling the hood of her coat up, Maddie ran across the nursery. Looking down at her wellington boots as she went, she splashed in as many puddles as possible, relishing the heavy patter of the rain as it bounced off her back and arms. A smile crossed her face for the first time in weeks. Her dad had always approved of her love of puddle splashing as she was growing up, and now, even at the age of twenty-nine, she still loved it. Some childhood habits were too good to break.

She couldn't remember the last time she'd been able to indulge in a proper welly walk; when she'd head out after a rainy day, bedecked in her blue and white stripy boots, to stamp the tensions of life away, jumping from puddle to puddle across the Devon countryside.

Maddie's smile faded. Now she had to manage The Potting Shed nursery without her father, she doubted she'd be able to do more than kick her way through the few potholes in the pathways between polytunnels whenever the urge to splash hit her.

Although he'd been gone for almost two years now, she still expected him to turn up next to her, helping to prick out seeds or drag bags of compost from one side of the nursery to the other.

She swallowed hard. No one had seen the heart attack coming – well – no one except her father himself. He'd known there was a chance – but even his doctor was surprised by how soon it had happened. Only three days after their family meeting to discuss changing his will, he'd gone.

Blowing out a ragged breath, Maddie came to a standstill and looked up. The rain, blowing in off the Blackdown Hills to the north, bounced off her face like a cold shower. 'At least Sabi was happy to keep things as we discussed rather than going with what your will actually states, Dad.' She wiped a gloved hand across her wet face. 'But we haven't got anywhere with upgrading The Potting Shed yet. The pandemic that hit China did reach us, just like you said it would – and then, well, nothing happened. Everything went on hold. But I'm going to make it happen, Dad. The Potting Shed *will* grow from a nursery providing plants for shops and hotels into a garden centre. A space for the community, just as we planned. I promise.'

'Queen of the Night?' Jake extracted the label that had been stuck into the box of bulbs as his boss arrived in the polytunnel. 'Your dad's favourite.'

'So they were.' Taking off her coat, Maddie gave it a good shake, spraying raindrops everywhere before hanging it over the handle of a fork that was propped by the doorway. She kept her eyes fixed on the tray of tulip bulbs, determined not to let the tears, which had flowed on and off with uncontrollable regularity for the past fortnight, return after her moment of welly booted elation.

Concentrating on the comforting patter of rain as it danced off the polytunnel's roof, Maddie slid a temperature gauge between the carefully netted bulbs. Inhaling the familiar scent of soil and stale, trapped air, she withdrew the device and examined its digital reading. 'At least these have stayed at the right temperature all autumn.'

Shifting his weight from foot to foot, Jake lifted a stack of flowerpots onto the work bench. 'Would you like me to pot them up for you?'

'No thanks, I'd rather like to do them this time if you don't mind. If you could make a start on checking to see if the other tulip bulbs have survived, that would be great. Normally we'd have these all potted on ready for spring by now, but...'

'No problem. I get it.'

Jake, clearly relieved at not having to make sympathetic small talk, strode to the far end of the tunnel. Maddie watched him through her rain-dampened fringe. Her father had been very fond of Jake, treating him like a son since he'd taken him on as a Saturday boy, four years ago, when he was just sixteen. She was sure he was still finding her father's absence from their lives as hard as she was, but accepted that he'd never say so. Expressions of emotion didn't match the tough-guy image Jake perpetuated; an image Maddie knew to be completely false.

Opening the net bag that had kept the tulip bulbs

protected since they'd finished flowering, Maddie laid them across the soil tray before her. The Queen of the Night tulips were well named. Their dark purple petals, with a slightly glossy sheen, made them a popular choice amongst the shopkeepers who came to her father's nursery to buy plant stocks to sell on.

My nursery now. Listening to the howling wind that had joined the rain hammering down outside, Maddie dug her fingers deep into the soil, savouring its texture and its warmth. Throughout her life, whenever she'd thought about her dad, she had always pictured him here, in this exact spot, with mud smeared over his hands, his fingernails so engrained with soil that the tips of his fingers had been permanently stained a dark brown. Tony Willand was usually whistling something tuneless as, with rolled up shirt sleeves, he potted bulbs, coaxed seedlings and muttered encouragement to their many plants.

Keeping her voice low, Maddie whispered to the tulip bulbs. 'You will grow for me, won't you? Dad was very fond of you. We can't let him down, can we?'

Taking a flowerpot in her hand, Maddie scooped up a portion of mud, knocking the pot edge against the side of the tray 'to settle the soil'. Her heart constricted as she heard her father's words in her ear. He'd taught her everything she knew about plants, her love of nature rivalling his own – so much so that she'd made it her career. Her degree in horticulture was as much his pride and joy as hers.

Gently lifting the first tulip bulb, Maddie checked it for signs of damage, before pushing it into the pot and covering it with more soil.

Dad's soil. His special mix. Part compost, part topsoil, part local soil. Organic.

Getting into a rhythm, filling one pot at a time, checking the bulb, and then lovingly bedding them into their new soil covered homes, ready to sell in time for flowering in late spring, Maddie felt some of the tension ease from her shoulders. This was ordinary. This was what she'd be doing even if...

He's gone. He's been gone for ages.

She thought back to their family meeting, when their expansion ideas had been mulled over and agreed, while eating biscuits in the kitchen of the house she and her father had shared. But those plans had never been formalised beyond scribbled notes on the backs of old envelopes and unwanted junk mail, and now...

'It's freezing in here.'

'Of course it is.' Maddie heard the distinctive sound of her sister's high-heeled boots as they made their awkward way across the uneven, wooden-planked floor. 'It's November, we are located in the dip between Exmoor and the Blackdown Hills, which is basically a wet weather trap, and the doors are open.'

'No need to be sarcastic, Mads.'

'Sorry.' Maddie threw her sister an apologetic look. 'Honestly, every time I think I have a handle on Dad not being here...'

'I know.' Hugging her thick Superdry coat around herself with one arm, Sabi dragged a paint-stained stool out from under the work bench, wiped the top free of soil ready to sit on it, before thinking better of the idea and pushing it back. 'The probate for the will taking so long to sort hasn't helped.'

'That's true.' Maddie kept her eyes on her work.

Sabi rubbed her hands up and down her arms. 'How can you be warm enough in just jeans and a jumper?'

'I'm busy. Work keeps me warm. Besides,' Maddie gestured to the small heater at her elbow, 'this helps, and it's a very thick jumper.'

'One of Dad's.'

Maddie nodded and carried on placing tulip bulbs into their pots.

Unable to put off the reason for her visit, Sabi spoke gently. 'I've heard from Lyle and Tate. Here.'

Maddie brushed soil from her palms before reluctantly taking a letter, addressed to them both, from Sabi's hands. A second later she thumped down onto a stool. 'Oh my God. That's a fortune. How can sorting Dad's will have cost so much?'

'It's not just that.' Sabi took a deep breath before pulling an envelope from her bag. 'A second bill came. For the inheritance tax.'

A cold sweat broke out on Maddie's brow as she extracted a sheet of paper from the envelope. 'How are we supposed to pay this? I mean, no one's been earning proper money over Covid and…'

Ignoring the mud, Sabi sat next to her sister and put a hand over her palm. 'We'll pay half each, yes?'

Maddie nodded dumbly.

'But…' Sabi licked her lips, '… the thing is Mads…. you'll have to sell. I mean, *we'll* have to sell.'

'Sell The Potting Shed?'

'It's the only way you'll be able to raise your half.'

Nausea vied with incomprehension in Maddie's head as she mumbled, 'You and Henry can afford your half then?'

'We have some savings that should cover it.'

Maddie's mind raced. 'You have savings, but I have to sell my livelihood?' She shook her head. 'No. There has to be another way. I'll get a loan.'

'But…'

'I'm not selling Dad's dream, Sabi. No.'

Sabi ran a hand through her hair. 'But you can't keep going, I mean, even without this blow The Potting Shed is in trouble. I've seen the books.'

Maddie's hands returned to her potting as she shook her head. 'Now the world is opening up again, things are improving. Jake and I have kept things ticking over. The local greengrocers still want the veg we grow to sell on. The two garden centres we supply in South Devon need the seedlings we set to sell to their customers. The hotels are reopening. Tim Robertson from the Blackdown Hotel has already been in touch to renew part of his regular veg order.'

'But, Mads…'

'No Sabi.' Maddie looked into her sister's eyes. 'You aren't here day after day. You aren't talking to the customers who tell us how glad they are that we are here. People came just for an excuse to walk around while we were mid-pandemic. Most of them bought something, even if it was just a handful of spuds for dinner.'

'I don't doubt it Mads.' Sabi sighed. 'And I agree. Goodness knows what I'd have done without my garden. My heart bleeds for people who were stuck in flats. How they've coped I do not know.'

A frown crossed Maddie's face. 'But you didn't come here much, did you? I thought you might have helped out. Work a bit, you know, just for fresh air if nothing else.'

Sabi bit her bottom lip. 'I wouldn't have wanted to be in the way.'

Maddie's eyebrow's shot up in surprise. 'Why would you have been in the way?'

'Well I…' Sabi stood back up. 'It doesn't matter, but these do.' She retrieved the bills from where Maddie had dropped them. 'These need paying.'

'I know.' Maddie gulped as she considered the sum again. Staring at her father's favourite plant bulbs, a new resolve took over. 'And the sooner we pay the better. Then I can get on with implementing Dad's dream. We've already delayed far too long.'

'What?' Sabi exhaled in surprise. 'Surely you can see that this place becoming a garden centre is impossible now?'

'Why not? It's what Dad wanted.' Maddie gaped at the closed expression that had settled on her sister's face. 'It's what I want too… and in the will it says…'

'It says that we have inherited half of the nursery each.'

Maddie couldn't believe what she was hearing. 'But we talked about it. Together. All of us. You, me, Henry and Dad. It was agreed that you didn't want to work at The Potting Shed, so I'd run the nursery and have the house, while you'd get all Mum's furniture – which is the only good stuff we had anyway – and you'd get a hefty chunk of the profits I make.'

'Yes, well… Dad didn't change the will did he?'

'We *agreed* though. We said that we'd act as if the will

had been changed. We…' Exhaustion hit Maddie in a wave, as the bulb she held slipped out of her hand, landing on the compost below.

'At the time we didn't know that the pandemic would hit Britain. So much has changed, and I've come to see that how things have been left is best for everyone.'

'Define "everyone".' Maddie lifted her head towards the lone figure of Jake in the distance, grateful that the headphones pumping music into his ears meant he wouldn't have heard their conversation. She could see his hands moving as he potted up trays of the variegated tulips they sold to the local greengrocers, who then did a roaring trade in selling them on.

'Don't be difficult, Mads.'

'Difficult?' Maddie pressed her palms flat into the soil.

'This place can't afford staff, and I am not willing to pay wages to those who don't deserve them.'

Taking hold of her sister's arm, Maddie grabbed her coat and towed Sabi from the polytunnel to the nearby shed-cum-greenhouse that doubled as a shop for their occasional customers.

'Don't you *dare* talk about Jake like that!'

'He's a lame duck! Dad only took him on because he felt sorry for him.'

Unlocking the shop's door at speed, Maddie shrugged off her wet coat and leant against the till's desk. 'Dad took Jake on because he knew the boy has a gift for plants. I have every intention of keeping him. I'd employ him full-time if I could afford the wages.'

'But he's a thug!'

'*What?*' Maddie wasn't sure she had heard right, and half-hoped that Sabi had said something else that she had misunderstood.

'Well, you only have to look at him.' Sabi pursed her lips in distaste. 'Shaved head, tattoo on his arm, grubby clothes...'

'Grubby clothes?' Maddie looked down at her own outfit. 'If grubby clothes make someone a thug, then you'll have to include me in that sweeping judgement – and Dad too, come to think about it! You can hardly spend all day working with soil and plants without getting a bit grubby, but we can usually be relied on to take a shower at the end of the day!'

Seeing Sabi's cheeks colour up, knowing that her sister was aware she'd let her prejudices run away with her mouth, but was too proud to backtrack, Maddie softened her tone. 'I don't want to argue, I really don't. Everywhere I look here I see Dad. I know it's a cliché but, even after all this time, I keep expecting him to walk through the door.'

'That's why I think my idea is such a good one. Honouring the will as it stands could help you move on from Dad's death. Let you get back to the life you had, before it went off course.'

'Off course?' Picking up a pile of post from the table, Maddie undid the first envelope, glad to have something to keep her fingers busy.

'You were a *head* gardener with the National Trust! You could go back. Doing a job you love, for good money. It had status and—'

'—and,' Maddie stood up the latest condolence card from a customer, 'it was something you could show off about at your bridge club: "my sister is a head gardener with the National Trust, you know".' She expertly mimicked Sabi's voice and mannerisms. It was cruel of her, she knew, but she couldn't help herself. Anyway, Sabi had asked for it by being so snobbish and superior.

'Don't be ridiculous, I can't stand bridge.'

Maddie's gaze fell on a pile of sympathy cards, stacked on a shelf beneath the desk, and sighed. 'I haven't been able to bring myself to throw these away.'

Taking one from the top, Sabi opened it, glanced inside, and sighed. 'Dad was popular, wasn't he?'

'And The Potting Shed still is.' Maddie looked around the cramped selling space. A rack of seed packets was propped against the opposite wall. A stack of poinsettias waited for new owners, ready to adorn Christmas tables in the coming weeks, and an order book for Christmas trees and holly sat open next to the till.

'But without Dad, it's unlikely to keep going.' Sabi lowered her gaze, not quite daring to look at her sister. 'Let's face it, custom has died right off without him. It's rather optimistic of you to have the shed open to the public outside of weekends. Dad never did.'

'True, but we need all the trade we can get now. Especially now.' She jabbed a finger at the rain-spotted bill Sabi clutched in her hand.

'But you can't sit in here all day in the hope of making a random sale. You have work to do with the plants so...'

'When I'm busy planting, I put the "Please ring the bell for service" sign up, but when I'm here sorting out stock lists and so on it might as well be open.'

'Makes sense,' Sabi conceded.

'I admit it's been slow rebooting trade, but we *are* getting there.' Maddie picked up the order book. 'See, we have loads of orders for fresh veg for Christmas. People are coming back. We had plans, Dad and I, you know we did, we were going to...'

'*Were* going to. Past tense, Maddie. Come on, be realistic. Dad's gone and there is no capital to do anything with, except get this place in good order so we can sell it.'

Maddie felt as if a bucket of cold water had been dumped on her head. She sat down heavily on the stool next to the till. She opened her mouth, but no words came out as Sabi carried on speaking.

'I miss Dad too, of course I do, but we have to face facts, the nursery is a small enterprise. You limped through lockdown, but be honest, it all but wiped out the nursery's finances and the solicitor's bills won't go away on their own. Henry and I have talked it over, and we've agreed it would be best for everyone if we sell up.'

'*You and Henry* decided?' Maddie checked her watch. 'When did you and your husband decide this?'

Folding her arms over her chest, Sabi pulled a face. 'We had a chat after this arrived this morning. Although...' Having the good grace to look sheepish, she added, '... we have talked about it before – thinking ahead to when probate was finally sorted and what that might mean for us all money wise.'

'And you didn't think to include me in any of these discussions about the potential removal of my livelihood. Not to mention your daughter's inheritance! Jem loves it here.'

Sabi sucked the cold air through her teeth. 'I do wish you wouldn't call her that. Her name is Jemima.'

'Don't change the subject! You know she loves it here. What if she wants to work here when she's older?'

'Come on Mads, by the time Jemima is ready to get a job this place will have folded! It's obvious.' Stamping her booted feet on the floor in an attempt to keep them warm, Sabi's voice became coaxing. 'Dad left you the house, so you could sell that too. You'd be quids in. Could buy anywhere you liked. Start again. Maybe find a man and—'

'Find a man? Start again?' Aware she was beginning to sound like a parrot, Maddie shook her head. 'I am not selling, Sabi. Not now, not ever. And as to a man… I tried that, remember. It didn't turn out to be for me.'

'I don't think you can dismiss all relationships just because you had one that didn't work. Broken hearts happen to everyone, Mads.'

'Well once was enough for me.'

'Umm.' Sabi ran a hand through her neatly layered bob. 'You probably need time to think. I understand that, but don't forget, you're already twenty-nine, if you don't move on from that toad Darren soon then—'

'I don't need time to think about him – *ever* – thank you. Dad dreamt of turning this place into a proper garden centre. A place for the community to come and learn about plants as well as buy them. I shared that dream, and I'm not going to let him down by giving up on it. That is what I need to think about.'

'Henry said you'd say that.'

'Your husband is a good person.'

'Meaning I'm not?' Sabi's eyes narrowed.

'Not at all.' Maddie was struggling to work out how they'd got to where they were. They'd always been so close – there for each other no matter what – but now… 'I simply meant that Henry understands how important the nursery was to Dad. *Is* to me.'

Sniffing, Sabi gestured around her. 'Look at this place Mads! *Really* look. The wooden fences are close to rotting, the polytunnels are tatty. Everything needs a facelift. The Potting Shed is not just failing, it's falling down. Sorting it out will cost money.'

Not wanting to see the truth of what her sister was saying, Maddie felt tears prick at the back of her eyes. 'How can you do this? Now? Just when I'm finally starting to turn this place around.'

'Because of these of course!' She smacked the bills onto the table. 'And because waiting isn't going to help pay them. If you want to save this place, you'd be starting from a place of being crippled in debt as well as feeling continuously bereft. Reminders of Dad are everywhere. Moving forward is the only way to deal with grief.'

Clutching a sympathy card to her chest, Maddie gritted her teeth. 'You're quoting to me out of a posh magazine aren't you?'

Not answering the question, Sabi fished a pair of leather gloves from her pocket and eased them over her slender fingers. 'I'll leave you to think.'

'Think?'

'Look Mads, I don't want to fall out with you over this, but the fact of the matter is that, despite what was said before he died, Dad ended up leaving The Potting Shed to us both. Equally. I appreciate you'll need time to adjust to the idea of selling up, so, in the meantime, I'll give you some breathing space.'

'But I...'

'I'll give you half of Mum's furniture back if it makes you feel better.'

'But...'

'Christmas. We'll do Christmas.'

'Why Christmas?' Maddie felt her throat go dry as she took in her sister's determined expression.

'We need to set a date, and Christmas seems as good a one as any. It'll give you enough time to sell off the existing stock and get your head around the idea of what you could do next. Then we'll put The Potting Shed on the market.'

2

'She made it sound like waiting until after Christmas was a generous gesture!'

The cloth-wrapped fruit canes made no response as Maddie made her way along the row, sweeping out leaves that had blown in between their pots.

'As if that would make giving up on Dad's legacy alright!'

Knocking the broom's head against the side of the polytunnel to dislodge some trapped twigs, Maddie brushed forward another raft of leaves, before getting onto her hands and knees and swapping the broom for a dustpan and brush.

'If only Sabi cared about the nursery like she did when we were kids.' Emptying a heap of autumnal foliage into a waiting bucket, Maddie's mind returned to the solicitors' fees and on to the solicitor himself.

Ronald Lyle had been The Potting Shed's legal representative since her father had started the business. Not that there had been much to do, but he'd been there, 'in case something crops up'. Ronald had known about the plans to develop the nursery, but there could be no denying the will hadn't been changed.

'Perhaps I should talk to Mr Lyle? See what he thinks

about me trying to keep going or selling up – if I have to. Maybe he'd let me pay his bill in instalments or something.'

Feeling disloyal to Sabi for even thinking about seeing their lawyer behind her back, Maddie swallowed. *I'm not being sneaky I'm just checking the facts – seeing what is involved in a sale. It's common sense.*

Brushing some soil from her palms, Maddie took her mobile from her back pocket. Since her father's heart attack her phone had seen more use than it had in years. Calls to the undertakers and solicitors in particular had become regular occurrences. Before that, with the exception of Sabi, Jake and Jem, Maddie's phone had only seen active service when summoning takeaways or ordering groceries for delivery.

Pressing the shortcut for the solicitor's office number, Maddie heard the line connect almost instantly.

'Good afternoon, Lyle and Tate, may I help you?'

'Hello, my name is Madeleine Willand, Mr Lyle oversaw my father's will and I wondered, well...' Maddie found herself floundering, unsure what she was asking for.

Clearly unfazed by the hesitation from their client, the secretary suggested, in a kind voice, 'You'd like to talk to Mr Lyle, perhaps?'

'Please.'

The sound of a few taps of a computer mouse came down the line. 'He has an appointment available on Friday next week.'

'Nothing sooner?' Maddie picked up a crisp fallen leaf and crumbled it through her fingers.

'I'm afraid not, he is very... oh, hang on... Yes. We had a cancellation last night that I haven't fed onto the system yet.

If you can come into Exeter first thing tomorrow morning. Nine o'clock any good?'

'That would be perfect, thank you.'

'May I ask what it's about?' The secretary calmly added, 'You are not obliged to tell me of course, but if I could give Mr Lyle some indication…'

'It's about my father's will. The way things were left was… unexpected. I have a few things to consider concerning the future of the family business.'

'Understood. I'll just say it's a consultation. That you are after advice rather than any sort of legal action.'

'That sounds ideal, thank you.'

'No problem, Miss Willand. We'll see you tomorrow.'

Sabi finished rubbing the gel into her hands and dropped the mini bottle of sanitiser back into her capacious handbag. The pub, on the outskirts of the village of Culmstock, boasted original Elizabethan fireplaces and period furniture, while the cushions, carpets and curtains gave the place an opulent yet homely quality that would have been any interior designer's dream. She could picture herself and her husband dining here on a regular basis, taking their time choosing from the Michelin-starred menu.

'It's beautiful, don't you think?' Miriam gestured a perfectly manicured hand around the room.

'It is. I can't believe I haven't come across it before. Henry would love it.'

'Historical chic. I'm thinking of writing a feature on the concept for *House and Home* magazine.'

Sabi raised the glass of raspberry gin that Miriam had

insisted she had instead of her usual glass of Merlot. 'I didn't know you were still writing articles.'

'Only when the subject is right.' Miriam brushed some non-existent dust from her lapel. 'I'm *so* lucky to have such great connections. They never say no when I send something in.'

Sabi sipped from the wide-brimmed glass and tried not to wince. It was far too sweet for her taste. Wishing, not for the first time, that her friend wasn't so definite about making decisions for other people, she said, 'Connections you worked hard to develop.'

'I knew you'd see that. *You* understand how challenging it can be to make sure the *right* people take notice. If only…' Miriam gave a dramatic sigh as she lifted her gin bowl and savoured the light scent of wild berries that it boasted. 'If only Petra would see that it takes time and effort to get where you want to be in life. Honestly, my daughter squanders every chance we give her.'

Sabi was taken aback that her best friend was admitting to any type of failure, even if that failure was her child's rather than her own. 'I thought Petra was doing well. A First, you said?'

'In English Literature. From Cambridge. Not an easy achievement. We wanted her to do Law, but we compromised and allowed her to study English on the agreement she did a solicitor's conversion course afterwards. *Far* more useful! But now she tells us, after all those years of us paying for her to do a pointless degree, that she never had any intention of becoming a lawyer.'

Sabi played with the stem of her glass. 'Not entirely pointless surely? Could Petra train to teach?'

'It would depend on the school she wanted to teach in. I don't need to tell you that some are very much better than others.' Miriam wrinkled her nose. 'You wait until Jemima is older. Anything and everything you do won't be good enough.'

'Believe me, I don't have to wait until then to feel like that. Jemima is fine – touch wood – but...' Sabi took a draught of gin, suddenly not sure she wanted to confide her own insecurities to the all-judging Miriam – but it was too late.

'Well, what, darling?'

'My father... I do miss him. Terribly. But he and Maddie had a way of making me feel I wasn't good enough. They talk – talked – about The Potting Shed being a family firm, but it wasn't. It's Maddie's and Dad's. They always made sure I was included, and yet, at the same time, I always felt that was *only* because they had to. They knew I didn't like getting my hands dirty and so I was in the way, even though there's much more to running a nursery than the actual gardening.'

'That was their failing.' Miriam gave a decisive shake of her head. 'You are perfectly good enough to do anything you put your mind to.'

'Oh.' Taken aback by her friend's forthrightness and confidence in her, Sabi was about to comment further, when Miriam lowered her glass to the table and leant forward, her voice conspiratorial.

'Sabi, I wonder, would you do me a favour?'

'If I can.'

'Whether you were made to feel unwanted or not, the fact is, you now own The Potting Shed...'

Shuffling deeper into the cushions on the settle, Sabi qualified her friend's statement. 'Part own, but yes.'

'Would you employ Petra? If she doesn't get out from under our feet soon, I'm going to go mad, and, frankly, it would teach her a much-needed lesson in how lucky she is. The idea of gardening would *appal* her, but if she had to do such a low-grade job for a while,' Miriam rubbed her hands, 'it might very well teach her a lesson while she's earning enough to pay for her own Christmas presents.'

Realising her confession had acted as an opening for Miriam to ask a favour, which she'd probably been intending to ask since they'd met that morning, feeling hurt that her father's livelihood was being belittled, and also grateful that Maddie wasn't there to hear her passion described as low grade, Sabi gave an internal sigh. But all the same, she had something she needed Miriam to help her with too, so...

'Of course. But you understand it will only be until we sell the nursery. There wouldn't be much for Petra to do.'

'I doubt she'll last a week. Thank you. Even having to put up with filthy, muddy clothes in the washing machine will be worth it to get her out of the house. I'll drop her off at nine o'clock on Monday morning.'

With a sense that she'd been railroaded, Sabi tried not to think about what Maddie might say. 'Actually, they start work at eight. And the pay isn't good.'

'Eight!' Miriam's over-plucked eyebrows shot upwards. 'In that case, Nigel will drop her off. The poor wages will be another good lesson for her. Now, talking of favours,' taking a last swig of gin, she scooped a set of keys from the table and swung them from the end of a red varnished fingernail, 'shall we take another look at that house?'

*

The drive curved to the right before straightening out and leading to the side of a detached Georgian dwelling, covered in wisteria. Bordered by a high stone wall, ensuring privacy, to Sabi it looked as if the doll's house she'd coveted while at school had grown to full size and was waiting for her to claim it.

The For Sale sign, which had *Superior Homes* emblazoned across it, was only recently installed. Miriam, who'd lined up the sale for the vendors, and knowing how Sabi had always admired the house, had warned her that the property would go fast. If she wanted to buy it, she'd have to put in a serious offer without delay.

Fighting the guilt nudging at her every time she remembered that she was only able to consider the purchase because her father had died before he'd had a chance to change his will, Sabi took the keys from Miriam's hand and, for the second time that day, slipped them into the lock.

Trailing a finger along the wooden bookcases that lined the wide hallway, suspecting they came from a library, and wondering if the absent owner would consider selling them with the property, Sabi made her way to the kitchen.

'You can see them, can't you?' Miriam beamed as she sat on a metal bar stool, smoothing her pencil skirt down a fraction as it threatened to ruck up and ruin the smooth line her slim body presented.

'Them?'

'Guests. Gathered around a polished oak table over there.' She pointed to a space by the large window that looked out over the part-lawned, part-paved garden.

'Chatting with friends and contacts from Henry's business, before moving through to the dining room, for meals and functions.'

As her friend spoke, Sabi could see it all. Even though it was smaller overall than her current home, it still had five bedrooms and a decent-sized garden. Everything about this house projected the image she'd been aspiring to since she'd left university. It had charm and character. Just one look at the exterior was enough to make any passers-by wish they lived there.

'Henry could have his own study.' Miriam jumped down from her stool and wandered towards the far right of the house.

'He already has one.' Sabi thought of the bedroom that they had converted into a study for Henry in their spacious modern home in the suburbs of Tiverton.

'Not like this he doesn't.' Miriam swung open the door, giving Sabi another glimpse of what would once have been, in a former age, the gentlemen's smoking room. A place in which the men of the house would drink port and smoke cigars, while the women retired to the drawing room to discuss the latest fashions and how to secure the best marriages for their daughters.

'Talking of Henry,' Miriam sat down in the desk chair – one that Sabi had already mentally replaced with a leather wingback armchair, 'what does he think? I wouldn't leave it too long before he comes for a viewing too.'

'Henry's busy this afternoon, catching up after losing the morning to the solicitor's appointment in Exeter. We'll discuss it this evening. I'm going to report back to him and we'll go from there.'

'Sensible.' Miriam opened the calendar on her phone. 'Shall I book you a joint viewing slot tomorrow?'

Mentally crossing her fingers, Sabi agreed. 'That would be lovely. Lunchtime if possible.'

Tapping her screen, Miriam scrolled through her diary. 'I can do one o'clock?'

'Perfect.'

'Excellent.' Miriam hooked a Dior handbag onto her shoulder. 'But don't spend too long thinking. To say thank you for helping me get Petra out from under my feet for a while, I will hold off other viewings for twenty-four hours, but after that, I'll have to open the sale to anyone and everyone.'

3

The kitchen table was always strewn with paperwork, seed packets, random lists scribbled on the backs of envelopes, bills and flyers for various unnecessary and unwanted goods. For the past year and a half, it had also been covered in drawings and lists. 'Plots and plans' her father had called them. They were all Maddie had left from their joint dream to expand The Potting Shed into something bigger than six polytunnels, a shed-come-shop, and a car park that, once a year, doubled as a sales area for Christmas trees.

Picking up the piece of paper nearest the top of the pile, Maddie felt her throat constrict as she read her father's handwriting out loud. 'Wild thought: convert house into flat upstairs and have a shop and café downstairs.'

Looking around her, Maddie knew it would have worked. There had been just the two of them and the house had four good-sized bedrooms. One could have become a living room and dining area, another a kitchen. That would have left them a bedroom each.

She hadn't touched anything on the table since her dad had died. Maddie had had to hold Sabi back from sweeping the whole lot into a black bin bag when she'd come around to help arrange the funeral.

Picking up a spider plant and weighing it in her hands to see if it needed more water, Maddie told it, 'I know Sabi isn't a bad person, but she never did understand Dad's need for clutter. It made him feel comfortable.'

Carrying the plant to the sink and adding some water, Maddie's eye caught a photograph propped up between two potted cacti in the windowsill. It showed her and her niece, Jem. They were standing next to two sunflowers that towered above them, wide beams on their faces.

'I *have* to make this place work. If I can show Sabi between now and Christmas that I can make a success of the nursery, then maybe she'll change her mind. Henry is minted, so it's not like she needs the money from the sale, and she'll get a share of our profits when they start to come in. I'd offer her a bigger portion of the takings if she'd let me keep going.'

Putting the spider plant back on its bookshelf home, she collected up her bag and slid on the only pair of shoes she owned that weren't covered in mud. Maddie had reached the front door when, on a whim, she turned back, gathered up her dad's notes for expansion, and threw them into her bag.

Refusing the secretary's offer of a cup of tea, for fear that she'd need to use the bathroom halfway through her meeting with Ronald Lyle, Maddie nervously fiddled with the page of a magazine she was pretending to read. She couldn't shake the idea that she was being disloyal to her sister.

She was disloyal first. Making plans for the future of the business without consulting me.

Even though that was true, Maddie didn't feel any better about sitting in the perfectly proportioned Victorian waiting room without having told anyone she was having this meeting. Her eye caught the carriage clock that sat at the exact centre of the mantelpiece. It was already 9.15am.

Perhaps I should just go.

Uncomfortable in her only pair of smart trousers and a crisp white shirt, Maddie lifted her handbag to her lap. She was about to make an excuse to leave, when she glimpsed her father's mishmash of plans lodged on top of her purse. A heavy sigh escaped her lips, making the secretary look up from her desk near the doorway.

'I'm sorry Miss Willand. I can't think where Mr Lyle has got to. He is expecting you.'

Blushing bright pink, Maddie got to her feet. 'Forgive me. I wasn't sighing at you. Perhaps I should come back another time. I really ought not...'

Maddie had just hooked her handbag onto her shoulder when the door to Ronald Lyle's junior partner's office opened.

'Miss Willand?'

'Yes.'

A tall, slim man, wearing a pale grey suit, was waving in her direction.

'My name's Edward Tate. Mr Lyle sends his apologies, but he's been called away. He asked me to see you, if you have no objection?'

'Oh, well I was just...' Maddie raised a hand towards the door, as if to indicate she was leaving.

'I have biscuits.' He jiggled a packet of chocolate digestives in a hand that had previously been hidden by the door.

Embarrassed on the junior solicitor's behalf, Maddie wondered how many of Ronald Lyle's regular clients preferred to wait a fortnight for him to be available rather than speak to his colleague. 'Sure, why not.'

Edward Tate's office was the polar opposite of his superior's. Whereas Ronald Lyle favoured an almost Sherlockian style, with deep seated wingback chairs for his clients to sit in, and a leather inlaid desk from which to attend to their needs, Mr Tate's domain was modern and light. It held comfortable, cream linen-covered Scandinavian-style chairs, and tastefully designed wall to ceiling bookshelves in a pale wood.

'Again, my apologies for not being Mr Lyle.' Edward Tate sat behind his desk, his large slim palms held out in front of him as if to emphasise his failure to be someone other than himself. 'How may I help you?'

'Well, it's a bit awkward.' Maddie shuffled forward, so she was perched on the very edge of her seat, as she struggled with a childish urge to make a run for the door.

'Trust me, Miss Willand, nearly everything I am told in this office is a bit awkward.'

Maddie gave an anxious smile. 'I'm sure.'

'My superior dealt with the contents of your father's will, I believe. My condolences.'

'Thank you.'

'Would you like some tea?' The solicitor smiled. 'It goes well with the biscuits.'

'Thank you.' Maddie dropped her tissue into a

conveniently placed waste bin. *I wonder how many tears get deposited in that bin?*

Getting up, Mr Tate headed, not out of the office to ask the receptionist to make the refreshments as Mr Lyle always did, but to a cupboard built into the wall nearest the window. As he flung open the door, Maddie saw a hotel-style setup of beverage-making equipment.

'I've offered tea, but it could just as easily be coffee or hot chocolate – if you don't mind the instant powdered variety?'

Maddie found herself smiling. 'Actually, an instant hot chocolate would go down a treat.'

'Excellent.' He picked up two sachets of hot chocolate powder. 'I can have one too, then.'

'Do you always choose the same drink as your clients?'

'To put them at their ease you mean?' Edward ripped open a packet, 'Sometimes. It depends on the subject and, to be honest, the age of the client in question. Today, I assure you, I genuinely fancy dunking a biscuit into hot chocolate. Will you allow me the indulgence of a dunk?'

Surprised to hear herself laugh, Maddie said, 'As long as I can dunk too, and I don't have to pay extra for someone to come and clean my crumbs from your carpet.'

'I promise, no cleaning costs will be added to your bill.' Stirring boiling water into two matching mugs, Mr Tate asked, 'So, what did you want to see Mr Lyle about?'

Taking the mug, its heat chasing away the cold in her hands, Maddie attempted to explain. 'I suspect I might be wasting your time. And mine come to that.'

'How about you tell me anyway? If I am unable to help, then at least you can go home knowing that you've got whatever it is off your chest and enjoyed a drink and a biscuit.' He took a tentative sip of his drink. 'How does that sound, Miss Willand?'

'Perfect. And please, call me Maddie.'

'Ed.'

Maddie blew across the top of her hot chocolate, sending the vapour dancing in wafts around her. 'Can I ask a question?'

'Please.'

'Lyle and Tate. A coincidence or…'

Ed laughed. 'Believe it or not, you are the first who has ever actually asked! Although sometimes we can see our clients *almost* asking – but not quite liking too. Surprisingly, I have not been the subject of "sugar" jokes since starting here, although my mates from uni had plenty to say on the subject when Mr Lyle took me on.'

'Suggesting Ronald only employed you as your surnames went together so well.'

'You've got it.' Ed grinned. 'Mind you, if it had been the other way round. If I'd been Lyle and he'd been Tate, he may have been put off by the dangers of infringing a trademark!'

Maddie laughed again as Ed picked up a sachet of sugar. 'See, we even use Tate and Lyle!'

'I should hope so too.' The moment's humour dissolved as Maddie remembered time was money in a solicitor's office. 'Maybe I should come to the point.'

'Fire away.'

'My father's will was left in a way that was unexpected. He died without having time to implement the changes he was about to make. Consequently, I find myself in a position of being pressured into selling the family business.'

'The Potting Shed nursery?' Ed pointed to his computer

screen. 'Mr Lyle sent me a few details over, but not, I should hasten to add, anything he considered too confidential. He wouldn't do that without your permission.' Ed ran a finger over the screen, as if underlining the point. 'And the permission of a Mrs Sabrina Willand-Harris.'

'My sister.'

'Am I to assume that Mrs Willand-Harris wishes to sell, while you do not?'

'That's right.' Maddie stared into her hot chocolate. 'I shouldn't be here really. She doesn't know.'

'I see.' Ed opened the packet of biscuits and eased a few onto a waiting plate. 'Please, help yourself.'

Taking a chocolate digestive, Maddie hovered it over her cup. 'My father and I planned to develop the nursery into a garden centre. It would be a prolonged process, developing a section of the site at a time.'

'And your sister does not wish this to happen?'

'The Potting Shed limped through the lockdown period. It didn't destroy us, but nor did it do more than cover the wages for my one member of staff and short-term subsistence. Consequently, we are not in the strong position we hoped to be. But I know Dad would have been determined to carry on anyway. He wanted to create a community space that was welcoming to everyone. Somewhere that would promote a love of nature, the outdoors and the beneficial qualities of gardening and being in the company of plants in general.'

Ed gestured towards the window. 'Human beings need the natural world, in all its forms.'

'Absolutely.' Maddie couldn't have agreed more. 'Well, my father, Sabi and I – with Sabi's husband, Henry – had a meeting two weeks before Dad died. In that meeting Dad and I explained our long-term plan for The Potting Shed. Sabi hasn't been interested in the nursery since she was a teenager, but her daughter, Jemima, loves it. At that meeting we agreed that the will would be changed, so that I would be left the nursery and the house, and Sabi would get a good cut of the profits, and so have a stake in the family firm, without having any say over how it was run. She'd also have inherited the few bits of furniture that had belonged to our mum.'

'And she was agreeable to these changes before your father died?'

'She was.' Maddie sucked at the edge of her biscuit for a second. 'But it makes no difference now. Dad had a heart attack before he could change his will and now, almost two years later, Sabi has decided she wants to sell. She has seen the company's books and knows the place is only just holding its own. The whole place needs a facelift and a massive dose of TLC.'

Ed picked up a pen, playing it between his fingers. 'And you came to see Mr Lyle today to enquire about belatedly contesting the will?'

Maddie clutched her mug tighter. 'No. The will was left how it was left. There was no double-dealing here. But it's taken so long to sort probate and the cost has been so high... then there's inheritance tax. Even having to pay half will wipe me out. I suppose I wanted to ask...' She paused. 'This is embarrassing.'

'Ask me anyway.'

'Could I have longer to pay my part of your fee? In instalments maybe, while we get back on our feet?' Maddie swallowed. 'While I get back on *my* feet I should say, and try to persuade Sabi not to sell, before she browbeats me into putting it onto the market after Christmas.'

'You intend to try and find a way forward? A way for you to implement your father's wishes and upgrade The Potting Shed despite the money issue?'

'I know it sounds mad, but I have to try. I suppose I could offer to buy Sabi out...' Her voice petered into silence.

'You'd rather that didn't have to happen though?'

'It's a family business. Dad would have loved Sabi to be part of it, and I'd still like Jem – my niece – to have some share of it in the future.'

'And to have any hope of that happening you need to prove to your sister by her imposed deadline of Christmas that you can turn the place around? Which, as it's the 24th of November today, is one month away.'

Daunted by hearing the short timeframe spoken aloud, Maddie took a bite from her biscuit as the solicitor continued.

'I can tell you that you are right about the will. Contesting it would not work. Realistically, has your sister given any indication that she might be willing to change her mind about selling?'

'No.'

Ed leant back in his seat. 'First off, you should be able to pay the inheritance tax bill in instalments. Secondly, I'll ask Mr Lyle if he'll consider an instalment system for payment. He might agree, but it's not something I can guarantee. I'm sorry.'

'Is that you being nice about saying there's not a hope in hell?'

'Possibly, but I will certainly enquire on your behalf.' Ed gave an encouraging smile. 'More positively, however, the bank might favour you. You could apply for a loan to pay off your debts – especially if the bank saw the nursery as a secure bet. A rise in profits before the end of the festive season would help impress them.'

'Would they give me enough to buy out my sister?'

'I couldn't say. However, you should be aware that would only be possible if she agreed to being bought out. The nursery is jointly hers.'

'Oh.' Digesting this information Maddie concentrated on dabbing some crumbs from her lap. 'I think I'll need a loan anyway, to pay for my part of the inheritance tax, make repairs and pay builders, architects and so on for the changes to the nursery we hoped to make. I had intended to ask my brother-in-law, Henry, to do that – he's an architect – but if they want to sell up, then that's no longer an option. I'm not sure the bank would lend me enough to do that as well as buy out Sabi – if she agrees to that.'

'Right then.' Ed took up a piece of paper and a pen. 'Let's get positive for a minute. In the short term the idea is to make the most you can of The Potting Shed as it is. Selling Christmas trees and so on in addition to your usual merchandise?'

'Yes. Holly too, but not mistletoe of course. I think it'll be a while before people are comfortable enough to encourage kisses from strangers.'

'I hadn't thought of that.' Ed's cheeks pinked and he muttered, 'What a shame.'

Maddie felt her face flush and her words speed up in response. 'I'm already doing well with poinsettias, and there's a lady in the village who sells her Christmas cards through me.'

'You may need more than that if you are going to bring in significant extra income.'

'Mr Tate, Ed, are you trying to tell me, in a nice way, that I may as well give in and do what my sister wants?'

'No.' Ed looked surprised. 'I'm sorry if I gave that impression. What I'm saying is, think through what else you could do to bring in revenue, because, even if you do ultimately intend to change The Potting Shed into a garden centre, if you haven't bought out your sister, you'll need her permission to do that.'

Maddie laid down her mug. 'I haven't thought this through, have I?'

'You are fairly recently bereaved and trying to keep hold of your father's dream. I'd say you are doing remarkably well on the thinking things through level.'

'Oh, thanks.'

'Now then, while I can't help you on the legal front, nor can I be the one to persuade your sister to keep things in the family, I have ten minutes before my next client, so I can help think up a few more ideas for boosting income. Sound good?'

4

Sabi held her breath. Usually, she had full confidence in her ability to persuade her husband to do anything she asked, but this was something rather more than a longed for holiday, or a dress she simply had to have. The second she'd seen the property come onto the market, the one she'd been in love with since she was a child, she should have called him. *Why didn't I?*

As Henry got out of the car and rested against its side, he gave his wife a knowing smile. 'How long before Miriam gets here?'

For a fraction of a second Sabi considered denying that her friend was coming, but thought better of it. 'How did you know?'

'Because you've been up to something for days, and we are parked outside a house with a *Superior Homes* For Sale sign outside.'

'Well, the thing is—'

'The *thing* is,' Henry interrupted as he pointed at the house, 'that this property is on the market with the same estate agents your best friend works for. How many times have you viewed it so far?'

'Three.' Sabi locked the car door. 'I know I should have said but...'

'But, as usual, Miriam has swept you along with the idea that we should be *seen* to be living in a certain way – her way, more often than not.' Putting an arm around his wife to take the sting from his words, Henry added, 'You do know that, just because you were close at university, that doesn't mean you have to do everything she says now.'

'I don't!'

'Darling, Miriam is a good soul at heart, but she has been steering your path for years. That was undoubtedly useful when you were the shy one at uni, who benefitted from a confident friend to get you through tutorials, but those days are gone. I don't mean to sound patronising darling, but you don't need to live in her shadow.'

'I don't! I'm not denying that her friendship at university was based on her inbuilt self-belief steering me along, but that was years ago. I still enjoy her company. Miriam and I like the same things and—'

Gently interrupting, Henry asked, 'Do you? Really? Have you told her you don't like flavoured gin yet? When was the last time you picked your own choice of food when you went to a restaurant with her, or came back from a shopping trip with the clothing you liked, rather than the clothing she liked you in?'

Neither confirming nor denying what they both knew to be the truth, Sabi waved a hand towards the beautifully proportioned home. 'Doesn't the wisteria look amazing? Even without its blooms and the leaves bronzed and semi-fallen, it's stunning. If I'm not mistaken, it's a Japanese

Wisteria. That means it'll produce a deep purple flower come spring. Royal Purple to be exact.'

'You learnt that from your father?'

'Yes.' Sabi lowered her eyes to the floor, as she produced a bunch of keys from her bag and waved them at her husband. 'Miriam entrusted the keys to me so we could take a look on our own.'

'Before we go in, can I ask, are we here because Miriam thinks you *should* like this house or because *you* like this house?'

Sabi looked her husband in the eye for the first time since they'd pulled onto the block-paved driveway. 'I've always loved this house. You know I have.'

'Darling, you may well have mentioned, on the odd occasion when we've driven past the place, that you think it pretty, but that does not mean that you haven't been influenced in that decision.'

Sabi drew her shoulders back. 'Henry, I promise you, I have *always* loved this house. The fact that Miriam works for the agents selling it is pure luck. Ask Jemima, she'll tell you. She loves this house too. It reminds me of a doll's house a friend at school had.'

Hearing that their daughter was also drawn to the house, Henry softened his tone as he studied the symmetrical windows that framed the front door. 'And that's why we're here? Because you want to check how much this place reminds you of said doll's house? A doll's house maybe you wanted and your parents couldn't afford?'

'It wasn't like that.' Knowing she was getting snappy because Henry was right, and feeling bad about not telling him from the start that she'd viewed the house, Sabi walked towards the front door. 'Shall we go in?'

Unlocking the door to the nursery's little shop, Maddie headed inside as she thought over the suggestions Ed had made. Ways that might boost The Potting Shed's income before Christmas. She doubted any of them would do more than give her a few more pounds' income, but it felt good to have something positive to consider.

Without bothering to go into the house to change out of her smart clothes, she perched on the stool by the till. As she looked at the piece of paper she'd scribbled Ed's ideas onto, she noted it was dotted with a light spray of hot chocolate. She hadn't remembered spilling any. 'Must have been when I was dunking my biscuit.'

It had seemed natural at the time, eating biscuits and sipping hot chocolate while mulling over ideas. Only now, back in the chilly reality of the nursery on a cool November lunchtime, did she realise it wasn't behaviour she associated with sitting in a lawyer's office. *Ed probably thinks I'm a slob.*

'He was only trying to help because I was obviously upset,' she told the row of cacti on the windowsill, each of which had been waiting to be sold for so long that she sometimes forgot thought they were stock rather than her own plants.

Picking up a pen she read through the list. 'Christmas trees we always do, so no changes there. Ditto poinsettias and bunches of holly. Mistletoe is a no again for this year at least.' Maddie decided not to dwell on the interesting colour Ed's cheeks had gone as they mentioned that plant. 'I'm not planning on being responsible for accidentally kicking off another surge in infections, but Christmas roses are good thinking.'

She started a new list, with 'Hellebores – a.k.a. Christmas Roses, various' at the top. 'Olive trees aren't a bad idea either…' Maddie made more notes.

'Christmas cacti?' She glanced back at the windowsill. 'Maybe not. Sorry guys, but you simply aren't selling, are you?'

Next on Ed's suggestion list was to make and sell Christmas wreaths. 'Nice idea, but do I have time? Would it be cost effective to make them, or cheaper to buy them readymade? Do I have the sort of customers who'd buy them? After all, most folk come here to buy stock or food for their businesses, not gifts for themselves.' She sighed. 'Maybe I should just concentrate on the veg and bulbs and stuff.'

Maddie looked back at the cacti. 'Well, you guys aren't exactly being helpful this morning. Some opinions wouldn't go amiss.'

Wishing her father was there to bounce ideas off, Maddie thought of the local shopkeepers who bought plants from her to sell on. Those that might want to sell festive wreaths had probably ordered them from elsewhere already. 'Would people who come here to buy their tree get one at the same time? And maybe some other goods too?' She drew a big question mark on the pad and moved onto the next item Ed had suggested. 'Bags of pinecones.'

She immediately found herself picturing the big chimney

breast in her sister's living room. Every Christmas she purchased new pinecones to sit pointlessly in two art deco bowls on either side of the hearth. 'Shame Sabi won't be supporting me, or she might help me sell things. I bet she could shift bags of pinecones as decorations to her yummy-mummy friends, especially if I sprayed them with some hideous fake scent or other.'

Maddie was just contemplating buying in some tinsel and baubles to sell alongside the plants, when common sense took over. 'Don't go too mad. First of all, find out how much it'll cost you to buy in the extra things on the list, then work out how much you'd have to charge for them to make it worth your while.'

Catching sight of her smart trousers as she looked down, Maddie got off the stool to go and change. Walking out of the shop she looked around her domain. There was not a soul to be seen. She only knew Jake was there because his heavy overcoat was folded up and shoved on a shelf behind the till.

With a heavy heart, trying to squash down the voice at the back of her head telling her Sabi was right, and the nursery was beyond saving, Maddie headed towards the reassuring comfort of a pair of worn-out jeans and a chunky jumper.

Henry looked out of the master bedroom's window in time to see a sleek black sports car park on the gravel drive. He knew it was Miriam even before she got out. It was a car he hadn't seen before, but that meant nothing. She changed her car as often as other people changed their mobile phones.

'She's here,' Henry called to his wife. 'Will you do me a favour?'

'Of course.' Sabi still felt guilty about the manner in which she'd sprung viewing a potential new home on him, and was relieved he had agreed to look round, even though he had firmly refused to make any promises about buying it. She stopped mentally planning where she'd place the new king-size bed they'd have to have for such a large room, and went to Henry's side. 'What's the favour?'

'Stall her.'

Sabi looked startled by the notion. 'I don't think that is physically possible.'

'Darling, I have looked at the house, and I have watched you looking at the house. I can see you're in love with it, but if you are just thinking you should love it because Miriam says you should…'

'Henry, I'd never…' She paused and rephrased her response into something more truthful. 'Not when it comes to our home, anyway.'

'Can you tell me what is wrong with our current home?'

Sabi was shocked. 'Nothing at all. I wasn't thinking of selling.'

Henry's forehead furrowed. 'Then why…?'

'Renting it out while we live here.' Sabi looked out of the window. Miriam was on her mobile. 'It's the best way to make money these days, and—'

'You want to go into property?' *So that's the seed that Miriam's planted in your head this time.*

'Yes.' Sabi smiled, her confidence returning. 'And with you being an architect and everything we'd be able to do our place up easily.'

Speaking fast, knowing there was a limit to how long even Miriam could spend on a phone call, Henry said, 'Our home does not need doing up, and even if it did, you know very well that my being an architect wouldn't help at all.'

'But it's a good idea isn't it, having a second home to rent out? Think of the things we could do with the extra money. The holidays we could go on! And it would help replenish our savings after paying Dad's inheritance tax.'

Henry wasn't sure if he felt exasperated, railroaded or both. 'Darling, while we are not short of money, we couldn't buy this one without selling our current place. Anyway, I'm not keen on moving out of Jemima's family home without consulting her first.'

'Obviously, I would include Jemima in any decision we made. But this place is perfect for us. You know it is.'

Henry looked around him. 'It is lovely, but be practical, we can't afford to buy this without selling our current home. It's not possible. Don't forget we have boarding school fees and a mortgage and, let's be practical, you do like the occasional shopping spree and holiday. There's no way the rent on our house would cover both the existing mortgage and the bigger one we'd have to get to buy this. I'm sorry, Sabi, we simply can't afford it.'

Sabi was filled with shame as she mumbled, 'We can once we've sold The Potting Shed. We'd be able to afford this *and* our current home. Especially if we rent our place out from the moment we've moved out to help pay the mortgage.'

'What?' A crease formed on Henry's forehead.

'I know we already have the money to pay to Lyle and Tate, but...'

'But we wouldn't get much for the nursery! It's rather

down on its luck to say the least.' Henry was looking dazed, as though someone had slapped him around the face repeatedly. 'And anyway, you said Maddie didn't want to sell.'

'I also said that she'd soon see sense. And I know it's not worth a fortune, but selling it now would bring us in more than if we wait for it to completely fall apart!' Staring around her, drinking in the perfect Georgian interior, picturing how she'd make it her own, Sabi headed down the stairs, calling over her shoulder. 'The Potting Shed has had its day, Henry. Now it's our turn.'

5

Jake stretched out his back and stood up straight. The spade he'd just scraped clean of mud rested against the wall, ready to be returned to its space in the tool shed. Wiping his hands on the old cloth he kept hanging from his leather belt, he peered around in surprise at the sound of a car arriving in the car park.

His heart sank as he recognised Henry Willand-Harris's Jaguar. While Jake quite liked Henry, his presence could herald the arrival of his wife, a woman who'd never made any secret of her dislike of his presence at The Potting Shed.

Wishing that Maddie hadn't chosen that moment to nip inside to fill a couple of flasks with tea, Jake braced himself for one of Sabi's disapproving looks. Seconds later, however, his mouth had fallen open and he was gawping.

A young woman had leapt out of the car, her expression one of deep concern as she called her thanks to Henry, before running towards the shed. 'Are you Jake?'

He was about to reply, amazed that a stranger would know his name, let alone a posh-sounding stranger with the face of an angel, but she was still talking.

'I'm so sorry! I wasn't late, Mr Willand-Harris was. And to be fair, he was only late because my mother got him talking about some house or other. Honestly! I wouldn't put it past her to have made me late on purpose. I'm Petra by the way.'

'Jake.'

'Yes, you said.' Petra looked around, her rush of conversation petering out. 'Is Maddie here?'

'Maddie?'

'Yes.' A crease formed in the middle of Petra's forehead. 'You did know I was coming, didn't you?'

'Um, no. Sorry. I'll fetch Maddie. She's just making tea.'

Leaving Petra where she was, Jake strode towards the house. He only just resisted the temptation to run.

Maddie was screwing the lid of Jake's flask down when her mobile burst into life. Her sister's name flashed across the screen.

'Hi Sabi.' Wondering if her sister had found out that she'd been to see a solicitor before she'd had the chance to confess, Maddie wrestled with keeping her voice light. 'I'm glad you rang. I want to talk to you about the nursery. I went to see if—'

'Never mind that now.' Sabi's words flew out in a manner that Maddie recognised from childhood. Her sister was about to drop her in it. 'I have a confession.'

Maddie's gut tied itself into a knot. *Has she already found someone to buy the nursery?* 'Go on.'

'I took on an extra member of staff and then got caught up with something and totally forgot to tell you.'

'You did *what?*!' Maddie rested her back against the

kitchen wall. 'Only two days ago you wanted me to get rid of Jake! Tell me you're joking.'

'Her name is Petra and—'

'Not Miriam's daughter?' Maddie couldn't believe what she was hearing.

'That's her. Anyway, she'll be with you any minute now.'

Maddie closed her eyes. 'With me, to do what?'

'Work. But don't worry, she won't last long. She just needs to be taught a lesson about knowing when she's well off.'

'And since when did The Potting Shed become a place to send spoilt children to be taught a—' The sound of Jake's boots being wiped on the kitchen mat stopped Maddie mid flow. 'Hang on Sabi.'

Turning to Jake, Maddie placed a hand over her mobile so her sister couldn't hear her. 'You okay?'

'There's a girl here. Says her name's Petra.'

Maddie fished her keys from her jacket pocket. 'Okay Jake. Maybe you could unlock the shop and ask her to wait in there.'

Jake hesitated, before asking, 'Is she working here now then?'

'Just go and check she's okay.' Maddie waved her phone in his direction. 'I'll let you know what's going on as soon as I find out myself.'

Hunching his shoulders, Jake took the keys, leaving at a rather slower pace than he'd arrived.

'Sabi, how am I supposed to pay another member of staff?' Furious with her sister, Maddie flicked the kettle back on, and took a third flask from the cupboard.

'Oh, it won't come to that.' Sabi dismissed the issue as irrelevant. 'I told you she won't last.'

'Can she garden? Does she know one end of a fork from another?'

'How should I know?'

'*What?* You agreed to this woman having a job here without checking her credentials?'

'It hardly matters now the place is going to close.'

Maddie felt sick as she protested. 'We haven't agreed to that yet. You said we'd leave it until after Christmas. I have every intention of showing you between now and then that this place is worth saving. I'd like us to meet up and discuss things.'

'We've already discussed it – why drag over it again? If you're worried, Henry will pay Petra's wages.'

Maddie opened her mouth to protest further, but the line was already dead.

Carrying three flasks bunched together in her hands, with an emergency packet of biscuits under her arm, Maddie was caught between seething anger and despair. While she and Sabi often had their differences, they'd never truly fallen out before – and although Sabi was much more comfortable living a life 'keeping up with the Joneses' and enjoying the benefits of her husband's substantial income than she was working at the nursery, she'd never been unsupportive of Maddie before.

When they'd been teenagers, they'd both enjoyed helping their father. Sabi had never minded getting her hands dirty and could cultivate the various flowers and vegetables with as green-fingered a touch as the rest of her family. It wasn't until she'd been to university, and seen the advantages that money could bring, that she'd swapped her jeans and wellington boots for designer trousers and heels.

Yet, even with their very different outlooks on life, Maddie couldn't square Sabi's current behaviour with the usual image of her sister. Even at her most unreasonable, she'd never simply foist a new member of staff on her – and the fact Sabi was willing to sell their family business without even giving her a chance to prove it could work again… It didn't make sense.

Maddie reined in her thoughts as she saw a young woman perched on the stool behind the till desk. Jake was nowhere to be seen.

Taking a deep breath, Maddie prepared herself to fire her latest employee before she'd even started.

Petra looked up at the woman approaching her. The nagging feeling that had started at the back of her mind on meeting Jake crystallised. 'You didn't know I was coming, did you?'

Wrong footed, Maddie almost denied it – almost blurted out that yes of course she knew, and she was so sorry for keeping her waiting – but something in her companion's expression stopped her. 'I didn't. At least, not until two minutes ago when my sister called me.'

Petra groaned. 'I'll swing for my mum one of these days.'

'Your mum?'

'It was her idea that Sabi employ me. I never dreamt that they hadn't asked you first.' A new thought hit Petra. 'You don't even need staff, do you?'

Putting the flasks on the desk, Maddie immediately felt sorry for the girl. If she'd been some sort of pawn in a game played by the formidable Miriam Reece, then she'd have stood very little chance.

'I don't.' Maddie waved a hand around the shed. 'As you can see, we are hardly beating customers off.'

'It's only half-past-eight in the morning.'

'Even so. During the week, unless I'm doing some paperwork in here, the shop is locked up. Anyone who comes to buy something rings the bell on the door and I hot foot it over from whichever polytunnel I'm working in.' Maddie pointed to the flasks. 'I didn't know if you liked tea, but I made you one anyway.'

'Thank you. I do.'

'Milk, no sugar?'

'Perfect.' Petra looked around her. 'Does a flask of tea mean I can stay and help today?'

Maddie looked at her unexpected guest with renewed interest. 'Would you like to? I got the impression that you'd been forced to come here.'

Petra smiled. 'Mum thinks this is a punishment. A way to show me which side my bread is buttered. She seemed happy to think that, so I let her think it. In fact,' Petra took a satisfying lungful of the damp peaty air, 'this is really rather wonderful.'

'It is?'

'I did an English degree. They wanted me to do law or medicine, but as I can't stand the sight of blood, that only left law.'

'But you did English?'

'After promising to do a conversion course later. A promise I've broken.'

'Ah.'

'I had several friends doing law. It didn't take long for me to know it was absolutely the last thing I want to spend the rest of my life doing. It sounded *so* dull!'

An image of Edward Tate munching biscuits and sipping hot chocolate flashed through Maddie's mind. 'Working in a nursery is rather different to that, or to studying literature for that matter.'

'I always wanted to work outside, preferably with plants.'

'Your parents wouldn't let you?'

'I never bothered wasting my breath. My path to adulthood was predestined from the second I was hatched and sent off to boarding school. I learnt early on which battles are worth fighting and which aren't.' Petra gave a wide smile at Maddie's appalled expression. 'Don't worry, I have a good life, had a great education, and my parents aren't bad people. They love me, I love them – but they are rather focused on what they think I *should* do with my life, rather than what I *actually* want to do with my life.'

'Ah.' Maddie's mind leapt to her niece. Sabi had posted Jem off to boarding school in the days after her eleventh birthday. *Was that simply because Miriam sent her child away to be educated, and Sabi likes to do what she does?*

'So, maybe this could be work experience or something?' Petra shrugged. 'Unless I'll be in the way. If that's the case, then I'll be on my way right now.'

Thinking of all the extra things she could be doing if Petra was happy to watch the till, Maddie said, 'Are you sure? Sabi said she'll pay your wages, but I doubt it'll be much.'

'It's fine, and anyway, I don't want to give my mum the satisfaction of going home without even completing the morning. I could paint the fence that runs around the car park or something.'

'Paint the fence?'

'It's a bit, um, flaky.' Worried she might have offended her new employer, Petra hastily added, 'I wasn't implying it was a mess or anything, I just thought…'

Brushing away the girl's discomfort, Maddie agreed, 'It does need painting. Has done for ages, but there's always something more urgent to do.' She placed the packet of biscuits on the desk. 'How good are you at social media?'

'Is that a trick question?' Petra grinned. 'I'm twenty-three – what do you think?'

'Fair enough.' Maddie laughed. 'What I meant was, I intend to order some Christmas stock, which should arrive at the weekend, but I haven't had the chance to advertise the fact. I wondered if…'

'On it.' Petra rubbed her hands. 'Laptop?'

'I'll fetch it.' Maddie smiled. Perhaps this wasn't such a bad idea. Having another pair of hands on site, even for a day, might be just what she needed – especially one she didn't have to pay for. 'Oh, if you get a customer, just ring the bell and I'll come running.'

'Or I could serve them. Is everything priced up?'

'Yes. And there's a bar code book for turf and soil and so on. But, as I said, customers outside of the weekend are not unheard of, but they are rare. Although we do get local shopkeepers coming by to collect stock they're pre-ordered.'

The sound of wheels crunching across the gravelled car park made Maddie check her watch as she got up and crossed to the doorway. 'That might be one of them now.'

Joining her new employer, Petra saw a small, thickset man with a friendly smile jumping out of a plain black van. 'Who's that?'

'That's Tim Robertson. He runs the Blackdown Hotel near Holywell. Gets stock for his kitchen from us direct.'

'Oh.' Petra's smile widened. 'I know Holywell. It's not too far from Wellington. Such a pretty village. I walk in the nature reserve up there sometimes.'

'Tim gets the majority of his root veg from us, and salad and herbs in season. He'll be here for his spuds.' Maddie waved a hand towards the approaching customer, before heading back into the shop with Petra. 'He'll go to the polytunnel first to pick up his sacks, then he'll come here to pay for them. The prices are in the book I showed you. Now I just need to show you how to use the till.'

'Oh, that's no problem.' Petra pressed three buttons and the dormant till sprang into life. 'Same make as the one I used when I worked at the Student Union bar.'

'Brilliant!' Maddie felt some of the tension in her shoulders begin to dissolve.

Petra winked. 'Only don't tell your sister I ever did anything as lowly as that!'

6

Jake was bent over a row of upright growing-sacks full of potatoes, adding extra canes to support the heavy stems of the leaves. Checking to make sure that the sacks were doing their job, and helping keep pests away, Jake nodded in satisfaction. In a few days he would cut the leaves back, and soon after that the late crop would be ready to harvest and sell on to the local greengrocer, as well as the two hotels that The Potting Shed had kept in winter vegetables for several years.

'Your tea.' Maddie placed a flask on the tunnel's work bench. 'You've done a fabulous job in here, thank you. Dad would've been proud.'

Jake ignored the thanks. 'Is that girl working here now?'

'Petra.' Maddie knew Jake wasn't going to find working with someone else easy. 'Just for a while. My sister sorted it. I didn't tell you because Sabi didn't tell me.'

Giving a short *humph*, Jake asked, 'What does she know about gardening?'

'I haven't had the chance to find out. For now, she's looking after the shop. I've ordered in a few extra things to sell in the run-up to Christmas, so Petra's doing some marketing for me while we can get on with tending to the nursery.'

I bet she's good at it too. I bet she's good at everything. Jake's eyes narrowed as he pressed his palms against the soil in the top of the potato sacks. 'As long as she keeps away from my plants.'

Maddie flexed her legs and stood up from where she'd been squatting, tidying the rows of raised beds. They were now, ready to be covered and left until it was time to sow new seeds.

Running an eye along the neatly tilled bed, Maddie would not allow herself to consider the job pointless. 'I will carry on as if we are going to be here in the spring. I have to.'

Sweeping the space around her feet clear of spilt soil, Maddie's mind flew back to the list she'd made of extra items to sell in the short term. It would have been nice to be able to talk through her ideas further, but Jake wasn't the most communicative workmate at the best of times, and Petra had only just arrived. Sabi would normally be her first point of call with anything remotely interior designish – a category Maddie threw Christmas decorations into. Now that she thought further, she could also buy in some garlands for draping across fireplaces. They might go down well if she had a way into the right sort of market to sell them too.

I wonder what Ed would say about...

Maddie stopped her thought mid-sentence and gave herself a shake. She'd been aware of her replacement solicitor popping into her head at regular intervals. *It was nice having someone of my own age to talk to – that's all – there's nothing surprising in that. It does not mean he'd be open to calls asking opinions on additional Christmas decor to sell!*

Tapping the contents of her dustpan into a bucket at the side of the polytunnel, Maddie found herself questioning when she had last had a conversation with a man who wasn't Jake, her father, or a customer – most of whom seemed to fall into the pensioner category. An image of her one and only serious boyfriend passed through her head. She shook the vision away.

I might like some male company every now and then, but I'm not going down the boyfriend route again – full stop.

Brushing the mud off her hands, deciding she ought to go and check on Petra, Maddie looked about her. The polytunnel she was in was ready to be shut down for the winter. She could hear her father's voice listing off the jobs still needing to be done in preparation for spring.

I can't give up this place. I can't.

The sound of voices in cheerful conversation floated across the open space between the nursery and the polytunnels. Maddie slowed her pace, torn between rushing forward to ensure Petra had all the information she needed to complete any sale she might be making, and not wanting to interrupt if she was in full flow with a customer.

Laughter followed a pause, and a moment later, Mr

Peters, one of The Potting Shed's regular customers, left the shop with a cardboard box full of purchases in his hands.

'How on earth did you manage that?' Maddie beamed at Petra as she joined her in the shed. 'I've never known Mr Peters buy anything beyond his weekly bag of mixed veg.'

Petra grinned. 'He's such a sweetie! I persuaded him his wife was in dire need of a houseplant or two. Something low maintenance to cheer up the windowsill during the winter months.'

Maddie followed the wave of Petra's arm. 'You sold the cacti! Wow! They have been here so long that I'd given up all hope.'

'Really?' Petra's eyebrows rose. 'But they're so lovely. Especially the ones with little flowers.'

'To be honest, it was pure fluke they were flowering. It doesn't happen often.'

'What a shame. So pretty.'

'I had wondered about getting in a few Christmas cacti – they are the only cacti that flower naturally in December.'

Petra picked up a catalogue from the desk. 'I've been flicking through this. Shall I see if they have them in here?' She started to thumb the thin pages of the thick volume. 'Do they have a special name?'

'Yes. Schlumbergera.' Maddie pulled out a stool and sat down. 'I'm sorry I abandoned you as soon as you arrived, Petra.'

'Not at all. I was landed on you, and I'm sure there are jobs that have to be done in a place like this on a daily basis.'

'The seasons do rather dictate the pace.'

'And the pace is always full on?'

'You've got it.' Maddie warmed further to the young woman. 'I can't thank you enough for selling something this morning.'

Petra's eyes widened, 'It can't be that unusual surely?'

'It's always a bit sluggish between the end of the autumn and the start of Christmas sales when it comes to drop in trade.'

Changing the subject, Maddie asked, 'Apart from performing a miracle cacti sale, how's it gone this last hour?'

'The postman came.' She gestured to a pile of mail on the desk. 'It looks like mostly junk stuff, although I haven't gone through it.'

'I'll flick through later. Thanks.'

Petra shifted self-consciously. 'And, umm, I hope you don't mind, but I couldn't help noticing you don't have the biggest sign on display outside. If I hadn't been searching for this place when Henry dropped me off, I wouldn't have seen it.'

Wishing she could deny it, but knowing she couldn't, Maddie admitted, 'It is a bit worn out, but most of the people that come here have been doing so for years, so they know where we are.'

Petra nodded. 'How about this instead?' She opened a tab on the laptop. 'It's not that expensive and, more to the point, it's big and the font is clear.'

A photograph of an arched sign with 'Greenways Lawnmowers' written across it in large script was both clear and inviting.

'You could get Jake to fix one to the front of the shop

– it's big enough, and would be high enough, to be seen from the road.'

Maddie looked thoughtfully at the sign. On closer examination she saw it was made of a thick plastic, although it looked like wrought iron and wood. 'How much would something like that be?' Maddie could imagine Sabi's reaction to her making such a purchase.

'There's a sale on, so they're one hundred and fifty pounds instead of three hundred. Half price.'

'Still not cheap.' Maddie's eye fell on the list of Ed's ideas on the desk near the till. 'But if I am going to turn the sales around and put this place on the map...'

As Maddie's words trailed off into thought, Petra said, 'If you're thinking of expanding the Christmas range then you'll need people to come and buy them. For that, you need to be visible.'

Petra's enthusiasm was infectious, and Maddie found herself saying, 'True enough. How long does it take to deliver, and is there a shipping cost?'

'Hang on.' Petra tapped a few keys before saying, 'No shipping fee during the sale. They are fairly local, so even with inscription time they'd be here in... three to six days.'

Maddie shuffled her stool closer to the laptop and pointed to a similar sign with a clearer script. 'I like how they have this one. We could have the same design, but with the wording saying, "The Potting Shed".'

'Sounds good. Shall I order?'

Maddie bit her lip. 'Do it!'

'Fabulous.' Petra's face lit up.

'Did you get an ad out on Facebook?'

Suddenly Petra looked unsure. 'I designed one, but I haven't posted it yet. Thought I should show you first.' Seconds later Maddie was looking at a professionally designed poster, which retained a beautiful simplicity, while still giving out all the information required about Christmas gifts being available soon, as well as a little map showing the location of The Potting Shed and their opening hours and email address.

'It's fabulous. Can you put it on our Facebook page?'

'Sure.' Petra tapped on the keyboard as she went on, 'I didn't put on a website address, because I wasn't sure what it was.'

'Ah.'

This time Petra was openly shocked. 'There isn't a website?'

'Never had five minutes to sort one out and...'

Petra finished the sentence, '... you had regular customers, so you didn't need one.'

'Hearing you say it makes it sound so feeble, but we were doing so well before and we couldn't have handled the extra trade.'

'I could sort one for you, but you'd have to pay out for a domain name and so on, and, well, the thing is...'

'The thing is?'

'I'd sort of assumed I'd be working with plants and so on.' Petra hastily added, 'Not that I mind doing this or anything, but...'

'But if you'd wanted to sit at a laptop all day, you'd have taken the law conversion course.'

'Yeah.' Changing the subject, Petra asked, 'Where's Jake?'

'He's tending the winter veg.' Maddie pointed to a row

of empty wooden boxes that ran along the left side of the shop. 'We'll soon be selling our winter potatoes. Jake's a dab hand with spuds.'

'He doesn't want me here, does he?'

Knowing she was right, Maddie tried to sound surprised when she asked, 'Why do you say that?'

'The less than thrilled vibe he gave out on my arrival for one. Then, he came in searching for you while I was doing the poster. Took one look at me and mumbled something about needing to see someone who knows what they're doing and left again before I found out what he wanted.'

'Oh. I'm sorry.' Wondering if Petra's ability to grasp a situation at speed was always such a good thing, Maddie said, 'He's worked for my father for four years. Part time, although he's often here far longer than he needs to be. Jake often turns up on Mondays, even though we are closed that day and he isn't employed to work then.'

'Part time.' Petra sucked in her bottom lip. 'Mum told me I was full time, but I don't have to be. If Jake is being distant because he's put out that I have longer hours than him, then I'll go to the nearest café and hang out until five.'

Maddie, who'd assumed Petra would be part time, privately cursed her sister further. 'Jake's only part time because I can't afford for him to be anything else. I know you said I didn't need to pay you, but you've already worked wonders, so not paying just isn't on, but full time is...'

'Impossible financially? I'll work full-time and get paid part-time. Simple.'

'I can't do that to you!'

'Alright, so I work part-time and volunteer part-time. Maybe you could pay me back by teaching me all you know?' Petra grinned, brushing a stray hair from her eyes. 'Problem solved?'

'Problem solved.' Maddie smiled at her newest employee, while wondering if Sabi really would persuade Henry to pay Petra, and what Jake would say when he found out Petra would be around all day.

More like problem half-solved.

7

Having left Petra with her business bank card ordering two dozen Christmas cacti, some Christmas roses, six small olive trees and a sack of pinecones, tinsel garlands, wrapping paper and gift tags, Maddie now stood in front of the house she'd shared with her father, trying not to think about the money that was about to be spent.

Built in the Seventies, it had been constructed with a view to practicality rather than to be pleasing on the eye. The part-brick, part-white boarded building formed a slim rectangle, with its front door in the middle of the short end, rather than in the centre of the long side. Realising she hadn't truly looked for years at the place she'd lived in all her life, she knew that if she'd been a child drawing the house, she'd instinctively have put the door in the centre of the long side of the house.

'Would that be where it would have to be if I converted the building to form the basis of the garden centre?' Maddie mumbled to herself, picturing a set of double doors before her, probably glass, to let in more light. 'The doorway could lead into a wide space full of seed-packet racks, decorative flowerpots, small tools and, perhaps, wellington boots and gardening gloves.'

Mentally going through the non-existent doors, Maddie swivelled right, imagining a till, tucked in the corner, with a range of houseplants and cacti, along with a rack of information sheets on how to tend various aspects of the garden. 'Maybe I could provide information packs for children as well. How to grow cress, sunflowers and herbs and such... Maybe, they should have stickers in them? Perhaps some colouring-in sheets for the younger ones?'

Swivelling to her left, Maddie walked her mind into the rarely used dining room and began to convert it, linking it to the adjoining kitchen, to form a small café. A space she and her father had always imagined would be hired out to community groups as well as used by shoppers wanting a quick caffeine injection.

Squashing back the nagging voice at the back of her head that told her she was wasting her time, Maddie was just wondering how much work it would cost to convert the downstairs toilet into a public washroom, when the sound of boots crunching across gravel drew her from her thoughts.

'Ed?' A second's feeling of pleasant surprise at seeing her solicitor was immediately replaced with a sense of dread. *Has Sabi made steps towards the sale already?*

Holding his palms up in supplication, Ed gave a shy smile. 'No need to look so worried, this isn't official business. I was passing and my curiosity got the better of me.'

'Just passing?' Maddie returned his smile. Aware that her hands were streaked with mud, she was grateful that the idea of shaking hands hadn't come back into vogue after the lingering effects of the pandemic.

'Okay, I admit it.' Ed looked faintly embarrassed as he

confessed. 'I wasn't passing, I'm here on purpose. I was curious. You spoke so passionately about this place that I wanted to see it for myself.'

'Oh.' Maddie wasn't sure what else to say.

'Although, I can tell you that Mr Lyle is happy for you to pay our bill by instalments – but the inheritance tax needs paying in full on time.' He shrugged apologetically.

'Well, that's more than I hoped for. Thank you. And thank Mr Lyle for me.'

'My pleasure. I'll be in touch next week with a revised bill for your half. Your sister has settled her portion.'

Registering that Ed wasn't wearing a suit, so this had to be his day off, Maddie took in his navy jumper and slim-fit jeans. He seemed taller than he had in the solicitor's office. *Why has he chosen to come to see the nursery when he could be doing anything he likes?* Wanting to know the answer to her thoughts, but not wanting to ask in case he was simply lonely and bored and saw coming here as an alternative to daytime television, Maddie gave herself a mental shake.

'Any chance of a tour then?'

Suddenly conscious that she'd been staring up at him without speaking for rather too long, Maddie fell back on Ed's suggestion with a sense of relief. 'Yes of course. Sorry, I was miles away.'

'Planning how to save this place?'

'Sort of.' Maddie rubbed the toe of one boot against the back of the other as she gestured towards the house. 'I was getting a bit ahead of myself. Wishful thinking, I suppose.'

Ed flashed a quick smile before following the direction of her outstretched arm. 'There is nothing wrong with wishful thinking. Nothing would happen if people didn't dream.'

'Normally I'd agree, but my dream has every chance of becoming a fantasy.'

'There's nothing wrong with fantasies either.'

Maddie felt herself go hot. There was something about the way Ed had said 'fantasies' that was doing complicated things to her insides. Without looking at him, she swivelled to her right. 'I've closed this polytunnel for the winter, but you can have a look inside if you'd like to.'

'And the rest of the place?'

'Sure.' Maddie wiped her palms together. 'It's quite cold. Don't you want to grab a jacket or something?'

'I'm fine thanks. I've never really felt the cold.'

'But there's nothing of you.' The words had left Maddie's mouth before she'd had the chance to consider she might be insulting him. 'Oh, I'm so sorry, I…'

Laughing, Ed interrupted, 'It's true. I eat and eat, but nothing happens. Even though I'm thirty-three and haven't grown so much as a millimetre since I was nineteen, my mum still insists I've stretched another inch higher every time I see her. Dad tells me that my neighbours regularly hear her say, "My boy grows up instead of out".'

'Many would envy you that.' Maddie considered her decidedly average frame.

Ed grinned wider. 'If there was a way to bottle my metabolism, I'd make a fortune. As it is, I'll have to carry on sorting out wills, conveyancing and getting to grips with the finer points of business law.'

'While drinking hot chocolate in secret?'

'And dunking chocolate biscuits.'

'Naturally.' Maddie smiled as she recalled the conspiratorial feeling they'd had in his office – as if the consumption of anything other than a cup of tea in such surroundings was a deliciously shared secret. She checked the time on her watch. 'About now I tend to put the kettle on to make Jake and me a cuppa. Fancy having a hot drink to hand while I give you the grand tour?'

'I'd love one, thank you.' Ed fell into step with Maddie. 'Perhaps we should take one for the lass in your little shop too.'

'Petra.' Maddie was embarrassed to find she'd temporarily forgotten about her new helper. 'She started today.'

'New staff?' If he was surprised, he didn't show it.

'It's a long story.' Maddie was surprised to find she wanted to tell Ed all about it.

Sabi sat at her kitchen table, the winter sunshine streaming in through the window over her shoulder. As she flicked on her laptop, a sense of excitement shot through her.

It had been easier than she'd feared to convince Henry that they could move, although he remained adamant that her idea about renting their current home out rather than selling it to pay for the move was one dream too far. Yet Sabi remained positive that, once she'd done her homework, and showed him how much they could earn from using it as an exclusive holiday let for exhausted executives wanting to escape city living for a while, Henry would see how the rental they could charge would pay their new mortgage for them. *We've already paid our half of Dad's legal fees. Surely we can afford this too. And if we can't, the bank would give us a loan for the shortfall, which we'd pay off in no time.*

Sabi looked around the room, imagining future guests

savouring its beauty, and envying them for owning such a beautiful place. *If Henry is right, we'll have to sell it though.*

She loved her home, especially her kitchen. The Aga she'd coveted for so long had been in place for over a year now. Bright red, its constant steady heat was like a comfort blanket. Everything in the room complemented everything else in shades of cream, with an occasional hint of red picked up here and there in the tiles that formed a splash guard above the Belfast sink, and the ornate doorknobs that had been handcrafted by a local ceramicist.

Sabi experienced a tug of regret at the idea of leaving her perfect kitchen behind, until her eyes lowered to the laptop screen, and a picture of her dream house appeared before her. It would be fun making it into the home she'd always wanted. A blank canvas on which to unleash all her creative urges. Interior design had been both a skill and a passion since she was a teenager. She had always instinctively known what went with what, unlike her sister who, when it came to being indoors, had always been happy to live amongst a clashing cornucopia of colours and objects. In the garden, however, there was no doubt that Maddie knew exactly what went with what.

Thinking about Maddie sent a ripple of disquiet through Sabi. Whichever way she looked at it, she couldn't escape the certainty that, by insisting they sell the nursery, she would break her sister's heart. Yet at the same time Sabi was convinced it was the right thing to do.

'Cruel to be kind.' She muttered the words to herself, knowing full well that once she told Maddie that she and Henry intended to use the nursery money for a second home, she'd never believe the timing was coincidence.

How am I going to make her see that I'd have wanted to buy the house anyway, even if the idea of giving up The Potting Shed hadn't come up? Sabi pressed a few keys on her laptop, bringing up her email. 'I wish Maddie could see that I want to sell for her good as well as my own. The nursery has become a millstone around her neck. It's stopping her having the life she should be living.'

Saying the words out loud didn't make Sabi feel any better about the sale. She wasn't looking forward to telling her daughter about her plans either. Jemima loved her aunt and The Potting Shed. 'It's best for her too. Why should I risk my child being saddled with a failing business on the off chance that she turns out to be the only person Maddie can leave it to?'

The sound of some post being deposited through the letterbox sent Sabi to the front door. A minute later, she was opening a crisp white envelope, addressed to her and her sister.

Assuming it was from the solicitor's office, Sabi was surprised to find herself reading a letter which began:

RE: BIG: Interest in nursery purchase.

Two minutes later she picked up the telephone.

'Hello. This is Mrs Sabrina Willand-Harris. I've had a letter from a Mr Leo Creswell on behalf of the garden centre chain, Big in Gardens. Is he available to speak to me, please?'

8

'I don't even like broad beans.' Ed posted a bean into the space Maddie had made with a wooden dibber. Following her along the row, he popped a bean into each new dip and covered it with a handful of soil.

'Nor do I,' Maddie confessed as she made a hole in the final pot of the run of twenty-five plants. 'They sell well though. People buy them to plant in their allotments and gardens. They're so easy to grow – and some people find them delicious, even if we think they're disgusting.'

Ed laughed. 'My parents grow their own veg. It always tastes better than when you buy it from the supermarket.'

'It does.'

'Is this why the nursery is called The Potting Shed?' Ed smiled as he picked up a pile of flowerpots waiting to be filled from the potting bench.

'Sort of, although this polytunnel isn't the original "shed". When Dad started the business it was just him in the shed that is now the shop. It was simply a large wooden garden shed back then with a tiny sign over the door saying, "The Potting Shed". Dad would plant everything up in there, then move the plants to his one small polytunnel to grow on. The shed was extended into the part-brick, part-glass structure that is now the shop when I was ten. Same time the extra polytunnels went up.'

As Maddie looked at the completed set of plants laid out in a line before her, the camaraderie of their companionable stroll around the nursery, chatting about what needed improving, mending or expanding, suddenly became eclipsed by the same sinking sensation she'd experienced while preparing the seedbeds for the spring in the closed polytunnel.

'Are you alright?' Not caring that he was messing up his clothes, Ed smeared soil-stained hands across his jumper. 'You've gone a bit pale.'

'I'm not sure why I'm doing this.' She gestured to the pots. 'Reminiscing is all very well, but if Sabi has her way, this will all be someone else's problem by January.'

Ed picked up the nearest pot, studying the space where, in time, a broad bean plant would emerge through the earth. 'It does seem a shame, I've only been here an hour and I can see how much potential The Potting Shed has, not to mention how much you love it.'

'Yeah, well,' Maddie sighed, 'fun as it was talking about my dreams, Sabi is right about the nursery suffering after the lockdown. I am sure Dad and I could have made it work properly again, but without him, and with Sabi so keen to sell...'

Ed surveyed row after row of pre-potted plants. 'It isn't my place to say, but have you talked to your sister about your passion for this place?'

'She already knows.'

'Knows from before, from the fact you gave up working as a head gardener at the National Trust to work here with your father? Or knows *now*? Knows about how determined you are to make this place work on a larger scale, despite your recent bereavement?'

Touched that Ed had remembered that she'd told him about her former job at Killerton House, Maddie said, 'We haven't spoken properly since Sabi came here after the meeting about the will. And that was more a case of Sabi speaking and me listening while in a state of shock. Once Sabi has made her mind up about something she isn't easy to dissuade.'

'You ought to try, though.' Ed crossed his arms over his chest and leant back against the workbench. 'If you'll forgive me sounding like your solicitor for a moment, from the state the business is in now, it won't be easy to do what you hope to do here long term, but it isn't impossible. This place was a going concern – and will be again with a little work – work you're obviously keen to put in. A well put-together business proposal should see a favourable response from your bank manager.'

'You think so?'

'I do.' Ed gave a half-smile. 'I can't promise I'm right, but new businesses are being encouraged and supported more than ever.'

Knowing Ed was right, Maddie's shoulder muscles tightened at the idea of trying to change her sister's mind, when a thought struck her. 'Are *you* The Potting Shed's solicitor now then?'

'That's something I need to talk to you about. And your sister.' Ed shuffled awkwardly. 'Mr Lyle has asked if I'd consider moving you onto my books. He's close to retirement and wants to lighten his case load. You'll be getting a call from him in a few days' time.'

'Oh. Right.' Maddie felt foolish. She'd been having such a nice time in Ed's company, sharing ideas she hadn't even mentioned to Jake yet – but now she saw he wasn't curious about this place on a personal level, nor had he wanted to see her again for her own sake. He hadn't just been passing at all. He'd needed to talk to her about taking on the business as his client, and had come to take stock of the situation before he agreed to saddle himself with a lost cause.

Face it, you imagined that shared hot-chocolate chemistry. Ed's here because he's a young lawyer trying to impress his senior partner by visiting one of the businesses they represent. End of.

'Maddie? Are you with me?'

'Sorry, yes.' Staring at her fingernails, feeling rather foolish, Maddie concentrated on flicking out the mud. 'I'd be delighted if you'd be our solicitor. I can't see Sabi objecting. It's not like she knew Mr Lyle personally. He was the business's solicitor, and until Dad died, she kept out of things. But you can never tell with my sister.'

'Mr Creswell?'

'Please, call me Leo.'

'Leo then,' Sabi spoke carefully into her mobile. 'In the letter I received from Big in Gardens I was asked to call you.'

'I'm very glad you did. I am BIG's chief legal representative. Before I get to the point, may I enquire, are you and your sister familiar with the Big in Gardens chain?'

'We are.' Sabi looked at her laptop screen. She'd found the BIG website while waiting for her call to Leo Creswell to connect. 'Fifteen large site garden centres across the Midlands and South of England.'

'And growing all the time.'

They're ripping the heart out of the family nurseries and garden centres.

The memory of her father's voice echoed at the back of Sabi's mind. It had been five years ago. She'd arrived at a family dinner after a trip to friends in Nottingham, with a plant with BIG written across the pot. She'd meant to give him the rose – a new variant in the UK – as a surprise. She'd even thought it might give him ideas for new items they could sell at The Potting Shed. Instead, her father had taken one look at the branding on the pot and hardly spoken a word for the duration of the meal.

That was the start of it. The moment my father and sister stopped asking for my opinion about the nursery. Stopped including me.

Keeping her voice level, Sabi said, 'The letter was addressed to me and my sister. Has Maddie been sent a separate letter?'

'She has.'

'Good. I can see why BIG are popular. I've visited a couple of the stores myself.'

'Then you will know that the company I represent is trustworthy and ambitious.'

'Trustworthy? That's an odd choice of word to highlight, Mr Creswell. Ambitious I do not doubt.'

'Just reassuring you of my employer's good intentions, Mrs Willand-Harris.' There was a tapping noise down the line, as if the lawyer was playing a pen against his desk. 'It has come to our attention that the owner of The Potting Shed, Mr Tony Willand, has passed away. My condolences.'

'Thank you.' The muscles in Sabi's shoulders tensed. 'May I ask how you heard of my father's death?'

'He was a respected man in the local gardening community. The word spread around his suppliers and eventually reached us.'

'Indeed.' Remembering how a tearful Maddie had told her that having to call the suppliers, to explain that bills should be addressed to her and not her father, had been heartbreakingly difficult, Sabi asked, 'And your interest in our business is what exactly?'

'As our communication indicated, we, that is, my client, would like to buy your father's nursery.'

Sabi frowned. 'And you think a garden centre would do well where The Potting Shed stands?'

'It's an excellent location. Just off the A38, not too far from the M5 motorway, but far enough out of town to make visiting an event. A trip that would give the customer a sense that going out was an occasion, even if they were just wandering around plants and having a cup of tea and a slice of cake. BIG have been considering expanding into Devon and Somerset for some time.'

'And as The Potting Shed is in Devon, but only fifteen miles from the Somerset border, this would provide the best of both worlds?'

'Precisely, Mrs Willand-Harris.'

Grateful that Maddie wasn't there to hear Leo Creswell confirm her claim that the nursery was well placed geographically when it came to her father's plans for expansion, Sabi asked, 'Can you tell me *precisely* what you're proposing?'

'That BIG would, should you agree, buy the land that The Potting Shed sits on, effectively stopping it trading as a nursery. We are aware that your father had plans to upgrade his business into a garden centre, and obviously my employers would not wish to have local competition.'

Sabi felt confused and in need of clarification. What exactly were BIG proposing, in that case? 'So, the proposal *isn't* to turn The Potting Shed into a new BIG garden centre, but to buy the land it's on so it can't be used as a nursery anymore?'

'That is correct. BIG are negotiating to purchase a large expanse of land nearby.'

'I thought you just said The Potting Shed land would be a good place for a garden centre?'

'I did, and so it would be. However, it is the land on the opposite side of the road that BIG are intending to develop. The Potting Shed land would be used for storage and as a space where deliveries of new stock can be made, and items sorted and priced before sale.'

Sabi tried to make sense of what she was being told. 'My sister lives on the land in question. What would BIG do about her home?'

'Your sister, Miss Madeleine Willand, would be at liberty to stay in the house. She'd be left a reasonably sized garden area, on the understanding that she didn't continue to trade from it.'

'Has my sister contacted you yet?'

'No. I would encourage you to suggest she does so with

some haste, Mrs Willand-Harris. There is a considerable sum of money involved here.'

'Considerable sum?'

Leo cleared his throat. Sabi tried to ignore the hint of triumph in his tone as he stated a figure that made her jaw drop. 'Can I clarify, Mr Creswell, Leo – is that figure the money you are offering for the site BIG intend to build on, or is that the figure you are offering for the land upon which The Potting Shed sits, on the understanding that we cease trading?'

'That is the sum my employers are prepared to offer yourself and your sister.'

An image of the house in Culmstock took centre stage in Sabi's mind.

If we say yes, then Henry and I could do what I wanted – we could rent out this place and live in our new home.

A vision of the first set of executive-style guests parking their sports cars on her drive, for a week of relaxation and recreation, drove away all thoughts of how her sister would take the news.

Perhaps we should get our future guests a hot tub for the garden?

'Mrs Willand-Harris, are you still there?'

'Please, call me Sabi.'

9

Jake hesitated. Twelve o'clock had come and gone. It was time for him to go home, but his coat was in the shop – and so was Petra.

All you have to do is go in, pick up your coat and leave. You don't need to say anything.

Contemplating going home without his coat, Jake hesitated. He knew that his mum would make her feelings about that very clear. He might have been twenty years old, but that didn't stop his lone parent having plenty to say whenever he failed to live up to her expectations.

Not sure why he felt so unsettled by Petra's presence, Jake sighed. He'd never been comfortable with other people. Tony Willand had understood that. He thought Maddie had too, yet she had taken on Petra on the whim of her sister without giving him any warning.

Stepping back a fraction, Jake stood between the two polytunnels nearest to the shop. He could see Petra perched on the stool by the till. She was flicking through a plant catalogue and periodically tapping into the laptop.

A wave of inadequacy washed over Jake. He'd never used the nursery's computer.

He watched as Petra tucked a stray strand of golden hair

behind her ear. It had escaped from the ponytail she wore. Seconds later it broke free again, and she twirled it around her little finger instead. Jake found himself momentarily hypnotised by the motion.

Shaking himself he took a deep breath. *It's cold, I need my coat, and if I don't hurry up, I'll miss my bus.*

Petra looked up at the sound of footsteps. Expecting it to be either a customer or Maddie, she threw out her best 'can I help you' smile. A smile that became uncertain as Jake stepped inside the shop.

'I need my coat,' Jake mumbled as he dashed past the desk.

'I'm not surprised, it's perishing out.' Petra stroked the scarf around her neck as if in solidarity from suffering the cold. 'Have you had a good morning?'

'Sorry?' Jake tugged on his coat at high speed.

'Your morning at work, has it been good?'

'Suppose so.' Jake eyed the door. 'You been okay?'

'I've had great fun.' Petra lifted up the catalogue. 'There is so much to choose from. I bet you love browsing through this.'

Jake eyed the book as if it was dangerous. 'Maddie does all that.'

'Have you been planting?' Petra sounded wistful. 'I'm dying to do some actual gardening. Maddie's promised to teach me. I'm keen, but I suspect I'll be a bit useless.'

Surprised that Petra could consider herself useless at anything, Jake said, 'I was tending the potatoes.'

'You're so lucky.' Petra patted the till. 'Don't get me

wrong, I don't mind doing this for Maddie, especially as she's had me dumped on her. But I'd much rather be getting my hands dirty.'

'You would?'

'Sure.' Petra smiled wider. 'My parents are convinced I'm destined for a life of sterile offices and computers. I can't think of anything worse. But hey, parents huh.'

'Yeah. Parents can be... challenging.' Jake checked his watch. 'Got to go. Bus.'

'See you tomorrow,' Petra called after Jake, but he'd already gone.

Maddie tried Sabi's phone again.

'It's still engaged.'

Ed rested against his car door as Maddie abandoned her third attempt to call her sister.

'Don't give up. You need to talk to her and her husband. Henry, did you say his name was?'

'That's him.' Maddie smiled at the thought of her brother-in-law.

'Do you think he'd be on your side? If you were able to prove you could make this place work?'

'It's possible. It's not as if they need the money from the sale for anything. And Henry knows how much Jem likes this place too.'

'Jem?'

'My niece. She's only eleven, but she loves it here. As I don't have kids, The Potting Shed will go to her.'

'And if you did have children one day?'

'That's hardly likely.' Maddie averted her gaze to a nearby

bird table, where a robin was making a feast out of the rind she'd cut off her bacon at breakfast. 'Anyway, I've got enough on my plate without finding an instant relationship and having an instant child, just so I can plead with Sabi to think of my child's inheritance.'

'You're young. You could still have a family.'

Not sure how to respond, Maddie said, 'I'll keep trying Sabi anyway.'

'You know, perhaps we're over-thinking this. As I said, you could always offer to buy Sabi out.' Ed opened his car door but made no move towards getting in it.

'I'd never get a loan for that much, surely, even if she agreed? Not if I needed money for the expansion too.' Maddie stared at her slightly crumbling empire. 'And even if I don't expand, I'll need a fair bit just to do this place up. Petra said something to me this morning about the sign being hard to spot. Since then I've started to see The Potting Shed through other people's eyes. I hadn't noticed how much TLC it required before.'

'We rarely see what's under our nose all the time.' Ed followed her line of sight. 'It's not that bad though, and I'm sure Jake and Petra would lend a hand with low-level maintenance, like painting the fences and generally tidying.' He paused. 'And so would I, if you wanted me too.'

'You would?'

'Sure.'

'Oh. That's very kind, I...' Maddie's words petered out as she felt Ed's heated gaze flick from her to the fence and back again. 'You also noticed how badly the fence around the car park needs a coat of preservative then?'

Maybe he didn't pop by to tell me he's going to be my new solicitor after all?

'Dad and I have had the fence's upkeep on our to-do list for years, but there was always something else to do. The plants always need looking after. Then there are the veg boxes we deliver to the local old folk; that all takes... And then...'

'Maddie!' Ed reached out a hand to her shoulder but drew it back before he made contact. 'I didn't think that the place needed a fresh lick of paint because it had been neglected or you had your feet up half the time.'

'Right. Sorry, I get these guilt hits.'

'Because it feels that whatever you do, it'll never be enough?'

'Yes.' Maddie refocused on the hungry robin. 'What you were saying about buying Sabi out, do you really think the bank would go for it?'

'I think it would be worth enquiring. You'd need a solid business plan, but it would be unwise to dismiss any possibility at this stage.'

'It's such a shame. I'd prefer it to be a family business. For all her stubbornness and high-handed manner, I love Sabi. She's my sister. We were close when we were children.'

Ed nodded. 'Perhaps that's the issue. Perhaps Sabi wants to sell because she doesn't want to work here, but assumes she'll have to now she's joint owner. You could tell her you'd be happy to continue to run the place with her as a sleeping partner.'

'I hadn't thought of that!' Maddie stood up straight as she considered what Ed was saying. 'Maybe it is as simple as that. Sabi probably wouldn't want the hassle of helping turn the place around now I think about it. It's not the sort of thing to discuss over an overpriced gin and tonic at the golf club. Hardly fashionable.'

'She plays golf?'

'No, but she likes being around people who can afford the membership fee.' Maddie bit her lip. 'Sorry, that sounded bitter. I just meant Sabi likes to have the best. Henry is the one who's a member – although now I think about it, I don't think he actually plays golf.'

'Status at work? Business meetings, that sort of thing?'

'I've always assumed so.' Maddie smiled as the robin, finally full, flew into a nearby tree. 'He's a lovely guy, Henry. There's no side to him. But he knows how to play the game as a businessman.'

'Maybe you should talk to Henry first?'

'I can't.' Maddie shrugged. 'That would feel disloyal to my sister. I'll try Sabi again after lunch.'

'Will you let me know what she says?'

'So you can make notes as our solicitor?'

Ed looked straight at Maddie. 'No, so I know what's happening as a friend.'

'Oh.'

'A friend who was sincere when he said he'd help tidy up the place. If you like?'

'Um, well, yes. Yes.' Maddie smiled. 'I'd like that. But right now, I'd better go and make sure Petra's alright. It's her first day and I've rather abandoned her.'

'Once you've checked on her, get thinking about that business proposal. I've not met your sister, but from what you've said, you'll need a well thought-out plan to show her – something to prove you're sincere about keeping The

Potting Shed going.' Ed got into his car, and then promptly got out again. 'I don't suppose you fancy coming for a walk with me on Exmoor?'

'Exmoor?'

'Yeah. Fancy it? This weekend?'

'I work weekends.'

'Not at night you don't.'

IO

Henry placed his spoon by the side of his bowl of cereal and watched his wife as she poured coffee beans into the machine, ready to be ground. As the grinder burst into life, Henry opened the calendar on his phone to check his appointments for the day. The morning was full of meetings he didn't particularly wish to attend, but the afternoon was mercifully free. As the beans finished submitting to their fate, he broke the sudden silence.

'Why don't you call Maddie? She must have read her copy of the letter by now. We could go over to the nursery this afternoon, talk to her about BIG's proposal.'

'I see little point until we have decided what to do.' Selecting two cups from the cream-painted rack that hung just above eye level, Sabi continued her morning coffee-making ritual. 'Or should I say, until you decide. I already think it's the perfect solution for all of us.'

'So you've said – several times.' Henry took his cup from Sabi and inhaled the robust aroma of its contents. 'Don't you think it odd that Maddie hasn't called?'

'Well…'

'Sit down, darling. Please.' Henry tapped the table lightly. 'I know the offer from BIG would mean you get what you want, and I know you are convinced that letting go of the nursery would be the making of your sister, but have you thought about what it is you are asking Maddie to give up?'

'Near poverty, hard work for little reward, and no social life.' Sabi cradled her coffee cup between her palms as she sat with her husband. 'Oh yes, I'm an awful human being for wanting to take all that away from her.'

'Don't be petulant!' Henry snapped. 'Maddie loves her life, and just because it wouldn't suit you, don't assume she'd be happier without it.'

Sabi put down her cup and reached a hand to Henry, cupping his palm in hers. 'But if we took up BIG's offer we could have everything we ever dreamt of.'

'We could,' Henry got up, 'but at the cost of taking away everything Maddie ever wanted.'

Sabi's mouth dropped open. 'I'd never…'

Speaking more gently, Henry released his hand and hooked his suit jacket off the back of his chair. 'Look, I know you love your sister and think you are acting in her best interests as well as ours, but please, take some time to think about this. Think about how you'd feel if someone wanted to take away the land you'd been working on and left you living in a house on that land, yet unable to work it. Waking up every day to see the people who took your dream, making a fortune across the road.'

Sabi mumbled, 'I hadn't thought of that side of it.'

'Just consider the whole picture before you get carried away with your plans, that's all I'm saying. Then, we'll go and talk to Maddie together after lunch. The shock of the offer may have worn off a little by then.'

'Actually, she's coming here anyway.'

'Is she?'

'I got a text while you were in the shower. She'll be here about two. Wants to talk about the nursery's future.'

Henry picked up his briefcase. 'A statement that implies she is determined to make sure it actually has a future despite BIG's plans.'

'Except it hasn't.' Sabi tugged at the sleeves of her jumper in agitation. 'Let's face it Henry, even if we are stupid enough not to accept Creswell's offer, they are still going to build a branch of their garden centre on the doorstep. What chance would The Potting Shed have then?'

Maddie stifled a yawn and hid her notepad under an old potato sack as Jake came into the polytunnel.

'Petra came back then.'

'She did. She's really very nice.'

'She's very chatty.'

Maddie couldn't help but laugh. 'That isn't a bad thing.'

Jake grunted as he took off his coat. 'What do you want doing first?'

'I thought we'd paint the section of the fence at the back of the car park, the bit that people will see when they come to buy Christmas trees.'

'We?'

'All three of us.' Maddie didn't add that she fully intended to keep going and paint the entire fence between her other jobs, even though it would take at least a week to do it properly. 'It's got rather run down. Its tattiness might put people off from coming here.'

'I don't look at the fence when I arrive.'

'Well no, but we're here all the time aren't we.' Maddie got off her stool. 'Petra's right though, it isn't welcoming.'

'Petra? We're painting a fence because of *her*?'

Hearing Jake's hectoring tone, Maddie shook her head. 'No, we are painting the fence because it badly needs some preservative putting on before it faces the worst of the winter weather. It's going to either crumble or rot or both soon. Petra merely reminded me it needed doing. It's been on my list for ages.'

'Okay.'

'Thank you.' Maddie gestured towards the tool shed hidden behind the polytunnels. 'Could you go and fetch the brushes? There is a huge pot of preservative there too and some old paint tins we could use to pour some of the preserver stuff into, so we can spread out and do a section of the fence each.'

Jake relaxed a fraction. 'We won't have to stand together to paint then?'

'Not if you don't want to, no.'

'Right.'

'Oh, and Jake. We're expecting the delivery of a new signboard towards the end of the week. Can you keep an eye out for me in case I miss it or forget that it's coming?'

Jake frowned. 'What's wrong with the old sign?'

'It's faded to almost invisibility, and Petra noticed that—'

'Of course, she did.' Jake cut across his boss with a defeated grunt. 'I'll fetch the fence stuff.'

'Who was the cute guy in the oversized jumper that was here yesterday?'

Maddie dipped her brush into the pot of wood preservative as she contemplated how to reply to Petra. If she said it was her solicitor that might worry Jake, if she said he was a friend, she sensed that Petra would ask a barrage of questions Maddie couldn't answer. In the end she opted for a watered-down but still honest answer.

'That was Ed Tate. He's taking over from our old solicitor and, as he was passing, he thought he'd come and see the place.'

'Unusual to see a solicitor without a suit.' Petra crumpled her freckled nose. 'Once our studies were over, I swear every single law graduate I knew hit Cambridge's equivalent of Savile Row and bought a suit they'd live in from their interviews to the moment too many corporate lunches had squeezed them out of it.'

'I'm not sure Mr Tate will ever have that problem.' Maddie's smile faltered as she glanced to her left. Jake had stopped painting mid-panel. His brush hovered aimlessly in thin air.

'I don't suppose you'd pop inside to fetch the tea flasks, Petra?' Maddie fished the house keys from her pocket. 'Would you mind? I left them on the side in the kitchen.'

Petra nodded. 'Certainly. No problem.'

As her newest assistant headed towards the house, Maddie turned to Jake. 'You alright?'

'She would have gone to Cambridge, wouldn't she! Typical.'

His words had been no more than a mumble, but Maddie heard and suspected she knew what was going through Jake's mind. Suddenly very tired, and not having the mental wherewithal to bolster his fragile confidence when faced with high achievers, Maddie moved to his side. 'When she gets back, maybe you should ask her why she decided to come here and do this rather than go for a career where high wages are guaranteed?'

Jake opened his mouth, but Maddie got in first. 'Petra's only been here two minutes and I haven't had time to get to know her as much as I'd like to. Maybe you could help me out, you know, make her welcome.'

'Me? But I'm—'

Maddie cut through the excuses she knew were coming. 'You're a similar age to Petra. You'll have more in common with her than I do.'

'But she's clever and I'm…'

Maddie laid down her paintbrush and stepped closer to her assistant. 'You are a brilliant gardener. You are a good, kind person and – more to the point – you are very clever at what matters here and now.'

'That's what your dad used to say. That I was clever at the here and now.'

'And he was right.' Maddie pulled off her gloves and flexed her fingers. 'I know you find new people tough, but Petra is keen to help and very friendly. You're making an awful lot of assumptions about her without getting to know her first. How would you like it if she did that to you?'

'I bet she took one look at me and wrote me off.'

'And *I* bet she didn't.'

The combined sound of a van turning into the driveway and Petra crossing the car park with three flasks balanced on a tray interrupted any response Jake may have had.

'Oh, that'll be the sign!' Petra put the tray down on top of her large paint tin, ready to intercept the van driver.

'Already?' Maddie's eyebrows rose. 'I thought it said three-day delivery?'

Petra pulled her ponytail forward, laying it over her shoulder. 'I might have paid for next day delivery – and the sign itself – out of my money, not the business'.'

Maddie spluttered in surprise, 'You didn't need to do that. You must let me pay you back.'

'No way. You've been so kind, taking me on without warning. It's my way of saying thank you. And, umm, I've arranged for them to put it up as well.'

As the courier swung open the back of the van, Petra ran forward to retrieve her package before her employer could respond.

Maddie nudged Jake's arm. 'Could you go too, just in case Petra has to help carry it into position? It will be heavy.'

Jake's feet stayed where they were. 'She paid for all that so we could have a better sign faster?'

'Told you she was nice, didn't I.'

'I didn't say she wasn't.'

'Fair enough.' Maddie smiled. 'By the way, you'll be in charge this afternoon. I have a meeting with my sister.'

'How long will you be?'

'I'm not sure.' Maddie knew Jake hated being in charge, even though he always managed perfectly well on the few occasions she and her father had been absent from The Potting Shed at the same time. 'As soon as we've finished, I'll come straight back.'

'"Straight back".'

'Promise.' Maddie tried to sound encouraging. 'You are good with the customers when you start talking plants,

Jake. And Petra will be here to deal with the till and any small talk if necessary.'

'Suppose so.'

'Why not use it as a chance to make friends?'

Jake looked alarmed. 'I thought she was only going to be here for a while?'

'Here, yes.' Maddie dipped her brush back into the old paint pot. 'But Petra lives locally, so she'll still be around the area. Wouldn't it be nice to have a friend of your own age?'

Jake grunted. 'You'd better not be matchmaking.'

'As if I would!' Maddie pointed to where Petra had stopped talking to the courier, who definitely had a look of a man who'd like to spend more time in the blonde woman's presence. 'Go and help her with that sign, Jake, there's a good chap.'

Maddie read the papers she'd printed out for the second time. There was one typo, but she was prepared to take any criticism her sister might make about that. All she wanted in this first instance was for Sabi to agree to read the proposal and take some time to think about the option of being bought out.

As she swapped her chunky working jumper for the smart cashmere sweater Sabi had given her for Christmas, Maddie felt her stomach churn.

Come on, you're only going to talk to your sister. Henry will be there. He's a sensible businessman. He'll at least listen before he says no.

Picking up her proposal, grateful that she'd managed to find a cardboard folder that was both new and unstained by either soil or biscuit crumbs, Maddie slipped on her one and only pair of court shoes.

'Even if it all goes wrong,' Maddie told the spider plant in the bathroom as she applied foundation, to hide the worst of the dark shadows that had formed after weeks of poor sleep, 'at least I have a night walk on Exmoor with Ed to look forward to.'

Promising herself that later on she'd look up the Dark Skies group he'd told her that he was a member of, ignoring the voice that told her that going for a walk with a man she didn't really know, on a vast moor in the middle of the night, wasn't the most sensible move, Maddie found she was wishing she'd asked Ed to come to her sister's with her.

'Only because he is our solicitor,' she told the spider plant.

'You can think that if you like Maddie, but I'm not fooled,' came a leafy reply.

11

'Maddie, good to see you.' Henry swung open the front door, greeting his sister-in-law as she crossed the gravel drive. 'How are you coping?'

'Not bad in the circumstances.' Maddie fought her natural instinct to smile at Henry's habitually generous expression. If she didn't start with a business frame of mind from the off, she'd be beaten before she began.

Henry tilted his head to one side. 'Are you sure you're alright?'

'Let's just say I'm hoping I'll get a hearing before Sabi dismisses what I have to say out of hand.'

Henry took her coat. 'I can't promise she'll agree to whatever you're going to suggest, but I can promise I'll make sure you have a fair hearing.'

Giving Henry's arm a grateful clasp, Maddie kicked off her shoes. 'How's Jem? I haven't had time to write or get over to Taunton to visit her much since Dad went.'

'She's great thanks.' The worried edge Maddie had noted in Henry's voice lifted as he talked about his daughter. 'Doing a botany project in science at the moment. Seems to be really enjoying it.'

'Botany at school?' Maddie felt a surge of love for her niece. 'Rare these days. Benefits of a private school I guess.'

Henry pulled a face. 'I know you aren't keen on her being at a boarding school, but she is very happy, you know.'

'I know.' Maddie sighed. 'Take no notice. I just miss her being around.'

Henry had no time to reply, as a call of, 'Are you two coming in or not?' shot through their conversation from the kitchen.

Taking a deep breath, clutching the business proposal to her chest, Maddie nodded to Henry, before following him towards his wife's summons.

The smell of freshly roasted coffee was perfectly complemented by the scent of bread cooking in the bread maker that sat next to the Aga.

'You look nice.' Sabi sounded genuinely surprised.

'I hardly get the chance to wear this jumper, and it's so comfortable.'

'Where did you get it?' Sabi poured out two cups of coffee and a cup of tea for herself. 'It's a gorgeous shade of burgundy.'

Maddie picked up a cup. 'You gave it to me for Christmas last year.'

'Oh.' Sabi looked harder at the jumper. 'I'd forgotten. Anyway, it's good to see you out of a dirty top and tatty jeans. Must feel good to have a reason to dress nicely.'

Immediately seeing the angle her sister was taking, and regretting her decision to appear business-like rather than be herself, Maddie placed her folder on the table and ignored the dig at her usual lack of elegance. 'I'm glad you were both free this afternoon. We have lots to sort out, and I'd really like it if we could do so without bickering. Dad always hated it when we argued.'

Her sister simply nodded as Henry opened the conversation. 'You know Sabi thinks you should go with the offer to sell up, but if you have another workable idea, then let's hear it.'

Giving Henry a grateful smile, Maddie blew across her coffee cup's steaming vapour. 'As you know, Dad and I had plans to expand the business. And with that in mind, I have taken some advice and put together a proposal to—'

'I don't think so.' Sabi gave a blunt shake of her head. 'I'm sorry Maddie, but no. Whatever you say, we aren't going to change our minds. Especially now – surely the offer made sense to you too.'

The colour drained from Maddie's face. She glanced at Henry, who was looking daggers at his wife.

'Sabi, I promised Maddie we would hear her out.'

'What's the point? We have some news that will make anything Mads has to say superfluous, you know we do Henry!'

'Superfluous?' Maddie spoke slowly. 'Hang on…. you said offer – you aren't talking about your offer are you?'

Sabi stirred a silver teaspoon around her tea with increasing speed. 'BIG's offer.'

'What are you talking about?'

'The letter.' Henry frowned. 'You have had a letter from Big in Gardens, haven't you?'

'Letter?' Maddie's insides lurched with apprehension. 'From BIG? They're the sort of corporation that Dad hated.'

Continuing to regard her teacup rather than look at her sister, Sabi said, 'That's as maybe, but it does not change the fact that they have offered us a lot of money to buy The Potting Shed.'

'They've what?' Maddie suddenly felt sick.

'You didn't know?' Henry shot his wife a look which told her to go gently. 'We had a letter. You were supposed to get one too.'

'I haven't had a chance to look at the post for a few days.' Maddie felt as if she'd been punched in the stomach.

Sabi took an envelope from a pile of papers on the kitchen. 'Here, you should read this.'

The fifth customer of the afternoon was making his way to the car park, with a poinsettia in one hand and a new garden trowel in the other, as Petra left the till to re-join Jake at the fence. Her arms and shoulders were aching from the unprecedented amount of physical labour. It felt good.

Studying the progress they'd made since Maddie had left, Petra took pleasure in the sight of the six refreshed fence panels. There was still a long way to go, but it was already proving to be time well spent.

Her gaze fell on Jake and the moment's contentment dissolved. She'd made an extra effort to be friendly, but he'd clearly decided that they weren't going to get on. She'd tried not to be hurt by this, but was hurt anyway. Sensing he'd set up some sort of armour around himself to keep people away, Petra felt an urge to help him, even though she had no idea how or why.

Observing him out of the corner of her eye, she saw Jake roll up his jumper sleeves, revealing a Celtic cross tattoo on his right arm. *Nice.* The thought took her by surprise. *Mum would hate that. She'd certainly never approve of me being friends with Jake.*

Hot from her DIY exertions, Petra tugged off her jumper and, throwing it over her shoulder, strode purposefully forwards. *Jake may not want to talk to me, but I'm going to talk to him. I like him, whether he likes it or not.*

'We've sold another plant!'

Jake remained focused on the fence. 'You mean, you have.'

'Okay, so I did the actual selling bit, but it's a joint enterprise. I couldn't have sold it if no one had grown it in the first place. Did you grow the poinsettias?'

Taken aback by the observation, Jake paused mid-brushstroke. 'Yeah.'

'Are they easy to grow? They're seasonal, aren't they? Or are they?' Petra's forehead creased as she pondered. 'Perhaps I'm only assuming they are because I associate them with Christmas.'

'Are you *really* interested?' Jake ventured a glance at his colleague. Her face looked open and genuinely curious.

'Yes. I told you, I'd love to learn more about the work you do here.'

Remembering what Maddie had asked him about trying to make friends with Petra, and knowing that he wasn't overly endowed with pals, Jake tried to relax. 'Poinsettias can be a real pain. It's because they aren't really flowers. They just look like they are.'

'Not flowers?'

'The red petals are really leaves called bracts that have evolved to look like flower petals. The seeds come from the tiny part in the centre of the bracts. They develop seed pods there. We use them to grow new plants.'

'I had no idea!' Petra looked delighted. 'That's fascinating. So, do you just plant these pods once they have developed?'

'If only.' Jake continued to plaster preservative on the fence as he explained. 'The seed pods have to be stored in a paper bag in a dry place. Then the waiting begins. Only once the pods are brown and dry, can you pop the pods open and collect the seeds.'

'And was the plant I sold the result of you doing that?'

'Umm, yes.' Jake felt oddly proud as he saw Petra's impressed expression.

'You're amazing. I wish I knew about things like that.'

The paintbrush slipped out of Jake's hand and landed with a splash, sending tiny droplets of light brown wood preserver flying across both of them.

'Oh God! I'm so sorry!' Jake was horrified to see Petra's previously clean white t-shirt taking on a dappled look.

Rather than shouting at him, as he expected, Petra burst out laughing. 'Perhaps I could start a fashion trend? H&M t-shirts with a touch of Ronseal?'

'It looked new.' Jake dragged his hands across the back of his jeans. 'I should buy you a new one.'

'Don't be silly. It's my fault for taking my old jumper off. Anyway,' Petra shrugged, 'I have way more clothes than I need. This can now officially be my "getting my hands dirty" top.'

'You aren't cross?'

'It's just a t-shirt.' Petra ran a hand across her cheek, smearing a few drops of preservative that had spattered her cheek.

'You've got it on your face.' Jake felt his fingers itching to reach out and wipe them away.

'Really?' Petra came closer to Jake and peered into his face. 'I think you escaped.'

Hardly daring to breathe as Petra homed in on him, Jake felt his pulse accelerate as he mumbled, 'You want to go and wash them off?'

'Nah, adds colour. My mother is always telling me I'm too pale.'

Maddie had temporarily forgotten how to breathe. The letter from BIG remained in her hand. She could hear Henry telling her that, as half the sale price that BIG were offering them would be hers, she wouldn't be left penniless while she looked for another job. Meanwhile, Sabi was explaining, for the third time, that she'd still have her home, but that she'd understand if Maddie wanted to sell that too.

'But Dad hated soulless garden centre chains,' Maddie finally managed to mutter as she stared at her closed proposal folder on the table.

'I know.' Henry had the decency to look embarrassed as he reasoned, 'but if BIG set up shop opposite the nursery, your trade would be significantly diminished. It'll be a real struggle for The Potting Shed to keep going.'

'Lots of people don't like large corporate-style garden centres.' Maddie knew the words coming out of her mouth sounded feeble, even before her sister confirmed the fact for her.

'Come off it, Maddie. Why would anyone in their right mind come to The Potting Shed, with its rundown polytunnels and limited stock, when they could walk into the crisp, clean, air-conditioned environment of a modern garden centre?'

'Loyalty.' Maddie fought the urge to cry. 'You remember that concept, don't you Sabi?'

Seeing the meeting about to dissolve into a row, Henry stood up and refilled his coffee cup. 'Maddie, this isn't about loyalty, it's about being practical in difficult circumstances. This lawyer chap, Leo Creswell, is confident the BIG build will happen even if you and Sabi don't agree to let them take over your land for their storage facility. I'm so sorry.'

Without giving her sister time to respond, Sabi repeated a line she'd already used twice in the last ten minutes. 'Can't you see Maddie, our situation is better than it was before? You'll have a lump sum with which to start a brand-new life. It's exciting.'

The smell of her un-drunk coffee felt stale against Maddie's nostrils. As she listened to Sabi explaining how good for the local economy BIG would be, something inside her snapped.

I can't stay here a second longer. How can they dispose of Dad's legacy so easily?

Without a word, Maddie pushed her unread proposal into the middle of the table, dropped the letter, ran to the hall, grabbed her uncomfortable shoes, and exited the house, leaving the front door open behind her.

12

Maddie manoeuvred her car into a lay-by to answer her phone. She had been tempted to ignore it, assuming it would be either Henry or Sabi trying to persuade her to sign the nursery away again, but then, remembering that it could be Petra with a customer query or Jake with a worry, she opened her mobile's case.

She was surprised to see the number for Lyle and Tate solicitors flashing on her screen.

'Hello, Maddie Willand speaking.'

'Hi, it's Ed. How did it go?'

'Oh.' Maddie wiped the back of her hand over her eyes, wincing when she spotted her careworn reflection in the driver's mirror. 'I assumed it would be your receptionist wanting to talk about Ronald Lyle passing us over to you.'

'No, but I am in the office.' Ed was almost whispering.

'Why do you sound as if you're in a spy movie?'

'Do I?' Ed's tone became more relaxed. 'Sorry, I was calling to see how you got on with your sister.'

'Oh.'

'Are you alright? You keeping saying "oh".'

'Oh, do I?' Maddie picked up the bottle of water lodged in her car's cup holder.

'Did you see Sabi?'

'I did. Hang on.' Unscrewing the bottle, she took a long draught of liquid. 'That's better. Sorry, I was so dry. I think my throat would have closed in on itself if I hadn't had a drink.'

'That doesn't paint a picture of a family chat over coffee and cake.'

'I think you could say it was a disaster, although not entirely for the reasons I suspected it would be.'

'How do you mean?'

Maddie found herself picturing Ed at his desk, his long legs stretched out beneath the desk, a mug of hot chocolate within reach. 'Well, basically—' Maddie broke off as a loud knock on Ed's office door cut through her sentence.

'Damn.' Ed's voice dipped again as he muttered, 'Sorry Maddie, my next client is here. Fancy dinner tonight? You can tell me all about it.'

'Dinner?' A massive yawn escaped Maddie as she slouched back against the car's headrest. 'Sorry. I'm not sure I'd be the best company. And I'm shattered.'

'That bad huh?'

'Worse.'

'Tell you what: I'll drive by the nursery at closing time. If you're up to it we can go out, if not, maybe we could grab a takeaway.'

Ed had put the phone down before Maddie had registered that she appeared to have a dinner date with her solicitor.

Jake scrubbed his fingernails with the nailbrush Maddie had bought for him. It had its own dish, next to a bar of coal-tar soap, in the downstairs washroom of her home. It sat on a slim glass shelf Maddie had screwed into the wall above the small basin.

Next to Jake's shell-shaped dish sat a similar one that held a brush for Maddie – ingrained dirt and filthy fingernails being an occupational hazard for them. His eyes rested on the third dish. The bar of soap remained, but Maddie had thrown away the nail brush. Its absence hurt Jake every time he went into the washroom, although he knew the brush had needed dumping and replacing long before its owner had died. It hadn't taken Tony more than a few scrubs with it to bend the bristles, rendering them permanently out of shape.

Pausing to wash fresh water over his fingernails, glad to see that the preservative that had splashed over his hand had come off with remarkably little effort, Jake wondered if Tony's soap dish would become Petra's now. He was surprised to find the idea didn't bother him as much as it would have done only a few hours before.

Perhaps Maddie's right. Maybe it would be nice to have a friend of my own age.

Jake stared at his reflection as he dried his hands. 'Who am I kidding? She'll get to know more about me, and then she'll disappear like all the rest.'

'Did it all come off?' Petra was back at the till, periodically stretching out her arms so her shoulder and neck muscles didn't seize up in the night.

'Yeah.' Jake dared a quick stare at his companion's flawless skin. 'Looks like you got all the fake freckles off too.'

'Shame the real ones wouldn't come off, but you can't have it all.'

'They suit you. I love freckles.' Jake quickly looked away, amazed at himself for making a personal comment.

Flattered by his awkwardness, Petra pretended she hadn't noticed his discomfort. 'I made tea. I wasn't sure how you had it. I assumed milk, but I brought the sugar with me. Sorry I forgot it last time.'

'Doesn't matter. Sometimes I have it with, sometimes without.' Digging a teaspoon into the bag of sugar, Jake put two hefty servings into his mug and gave it a stir. 'Thanks. I'm parched.'

. 'That's a hell of a mug,' Petra nodded towards Jake's tea. 'I don't think I've ever seen such a big one.'

Jake struggled to keep a straight face as Petra burst into giggles.

'I must be tired! I promise my innuendos are usually more subtle than that!'

Jake raised his giant mug in a toast. 'Ah, but how did you know the big mug was mine?'

'Wishful thinking?' Petra blushed as her giggles became a hearty laugh.

Jake hadn't realised he was laughing in return, until the sound of footsteps approaching cut through their unexpectedly relaxed merriment.

'That could be Maddie back.' Petra hopped off her stool and went to peer through the open doors, with Jake close behind her. 'No, it's another courier. You couldn't deal with him could you? I'm suddenly dying for a pee!'

'Oh, but... actually, I don't... umm. Maddie always deals with that side of things.'

'All you have to do is check it's the right stuff and sign.' Petra did a little jig to show she was serious about needing the bathroom. 'I should not have stood up!'

'What is it supposed to be?' Jake looked increasingly uneasy. 'Maddie never said about a delivery beyond your new sign.'

'I've no idea.' Petra waved at the courier who was walking towards them, a docket in hand. 'I must dash.'

'Two dozen?' Jake counted the bags of manure, hoping that the mild shake that had started in his shoulders wasn't visible to the delivery man who had just dropped the last bag onto the ground before him.

'That's right mate. Here.' Passing a clipboard to Jake the courier fished a pen from his pocket. 'Sorry it's old school today. The computer system is down, so the tablet isn't working for signing.'

Jake's eyes narrowed as he gingerly took the pen. 'Do I have to read anything?'

'No mate, just sign at the bottom.'

'And Miss Willand ordered this, did she?'

The courier made a show of checking the time. 'I have no idea.' Taking back the clipboard, he scanned the sheet. 'Here, look, it says here it was a Mr Willand, just over a month ago. The order was delayed for some reason.'

'*Mr* Willand? It should be Miss Willand.'

'Look mate, I don't care which Willand it is. I'm getting behind here. Are you gonna sign, or have I got to put that lot back on the van?'

His cheeks blazing red, Jake scribbled his signature on the bottom of the page.

'Thank you!' The courier mumbled as he slammed the van's backdoors shut and dashed round to his cab.

'How rude.'

Jake hadn't heard Petra come up behind him.

'How hard can a bit of politeness be?' She bent to the bags of manure. Even though they were well wrapped, they still had a distinctive hum about them. 'Bet these will be fragrant when the wrappers are off.'

Jake couldn't bring himself to look at her. *How much of that did she hear?*

'Sorry I had to dash off.' Petra tapped the bags. 'Where would Mr Willand have wanted these?'

'You heard that he thought these were for Tony then?' Jake felt defeated. For a few minutes he'd shared a laugh with an attractive woman of his own age. Now she was probably privately laughing at him. Or worse – feeling sorry for him.

'I did, yes. Whoever took the order obviously wrote it down wrong.' Petra frowned. 'Are you okay, Jake?'

'What do you think?' He kicked a foot against the gravel.

'Look, I'm sure you miss Maddie's dad. I'm so sorry that—'

Spinning round, Jake snapped, 'Of course I bloody miss him. He was like a father to me! And, to spare you wondering how to ask me about what just happened, I'll tell you – I'm rubbish at reading and writing, okay!' Even though Petra was staring at him with hurt incomprehension, Jake found, now he'd started venting, he couldn't stop his lips moving.

'Yes, that does make me thick and stupid. But there you go – now you know. *Still* want to be nice to me?'

'I...'

'No? Thought not.' A second later Jake was storming across the car park to the safety of the polytunnels, trying to forget how relaxed he'd been in Petra's company less than ten minutes ago.

Maddie pulled into the private parking bay and stared at the side of the house. Her heart constricted. She'd lost her father and now her home was in danger of being taken away as well; there was no way she could live there if the nursery had to close.

How am I going to tell Jake?

The thought made her close her eyes. An image of Ed came to mind. She wasn't sure if she was looking forward to seeing him later or not.

I am looking forward to seeing him – but do I want to talk to him because I like him or because I need his advice as my solicitor?

There had been no cars in the car park when she'd arrived back at The Potting Shed, and having checked the time, and seeing it was already four o'clock, she decided she'd send Jake and Petra home and close early.

After all, what difference is two hours lost trade going to make now?

13

'What time is the bus into Wellington?'

Jake spun round to see Petra standing behind him. Her fair skin looked even paler than usual, making her freckles stand out.

'You live in Wellington too?'

'Yes.'

'Won't you be getting a lift?' Jake stared up the road, willing the bus to appear a miraculous ten minutes early.

'No.'

'I'd have thought you had a car of your own.'

'Why?' Petra wrapped her arms around her chest.

'Your sort always have nice things from an early age.' Jake could hear the resentment in his voice. He knew Petra didn't deserve what he was saying, but he was too angry at himself to swallow his pride, apologise or calm down.

'My sort?' Petra brushed her ponytail over her shoulder before sitting on the thin strip of plastic beneath the bus shelter that pretended to be a seat. She knew she ought to be cross, but instead she felt sad. 'I don't know what I did to offend you, Jake, but I'd appreciate it if you'd stop talking to me like I was something stuck to the bottom of your shoe.'

'Me? You're the one who—'

Petra stood up again, looking up at his averted face. 'I'm the one who what? Made you a cuppa? Offered to help move the manure? Painted the fence? Enjoyed a laugh with you between customers? All those hideous crimes that they didn't teach me about on my boring law course at uni.'

'*Boring?* At least you went to uni. Some of us would have given anything for a chance like that!'

Petra couldn't believe what she was hearing. 'I'm sorry you didn't get it, but that's hardly my fault, is it?'

'People like you just have no idea how lucky you are—'

'*No.*' The word came out as a hushed shout, taking Petra by surprise with the force with which she'd delivered it. 'I *do* know how lucky I've been, but I didn't know you found reading difficult – which I'm assuming is what happened with the courier and why your knickers are in a twist. But I'm not judging you for the way your life has been, so maybe you could return the favour and not judge me for mine without getting to know a bit more about me first!'

The sound of the bus coming in the distance made them look up. Sticking her arm out so the driver knew to stop, Petra went on. 'I was enjoying your company before that delivery came. And just so you know,' she stepped back as the bus drew up in front of her, 'I couldn't care less if you can't read or write or whether you secretly have a double first in nuclear physics for that matter. I found myself liking you because I thought you were a nice person. Maybe you're not so nice after all.'

Leaping onto the bus, Petra flashed her bus pass over the scanner, twisting round to face Jake as he followed suit. 'I'm going to sit upstairs. Don't follow me. I thought we might be friends, but it seems you don't want that'

Henry had left two messages on her mobile while she'd been taking refuge in the shower, but Maddie hadn't listened to them. She couldn't imagine they'd say anything that her sister hadn't said on repeat earlier that afternoon.

Since she'd closed up the shop, she'd almost texted Ed a couple of times to cancel dinner. In the end she'd decided to go with the flow. She knew she needed to talk to someone.

'If Dad hadn't gone, then I wouldn't be in such a mess anyway.' Pulling on a clean pair of jeans and a shirt, Maddie dragged a brush through her tangled hair as she addressed the fern that sat on the overcrowded windowsill. 'If his heart attack had come two weeks later, then the nursery would have been mine.'

The plant, jammed between a pile of gardening magazines and a collection of coffee mugs waiting to be taken to the kitchen, seemed to reply, 'But that wouldn't have changed the BIG situation, would it. They would still want your land and be about to build nearby.'

Sinking onto the side of her bed, Maddie ran both palms over her face. 'This is ridiculous. I can't go out tonight. Ed's my solicitor, for heaven's sake. If Sabi sees us she'll assume we are plotting behind her back.'

The fern stared at her across the room. 'Even if you go to a restaurant, it is highly unlikely to be the sort of place Sabi would go.'

'True.' Maddie checked her watch. It was two minutes to

six. If Ed was on time, then he'd be there soon. 'We could stay here and have a takeaway.'

One look around her bedroom put her off. 'Not that I have any intention of Ed coming in here, but the mess does rather echo the state of the house in general.'

Suddenly wanting to be away from the nursery, even if for only a little while, Maddie stuffed her phone into her mini backpack, and headed downstairs, through the kitchen and out into the car park to wait for Ed.

'This is lovely.'

Maddie looked out of the picture window next to their table for two. The River Exe tumbled beneath a stone bridge. The wind that had picked up since they'd arrived stirred its flow into mini white-topped waves as the water navigated around and over the rocks hidden beneath the surface.

'One of my favourite spots for dinner.' Ed picked up a menu. 'I hoped you'd like it too. Close to town, and yet most definitely in the countryside. Sometimes you can see a heron fishing, just there.'

As Ed pointed to a flat stone that sat on the opposite bank, Maddie felt a strange sense of disquiet. Was she one in a long line of women he'd sat here with, looking at the view and hoping to watch a heron go fishing?

'You come here a lot then?'

'My parents love it. I bring them whenever they're down from Scotland.'

With a sense of relief she told herself she had no right to, Maddie asked, 'You're Scottish?'

'Ish.' Ed grinned. 'But please don't ask me to do the

accent, because it is truly awful and would be an affront to anyone from north of the border.'

'How can you be Scottish-ish?'

'I was born in Inverness, but to English parents.'

'Hence no accent?'

'I always assumed so. Although I was surrounded by a beautiful local brogue, I never picked it up. We came back to England when I was eleven. My father's job was relocated. He was in the Ministry of Defence doing something.'

'Something?'

'I imagine it was terribly dull, but the fact he could never tell us what it was gave him a hint of intrigue.' Ed flicked his eyes back out to the river. 'They moved north again once Dad retired.'

'Did your mum work?'

'She was a part-time gardener.'

'Seriously?'

'She'd tidy pensioners' gardens when they could no longer manage the work, plant up hanging baskets, clear weeds and so on. Nothing heavy, but she loved it.'

Maddie turned back to watch the water. Its presence was both soothing and mildly hypnotic. 'Perhaps I could do that? It sounds rather nice, and I suppose I'd have money if I sold, so…'

'Have money? *Sold?*' Ed put his menu down. 'Whatever happened at your sister's house?'

Two plates of beer-battered cod and twice-cooked chips arrived just as Maddie explained how she'd left Sabi without any agreement being made over the nursery's future.

'Although, if BIG really are going to build a garden centre on the fields opposite The Potting Shed, then I have to agree with Sabi, it could all be rather pointless anyway.'

Finding himself fighting the urge to take Maddie's hand and tell her it was going to be alright, even though he wasn't sure it would be, Ed speared a chip with his fork. 'And your sister and her husband are happy to sign the land over to BIG for their storage area?'

'I'm not sure happy is the word in Henry's case, but Sabi certainly is. She's convinced that it's a blessing for me – doing me a favour by getting rid of the nursery, which she sees as a burden, and giving me a chance to get a life – which in her mind equals a husband, kids and a job that ends at five o'clock.'

'A rather old-fashioned attitude.' Ed chewed his chip thoughtfully.

'It probably comes from a good place, but I've never wanted the same things from life as Sabi. She has trouble seeing that.'

Ed spooned a dollop of ketchup onto his plate from a small glass bowl. 'This lawyer you mentioned, Leo Creswell.'

'What about him?'

'I'm sure I've heard the name before, although I can't think why.' Swirling some fragments of batter through a puddle of tomato sauce, Ed added, 'You'll need to talk to him too. Make sure you have all the facts and finer details. Do you know exactly where this BIG garden centre will be built? Is it exactly opposite or is it a few fields away? The land opposite The Potting Shed is fairly open until you reach the motorway.'

'From what Sabi said, I took the build to be directly over the road, but I haven't seen any plans so...'

'Then you need to request plans. There will also be an application at the town hall lodged for planning permission. Not even enterprises as wealthy as BIG can build without all the legal hoops being jumped.'

Maddie's fork wavered on its way to her mouth. 'There might be objections to it being built?'

'There are always objections to anything being built, although, at the risk of being defeatist, I imagine the local council would welcome BIG on an employment level, but we could check.'

'We?' Maddie couldn't help but smile. 'As my solicitor or my friend?'

'Both.'

Maddie gave a small sigh. 'I think, right now, I need a friend as much as I need a solicitor.'

Ed met Maddie's eyes for a second, before concentrating on his depleted dinner. 'I hope that means you'll come for a walk on Saturday night?'

Maddie picked up her glass of lager. 'Are you sure your Dark Skies group won't mind me tagging along? I'd hate to be in the way.'

'We're always after new members, so there's no question of you simply tagging along. I promise it's a friendly group.'

'And you walk across Exmoor and look at the stars once a week, during autumn and winter?'

'That sums it up.' Ed hooked a chip up between his fingers. 'We usually walk to a pre-planned spot and then sit down – or lie down – and stare at the constellations. As there's no artificial light, you'd be amazed what you can see.'

Images of lying in the open, in the middle of the night, next to Ed, were blocking out all other thoughts. 'That sounds very peaceful.'

'It is.' Ed nodded. 'We tend to chat as we walk, but once we stop to look, everyone is quiet. There's no rule about silence or anything, but somehow the sense of the place takes over and there's no need for words.'

'Do you know a lot about astronomy then? Would I need a telescope or anything?'

'All you need is your eyesight and something to lie on. A travel rug or thick towel. And a hot drink is a good idea, it can get quite cold.'

A new image of snuggling up to Ed as they watched the stars took up pole position in Maddie's mind, and for a moment she wondered if he was having exactly the same thought. 'I think perfect peace sounds delightful at the moment.'

'Good. I'll collect you if you like.'

'It's okay, you'll have to drive miles out of your way.' Suddenly unsettled by the uncharacteristically romantic route her mind was taking, and wanting to be seen to be independent, Maddie said, 'I'll meet you there.'

'If you're sure. It can be quiet hairy driving to the meeting spot in the dark.'

'I'll cope.'

'Fair enough. I'll email you the details.' Forking up his last mouthful of fish, Ed returned the conversation to the nursery. 'Look, if you don't want to talk about it now, just say, but if BIG do buy your land, have you thought what you'll do?'

'I won't be able to stay in the house.' Her appetite diminishing, Maddie laid her cutlery down. 'It would kill me to see them on my dad's land. The thought of not fulfilling the dream we set ourselves makes me sad.'

'Have you thought about setting up your own place from scratch somewhere else?'

'I hadn't.' Maddie drained the remains of her lager. 'To tell you the truth, I think I'm still in shock.'

'I'm not surprised.' Ed put down his glass. 'Let's think about something else for a minute. Tell me about you, Maddie?'

'What do you mean?'

'We've talked about my life and my hobby, but what do you do when you aren't at work?'

Maddie only just stopped her hollow laugh in time. 'I'm never not at work.'

Hearing how negative that sounded, she hastily added, 'I don't mean that as a complaint. I love my job, but The Potting Shed is a 24/7 operation for me. The perils of being self-employed.'

'But surely when your father was alive you had time off?'

'Occasionally…' Maddie paused, '…mostly we enjoyed working together, and when we got really busy, then he and Jake would often need a third pair of hands, so even if I'd planned to take some time to myself, I'd stay to help.'

'And when they didn't need your hands?' Ed cocked his head to one side. 'Why do I get the feeling you don't want to tell me what you get up to when you aren't covered in soil?'

Staring at her plate, Maddie said, 'You'll think I'm mad.'

'Why?'

'Because it's silly.' Maddie bit her lip.

'Now I'm intrigued, but if you won't tell me, I'll have to guess.' Ed picked up the pudding menu as he pondered. 'Belly dancing, ballet, Thai food cooking, macramé…?'

Maddie couldn't help but laugh. 'Do I look like a belly dancer to you?'

Wiggling his eyebrows playfully, Ed said, 'Give those hips a jiggle and I'll let you know.'

'Not likely!' Maddie grinned. 'I'm no dancer.'

'Well that crosses ballet off the potential list too then.'

'And I'm a terrible cook, so it's a no-go with the Thai cooking.' Maddie looked down at her plate. 'Although a class wouldn't be such a bad idea. Perhaps if I learnt to cook things that weren't served with toast Sabi wouldn't think me quite such a hopeless case.'

'Do you like eating stuff on toast?'

'Yes.'

'Doesn't matter what your sister thinks then. You're not entertaining those high-flying suited businessman types I suspect Sabi's husband needs to wine and dine sometimes – I'm assuming that happens?'

'It does.' Maddie felt a twitch at the corner of her mouth. 'But Ed – *you're* a suited businessman.'

'Ah yes,' Ed leant forward conspiratorially, 'but I'm in disguise.'

'Not at home in a suit then?'

'I think of the clothing as an occupational hazard.' Ed surveyed the dessert options as he said, 'It's got to be macramé then.'

'Pardon?'

'Your unspoken hobby.' Ed sounded victorious. 'I shall

expect The Potting Shed to be selling woven hanging devices for pot plants any day now.'

Maddie's smile dipped. 'It may yet come to that if we want to keep going.'

'I'm sorry.' Ed reached out a hand, touching his fingers lightly on the back of hers, before withdrawing them. 'I was trying to change the subject and failed spectacularly.'

Staring at the spot where his fingertips had been, Maggie mumbled, 'Welly walking.'

Ed leant forward again. 'Did you say welly walking?'

'Uh-huh.'

'Is that with a group then?'

Maddie risked raising her eyes to meet his; they looked back at her with interest rather than disbelief. 'You aren't laughing?'

'Why would I? I go onto the moors late at night, lie on my back and look at the sky – walking in welly boots is normal by comparison. So, where do you walk?'

'Various places. Depends. Killerton mostly. Having worked there for so long, I know the grounds like the back of my hand. It's easy to disappear into the peace and quiet of the countryside. Sometimes I hit the Blackdown Hills instead. Anywhere where I can be guaranteed good puddles.'

'Puddles... Oh, I see, not so much welly walks as puddle splash hunts.' Ed's eyes lit up. 'I used to love splashing in puddles when I was a kid.'

Maddie's cheeks heated with embarrassment. 'That's what I thought you'd say. It's what everyone says just before they start looking at me as if I'm either nuts or with pity. As if I'm someone who hasn't noticed they aren't eight years old anymore.'

'Well, I think it sounds fun and rather freeing.'

'It is.' Maddie spoke into her glass. 'Very good for relieving stress. Somehow the hunt for good puddles, then the pleasure of actually jumping in them – wading through them…' She stopped speaking. 'God, it sounds so mad. You can understand why this is a pastime I do not talk to people about!'

Ed was thoughtful as he contemplated the ice cream options. Finally, he said, 'I think there is something very pleasing about the sound a deep puddle makes when you wade through it, don't you?'

In that second, it was all Maddie could do not to run around the table and hug him. An hour later, she was still wondering why she hadn't.

14

Petra clasped her shoulder bag to her chest as she marched from the car park to the nursery's little shop. Seeing no sign of Jake, she spun on her heels and headed to the nearest polytunnel, fully intending to visit each one until she found him.

Spotting him, semi-hidden by a forest of evergreen grasses and ferns, a stooped figure bent over a potting table in the third polytunnel she tried, Petra paused as nerves fluttered in her chest.

Come on, there's no way you can leave the situation like this.

Hoping that he felt as bad as she did about how they'd left things the afternoon before, Petra walked into the tunnel. The change of atmosphere was instant. The cutting wind, which sliced through the cool air outside, disappeared within the cocoon of the thick plastic walls, only to be replaced by a mild humidity, afforded by freshly watered plants and artificial heating.

'Jake?'

He stood abruptly, making Petra think he'd been so absorbed in his work that he hadn't heard her coming. 'Does Maddie need me?'

'I don't know. I haven't seen her yet.'

'Oh, well, I'm busy.' He bent back over his work.

Knowing he'd expect her to walk away, Petra stood her ground. 'Listen, I'm sorry I lost it yesterday. I should have realised you weren't in a good place. I'm guessing you haven't been for a while, in fact.'

Jake's hands paused in their work; one palm full of topsoil, the other became motionless in the act of picking up a pot. 'Why shouldn't I be in a good place?'

Petra took a deep breath. 'You lost your employer. Your friend. I don't think there's been anyone you could talk to about how you feel, has there?'

'What?'

'You couldn't talk to Maddie, could you – Tony was her father, and you didn't want to add to her grief and upset her further. So, you've had to keep your feelings bottled up. I just thought you'd like a friend to talk to. I hoped that I could be that friend – if you want.'

Feeling uncomfortable, but recognising that Petra was offering him an olive branch, Jake gulped, 'I'm sorry about the "your sort" comment yesterday. I didn't mean... Look, let's face it, I'm stupid, and you're really clever. I suppose I thought you wouldn't want to know someone like me who can't even read properly, when you know so many other clever people.'

Petra tried not to snap. 'I told you yesterday, only you weren't listening. I liked you because I thought you were a nice person. It doesn't matter to me that you can't read properly.'

'People always say it doesn't matter, but they never mean it.'

This time Petra did snap. 'I'd be grateful if you didn't lump me in with whoever *they* are, thank you very much. I'm not "people", I'm me, so perhaps I could be allowed to know what does or doesn't matter to me.'

'Yeah, well, as I said, I'm sorry.' Shamefaced, Jake started to rearrange some plant pots. 'I shouldn't have judged you. I just didn't expect someone like you to be interested in me.'

'Again, "someone like me"?' But this time there was a humorous twist to Petra's lips and a sparkle in her eyes. 'Maddie likes you. Tony liked you. I'm not that different from them.'

'Sorry.'

'And stop saying sorry!'

'Sorry – I mean, not sorry. I mean, yes I am but... what I mean is, you're right, I could use a friend, if you still want. Can we start again?'

'Of course. And this time, we'll both try and not jump to conclusions. Deal?'

Jake's shoulders relaxed as he smiled. 'Deal.'

'What are you doing?' Petra came to his side, watching how he pressed some soil into place with firm but gentle fingers.

'Bulbs for the spring. Hyacinths. They would normally be planted in October. These got overlooked, but as the temperature in this tunnel is kept at a steady heat, they should manage okay if I look after them.'

Petra picked up one of the bulbs, 'Weird things aren't they. They're so hard – crisp even. It's like they're dead.'

'That's how they need to be. It's more like they are dormant. Think of it as hibernation.' Jake took the bulb from Petra and eased it into the compost. 'They have to be in a leafless, rootless state, to stand any chance of growth.'

'It always seems a miracle that anything can go from appearing almost desiccated, to producing such beautiful flowers.'

'Well, if you come by in the spring, then you'll be able to see these in all their glory.' Jake picked up a permanent marker and passed it to Petra. 'Here, you can have this one. Write your name on the pot and I'll keep it safe for you.'

'Really?'

'Yeah,' Jake shrugged. 'My way of saying sorry for being an idiot.'

Petra smiled. 'Okay, but I have two conditions.'

'Even I know that conditions attached to receiving a gift isn't normal.'

'Even so.' Petra twirled the pen between her fingers. 'The first condition is that you are never *ever* to call yourself stupid again. You are far from stupid. And the second is that you write my name on the pot.'

Jake's eyes immediately flashed with panic. 'I told you, I can't…'

Petra held up her hand. 'I know, but I wondered, can you write individual letters?'

'Well, yes.'

'Okay. So, the first letter is a P.' She held the pen out to him, 'Try? I'll make you another giant mug of tea as a reward.'

'That's bribery.' Jake reluctantly took the pen.

'Don't knock bribery, bribery moves mountains.' Petra gave him an encouraging nudge, noting how foreign the pen looked in his large fingers. 'No rush. So, P.'

Jake gripped the pot in his hand, and twisting his body away, so his companion couldn't see, ran the tip of the pen over the pot. 'Okay.'

'E.'

Petra clamped her mouth shut, resisting the urge to let the rest of the letters tumble out of her mouth before he was ready.

'Next?'

'T.'

'And?'

'R.'

The pause was longer this time. Petra could hear the squeal of the pen's tip as it was methodically dragged over the curved plastic surface.

'Are there anymore?'

'Last letter now. A.'

A moment later, Jake stood up straight. His height took her by surprise. 'Blimey, you're so tall. Why don't you stand up straight more often?'

'What?'

'You should shove those shoulders back. You're a good-looking bloke.'

'Oh.' Jake didn't know what else to say until he noticed the sudden pink tinge to Petra's cheeks. 'You're blushing.'

'Might be.' She grinned, peering up at Jake as he passed her the pot. 'This is fantastic. Thank you so much.' The writing resembled that of a child attempting capital letters for the first time, but she was thrilled nonetheless. 'Where does this go so it will grow?'

'Over there.' Jake pointed to a bench near a heater. 'I'll put it with the others when I'm done.'

'You'll look after it for me, won't you?'

'Will you remember to come back for it in April?'

'Definitely. Hopefully, I'll have learnt to grow them, and lots of other things, myself by then.'

Her determination took Jake by surprise. 'But you could do anything you wanted?'

'I could, but I think I'd quite like to do this.' Petra picked up an empty pot, 'I'd better go and find Maddie and see what she needs doing. Shame really, I'd rather stay here and help you.'

'You would?'

'Yes.' Petra gestured to her pot. 'That's my name. *You* wrote it.'

'That hardly makes me literate.'

'It proves you are not illiterate.' Petra put her hand into her bag and hesitated. 'Look, don't go all offended on me again, but I stopped by the library on my way home last night.'

'Sensible place to go if you can read and want a book.'

'I got you these.' Petra took a flyer out of her bag and dropped it onto the worktable. 'I'd help you, if you wanted me to. You don't even have to tell anyone. Anyway, have a think about it.'

Departing at speed through the polytunnel's doors, Petra left Jake staring at a leaflet for adult literacy workshops. She didn't see the thunderous look that crossed his face, or she would have waited a bit longer.

Maddie hadn't expected to sleep, but a combination of sheer exhaustion and a pint and a half of lager had pulled her into a dreamless oblivion as soon as her head hit the pillow. Now, however, the cold light of day brought with it the reminder that she had to talk to Jake and Petra about the future – or lack of – of The Potting Shed. She wasn't worried about Petra's reaction, but Jake…

If I started a new nursery, he could still work for me.

Maddie groaned. The thought of uprooting hadn't become less daunting because she'd slept well. *And the fact remains, I don't want to start again. I love it here.*

Moving around the kitchen, making up the daily flasks of tea and coffee that kept her and Jake going, Maddie was trying to remember if Petra had sugar in her tea, when she caught sight of the envelope she'd found amongst the heap of post Petra had gathered up in the shop. She didn't need to read its contents again. Every word of BIG's letter, identical to the one her sister had received, was seared onto her heart.

Petra's smile was missing. Maddie felt a twinge of unease as she walked into the shed shop. *Does she know already?* Maddie dismissed the thought. Sabi would never have spoken to Miriam about this, not before a decision had been made within the family.

'Are you alright?'

'Not really, but it's my own fault.'

'You want to talk about it?'

Shaking her head, Petra's ponytail wobbled against her shoulder. 'It's okay. I was trying to help someone, and it didn't work. That's all.'

'I can think of worse crimes.' Maddie slid the loaded tray onto the till's bench. 'I couldn't remember if you took sugar.'

'No thanks.' Petra picked up the packet of biscuits

Maddie had brought alongside the tea. 'I'll make up for it by eating too many of these.'

Maddie felt her fake smile blossom into a real one. She's only been here a minute, but already I'm going to miss her.

'How about you, Maddie?' Petra tilted her head to one side. 'Your smile is looking a tad strained too. You sleeping okay?'

'On the whole, no.' Maddie sat at the desk, and patted the stool next to her. 'While it's quiet, I've got something to tell you.'

Petra sat down. 'You can't afford for me to stay, can you?' Her eyes roamed over the till. 'It's okay. I know I was thrust upon you. But I was going to tell you anyway – I was just summoning up the courage.'

Feeling as if she'd taken a wrong turn in a conversation she hadn't even started yet, Maddie asked, 'What were you going to tell me?'

'Even though the job was only until after Christmas, I can't stay. I want to. I already love it here, and I am definitely going to look for gardening work if I can find someone to give me a chance, but I can't work with…' Petra's voice trailed off. 'I can go now if it's easier for you?'

'Go now?' Maddie tried to process the avalanche of information she'd just heard. 'Jake?'

'Uh huh.' Petra unscrewed her flask. 'As I said, I tried to help. But it went wrong – although I'm not sure how. Either way, it would be awkward if I stayed, and as Jake clearly does not cope well with awkward situations – or people come to that – it's better for me to be the one who moves on. I'd hate an atmosphere to develop which might put off your customers.'

Maddie cursed inwardly. 'I should have warned you about Jake – he's lovely, it's just…'

'No people skills. I worked that out.'

'How did you offer to help him?'

Petra watched the vapour from her hot tea as it evaporated into the cold shed. 'I don't think Jake would like it if I said.'

'Fair enough.' Maddie gave a nod of understanding. 'I'm sorry you feel you need to leave, but as it happens—Hang on, how did you know I was going to have to let you go after Christmas? I was about to tell you that.'

Petra sipped her tea. 'As I was forced upon you, and you've been so kind, I never liked to bring the subject up.'

'You know about this place potentially closing down?'

'Closing?' Petra's forehead furrowed. 'No. I assumed you'd buy Sabi out. It's obvious you love this place. You can't close!' Petra looked aghast.

'But you knew that Sabi wanted out of the nursery?'

'Sure. She needs the money. I overheard Mum and Sabi talking about the plans for your sister's second home. Her getting me a job here was a favour in return for Mum holding off other vendors, so Sabi and Henry could buy their dream home. Mum's getting some sort of commission for facilitating the sale.'

Putting her flask down, Maddie spoke with exaggerated care. 'Can you say that again please?'

15

Maddie was driving her old Suzuki jeep towards Tiverton before she'd thought about what she was doing.

Sabi and Henry lived on Post Hill, on the outskirts of the ever-expanding market town. A long, bolt-straight road, dotted with large, detached houses, many of which belonged to businessmen and women who needed to be close to Tiverton Parkway Railway Station and an easy run to Taunton, Bristol or London.

'What the hell happened to us, Sabi? We used to be so similar. We'd play together at the nursery, running around the polytunnels, helping Dad. But now...' Slowing while the car in front of her overtook a cyclist, Maddie struggled with her incomprehension and hurt, '... now you want to sell our father's life's work so you can own a second house. You already have a home that's way bigger than you and Henry will ever need!'

Turning off the link road, and driving towards Samford Peverell, Maddie eased the car down to thirty miles an hour, along the winding stretch leading to the village of Halberton. Passing the bridge that spanned the Great Western Canal, the enormity of her sister's betrayal consumed her mind and knotted the muscles in her stomach and shoulders.

'No wonder Sabi's so determined to agree to BIG's offer. How convenient for her to have something come along to shoulder the guilt of taking my home and business away.'

As she passed the sign for Tiverton Golf Club, Maddie flicked on the car's indicator and manoeuvred onto Sabi and Henry's gravelled drive. Her insides fizzed as if she'd consumed an entire packet of sherbet, leaving her edgy and nauseous. Maddie wasn't sure if she was relieved or disappointed that only Sabi's car was in the drive.

'Henry must be at the golf club or something.'

Remembering her brother-in-law's messages, Maddie clicked on her mobile's answer phone. Staying in the driver's seat, steeling herself, she listened as Henry's recorded voice filled the car.

'I'm so sorry Maddie. Sabi and I honestly thought you'd know about BIG already. I hope you can forgive us once the shock has passed. Who knows, this really might be for the best.'

Maddie rolled her eyes as the second message began to play.

'Forgot to say, you left an old folder on the table. Let me know if you need it and I'll drop it over next time I'm passing.'

'An *old* folder.' Maddie got out of the car and slammed the door behind her. 'Neither of you bothered opening it then!'

Marching to the front door, hoping her indignation would hold for long enough to say what needed saying, before she fell back into her habit of doing what Sabi wanted because it was so much easier, Maddie rang the bell.

'And if you want to buy a mansion, Sabi, you are perfectly capable of working hard and earning the money to buy one like everyone else!'

Sabi took a step back from Maddie's ire. Her sister had been railing at her across the kitchen table for what felt like forever. As yet, she hadn't managed to get a word in edgeways.

'How dare you!? You didn't even give me a chance to explain my ideas to make Dad's business work when I was here last time.' Maddie picked up the folder that still sat on the table and slammed it down again. 'Oh no, you'd rather simply buy your dreams using money that robs me of my livelihood and your personal contacts. If it wasn't for Miriam, you'd never have got a look in with that house – a *second* house! When were you going to bother telling me about that by the way?'

'I...'

'Oh forget it.' Maddie picked up the folder and waved it at her sister. Deflated, she gave a ragged sigh. 'We could have worked together. We could have built The Potting Shed into something unique and exclusive. Wouldn't you rather do that than drift around an empty house all day turning yourself into a clone of Miriam? I simply cannot believe you're happy to let BIG destroy Dad's business – it's bad enough that you were willing to sell up – but to *them*!'

Banging the folder back on the table with a thump, Maddie pointed a finger at it. 'You might as well recycle this lot. Saves me the trouble of adding it to the skip I'll have to hire when I start clearing Dad's things prior to moving out, because if you think that I could live there once the nursery has been destroyed, then you clearly don't know me at all.'

Spinning round on the balls of her feet, Maddie left Sabi leaning against her polished granite worktop, two unused cups in her hands, listening to the empty echo of the front door slamming as Maddie left the house.

Maddie was still shaking as she drove the jeep back into the nursery car park. Even the sight of half a dozen customers' cars didn't lift her spirits.

Taking deep breaths of crisp, cold November air, Maddie's eyes fell on the fence. It looked better than it had, although another coat of preservative would improve things further. *Is there any point, though?*

A couple crossed the car park before her. An elderly gentleman was carrying a cardboard box, the contents of which were hidden from view, but whatever it held, his wife was clearly pleased, as they trotted happily towards their car.

I don't want to lose that. Maddie swallowed. *I like growing plants that will make people happy.*

Tugging a woolly hat over her head, Maddie tried to ignore the sound of her own voice at the back of her head. It was rehashing her one-sided conversation with Sabi. *Perhaps I should have let her speak.*

Maddie thought of all the work she'd put into the proposal she'd left at her sister's house. But what would have been the point? It would only have become a row. Sabi was determined to sell even before BIG came along.

She gave an inward groan. *I hate that Sabi is right about there being little point in trying to keep going if BIG are next door, but I don't suppose it was her fault they came along. I shouldn't have shouted at her.*

Petra was handing over some change to a woman buying a big bag of red onions as Maddie arrived back in the shop.

'And don't forget, the Christmas trees will be here in early December. If you want to bag a good one, I wouldn't hang about if I were you.'

The woman picked up her bulging paper bag. 'I'll be here. I need one at least seven foot tall, and they can be so hard to find.'

'Don't worry, we'll have all sizes, but only the best shapes.' Petra bid her customer goodbye and closed the till.

Maddie took off her hat. 'I'm impressed.'

'Thanks. I'm really enjoying selling things.'

'Something you are clearly good at. Your sign is already proving to be a godsend.'

'It's been steady so far today. Not busy, but steady.' Now the customer had gone, Petra looked worried. 'You weren't gone as long as I thought you might be. Are you okay?'

'In all honesty, I have no idea.' Recalling how Petra had come to tell her about Miriam and Sabi's house plans in the first place, Maddie asked, 'And you? Spoken to Jake yet?'

Petra's smile faded as she pointed to a leaflet in the wicker wastepaper basket under the desk. 'As I said, I tried to help. That help was not welcomed. He popped by to reinforce the point.'

Maddie fished the pamphlet from the bin. 'Adult literacy

information? He told you he couldn't read or write very well?'

'He did.'

'Wow. He never tells anyone that. I only found out by accident.' She studied Petra more closely. 'You know, if he told you, then that's a big deal. He must like you.'

'And yet all the evidence points to the contrary.' She shrugged sadly. 'Anyway, I found out by accident too.'

'What happened?'

By the time Petra had told Maddie about the courier and the hyacinth bulb, Maddie was stunned. 'You have a hell of a gift with people, Petra.'

'Really?'

'Jake never trusts anyone, and not only did he tell you about his writing once you'd worked out he doesn't read very well, but he wrote your name on a pot. That's huge!'

'I knew it was a big deal for him. I respect that. I thought he understood I respected that, but only ten minutes after you'd gone, he came here and dropped it in the bin right in front of me without a word.' Petra muttered, 'I wouldn't be at all surprised if he'd consigned my hyacinth to the compost pile too.'

16

The decision to put off telling Jake he was losing his job in the near future wasn't difficult, especially as she now had something else to talk to him about. Something that, if he wasn't going to be working at The Potting Shed for much longer, was about to become important.

'You've been busy while I've been out then.'

'Yeah. Customers needed soil and stuff carrying to their cars. Even sold some of the manure bags that arrived this morning.'

'Were they regular customers?'

'A couple of them.' Jake picked up a dustpan and brush and cleared up a sprinkling of spilt root powder. 'Some new.'

'You know why we have a few new customers, don't you?'

'The new sign and the social media stuff.' Jake laid down the dustpan. 'I'm not that stupid, Maddie.'

'You aren't stupid at all, but it seems that you are ungrateful.'

Blanching, Jake opened his mouth to reply, but no words came out. Maddie had never so much as raised her voice to him before. 'What do you mean?'

'Petra must have gone out of her way to get that information for you, and you threw it in the bin.'

'It's too late for me.' Jake picked up a stack of pots, their familiarity comforting between his fingers.

'You're twenty years old. That's nothing!' Maddie brushed her hair from her eyes. 'But if you are determined not to accept Petra's help, then you could have got rid of them in private to spare her feelings. But no, you went over to the shop and dumped it into the bin right in front of her. How do you think that made Petra feel?'

'She shouldn't interfere. It's none of her business.'

'Then why did you tell her you couldn't read or write well in the first place?'

Jake hugged his arms around himself. 'There was a courier and—'

'I heard. Hence the new bags of manure to sell. I also heard you wrote Petra's name on a pot.'

'She likes hyacinths.'

Dragging her hands through her hair, a few knots snagged on her fingers as Maddie felt her temper, so rarely riled in the years preceding her father's passing, rise again. Battening it down, knowing that it would only make things worse where Jake was concerned, Maddie spoke firmly. 'I suggested that it would be good for you to make a friend of Petra. It sounds as if you'd taken my advice.'

'Well, yeah.'

'And you like her, don't you – as a person.'

'She's alright.'

Picking up a broom that was propped against the workbench, Maddie swept the area around her feet while she spoke. 'Petra must have gone out of her way to get that information for you. I imagine she offered to help you learn. Am I right?'

'I don't want—'

'Am. I. Right?'

'Yeah.'

'I'm sorry if I seem short with you, Jake, but I'm very tired. Since Dad died, I've not slept well and I've got a lot on my plate. I know you won't think this is any of my business, but I care for you, so…' Pausing in her work, Maddie rested her weight on the broom's handle, '…I am going to say this anyway. It's high time you tackled that chip on your shoulder. You and Petra get on – she is a kind person who tried to help you.

'Ask yourself, did Petra recoil in horror when you told her about your literacy issues? Did she shout "unclean" or say something unkind? No. She tried to help and all you're doing in return is giving her the cold shoulder.'

Jake started to place the pots on the workbench into a neat line. 'I don't like people trying to fix me.'

'Did you explain that?'

'Well, no.' Jake looked at his boss. 'I haven't had anyone try to help me for so long. Not since you and your dad and… I don't know how to…'

As Jake's words trailed into the still air, Maddie felt herself relenting. 'I know. Look, why not ask Petra out for a drink or something? Women like her do not come along every day.'

'A drink? As in a date?' Jake was horrified by the prospect.

'Why not? She's lovely.'

'And way way *way* out of my league. Blokes like me do *not* date woman like her. They just don't.'

'Do you like her?'

'Makes no difference now, does it?'

Maddie passed him the broom. 'I've got to get on. Just think about it, okay Jake? At the very least apologise and tell Petra why you reacted like you did. I would be very surprised if she didn't forgive you.'

The pot in which the tea was served was of the finest silver. Sabi was itching to lift it up to study the hallmark she was convinced she'd find on the base.

'I'll pour, shall I?' Leo Creswell lifted the pot, hovering it over a bone china teacup.

'Please.' Sabi breathed in the scent of lavender as the herbal tea they'd chosen from an extensive list of flavours landed in her cup.

'I, or should I say, we, appreciate you agreeing to meet in person.' Leo added a drop of milk to his own tea, after Sabi had declined, opting instead for a spoonful of runny honey. 'It's so much nicer to talk business in person.'

'My pleasure.' Sabi looked around the busy hotel lounge. She'd often meant to book afternoon tea here, but as yet, hadn't had the occasion or excuse to warrant the price, hefty even in exchange for unlimited finger sandwiches, cake, tea and silver service. 'I was hoping to have the opportunity to talk to you. Your offer came out of the blue, so, as you can imagine, since then, my husband and I have thought of a lot of questions to ask you.'

'Hence this meeting. To give you a clearer picture of the

situation and for you to ask me anything you like.' Leo took a sip from his tea. 'I am assuming that you are intending to accept BIG's offer.'

'We are considering it.' Modelling her responses on those she imagined Miriam would give in the circumstances, Sabi added, 'I am keen to proceed, but you must remember that the decision isn't entirely mine. My sister remains wary about losing the family business.'

'An understandable sentiment.' Leo looked at the two empty chairs at the table. 'I assumed Miss Willand and, possibly, your husband would be joining us.'

Hoping he didn't guess that she hadn't told either her sister or husband about their meeting, Sabi stirred her tea and murmured, 'The run up to Christmas is a busy time at The Potting Shed, especially on a Saturday, and my husband is lunching at the golf club.'

'Of course.'

Sabi had the feeling that Leo was mentally rubbing his hands at the thought of the Christmas trade that BIG might conjure in the fullness of time. 'I have a few questions, if I may?'

'You may, but first, I should bring your attention to a *minor* change of plan and reassure you on a few matters.'

'Change of plan?' Sabi reached out to a three-tier rack of the finest, slimmest sandwiches she'd ever seen. Selecting a cucumber one, she put it on her plate.

'As you know,' Leo stretched out his little finger as he drank from his teacup, 'the intention of my employers was to build one of their deluxe garden centres on the fields opposite The Potting Shed and the storage buildings on your nursery's land. However, having done further investigative work, they have decided – should you and your sister agree to sign the papers – to pull down your nursery buildings and build a BIG garden centre over it. Eliminate the competition, as it were – while recompensing them handsomely.'

Sabi's intake of breath was so sharp that a nearby waiter scuttled to her side to make sure everything was alright. Having assured him that no fish bones had conned their way into the salmon sandwiches, Sabi took a mouthful of tea. She took her time topping up her cup from the pleasingly weighty tea pot before responding.

'My father's business closing is one thing, having the entire site destroyed...'

Leo leant forward, a suitably sympathetic expression on his face. 'I do understand. Here we are, swooping in just after your father passed away. I'm so sorry.'

Sabi took another sip of tea, as she tried to stop thinking about Maddie's reaction to this development.

'Naturally, as this would be a slightly *bigger* upheaval,' the lawyer chuckled, 'if you'll excuse my little pun – then you would receive a larger recompense.'

'And my sister's home?'

'Would remain. Although, I should mention that the area of garden left to her would be smaller. We promised the house itself would be untouched, and so it would be. Here,' Leo flicked open the briefcase he'd balanced against the side of his chair, 'you can see the plans.'

Sabi could hear Henry's voice echoing in her head, asking how come the plans had already been drawn up. In all his years as an architect, his constant bugbear had been that plans, even in the technological age, took ages to be drawn up and even longer to be signed off.

Why didn't I tell Henry about this meeting? If I'd phoned him, he'd have come with me. Sabi's mind raced as the truth unhelpfully waved a flag in her direction. *Because you were afraid he'd hear something that would stop you being able to have what you want.*

'So, you can see,' Leo ran a manicured fingernail over the edge of the plans, 'your sister's home would be on the very edge of the rebuild.'

'Would she have private access to her home?'

'Naturally.' Leo traced a finger along a line from the house to the main road, which ran a little to the right of the site. 'A new access point would be constructed so Miss Willand could come and go without having to cross the garden centre land.'

'And the additional remuneration you mentioned would be what, exactly?'

Leo took another sheet of paper from his briefcase and passed it to Sabi with an exaggerated flourish. 'A not inconsiderable sum.'

We could buy the house in Culmstock outright. Sabi could already see herself arranging new furniture and poring over paint charts.

'To receive that,' Leo broke through her daydream, 'we would need both yours, and your sister's, signature on this contract by December 4th.'

Sabi came back to earth with a bump. Maddie already hated her for considering selling the land – she could just imagine her response to knowing the nursery wouldn't just be forced to stop trading but would also be dismantled and turned into a BIG centre.

'You mentioned reassurances?'

Leo lounged back in his chair; a slender finger of Victoria sponge lodged between his fingers as if it was an expensive cigar. 'During the course of the buyout, it may well come to light who some of the shareholders are, therefore I am duty bound to inform you that I have shares in the business, as well as being their legal representative. I must assure you, however, that there will be no conflict of interest; I'm not on the board of directors or anything. However, I do take my job very seriously, and any money I may make when the share price rises is purely a perk.'

Sabi's throat went dry. 'What you are telling me, Mr Creswell, is that it would be in both our interests for the sale of The Potting Shed to go ahead.'

17

Sabi sat in her car and stared at the house. It was perfect. Her forever home. She could imagine herself and Henry growing old there, pottering around the garden while planning various retirement holidays.

Steeling herself for Henry's reaction when she told him about her meeting with Leo, Sabi pushed back thoughts of her sister's inevitable response. She was still reeling from how angry Maddie had been that morning. The look on her face had been pure fury and uncomprehending pain.

Maddie hardly ever gets angry – at least, she never used to.

'Perhaps I should have asked why the plans had been changed to build over our land?' Sabi muttered to herself as she got out of the car. 'But it's for the best... I'm sure it is. And now it's out of my hands anyway. BIG will ensure that The Potting Shed will not be there to save.'

But, if Maddie doesn't agree to sign, and insists on trying to buy us out, then BIG can't destroy the nursery ... although they could still build nearby. She'd never survive with them as competition.

Sabi took her mobile from her handbag and pressed a few keys. 'Miriam, hi. Just to let you know. I'm taking one last look. Then, if you've got a free moment, I'll pop into the office to give back the keys.'

Maddie gave Jake a pointed look as she passed him on the way from the shop to the house with the day's takings. He could almost hear her unspoken reproach. 'You haven't said sorry yet, have you?'

Even though he knew he looked like someone who'd be the first to dive into a pub brawl, Jake had never been good at confrontation. He'd developed a bully boy persona to protect himself – to keep people away – and it had worked. Perhaps too well.

Life had been so much easier when Tony was alive. He'd let Jake do his own thing around the polytunnels, leaving the people side of life to himself and Maddie. It had just been the three of them, all getting on with life. Sabi rarely stuck her oar in, and there'd been no new members of staff.

Jake thought of the leaflet that Petra had got for him. *Stupid idea. How can someone who can't read properly read a leaflet about learning to read?*

As he reached the shop he could see Petra sweeping the floor. He checked his watch. It was six o'clock exactly.

Skirting around to the car park Jake dragged the sign away from the entrance. He knew he was running out of time to avoid her, especially if they ended up waiting at the bus stop together again.

With his heart beating fast, Jake marched towards the shop. Maddie had been right, he had to apologise. Hooking his fingers into his belt loops, Jake told himself that even if Petra did tell him to get lost, he'd cope. He was used to being alone.

A small smile unexpectedly crossed his face as he remembered Petra getting annoyed with him at the bus stop. It hadn't been like when his mum was mad with him; it had been as if... as if she cared. The thought made him slow his pace.

Maddie got cross with me today too – she never gets cross – she said it was because she cared too.

He frowned. Maddie hadn't been herself for ages. Understandable in the circumstances, but Jake had a sense that he was missing something. That there was something more going on than grief for her father. *No, she'd have told me.*

Arriving at the shop door just as Petra was getting ready to lock up for the night, Jake dived straight in. 'I'm sorry. You were trying to help, and I was ungrateful.'

Petra weighed the keyring in her palm. 'Apology accepted, but only if you'll come out for a drink with me tonight.'

Jake's mouth dropped open. 'Out with you?'

'Why not? It's Saturday night. I promise I'll have a wash first.' Petra grinned. 'Do you know the Red Lion on Wellington Road?'

'Yeah.'

'Eight o'clock. Don't be late.'

Maddie lay on her bed and stared at the crack in the ceiling's Artex surface. She'd been meaning to mention it to her father for months – years, maybe.

'The nursery had its best day for ages today, Dad. Petra

has one of those smiles that customers are already coming back to see again. I think you'd like her.'

Closing her eyes, telling herself a rest was wise before heading out at nine to meet Ed and his Dark Skies friends, Maddie took some steadying breaths. Hoping an attempt at meditation would help un-muddle the thoughts, instead she found herself replaying the scene when she had stormed into Sabi's home. Giving her sister a piece of her mind might have been justified in the circumstances, but she still felt guilty for behaving so badly.

Pushing her back further against the bed, Maddie repositioned herself and tried to relax, but as she exhaled, trying to 'puff away her troubles' in a manner her university yoga teacher had advised, a picture of Jake's confused face when she'd told him to tackle the chip on his shoulder jumped to the forefront of her mind, adding its weight to her conscience.

'I don't know what to do, Dad.' A tear escaped from the corner of Maddie's right eye. 'Sabi wants to sell The Potting Shed and BIG want to buy our land. I know how much you hated chain stores of any sort, and so does Sabi. Not that it seems to be bothering her.

'I don't feel like myself anymore. Arguing, being snappy and sad.' Rolling onto her side, Maddie let the tears flow faster. 'I hate being at odds with Sabi. We ought to be pulling together. I thought maybe, now you've gone, Sabi would take more interest in this place.'

A growl from the pit of Maddie's stomach reminded her that she hadn't got round to having lunch. Knowing she ought to eat before she went out, she forced herself off the duvet. 'I think you'd like Ed, Dad. He's taking me out to watch the stars tonight. It's not a date or anything. We're just friends, but…'

She stopped talking and gave herself a shake. *But I'd like it to be a date. I think.* The thought made her frown. *No, no, I don't do dates anymore.*

Henry picked up the oven gloves and opened the Aga door. Taking out the baking tray, he loosened the tinfoil that was wrapped around the salmon and added a twist of black pepper to its buttery surface. Satisfied, he popped the fish back into the oven and eased the heat down. Then, checking that the new potatoes he was boiling weren't about to go soft, he chopped the ends off some mini pak choi, ready to flash fry it in olive oil.

The shrill ring of the house's landline took him by surprise. He couldn't remember the last time it had rung.

'Henry Willand-Harris.'

The voice at the other end of the phone announced itself as Jayne Davidson, a colleague of Miriam Reece's. She was pleased to inform him that the offer he and his wife had put in on the house in Culmstock had been accepted, and if they would like to come into the office on Monday, Miriam would be happy to talk through what would happen next.

Laying down the knife he held in his hand, Henry considered asking if there'd been a mistake, but knew there hadn't been. Miriam had many faults, but she did not make mistakes that involved money. Thanking Jayne, he informed her that his wife would call the office on Monday to book an appointment with Miriam and hung up.

Henry stared at the Aga. The dinner he was cooking was one of Sabi's favourite meals and he'd always loved making it for her. Now he had the urge to throw the whole lot in the bin. Not sure where to start with the conversation he now had to have with his wife, he carried on with cooking anyway. Sliding the pak choi into the frying pan, Henry found therapy in the act of stirring the green leaves, making sure each was coated in olive oil.

Knowing arguing with Sabi was never wise on an empty stomach, Henry gritted his teeth and called out, 'Sabi! Dinner will be ready in a few minutes.'

Jake was aware that people were looking at him. For the first time in living memory, he didn't mind. He'd been a semi-regular at the Red Lion since he was sixteen. Usually he'd sit, cradling a pint in the corner of the snug on his own, making it last, putting off the moment when he'd have no choice but to go home. Today, however, he was in his usual spot, but with a beautiful woman who was actually laughing with him, and not at him. His smile was so out of practice that his facial muscles were aching.

'I would never have had you down as a Guinness drinker.'

Petra wiped the back of her hand across her mouth in case she had a foam moustache. 'Let me guess, you had me down as a prosecco girl – or maybe Buck's Fizz?'

'Champagne at the very least!' Jake laughed as he lifted his pint.

Petra grinned. 'Preconceptions are dangerous things.'

Jake felt the pull towards a conversation he'd been

hoping to put off, but found he wasn't so daunted by telling Petra about his life as he thought he might be. 'And we all make them, even when we don't mean to.'

'Very true.' Petra laid down her glass and lowered her voice, 'I think this is the bit where you tell me what happened to stop you getting a decent education.'

Jake held his pint closer to his chest. 'It's no big disclosure, just a combination of ordinary stuff.'

Petra shuffled closer to him. 'Go on.'

The touch of Petra's denim-covered leg against his did nothing to make the task of telling her his story easier, but Jake wasn't going to complain about that. His brain was screaming at him.

There is an attractive, kind, clever woman sat with her leg against yours. Do you know how long it has been since you were within touching range of a woman who wasn't your boss? Five years. And that led to having a slap around the face.

'Jake?' Petra coaxed.

'Yeah, sorry, just deciding how to start.' Clearing his throat, Jake fixed his eyes on their touching knees. 'I was okay until I was about seven. Then one of my teachers noticed that I wasn't keeping up with the other children. Mild dyslexia they said.'

Petra, who was resisting the urge to lay a hand on his leg, said, 'It's so common. I hope you got help.'

'At first, yes. Extra reading time and I had help for my spelling. It was a bit embarrassing being hauled out of normal lessons for these "special classes", as my teacher called them. I did catch up a bit, but not long after that I began to have trouble concentrating. My parents weren't getting on and my dad left. I was eight by then.'

'I'm so sorry.'

Jake took a gulp of his drink. 'Mum's okay, but she's a bit... Umm...'

Petra spoke gently. 'You don't have to tell me. I wasn't being nosey. I just wanted to give you the chance to talk – but only if you want to.'

'I'm sorry about earlier.'

'That's okay.' Petra rested a hand on his leg.

'Oh.' Jake looked up at her.

'Should I move it?'

Shaking his head, not trusting himself to speak, Jake gingerly placed a palm over hers, and held it tight.

18

Sabi put down her knife and fork. 'I am so spoilt with your cooking Henry. That was truly delicious.'

'I'm glad you enjoyed it.'

'I always do, it's my favourite.'

'I know.' Henry twisted the stem of his wine glass between his fingers. His voice was a study in practised calm as he said, 'You almost didn't get it. It was destined for the bin, but then I convinced myself that it must be a mistake. That I had misunderstood somehow. That you'd *never* do something like that without speaking to me first.'

Sabi's insides clenched. 'What do you mean?'

'You're really going to sit there and pretend you don't know?'

Lifting her fork back up, Sabi played it through her fingers. 'I was going to tell you about the meeting after dinner. Over coffee, once we'd stacked the dishwasher.'

'What meeting?' Henry's brow furrowed.

'You *weren't* asking me about the meeting?'

'No. I was going to ask you what made you think that it was alright to put an offer on a house without talking to me first. An offer that has been accepted by the way.'

'Accepted?' Sabi bit back her rush of elation as she

saw her husband's face. Picking up her wine, she took a gulp, more as a delaying tactic than because she wanted a drink. 'I *was* going to tell you, but it all happened so fast and—'

'—and I might have said no.'

'No. Well, I suppose you might have, but that isn't why…' She could feel Henry's eyes boring into her and sped up her response. 'I had a call from Leo Creswell. He wanted to give me the chance to ask any questions we might have had about the sale – at least, that's what he said.'

'At the meeting you didn't tell me about?'

'Umm, yes.' Sabi shifted uncomfortably in her seat.

'But that isn't what he wanted?'

'That was what he said on the phone, but when I got there, he told me that BIG have changed their plans.'

'Plans that sent you rushing to Miriam to put an offer on the Culmstock house.'

'No.' Sabi's voice took on a hectoring tone. 'I was passing the house on the way home from seeing Leo and decided to have one more look. A last look – I was thinking of Maddie and how she'd react to the new plans from BIG, but once I was in the house again, I knew I couldn't give it up.'

'That is no excuse for acting without talking to me first.'

'I know.' Sabi looked drawn as she confessed. 'I even went to the estate agents to hand back the keys. To say we had changed our minds. I was intending to do the right thing. *Honestly.* I wanted to talk to you and Maddie first. But then Miriam told me someone else was interested. I love that house so much Henry and—'

'—and you panicked and put in an offer.' Henry lowered his eyes, knowing that if he looked at his wife, he was liable to give in. Sometimes he wished he didn't love her quite so much.

'Yes.'

Heaving himself off his chair, Henry switched on the coffee machine. 'I'm going to make us a hot drink, then we are going to sit in the living room, and you are going to tell me everything about this meeting. Then you will tell me how much the offer is on this house we appear to be buying.'

'Alright.'

'And Sabi.'

'Yes?'

'I am not promising you anything about the house. I love you very much, but this is our future. But not just ours and Maddie's – but also Jemima's. When it comes to the family business, what is right for our child will come first. Yes?'

Petra had been tempted to order a prosecco, just to make Jake laugh, but she'd never liked it much, so she stuck to stout for her and lager for him. As she waited for the barman to pour their drinks, she reflected on what Jake had told her so far. It was heart-breaking. His mother, bitter and struggling for money after his father had left them, had taken out her frustration on her son. To Jake, it must have felt like he'd been alone since he was eight years old.

Having collected their drinks, Petra placed Jake's drink in front of him and sat herself exactly where she'd been before. She hoped he'd take the hint and put his hand back where it had been before. He didn't. Instead, he reached out and wrapped her hand in his, holding on to her as he carried on from where he'd left off.

'As you can imagine, I was bullied at school. Mum had stopped caring. I wore dirty clothes. I suspect I smelt. Before long, the few friends I'd had distanced themselves and, to be frank, I don't blame them.'

'And the extra reading classes?'

'They continued while I was at primary school. Got me to the point where I could read basic stuff. Do you remember the Biff and Chip books?'

Petra's face lit up. 'I do! The Oxford Reading Tree! I learnt with those! Wilma and Kipper and... What was the dog's name again?'

'Floppy.'

'So it was. It was years before I worked out that Biff, Chip and Kipper were nicknames and not their real names. I loved those books.'

'Me too.'

As Jake lapsed into silence, Petra coaxed, 'I take it secondary school was not a good time for you?'

'I started by being bullied on the first day. It was like primary school but with harder punches. By the third day something inside me broke.' Jake lifted their entwined hands and looked at them as if he couldn't believe what he was seeing. 'I'm going to let go of your hand. If you want to hold it again after I've told you the next bit, then I'd like that. If you walk out of the door instead, I will totally understand, and I won't chase after you.'

Oddly bereft without his palm in hers, Petra anxiously waited for Jake to speak.

'I remember being so tired. I was only eleven years old, and I was exhausted from fighting. Not physically, but mentally. I hated who I was. I hated that I was starting a new phase of my life at the very bottom of the pile. The stupidest kid in the lowest set at school. I could just about add up, I didn't know anything higher than my three times table, and as for spelling...' Jake gripped his glass tighter. 'So, I turned the tables. I wasn't a bully in the sense that I searched for weak people to pick on, but if someone had a go at me or made fun, I didn't sit and take it anymore.'

Petra's pulse raced. She knew she'd had a privileged upbringing, but that didn't mean she'd not witnessed bullying, nor had she totally escaped its evil herself. There had been a short time when she was fourteen when being seen to be clever had not been a good idea. Her heart bled for him as Jake went on.

'I started to get into trouble for fighting back, and soon I had a reputation for being a thug. Rather than object, I used it in my favour. It kept other people away from me, and that worked out best for everyone.'

'But surely your teachers...'

'In a small town, with too many pupils, not enough staff and no parental support to back them up? Nah, they weren't bad people, they just had no energy left for me.' Jake took a drink, licking lager from his lips. 'Even the welfare officer gave up in the end. I remember her saying, almost in despair now I think back, "You could do anything you wanted, but I can't help you if you won't help yourself".'

With an overwhelming sense of sadness for the man next to her, Petra whispered, 'But you didn't help yourself.'

'No. I liked that no one spoke to me. Or even noticed me.'

'Did you play truant?'

'No need. If I was in class I was left to my own devices. The staff stopped expecting anything of me.' Jake shrugged. 'I wasn't out for trouble. I just wanted to be left alone. And it worked.'

'The price being that your formal education stopped before it started.'

'Yep.'

Petra looked at Jake's hands. One held his pint glass, the other gripped his knee. She could see his knuckles whitening.

Changing the subject, Petra asked, 'When did you discover your love of gardening? You have a natural skill there, that's obvious.'

'Is it?' Jake glanced at her in surprise.

'Very much so.' Petra gently took back his hand. 'Tell me where the gardening thing came from?'

'My dad. Before he took off, we used to work his allotment. We went for walks on Exmoor and explored all over. I only remember it faintly now, but I know I felt safe and happy when we were outdoors together.'

'Why did he...'

'Leave?'

'Yes.'

'When I was little, I thought it was my fault. That I had made him unhappy, and he'd left me as a punishment.'

'I'm sure that wasn't the reason. A lot of children think that way, but they're always wrong.'

'I know now that it was my mum he'd had enough of.

But he still left me behind. He could have taken me with him rather than leave me with her.'

'You don't get on with your mum?'

'Let's just say she is not easy to live with.'

Henry's coffee cup had been empty for some time. He was beginning to wish he'd made it considerably stronger as Sabi recounted her meeting with Leo Creswell.

'And what will make Maddie angrier do you think, hearing that the nursery site will be built on by BIG *if* we sign, or the fact that she should have been at the meeting to learn that fact first-hand? For heaven's sake! You're withholding vital information from your own sister!'

Kicking off her slippers, Sabi tucked her knees defensively under her chin as she sat on the sofa. 'I know I've done this all wrong, and I know it's going to take a lot to get Maddie on side, but BIG building on the nursery, rather than using the land for storage, doesn't change anything. Even if Maddie insists on keeping going where she is, BIG *will* build next door as per originally planned. The Potting Shed won't last five minutes. You know as well as I do that we'd all be better off taking the money, and this way we'll get even more.'

Henry regarded his wife in silence for a moment, before abruptly stating, 'You're bored, aren't you?'

Sabi's legs shot back onto the floor. 'I'm never bored.'

'So, this need for a house to make right for us to live in while making this place into a holiday let – that's simply a project because you need to stretch your intellect?'

'I... I would like a new challenge.' Sabi closed her eyes

for a second, as she remembered Maddie shouting at her, telling her she should earn her own money if she wanted new things.

'And your heart is set on running this place as a holiday let?'

'It would be a challenge. And we'd make money on it. Plus, we'd own two homes, one of which Jemima could have in time.' Picking up a cushion, Sabi squashed it against her chest. 'Do you think I'd be up to it though, Henry? I've not worked for so long. Dad and Maddie didn't really ever need me around the nursery and Miriam – she's so successful. She has such a lovely home and....'

'And she shows all those things off – making you feel as if you're not good enough somehow. Like you need things of equal value to be worth her while as a friend?'

'Well, I...'

Henry shook his head. 'And yet she's the woman you aspire to be.'

'I don't.' Sabi blanched at her husband's bluntness. 'I like being me. I wouldn't want...'

'Darling, as I said, I love you to pieces, but if they gave a prize for trying to keep up with the Jones – or the Reeces in this case – you'd win hands down.'

19

Having made the mistake of wondering how she'd manage if she needed the loo once she was on the moor, now it was all she could think about, and she desperately needed to pee.

'Talk about the power of suggestion!' Maddie parked her jeep next to the toilet block on the edge of Haddon Hill's car park.

The rest of the car park was deserted but for a short row of vehicles on the far side of a large gravelled area. Spotting Ed's car, Maddie dashed into the washroom before anyone could see her. Staring into the mould-spotted mirror that hung at a jaunty angle over a surprisingly clean sink, Maddie allowed herself thirty seconds to gather herself together as memories of how she'd felt when Ed had touched her hand in the pub assailed her.

'For goodness' sake woman, there was less than a second's contact. He's your lawyer! He's just someone who happens to like the outdoors as much as you do and has offered to introduce you to other like-minded folk. End of.'

Five minutes later, Maddie was back outside, aware that her personal pep talk hadn't worked, and that she was becoming increasingly nervous about meeting new people and anxious about how to be with Ed. Not giving herself a chance to sneak back to her car before she was spotted, she forced herself to stride forward.

If you lose the nursery, you'll need a new life. New friends would be a good place to start.

'Maddie. I'm so glad you made it.' Ed waved as the crunch of her walking boots over the loose chippings alerted him to her approach. Reaching out a hand, he lowered it again as she got within touching distance.

Pretending she hadn't noticed, and surprised by the sense of physical disappointment she felt, Maddie asked, 'I'm not holding you up, am I?'

'Not at all. We're waiting for Jo. He's a definite regular – you'll like Jo, he's one of life's good guys.' Ed tapped his backpack. 'Do you have a hot drink and something to lie on?'

'All present and correct.' Maddie gestured to her rucksack, before spotting the large flashlight in Ed's hand. 'I didn't think to bring a torch though.'

'Not a problem.' Ed flicked on the beam of light. 'You can share with me. If you don't mind sticking to my side that is. I'd hate you to fall over as we climb up to the top.'

The thought that perhaps Ed had deliberately failed to tell her to bring a torch so she could stay near to him sent a wave of something that might have been hope through Maddie. 'I know Haddon pretty well, but I've never walked here in the dark.'

'Then keep close.' Ed's voice became serious. 'The terrain here isn't difficult, but all it takes is for you to catch your foot in a rabbit hole, and you'll be nursing a broken ankle.'

'Which I absolutely do not have time to do.' Privately

vowing to stay glued to Ed's side, Maddie stared up at the sky. It was alive with more stars than she'd ever seen. 'Wow.'

'Incredible, isn't it.'

'You should see it once we get up the hill.' A man who had been talking to another group member approached Maddie. 'I'm Ivan, pleased to meet you.'

'Maddie. Likewise.' She adjusted her weight from foot to foot. 'Thank you for letting me join in.'

'It's great to see a new face.' Ivan gestured to the black Labrador at his heel. 'This is Sheba. You comfortable with dogs?'

'Definitely.' Maddie reached out to the dog, but then stopped. 'Is it okay to stroke her?'

'It is.' Ivan scrubbed a hand through his beard. 'Thank you for asking first. Few bother.'

Maddie crouched to the dog. 'Aren't you beautiful?'

'She is that. We've been inseparable for the past eight years. Sheba loves coming up here with this lot.' Ivan gestured to the assembled group. 'They spoil her rotten.'

'I'm not surprised.' Wishing she could stay where she was and continue to make a fuss of the dog rather than have to talk to the other humans, Maddie stood as Ed introduced her to the rest of the group. She was wondering how she'd remember everyone's names when a van pulled up next to them.

'Ah, and here's Jo.'

Maddie found herself smiling as a bright orange VW camper van arrived in the car park. 'Now that is a cheerful vehicle.'

'Great isn't it.' Ed grinned. 'Jo runs a business from it.'

'Really?'

'It's a coffee van.' Ed bent to give Sheba a stroke. 'Well, more like a mobile café. You'd be amazed by how much stuff is stacked in there.'

'How fantastic.' Maddie was wondering how Jo operated a café from such a tiny space when Ivan stepped forward, clipping a lead onto Sheba's collar.

'Jo's great. I don't know what I'd do without him.'

'Jo works for you?'

Ivan laughed. 'I'm not sure Jo would see it like that. He's very much his own boss, and an essential part of my business .'

Maddie was about to ask what business Ivan was in that depended so much on a coffee van, when the slamming of a sliding door indicated that Jo was about to join them.

'Obviously that's Orion,' Ed whispered as they lay next to each other on their travel rugs. 'You can see the three brightest stars on the belt so clearly tonight.'

Maddie nodded, and then remembered Ed couldn't see her. Since they'd all lain down at the highest point of the hill and switched off their torches, a blanket of darkness had covered them. It had felt oppressive for a few seconds, and Maddie had found herself automatically reaching out for Ed, who'd briefly squeezed her hand before letting go again, promising her that the claustrophobic feeing would pass very quickly.

'I can't get over how much we can see.'

'It takes my breath away every time.' Ed's hand was a dark shadow as he gestured upwards again. 'The stars on Orion's belt are called Alnitak, Alnilam and Mintaka.'

'You know a lot about the constellations.'

'Not as much as the others, but I'm learning.' Ed rolled onto his side, so he was facing Maddie rather than the sky. 'For me it's more about being here and enjoying the view.'

Conscious that even though she couldn't see the others, they were there, Maddie whispered, 'You're not looking at the stars though.'

'And yet the view is still stunning.'

Not sure what to say, Maddie felt a long-forgotten buzz of happiness zip through her as she stared upwards. 'How long have you been doing this?'

'A couple of years, each autumn and winter. It's too light in the spring and summer.' Ed sat up and reached for his thermos. 'Coffee?'

Aware that there was an increase in movement around them, and that the others must be having a break too, Maddie reached for her flask.

'It won't be as good as Jo's, mind.'

'Why, thank you.'

A faint rustle a little to the left caused Maddie to look round as Jo responded to Ed's compliment.

'I'd fire up the van, but it's tricky to make good coffee in the dark.'

'Which is a greater shame than you can imagine, Maddie, for Jo makes the best coffee in Devon. His own blend.'

'You do?'

'Sure.' Jo moved a little closer. 'If you have an empty cup there, I have far more than I need in my flask. Would you like to try some?'

'I couldn't possibly. That's your coffee.'

Ed laughed. 'When Jo says there's plenty, he mean's he

has a flask three times bigger than yours plus another in the van, right Jo?'

'Two more in the van.' Jo gave a mock bow. 'I'm caffeine fuelled, and I always try to have some on hand for folk to try. Everyone's a future customer.'

'Well, in that case.' Maddie passed over her tin mug. 'I'd love to try it.'

'I'll just alert the others to shield their eyes.' Before Maddie could ask what they meant, Jo called out, 'I'm going to switch my torch on.'

Maddie found herself blinking hard as a circle of light, its brightness a shock after the intensity of the dark, filled the space around them.

'Here.' Jo poured some coffee into Maddie's cup. 'It's black, is that alright?'

'Perfect.'

'I'd give it a moment. This flask keeps things at scalding heat.' Jo gestured to Ed, 'I assume you want a Jo special?'

'As ever.' Ed lifted up his cup. 'How's business, mate?'

'Quiet. The season is over and although I've a few gigs over Christmas, not much will happen now until the bluebells come out in May.'

'The bluebells?' Maddie drew in the comforting aroma as she blew across the top of her coffee.

'Several of the local estates open their gardens to the public when the bluebells bloom. They like to hire a pop-up café like mine to help lure in the punters.'

'That's an excellent idea.'

'It's good fun too.' Jo took a tentative sip of their coffee. 'It's safe to drink without getting third degree burns on your lips now.'

Doing as she was told, Maddie took a quick drink, before immediately diving in for another. 'Wow. That's like… like velvet and coffee and… chocolate?'

Jo laughed. 'That's a great description. It is all of those things.'

'But how…?'

Ed laughed. 'You can ask Jo all you like, but he'll never tell you.'

'Trade secret.' Jo adjusted the grey beanie hat so it sat lower over his ears.

'Do you travel from event to event then?'

'Markets, fairs, you name it.' Jo gestured to the van. 'People seem to like the coffee, and obviously I provide tea for the less refined amongst us.'

Maddie couldn't help but laugh as she thought how Sabi might respond to such a comment. Tea was, in her sister's mind, the preserve of the refined.

'And if you think the coffee is good,' Ed knocked back the remainder of his drink, 'you should taste Jo's pastries.'

The walk back to the car park was slow as they took care not to take a badly placed step while wandering down the hill.

Shining his torch before them, Ed hooked his arm through Maddie's as they made their way along.

'Did you enjoy that?'

'I loved it. I can't believe we saw so many stars. They were beaming holes in the sky. Does that sound silly?'

'Not at all.' Ed lowered his voice, 'I hope you'll come again.'

'I will.' Maddie held his arm tighter as her foot hit a loose stone. 'I can't tell you how long it's been since I went out with a group of people.'

'When was the last time you went welly walking then?'

Touched he'd remembered their conversation about her secret hobby, she frowned. 'Must be nearly two years.'

'As long as that?'

'I've not had much time.' Until that moment, Maddie hadn't realised how long it had been since she'd last kicked her way through a satisfyingly deep puddle.

'But surely you must have had a day off in the last two years?'

Maddie felt her smile wane as thoughts of the nursery nudged their way back to the forefront of her mind. Easing her arm out of her lawyer's clutch, Maddie dived her gloved hands into her pockets. 'Well, yes, technically we close on a Monday, but obviously I still have to tend the plants and suchlike. I don't get much time away.'

Ed peered down at their walking-booted feet. 'Don't you find walking in wellingtons a bit uncomfortable after a while?'

'They can be if they don't fit properly. My one indulgence is an expensive pair of boots and cosy boot socks.'

'I trust they're jaunty and not plain green or black?'

Finding her grin returning, Maddie said, 'My current pair is stripy – navy and white. The last ones were blue with red dots. I do *not* do boring wellies.'

'I'm very glad to hear it. You never told me about the group you go splashing with.'

'That's because there isn't one. It's just me.'

'Would you take me?' Ed asked, before quickly adding, 'if you'd like company. If you prefer to go alone then—'

'No. I mean, yes... you'd be very welcome.'

Ed smiled. 'Good. When?'

Maddie shrugged. 'No idea. I'd like to say soon, but...'

'I know. You're busy.'

'I am, but it isn't just that.'

'What is it then?'

'It hasn't rained this week. For puddle splashing, you need puddles.'

They were almost at the gate to the car park before Ed spoke again. 'So, this "you not going out much", does that include dates?'

Feeling awkward, Maddie flexed her hands within her pockets. 'As I've said, the nursery takes all my time and energy.'

'I can imagine.' Ed was quiet for a moment, before saying, 'If I asked you out to dinner again, would you come?'

'I would.' Maddie suddenly felt out of her depth 'I, umm... it's nice to have a friend.'

Ed took her arm again, gently holding her back so they were distanced from the group. 'And if that friend was to say he might want to develop that friendship to something more – in time?'

Maddie could feel his presence, his closeness, his desire. She wanted him to kiss her, to touch her...

Do you really want to open yourself up to being hurt by a man again? And anyway, do you have time for a boyfriend right now?

Suddenly unsure of herself, Maddie said, 'Let's just go for dinner sometime and see what happens.'

'Okay.'

Hearing the disappointment in Ed's voice, Maddie hastily added, 'It isn't that I don't want to have dinner – it's just, well, I have so much going on and…'

'I understand.' Stepping further away from her, Ed abruptly transformed from friend to solicitor. 'So, tell me, how is the nursery situation?'

20

'Sorry for the early call, but I wanted to make sure you were alright after all that happened with BIG and your sister yesterday. I also wanted to say thanks.'

'Thanks for what?'

'For coming out last night.'

'I loved it.' Maddie put down her cereal bowl. 'Are you at work already?'

'In the car, about to go inside.' Ed paused. 'Look, I know you don't want to do anything heavy date wise at the moment, but you know I'm here don't you?'

Warmth filled Maddie as she found herself wondering if he was wearing the same suit she'd seen him in when she'd visited his office. 'Thank you. And likewise.'

'Good. So, what's the plan? Finding new premises? Something I would be happy to help with.'

Maddie got up to put a carton of milk back in the fridge. 'I suppose it's an option I'll have to consider, but the thought of relocating The Potting Shed is a nightmare. Before I give in and do that, I'm going to talk to Sabi properly. I still want to offer to buy her out. I've been up since dawn putting a new proposal together.'

'Wow. You must be shattered.'

'I'm okay. I was having trouble sleeping, so I thought I'd use the time wisely rather than toss and turn.' Maddie stifled a yawn at the mention of sleep. 'I had a few ideas as I drove home last night that might help keep The Potting Shed's head above water while trading against BIG. Must have been the clean air and good company.'

Maddie was lacing her boots, ready to open the nursery, when her mobile burst into life for the second time that morning. Half-expecting it to be Ed again, she was surprised by the level of disappointment she felt when it wasn't.

'Henry, how can I help?'

'I wondered if – *we* wondered if – you'd meet Sabi today. You two need to talk.'

Maddie slid her left foot into the waiting boot. 'I have no problem with talking, Henry, but will Sabi listen?'

'Of course she will. Sabi misses your father too you know.'

The positivity she'd felt when talking to Ed ebbed away. 'And yet she has wasted no time in ensuring his business folds.'

'Maddie, it isn't like that. Sabi didn't contact BIG, they came to her. To both of you,' Henry paused, 'and you two shouldn't fall out over it. You're the only immediate family you have left.'

'Which is why Sabi getting rid of Dad's legacy is so unbelievable.' Maddie drew breath. 'I've been working on a few ideas to sort things out actually. I know I left a proposal with you before, but that was written prior to me knowing you were planning to spend the money from the nursery on a second home.'

'Maddie, that's just so that Sabi can have...'

'Whatever she wants, yes. No change there.' A stab of sadness hit Maddie as she felt her hackles rising. 'I hate this, Henry. I just want us all to work together.'

'I know. I hate it too, but...'

Cutting across Henry, knowing she had to keep talking before tiredness got a grip and she burst into tears, Maddie continued. 'Anyway, as I said I've put together a better proposal. One that is more practical, given your step into property. I need to get a few figures from the bank manager.'

Stifling a groan, Henry pleaded, 'Please Maddie, just come over and have a chat. You don't have the whole picture yet.'

'I'm very busy. Can't Sabi come here?' Maddie stood up and headed for the door. 'This place doesn't run by magic.'

'About two o'clock? Here. *Please* Maddie.'

'Why didn't Sabi call me herself?'

'She's busy too.'

'Busy?' Maddie scooped the keys to the nursery off the table by the front door. 'Come off it, Henry.'

'Say that again, but much, much slower.'

'Saying it slower isn't going to change anything, Maddie.' Sabi fiddled with her wedding ring as she sat at the kitchen table. 'Will you stop acting like I've engineered this?'

'But you aren't fighting it, are you? Quite the reverse. BIG's plans are a gift from the gods to you. A way to get on the same level as Miriam and the other corporate wives who have to be seen to have it all.'

'It isn't like that!' Sabi lowered her eyes. 'Please, I don't want to fall out with you.'

Maddie chewed on her bottom lip. 'I don't want to fight either. I hate being cross.'

'I know, and I know I've gone about everything the wrong way, but the fact remains, BIG want to build over The Potting Shed.'

Massaging her forehead with her palms, Maddie couldn't find any words to respond as her sister leant across the table.

'It might feel like the end of the world right now, but it needn't be.' Sabi hesitated before pressing on. 'Have you thought about that fresh start I mentioned? Finding someone maybe – getting a job where you don't have the pressure on your shoulders 24/7. Wouldn't you like that?'

An image of Ed flashed through Maddie's mind. 'Right now, I'm still trying to process the fact that you had worked out how to spend your half of the nursery sale money *before* this new development – and only seconds after BIG approached you in the first place.'

Sabi got up to click the kettle on. 'It was a coincidence. I promise.'

'And if BIG hadn't come along when the house in Culmstock came on the market?'

'We'd have sold here and put an offer in anyway.' Sabi spooned beans into the grinder to make Maddie a coffee as she added, 'We aren't doing this because I want to show off having two homes. I want a project. I want a business of my own to run.'

Maddie opened her mouth, the tumult of possible responses all getting caught in her throat before any of them could come out. *You have a business. One you share with me.*

Screwing the lid of the grinder into place, Sabi went on,

'It's an investment. Jemima will reap the benefits when she is older. One of the houses will be hers. We have her to think about her as well as you, you know.'

Maddie let the implied accusation that she didn't care about her niece's future go as she finally found some words. 'That's why you're so keen to let BIG close The Potting Shed down. So that you can be a property-let executive?'

'And so Jemima has a home in the future.'

The frown lines on Maddie's forehead deepened. 'Have you asked Jem about this? Perhaps she'd like the family business to be there for her when she's finished her A levels.'

'Don't be silly, she'll go to university.'

Maddie bit the inside of her cheek against voicing the thoughts swirling in her head. *I went to university and I'm working there.*

Oblivious to her sister's indignation, Sabi switched on the deafening grinder, only to start talking again the moment it was done. 'I wondered, afterwards, would you like to be our gardener? We'll have two places to keep up and you're so good at it. The new house will require its grounds landscaping. We'd pay you properly and—'

'Sabi.' Maddie didn't shout, but the defeat in her tone was enough to cut through her sister's stream of words as she placed a tea and coffee cup on the table. 'I take it you haven't read my original proposal then?' Maddie looked around. 'Where is it by the way?'

'Proposal?'

'I left a folder here for you and Henry to read. My plans to keep the nursery going. Ways we could make it work. Together.'

Sabi's mouth dropped open, but no words came out as

powdered skin blanched. 'I thought you'd just left some work behind.'

'You didn't even open it?' Maddie rocked back in her chair as a new thought occurred to her. '*When* did BIG tell you of their change of plan?'

'Yesterday, late morning.'

'Yesterday? 'So, you've had over twelve hours to tell me about it. Was it by phone? Zoom?'

Not looking at her sister, Sabi muttered, 'In person.'

Maddie grabbed her coffee, concentrating on keeping calm. 'An *actual* meeting. Why wasn't I invited? Why wasn't I even told?'

'It happened so fast, and you were working. Saturdays are the nursery's busiest day and I thought—'

'You thought that if I was there, I'd stop you getting what you wanted.'

Sabi winced to hear her sister repeat her husband's earlier accusation. 'No! Honestly, you were at work and Leo Creswell called out of the blue. I thought he was going to explain how the takeover would happen, but he had this other news.'

Maddie couldn't believe what her sister was saying. 'But I haven't agreed to sell. I haven't agreed to *any* of this.'

'But Maddie...' Sabi pulled out her chair, her voice almost pleading as she sat down, '... can't you see, with the money they are offering, you could restart The Potting Shed somewhere else or have a totally new life doing anything you wanted.'

'So you *keep* saying.'

'And I could have my house.'

'*You* have *your* house? Not Henry and you? I thought

this was for Jem. No mention of her now then? This is all about what you want, Sabi.'

'No, I—'

'This is pointless. We are going around in circles.' Maddie jabbed a finger towards her new proposal. 'That, if you are interested, is how I intend to earn enough money to buy you out, if you'll agree to that, and keep The Potting Shed going. Something I worked on *before* you verbally agreed for them to obliterate all that Dad and I have worked for at a meeting you didn't tell me about. I take it you *did* verbally agree?'

Sabi opened her mouth, but no words came out as her sister stood up.

'And why do they want to build over our land anyway all of a sudden?'

'I ... I didn't ask.'

'What happened to you, Sabi? You were my right arm when we were teenagers, my friend! Well, I'm not signing any paperwork that would agree to selling the business. Not for you or BIG or anyone.'

21

Maddie had managed to hold herself together while she'd been driving. She had even given a cheery wave to Petra as she'd passed the shop on the way to the nearest polytunnel. But once she was safely inside and had placed a 'staff-only' sign on the door, she allowed her concentration to wane and her emotions to take over.

Sat on a wobbly stool, her elbows resting on the bench before her, the tears she'd been holding back flowed freely. She wasn't sure what had upset her more: BIG's updated plans, or the fact that Sabi hadn't told her about the meeting with Leo Creswell in advance, even though she'd admitted that he'd invited her too.

Trying not to think about how many hours she'd wasted reworking her business proposal, not just last night, but all morning, Maddie felt the faint hope she'd experienced when putting it together – that maybe they could create a garden centre that could hold its own with a branch of BIG across the road – melt away.

Her mind spun from anger to blank hopelessness as she pictured herself starting all over again. It wasn't so much the premises; it was the people. The clients who'd been coming to The Potting Shed for years. Her father's blend of soil remained popular, the local shops that bought hanging baskets to hook outside their shop fronts every spring and again in the summer. The one remaining greengrocer in Wellington who always bought cabbages, onions and herbs from them along with the local bed-and-breakfast and hotel proprietors. Mr and Mrs Pickle, who rejoiced, each September, in coming along to buy pickling onions, so they could honour their names by pickling them in time for their Boxing Day supper. The idea of any of those customers in BIG simply didn't compute. They'd never get a service that was tailored to their personal needs.

Frustration at BIG's change of plan and anxiety about the future sent a choked sigh whooshing from Maddie's lips as the unexpected sound of giggling lifted her from her emotional haze.

Looking up from the row of untouched pots, she saw Petra and Jake crossing the nursery together. Her first thought was that she couldn't believe it was already closing time. If Petra had left the shop, then it had to be gone six; a fact confirmed by a quick check of her watch. *I've been sat here for two hours!* The second thing Maddie noticed was that they were holding hands.

'At least someone listens to me. Well done, Jake. I bet that took guts.'

The happiness she felt for her helpers was immediately dimmed by the knowledge that they might soon be jobless.

'At least they'll be able to comfort each other.' Maddie thought back to her evening with Ed and his Dark Skies friends. She knew he'd have kissed her there and then if she'd let him. 'Maybe I should have.'

Knowing he'd be waiting to hear how the meeting with

Sabi went, Maddie addressed the row of plants in front of her. 'Ed's a lovely guy. He's good looking and fun to be with. He could have anyone. Why on earth would he want a relationship with a woman who gave up a great career to run a nursery that is unlikely to last beyond Christmas?'

Sabi hadn't moved for some time. Her sister's reaction to the news she'd imparted had been as she'd expected it to be – but not as she'd hoped it would be. Part of her had banked on Maddie embracing the idea once she'd mentioned how Jemima would eventually benefit from her investing in property.

'Why shouldn't I have another home? Henry works so hard. He earns it so…'

Sabi stopped talking. Her words trailed into the sterile air of the kitchen as her imagination filled in precisely what her sister would say if she'd been there to hear her.

'Henry earns it – Henry works so hard. What do you do?'

'But *I* want to do something, that's the point!' Sabi regarded the two cups before her. Hers was empty, but for the second time in only a few days, Maddie's sat untouched and ice cold.

Sabi's eyes moved from the cups to her mobile. A message from Henry had been waiting for her attention for the past hour. She knew it would be asking how the chat with Maddie had gone.

Without picking up the mobile, she rehearsed what to say. 'It was a disaster, Henry, and it was my fault. Maddie was furious and I can see why… but this is such a good chance for us.'

Sighing as she listened to herself, Sabi tapped her fingernails against the table. 'I'm sorry, Maddie.' She picked up the folder that had been so unceremoniously slapped against her table. 'But whatever you've got in here is pointless.'

Unless I don't agree to BIG's offer either.

'But the nursery is on its knees,' Sabi pleaded to her sister in her absence, as she absentmindedly opened the proposal. A few seconds later she was engrossed.

'Upgrade house into a flat and shop… turn the downstairs bathroom into a public toilet…' Sabi flicked over the page to see a brief rundown of possible costings next to a note about a café. 'Café – a plan for the future. Too expensive in the first instance.'

Sabi found herself nodding. 'Not too far into the future though, Maddie – a café is always a sound move in a garden centre.' Running her finger down the page, Sabi smiled as she pictured how the site might look. 'I'd have the till area near the café, so people are tempted to linger by the sight of cake and…'

Her pleasant musings were halted as she read the next line aloud. 'Designer and architect of new layout arranged.'

She sank back in her seat. 'Arranged? Arranged with whom? Henry's an architect and I love interior design, but I'm… I'm nothing!'

Slamming the proposal closed, Sabi pushed it away. 'You and Dad never did want me around, did you Maddie?'

'I wanted to help, and this seemed the only positive thing to do.' Ed waved three property flyers in Maddie's direction, each one detailing a potential alternative site for the relocation of the nursery.

'Thanks.' Maddie slid them into her bag. 'I promise I'll look at them. I just need a little longer to get to grips with what Sabi's done.'

'I'm so sorry.' Ed rested against the side of his car, his head lowered. He peered at her through his fringe as he added more tentatively, 'From what you've said, surely it's BIG that have moved the goalposts. Your sister has—'

'Already spent the money she'll get by putting an offer in on her dream house.'

'Oh.' Ed risked meeting her eyes and saw the traces of tears already shed. 'You didn't mention that before.'

'I'm sorry, it's just…'

'No need to keep apologising.' Ed held up a hand in reassurance. 'How about sharing a takeaway tonight? We could make a plan.'

'There's not much of a plan to make now. Sabi gave me the impression that she's told Leo Creswell we are up for the sale. All they need is my signature and it's over.' She turned to face the nursery, flapping a hand towards the polytunnels. 'Everything Dad and I worked for will be lost under a flat-pack set of buildings and a corporate image.'

Ed picked up his mobile. 'You need food, and I'm not taking no for an answer, even if you want me to go so you can eat alone. Chinese takeaway or pizza?'

'Chinese. It's my favourite.' Maddie smiled meekly. 'Sorry Ed. I promise I'm not normally this ratty.'

'You're in shock.' He typed a few numbers into his phone. 'So, do I order for one or two?'

*

Having shoved the detritus that covered the kitchen table to one side, Maddie laid out two sets of cutlery. She had expected Ed to arrange for delivery, but when he'd said he'd go and fetch the takeaway, she'd been glad of the time to gather herself.

Maddie knew she'd only invited him to stay because she felt she ought to. *No, that's not true – you want him here. But...*

Her thoughts expressed themselves in a groan. Even though she'd only known him for a short time, she knew she was beginning to rely on Ed's solid, comforting presence.

Thinking back to her last boyfriend, Pete, a chap who worked at a nearby petrol station, Maddie realised with a start that that two-month event had been three years ago. There had been no one since. And even that had been against her better judgement. An experiment if she was honest – to see if she could cope with having a boyfriend after Darren.

She had been honest with Pete, and he'd been fine with a sex-and-small-talk relationship, but it hadn't been serious for either of them. Apart from a few memories of bedroom fun, all their association had done was left her preferring the company of her plants and the hassle of finding a different garage to use whenever she needed petrol.

Ed isn't like Pete. You have things in common beyond attraction. He is definitely not like Darren.

Maddie stared at the cutlery on the table. The knife and fork she'd put out for Ed were in her dad's place. She closed her eyes as her head started to ache. Anything beyond friendship suddenly represented a decision she wasn't ready to make.

But how do I know he's not like Darren? He was kind and generous and made me laugh – at first... Ed could be the same – but when he touched my hand...

'Sorry it took so long.'

Ed put the white carrier bag on the table before heading to the sink to wash his hands. 'There was a tractor on the link road and no chance to overtake. Hope it's not gone cold.'

Maddie opened the lid of the carton of egg fried rice. 'Steaming hot.' As Ed grabbed a serving spoon to help ladle out the sweet and sour chicken, she held up two bottles of lager. 'I only have alcohol free. That okay for you?'

'Perfect. Driving and all that.'

Levering off the bottle tops with the end of her can opener, Maddie passed one to Ed. 'I wasn't sure I'd be able to eat, but all of a sudden I'm famished.'

'Here.' Ed passed her a packet of prawn crackers. 'These were thrown in for free.'

'I'm not surprised.' Maddie surveyed the mountain of food before them. 'There's enough to feed the five thousand.'

'I wasn't sure what you liked.' Ed started to open the cartons of food. 'Anyway, I tend to eat a lot.'

'But you're so slim.'

Ed laughed. 'I told you, slim with a crazy metabolism. Calories don't stick.'

'You lucky...'

'I know.' Ed winked.

Laughing, Maddie scooped up a forkful of rice. 'Thanks for the property flyers and dinner.'

'No problem.' Ed chewed a prawn cracker. 'Did you take a peep while I was gone?'

'The land on the outskirts of Broadclyst is the only real possibility.' Maddie gestured towards the papers on the edge of the table. 'The other two are that bit far from a connecting road, whereas Broadclyst isn't too far from the motorway or Exeter.'

'Makes sense.' Ed brandished his spoon towards the particulars. 'As it happens, the planning permission for building on that site looked the least problematic of the three. I asked a mate in the planning office.'

'You did?' Touched by how much effort he'd put into researching the sites, Maddie said, 'Thank you. That is a major point in its favour. As is the lack of any other garden centre within a fifteen-mile radius.'

'As far as that?'

'I did a Google Maps search. The site is six acres, which is more than enough for what I have in mind, so I could even hire out an acre at the back for stabling.'

Ed's eyebrows rose. 'How long was I gone? You've really thought this through.'

Her appetite fading away, Maddie laid down her fork, trying not to dwell on what else she'd thought about while he was out. 'I can be quite practical when I have to be. I could do a lot with this space.'

'But?'

'I don't want to.'

'That, I can understand.' Ed paused in the act of adding some prawn toast to his plate. 'Maybe I shouldn't have got these for you. I just wanted to do something to help.'

'And you have, and I'm grateful.' Maddie gave him a brave smile. 'It's so good to have a friend right now.'

Ed opened his mouth to say something, but thought better of it, crunching through his prawn toast instead.

Sensing the need for a change of subject, Maddie said, 'I enjoyed the Dark Skies trip.'

'I enjoyed you enjoying it.' Ed's eyes met hers and held them for a moment. 'Everyone liked you.'

'I liked them too.'

'Because it's good to have new friends?'

There was something about the way Ed asked the question that made Maddie's pulse increase. She found she dare not look at him. 'That's always good, isn't it?'

'Yes. It's just…'

The abrupt ring of Ed's mobile made them both jump.

'Sorry, it's my boss. I'd better take it.'

Maddie was about to say that was perfectly alright, but Ed had already left the room to take the call in private. Five minutes later he was back.

'Sorry Maddie, but Ronald needs me at work. Something urgent has come up.'

'It's seven o'clock.'

'Even so.' He waved a hand at the remaining food as he bolted for the door. 'Enjoy.'

22

Maddie threw the property flyers onto the table. The land in Exeter might well be a feasible place for her to start a new business from, but until she had got to grips with losing The Potting Shed, she knew she wouldn't be able to give any location fair consideration.

She'd half-expected Ed to call her once he'd finished dealing with whatever his boss wanted him for, but he hadn't.

'He had to go. It was work.' The fern on the windowsill was quite definite on this point.

Disquieted by Ed's abrupt departure, the food they'd enjoyed the night before now heavy in her stomach, Maddie pulled a jumper and some jeans over her pyjamas, grabbed her housekeys and ran downstairs. 'It might be only five o'clock in the morning – but right now I need my plants!' Pushing her feet into her boots, torn between what she wanted to do with the nursery, what she thought she ought to do, and what it was possible to do, she pulled her coat off a hook by the front door and made a determined beeline for the vegetable polytunnel.

'*When all else fails and nothing makes sense, head to the garden., Maddie lass.*' With her father's words ringing in her ears, Maddie shoved her sleeves up past her elbows and sank to her knees. Seconds later she was totally engrossed in hooking out the tiny fledgling weeds that were attempting to take hold around her onion sets, all other thoughts drowned out by the methodical calm of her work.

Petra waved through the window as her bus pulled into the stop nearest the nursery. Her heart did a happy cartwheel as she saw Jake waiting for her, a self-conscious grin on his face.

'Sorry I missed the bus you were on. Mum was being awkward.' Petra checked her watch as she jumped off the bus. 'At least I'm not late.'

'Don't worry, I got your text.' Taking her hand in his, Jake regarded her with a sense of wonder. 'I didn't dream it then, you really are okay about being seen with me?'

'And why wouldn't I be?' Petra flicked her ponytail to one side as they walked towards the nursery.

'I thought the confessions of my youth might have put you off, once you'd had time to think about them.'

'Well, they haven't. Still up for going to the pub again tonight?'

'Definitely.'

Enjoying the heat of Jake's palm in hers, Petra said, 'I have been thinking though.'

'About?'

'Ways to help.' Petra added more quickly, 'If you wanted me to.'

Jake bit the inside of his cheek. 'Is this about my reading again?'

'Sort of.' Petra looked at him as they crossed the car park. 'I know you're nervous about it, but well... I found a class that might be good at the adult education college. Something light that would improve your writing in case you needed to. Who knows what Maddie will do with this place and ...?'

'We've been through this.' Jake groaned. 'Maybe you could let me get on with being who I am.'

Watching their trainered feet marching along together, Petra felt as if she'd been mildly told off. 'I wasn't trying to change you Jake, just help you.'

Unpeeling his fingers from hers, Jake stepped away from Petra; he stared out across the nursery. 'I know that's what you think you're doing, but it comes down to the same thing in the end and I can't change. I simply can't.'

'But...'

'I've got to sort out the winter veg today. I promised Maddie.' Jake thrust his hands into his pockets and marched away, leaving Petra standing where he'd left her.

Sabi watched as Henry laid his black leather portfolio folder in the boot of his car. Alongside the designs for an office block upgrade in Bristol sat the particulars for the house in Culmstock.

'Are you sure I can't make you some coffee for the journey?'

'I'm going to Bristol, not Outer Mongolia.' Henry slammed the boot shut. 'It's an hour away at most.'

Sabi nodded. 'I hope it goes well – that you get the commission, I mean.'

'So do I. The contract is a lucrative one and the way you've been spending our money of late, we may well need it.'

'Henry, I…' Sabi stopped talking. They'd been over her conversation with Maddie so many times it had become a blur through constant repetition. Crossing her arms over her chest, she mumbled, 'Do I withdraw the offer on the house then?'

'We'll talk later.'

'But Miriam needs to—'

'Bugger Miriam!' Henry took a deep breath. 'We will talk about it tonight. In the meantime, go and see Maddie. You've just lost your father. Do you really want to lose your sister too?'

Hanging up the phone, Maddie scribbled a note on the pad by the till. 'Fifty Christmas trees, various sizes, will arrive on the 30th of November.'

'That many?' Petra pulled her gaze back from where she'd been staring into space.

'We usually have eighty, but I'm late with placing the order this year, and with things as they are…' Maddie let her sentence fall away. 'Anyway, we'll need a series of posters with different prices on. Do you think you could do that?'

'Sure.'

'Are you okay?'

'I'm fine.' Petra picked up a pen. 'Prices vary with tree height I presume?'

'That's right.' Maddie tilted her head to the side. 'I saw you with Jake yesterday, you seemed happy.'

'That was yesterday.' Petra tapped her pen on the pad. 'What's the smallest sized tree we offer?'

Respecting Petra's right not to talk about whatever it was that had happened between her and Jake, Maddie said, 'Three foot. They'll be trees that come in at three and a half, so I tend to round things up. If a tree is three-foot-two, we charge the same as for a three-foot-tree, if it's three-foot-three, it'll be charged the same as for a three-and-a-half-foot tree.'

'And so on up to?'

'The tallest I've ordered is nine feet.'

'Wow. Tall.'

'There are several houses around here with high Victorian ceilings that take a big tree. I've only ordered a few of those. Most are in the five-to-six-foot bracket.'

'Prices?'

Maddie took a list from her pocket. 'This is what we charged last year. Add three pounds for each tree under six foot, and five pounds for all those over six foot.'

'Right.'

Maddie was about to leave, when Petra blurted out, 'Why doesn't Jake want to learn to write?'

'Ah.'

The young woman banged her pen onto the desk in frustration. 'If this place closes and he can't read or write properly, no one else will take him on.'

Maddie sat next to Petra. 'It will make it very difficult for him certainly.'

'He doesn't know yet, does he?'

'No.' Maddie stared out across the nursery, 'I'll have to tell him soon. I thought I might be able to save the place, but now… Let's just say the goalposts have moved. I'll tell you all about it as soon as I can. Promise.'

'I'm so sorry. I can see how much you love this place. If you can find a way to save it, and you need help, then I'm your girl.'

'Thanks, Petra.' Maddie opened the till and poured some change into its tray. 'Have you given any thought to what you'll do work-wise, long-term?'

'A bit.' Petra perched on the edge of a stool. 'Although I haven't spoken to my parents about it yet.'

'That makes it sound as if you have definitely decided not to do law.'

Petra made a face. 'I'd made that decision long ago, but convincing my mum that I'm serious about not wanting to play corporate games is continuing to prove challenging. We had another of her little chats about it over breakfast.'

'So?'

'I wondered about going back to college. Studying horticulture maybe.'

'I think that's an excellent idea.'

'You do?' The smile that had been wiped away by Jake's rejection of her help, edged back across Petra's face.

'Yes. I'm sorry you haven't had the chance to do much in the way of gardening. I'd get Jake to show you how we do things, but right now, there is only enough for Jake and me to do.'

'It's okay.' Petra doodled on the edge of the pad. 'I don't think Jake would want me to work with him anyway.'

'What happened?'

'I've seen this college course that would be perfect for him. Very light and easy going. No exams or anything, just guided help to improve writing, help with form filling and CV creation. Reading practice for those who want it. But...'

'But Jake immediately yanked the shutters down and walked away.'

'More like ran away.' Petra sighed. 'He thinks I'm trying to change him. I'm not. He is so good at what he does here, but outside of The Potting Shed...'

'I know.' Maddie bit her lip.

Speaking softly, Petra asked, 'Is there *really* no way to save this place?'

'If my sister wasn't so set on selling, then maybe, but she is fully committed to taking the money.'

'I'm sorry.'

'And I'm sorry about Jake. Perhaps if I'd told him about the nursery's uncertain future, he'd have understood why you wanted to help him.'

'It's not your fault.'

'Even so, I haven't helped.' Maddie hopped off her stool. 'I have the list for the week's potato orders, so I need to go and see Jake now. I'll try and talk some sense into him.'

'Thanks, but there's no need.' Petra lowered her eyes to the pad of Christmas tree prices. 'If he can't see I had good intentions, then he's not the man for me.'

'Are you insane?'

'What?' Jake looked up as Maddie jogged into the polytunnel where he was digging potatoes out of their sacks.

'I can't believe I'm having to say this again. Petra is funny, kind and likes you a lot, and what do you do? You make her feel like crap for offering to help you! All you needed to do was say no thanks if she was offering help you didn't want. Petra isn't a bully. She'd have left it at that.'

Taken aback by Maddie's second burst of anger in a week, Jake took a step back. 'You know I don't want to …'

'Jake! No one likes change, but sometimes it is forced upon us. Now for goodness sake, get over to the shop and apologise! Now.'

23

Maddie smoothed out the crumpled particulars for the land near Exeter as she glanced at the clock on the wall. It was almost eight o'clock in the evening. Ed hadn't been in touch all day.

But then, I haven't contacted him either.

Tempted to call and find out why Ronald Lyle had required his presence so late in the evening, Maddie resisted.

What would I say anyway? His work life is confidential and all I have to talk about at the moment is the nursery. He's probably bored of hearing me go on about it.

She re-read the price of the land at the bottom of the flyer. It seemed a hell of a lot for just fields. 'Plus, there would be building costs, planning permission fees and insurance to pay for.' Maddie got up from the kitchen table and looked out of the window across to The Potting Shed. 'I should have reined in my temper and stayed with Sabi long enough to hear just how much money there would be if we did sell.'

Glancing across to the fern plant, she addressed its mass of haphazard leaves. 'I don't think I've ever lost my temper so often in my whole life.' She stared down at her feet. 'I'm not sure I like who I am at the moment.'

'Then do something about it.' The fern stated the obvious.

'But what?' Her eyes fell on her stripy wellington boots.

Ed wanted to come for a welly walk.

Maddie suddenly longed for a night of rain so she could take out some of the tension she was carrying around with some major puddle splashing.

Even if it did rain, when would you find the time to go?

Reverting her attention to the fern on the windowsill, Maddie forced herself to be practical. 'Here is the situation. BIG want to build over this site. Sabi is happy for this to happen. I am not. My choice is therefore easy – I either refuse to sign and my sister never speaks to me again, and presumably BIG will go back to their original plan of building nearby and become challenging competition. Or else I sign and say goodbye to my home and my livelihood.'

Knowing she needed to speak to her sister and Jake, but too tired to face the prospect, Maddie continued to address her pot plant. 'I know it's early, but I'm going to bed. I'll switch off my phone and indulge in twelve hours of pretending that nothing bad is happening. Then, tomorrow, I'll grow up, face the situation, and call my bank manager.'

Jake felt the pub landlord's eyes boring into him. Shuffling self-consciously in his seat, his pint untouched before him, he was convinced he knew what the older man was thinking as he polished a pint glass.

Why isn't that pretty girl with Jake tonight? He blew that quickly. What did he expect? She was way out of his league...

Jake sipped his lager and grimaced. It tasted bitter.

Following Maddie's order, Jake had apologised again and, miraculously, she'd accepted his apology.

Petra said she'd come here tonight.

But she wasn't there. Eight o'clock had come and gone and Petra had not arrived.

I should have known better.

Jake put his half-full pint glass down on the sticky brown tabletop before him and headed for the door.

By the time he'd got home he knew what he had to do. Jake's hand trembled as he gripped the only pen he owned, staring at it as if it were a bomb about to go off.

I bet she never liked me anyway. I was just a project. Something for her to fix while she worked out what to do with her life. She felt sorry for me. That's all.

Humiliation leant wings to his determination, as with immense concentration, he wrote,

Deer Maddie,

I can't work for you no more.

Sorrie,

Jake

Folding the letter in half, he looked around his room. The walls rebounded with all the times his mother had told him off, told him he was useless, told him he'd amount to nothing like his father. He could imagine what she'd say about him leaving his job. '*How like you to throw away the one good thing you had!*' The echoes of her imagined words merged with all the taunts he'd suffered at school and suddenly, he needed to get away. To be anywhere but there.

Hoisting up a holdall, Jake stuffed a few items of clothing and his phone charger inside and left his bedroom without looking back and with no idea where he was going.

Walking towards the shop the following morning, Maddie felt more positive than she had in days. Her early night had paid off, and the resulting dreamless sleep had been a welcome surprise. Even her last conversation with Sabi hadn't haunted her slumber as she'd assumed it would. Although the reality of her situation hadn't become any easier to deal with overnight, she at least felt refreshed and brave enough to call the bank to talk about a business loan.

Over breakfast she had made three decisions. First, she'd call the bank; then she would call Ed to thank him for the takeaway and his kindness. Then she would contact her sister and ask for Leo Creswell's email and phone number.

'And I will do all of those things as soon as Jake and Petra arrive.'

As she stepped inside the nursery's shop, Maddie automatically turned to chat to the cacti in the windowsill, only to be reminded that they were no longer there – the first success of Petra's selling skills.

With a smile, she pushed the shop's door wide, ready to wedge it open for the day. Maddie was just kicking the doorstop into place, when she spotted a piece of paper that had caught against its underside. Bending to retrieve what she assumed to be a blown-in piece of rubbish, she was about to throw it in the bin when she noticed someone had written on it.

As soon as she saw the spelling 'Deer' instead of 'Dear' she knew it was from Jake. Two seconds later her intentions for the day disappeared as she tapped Jake's number into her phone.

'*Why*, Jake? Did Petra tell you about us maybe closing?' Maddie spoke to the incessant ring of the mobile. 'She doesn't know about BIG, so, unless Sabi told Miriam and she told her daughter…'

The phone kept ringing, but Jake did not pick up. Unease prickled at Maddie's neck. Jake hadn't missed a day at the nursery in four years. He loved it here. She'd always assumed he saw it as his safe space. He'd never taken any holiday, despite being entitled to it, nor had he had a sick day.

What on earth could have happened to make him hand in his notice?

Maddie spun back towards the door as the obvious answer hit her.

Petra.

Leaving a 'call me' message on Jake's answer phone, Maddie pressed Petra's number. The instant automated response of 'This phone is currently unavailable' stopped Maddie in her tracks.

She hadn't known Petra long, but she couldn't imagine her switching her phone off without good reason.

'If she and Jake have had another row, then perhaps she switched it off to avoid talking to him.'

Her intentions for the day crumbled to dust as Maddie checked the time. Providing the bus wasn't late, Petra would be with her in ten minutes. As soon as she arrived, Maddie would dig out Jake's emergency contact details and contact his mother.

★

The email was brief and to the point.

Dear Mrs Willand-Harris and Miss Willand,

The finance and planning department of Big in Gardens (BIG) are keen to proceed with the development of our Somerset/Devon border store.

With this in mind, please could we arrange a meeting of all interested parties for this coming Saturday, 4th December, at 11 o'clock. We would be willing to meet at the home of Mrs Willand-Harris, or The Potting Shed; whichever is the most convenient for you both.

Please confirm the convenience of this meeting at your earliest opportunity.

Best regards,

Leo Creswell

Sabi was about to reply to say that, yes, they would meet them – whoever 'they' were – when she stopped. She could just imagine what Henry would say if she responded to a communication about the future of The Potting Shed without consulting him or Maddie first.

But Henry doesn't know that Maddie was planning to work with another architect to upgrade the nursery. Maybe I should have told him, but I don't want them to fall out too.

Pushing the sense of rejection she felt whenever she considered who Maddie's preferred architect and designer might be, Sabi considered how Leo would take the news if her sister was still refusing to see the inevitability of The Potting Shed's collapse before the weekend. Sabi experienced a sense of disquiet.

Bit odd, having a business meeting on a Saturday.

Her brows knitted together as she pulled Maddie's business proposal towards her and opened it on the last page. Switching on Google, copying the words directly from Maddie's notes, she typed, Farmer's Market – Ivan Porter, into the search bar.

Perhaps I can prove to Maddie that I am worth having around by finding a way to help her make some money before the nursery closes down. And show her I'm not heartless at the same time.

Having sold two pre-ordered half-sacks of potatoes, a bunch of holly and three poinsettias, Maddie was getting worried. It was almost half-past-nine; there was no sign of Petra, and her phone was still off. Nor had Jake had a change of heart and made an appearance.

A fruitless call to his mother had left Maddie none the wiser and rather sad on Jake's behalf. She knew he and his mother weren't close, but the woman's disinterest in the whereabouts of her only child was disturbing. It had taken all of Maddie's persuasive tactics to get her to check he wasn't in his bedroom.

Calling Petra's home was the next obvious move, but Maddie didn't have the number. The only way to get it would be to call her sister for Miriam's contact details. Although speaking to Sabi had been on her day's to-do list, admitting that she'd mislaid her entire workforce would only add fuel to her sister's claim that The Potting Shed was doomed.

'I'll give it one more hour. Then, if Petra hasn't turned up or called in nursing a hangover, I'll call Sabi.'

The list that Sabi had been writing covered almost an entire side of A4. When the ring of her mobile broke through the tones of *Women's Hour* on Radio Four, she was surprised by how absorbed she'd become in her task. She felt oddly caught out when she saw Miriam's name flashing on her phone's screen.

'Hello Miriam. Sorry I haven't phoned to confirm the sale yet. We are going ahead, but Henry wants to—'

A sound of a ragged sob down the line broke through Sabi's excuses.

'Miriam? What is it?'

'Petra. It's Petra… Can you… Maddie. She doesn't know. She'll be worried.'

Sabi jumped off her chair and grabbed her car keys. 'Whatever is it? What has happened to Petra?

24

The beeping of the hospital machinery that surrounded Petra lent a sinister soundtrack to the already frightening array of equipment and the stark whiteness of the sterile room in which she lay. Her eyes were closed, her body unmoving.

Maddie and Sabi stood beside the door in silence as Miriam and her husband, Nigel, sat either side of their daughter's bed, each clutching a bare arm. They both looked as pale as their child.

Once Sabi had arrived at the nursery and delivered the news to Maddie they hadn't hung around. Operating like a well-oiled machine, they had quickly and quietly ushered out the few customers with polite apologies, closed the nursery, locked the till and jumped in their respective cars, having decided it was impractical to go in one in case they needed to leave at different times. Meeting again at the hospital's main reception, they were pointed in the direction of the private rooms on the third floor.

'Black ice is so dangerous. Dad used to grumble about it a lot.'

'I remember.' Sabi wrapped her arms around herself. 'According to the police, the car that hit Petra's didn't stand a chance. It wasn't speeding or anything; met the ice at thirty and swerved.'

'Anyone else hurt?'

'Just bruised and shaken apparently.' Sabi kept her eyes on her friend's daughter.

'That's something.' Maddie couldn't imagine how Petra's conscience would have coped if anyone had been badly hurt, even though it wasn't her fault.

Tapping her sister's arm, Sabi gestured to a row of chairs. 'We should wait over there. We'll hear when there's news.'

The metal and plastic chairs felt unseasonably hot as they sat down.

'I've never seen Miriam like that before.' Even though there was no one around, Sabi found herself whispering. 'She's never shaken, never unsure.'

'Hopefully, you never will again; especially not in this way.' Maddie cleared her throat, 'Thanks for coming to tell me.'

'That's okay.' Sabi kept her eyes on the door to Petra's room. 'Your assistant being in a coma isn't the sort of news I wanted to deliver by phone. It's a miracle no bones are broken.'

'But what about her insides? Any damage?'

'They didn't say. Thank goodness it was such a good car. The side airbag in its door probably saved her worse injuries, or even her life.' Sabi was quiet for a while before she mumbled, 'I'm sorry about how things are with The Potting Shed.'

'Okay.'

'I know it looks as if I'm enjoying this, spending the money before we even have it.'

Maddie briefly laid a hand on her sister's knee. 'It doesn't matter right now.'

Sabi swallowed. 'It's not as if I'm any use to you and—'

'What do you mean?' She fished her phone out of her pocket. 'I have to go outside so I can make a call.'

'You want to warn Jake that you may be closed tomorrow?'

'Closed tomorrow?' Maddie shook her head. 'Not something I can afford to do.'

'I suppose you and Jake ran the place on your own just fine before Petra. I'm sure you'll manage without her for a while.' Sabi felt awkward as she added, 'It's not as if there are many customers.'

'There weren't.' Maddie got up from her chair. 'But Petra was making a difference. The regulars like her. The bigger signage was her idea, and it's bringing in new people. The upturn is only slight so far, but it is happening. Now though…'

'She'll be alright.'

'I hope so.' Maddie looked around. The corridor was empty but for them. 'It doesn't seem a minute since we were sat on a similar set of chairs in another ward.'

'I know.'

Shutting her eyes, trying to block out memories of how they'd sat together waiting for news of her father as the medical staff had tried to save his life, Maddie mumbled, 'But this time it's my fault.'

Sabi turned to her sister. 'How on earth can this be your fault?'

'If I hadn't encouraged Petra to go, she'd never have been on the road in the first place.'

'You know where she was going?'

'To meet Jake. They were on a date.'

Sabi's eyebrows shot upwards. 'Don't be ridiculous. Petra would never…'

Maddie buried her head in her hands. 'I don't need you to air your views on Jake right now, thanks. You've never taken the trouble to speak to him properly, so how would you know what he's like?'

'You only have to look at him!'

'Judging by appearances. How very you.' Maddie's words were heavy with fatigue. 'The fact is, they get on well. They've already had one date, but then there was a row. I thought they'd sorted themselves out. They agreed to meet last night. That must be where Petra was going when…' Maddie jumped to her feet. 'That's why!'

'What's why?'

'Jake didn't come to work this morning. He…' Maddie stopped talking, knowing that her sister would be delighted to hear Jake had resigned, but knew she'd gone too far not to say something. 'He's never had a day off before.'

'You think he's nursing a sore ego because he thinks he was stood up?'

'It would make sense, and before you judge him further, it was a big deal for Jake to trust Petra enough to want to see her. To trust anyone. His life hasn't exactly been overflowing with kindness. Her not turning up—'

'But she's in a coma!'

'A fact that Jake is unaware of!' Maddie slumped back in her seat.

'Petra was only going to be with you for a while anyway. She'll be doing a conversion course to be a lawyer soon.'

Sabi spoke with certainty. 'You can think what you like, but no way would Jake make the right sort of partner for her as she climbs the ladder.'

Maddie felt the hysterical giggle escape before she could stop it and clapped a hand to her mouth.

'Maddie!'

'Sorry Sabi, but Petra has no intention of being a lawyer. Ever.'

'But her parents…'

The heaviness of the situation overtook Maddie's hysterical exhaustion. 'Her parents decided their daughter would be a lawyer. They didn't ask her first if that's what she wanted.'

'I'm sure they have her best interests at heart.'

'That doesn't mean they get to make decisions about her future. No parent has that right.'

Sabi looked stung. Leaving her words to sink in, Maddie moved towards the door. Whatever Jake currently thought of Petra, he was going to have to be found and told what had happened.

Maddie tapped out a text to Ed, explaining what had happened, while wishing she hadn't scuppered her chances of him coming over to give her a much needed cuddle. Then she called Jake's phone for a third time.

Convinced that her assistant would be hunkered down somewhere feeling humiliated and stupid, Maddie muttered to herself, 'Please let Petra wake up. *Please.*'

As she walked back towards the hospital's main doors, her phone vibrated in her pocket. Whipping it out fast, hoping it was Jake, Maddie saw a reply from Ed waiting her attention.

How awful. Let me know when there is news. Ed

She stared at her phone screen. She wasn't sure what she'd expected his reply to say – or even if he'd reply – but the lack of a 'how are you' stung far more than it should have done.

'Don't overreact. There's no reason he should have said anything more.' Maddie gave herself a shake. 'And all that matters right now is Petra.'

Sabi caught Maddie's arm as she arrived back in the ward's corridor.

'What is it?' Sick with apprehension, Maddie allowed her sister to escort her to the set of chairs they'd been sat on before.

'The scan results have come back. Extensive bruising, internal and external. No hidden fractures.'

'That's good…isn't it?'

'It's a miracle in the circumstances.' Sabi glanced over her shoulder. 'But – she hasn't woken up yet.'

'But they think she will – don't they?'

'Yes. But they can't promise, and they can't say when.'

Maddie felt shaky with relief. 'How's Miriam and…?'

'Nigel. They're as you'd imagine, but better now they know there is no brain damage or spinal injury.'

'Will they take the neck brace off? It makes Petra look so vulnerable.'

'No idea.' Sabi hooked her handbag up her shoulder. 'I'm going to fetch Miriam and Nigel some coffee. Do you want any?'

'No thanks.'

'Did you get hold of Jake?'

'No. His phone is still off. I need to look for him. Will you call me if there's any change?'

'Sure.'

'Thanks.'

Maddie was almost at the ward door when her sister called her back. 'Um, Maddie, I was going to phone you later, but with all this...'

'What were you going to call about?'

'I read your proposal. It's good.'

'Oh.' Maddie peered through the glass window in the door to Petra's room. Her young friend was so still, so serene, in her crisp white bed. 'Shame it was a waste of time. I don't want to sell, but I'm boxed in, aren't I. If I don't sell, you will be unhappy, and I don't want that on my conscience.' Keeping her eyes averted from her sister, Maddie added, 'You know, the Sabi I grew up with had fight in her. She'd never have given up something that was important to our family without exploring every angle.'

'But why should I, when you don't want me or...'

'Forget it.' Maddie brushed away the excuse she was sure Sabi was about to make as she saw Miriam soothe a palm over her daughter's forehead. 'Do something for me though.'

'What's that?'

'Ask Jem what she thinks about closing The Potting Shed. Include her. She may be in total agreement with you. She may love the idea of having a house on tap in the future. But she might not.'

'Here.' Sabi handed the takeaway coffee cups to Miriam. 'It's not that good, but it's wet and warm.'

'Thanks.' Miriam looked like she hadn't slept for years. 'I can't believe that's Petra in there.'

'I know what you mean.' Sabi watched through the open doorway as Nigel brushed a hand through his daughter's hair.

'I don't know what to do.' Miriam's hands began to shake, making the coffee slop dangerously close to the edges of the cups.

'Here.' Sabi took the drinks back. 'Why don't you sit over there a minute?'

Placing the coffee cups down on a chair just inside Petra's room, Sabi hurried to her friend's side. 'If I can do anything, you only have to ask.'

'I know. You've always been a good friend.'

Surprised by Miriam's candour, Sabi put her hand over hers. 'As you have to me. All that matters now is Petra. Can I call work for you or anything?'

'Nigel did that, but thanks.' A tear escaped from the corner of her eye, 'I'm always in control. I *need* to be in control. It's who I am... but this... I know sometimes I can be a bit... you know... but I always know what to do. Always.' She pulled a tissue from her sleeve and blew her nose. 'How can I be me, Sabi, if I don't know what to do to help my child?'

★

Maddie was running out of places to look. She'd tried Jake's home, but there'd been no reply from her loud knocks on the front door. She'd tried the pub she knew he favoured and left urgent messages there for him to call her.

Manoeuvring into her parking bay, Maddie watched as the clock on the dashboard clicked around to half-past-nine. She was so tired but knew there were jobs she had to do around the nursery before she could go to bed.

Climbing out of the jeep, Maddie had only taken two steps towards the first polytunnel to check the overnight temperature was set, when she stopped again. Suddenly, she knew where Jake would be.

'So obvious! I should have looked there first!'

Breaking into a jog, she headed for the polytunnel at the far end of the nursery. Slowing as she reached the entrance, Maddie saw her suspicion had been correct. Jake was there; his shadow showing him to be hunkered down against the tunnel's side, near to the small fan heater they used for extra warmth in winter.

Wanting to give him a chance to compose himself in case he'd been crying, Maddie made her approaching footsteps deliberately loud on the gravel and indulged in a brief fake coughing fit.

The shadow inside the polytunnel was already straightening up as Maddie walked through the half-unzipped door. She'd toyed with the idea of expressing surprise at seeing him but decided against it. He didn't need patronising on top of everything else.

'I had a hunch you'd be here.' Maddie took her gloves from her pockets. 'I wish I'd had it earlier, would have saved me a trek around Wellington.'

Jake's surprise was obvious. 'You went looking for me?'

'I was worried. Your phone is off.'

Jake gave a full body shrug and sat back down on the patch of soil he'd made his own.

Maddie gestured to his holdall. 'Were you planning to spend the night?'

Jake avoided Maddie's eyes. 'I'd have been gone before the nursery opened tomorrow.'

'There's a spare bedroom in the house. Come on.'

'What?'

'Come to the house. I have a spare room.'

Jake stayed where he was. 'But I resigned.'

'Because you didn't want to work here anymore, or for another reason?

Jake hugged his holdall to his chest. 'I love working here.'

With the knowledge that the nursery's days were numbered knocking at the inside of her brain like a malevolent woodpecker, Maddie said, 'As far as I'm concerned that note was never written.'

'Really?' Jake's face lit up for a second, but then it dulled again. 'I still can't work here. Not with…'

'Let's go inside. I need to talk to you about Petra.'

'And he wants to have this discussion about BIG's plans on a Saturday? This Saturday?' Henry raised an eyebrow. 'Odd day to choose.'

'That's what I thought.' Sabi climbed into bed and picked up her novel and reading glasses. 'And before you say anything, I didn't say earlier because I found out about Petra shortly after I'd read the email and forgot all about it.'

Wrapping an arm around his wife, Henry lifted the book from her fingers. 'No need to be defensive, I wasn't about to accuse you of withholding information.'

'Sorry.' Sabi rested her head against Henry's shoulder. 'It's been such a horrid day. I'm sure Maddie didn't mention today's email for the same reason.'

'She would definitely have got the email?'

'I gave Mr Creswell her email address when I gave him mine, so I assume so. The initial letter was sent to us both wasn't it?'

Henry nodded as he asked, 'How are Miriam and Nigel holding up?'

'Better now they know there is no internal damage. Petra was so lucky, especially when you consider what might have happened…' Sabi's voice cracked. 'I was thinking, perhaps we could go and see Jemima this weekend.'

Henry kissed the top of his wife's head. 'I was thinking that very thing.'

'I know it's daft, but I need to make sure she's okay.'

'It's not daft at all. Jemima is often on my mind, but today I've been fighting the urge to drop everything and go to check that all her limbs are where they ought to be.'

Snuggling closer to her husband, Sabi sighed, 'But if we have a meeting with Leo on Saturday, then…'

Henry stroked her hair, 'Jemima is our child. We don't have to wait until Saturday. I'll call the school in the morning. Dinner at the Chinese in Tiverton tomorrow night?'

'Jemima's favourite.'

'Exactly.' Henry grinned. 'I'm rather partial to the food there myself.'

'Me too.' Sabi felt foolish as she muttered, 'It's Maddie's favourite too. Miriam would never go there.'

'Not posh enough.' Henry pulled a face. 'Look love, I know Miriam is a friend, and you are right to be there for her just now, but you don't have to *be* her. I don't *want* you to be her. I want you to be you. My beautiful, intelligent, kind wife.'

'I'm sorry if I've been a bit…' Sabi knew she didn't have to finish the sentence.

'With your dad, then BIG coming out of nowhere, flipping everything upside down, you're bound to be a bit off kilter.' Henry smiled. 'We could ask Maddie to come tomorrow too. Proper family dinner.'

'Actually, would you mind if we didn't.'

'I thought you two got on well today?'

'We did, but there's something I want to ask Jemima about, without Maddie being there.'

25

December

It had taken all her persuasive skills to stop Jake dashing off to the hospital the previous night. Even though she'd promised to close the nursery early and take him into Exeter as soon as evening visiting hours started, Maddie wasn't that surprised to find a new note on the kitchen table at breakfast time.

Gonne to Petra.

'Oh Jake, they won't let you in until this afternoon.' Maddie peered at the kitchen clock. It was barely seven o'clock in the morning.

Contemplating checking to see if he was at the bus stop, waiting for the first of the three buses he'd need to take to reach his goal, Maddie stopped herself. Jake was an adult, if he wanted to sit outside the hospital all day, then that was his choice.

'Although, goodness knows how Miriam will react when she sees him!' Maddie tutted to herself.

Picking up her phone to see if Sabi had sent any news about Petra overnight, she saw she'd missed a text, not from her sister, but from Ed. It had been sent at just gone midnight.

Any news on Petra?

'I should have texted him.'

Sorry for delay. I had a situation with Jake. OK now. Petra in coma. No internal injuries.

Pressing 'send' Maddie realised she hadn't asked how he was. She lifted the phone to send a follow up text, when it burst into life.

'Sabi. Any news?'

'Miriam just called. Petra is still unconscious, but the doctor's hopeful that it's just a matter of time.'

'That's great.' Maddie rested her back against the kitchen sink. 'Do you think it'd be alright if I pop by later? I wouldn't want to be in the way.'

'I'm sure it's fine. Miriam and Nigel are going back in this evening. Apparently, they are too busy with work to go before then.'

'Excuse me!'

'I know.' Sabi shared her sister's shock. 'I couldn't believe it either. If it was Jemima, I'd never leave her side.'

'And I'd be there with you!'

'I know you would.' Sabi tutted down the line, 'I am surprised at Miriam to be honest. She was so choked up when we spoke yesterday. Said she didn't know what to do. That she felt out of control. And now she isn't even visiting her child until this evening.'

'Perhaps it's her way of coping, you know, by spending the day doing something she can control she'll feel less lost and afraid.' Surprised to find herself defending Miriam, Maddie added, 'It wouldn't do for me though.'

'Nor me.' Sabi's voice became small. 'I'm going to do what you asked, we are seeing Jemima later. I'm going to ask her opinion on a few things.'

Maddie smiled. 'Thanks Sabs.'

'Sabs? You haven't called me that for ages. Sabs and Mads.'

A chuckle escaped Maddie. 'Neither of us could say Madeline or Sabrina when we were tiny.'

Sabi felt a lightening of her spirits, only to risk losing the sensation by saying, 'You know, Jemima might not think saving the nursery is a good idea, Mads.'

'True, but I appreciate you consulting her. The Potting Shed is a family business, after all.'

A nurse Maddie hadn't seen the day before came to her side as she arrived at the door to Petra's room.

'The young man arrived just after nine this morning, wouldn't take no for an answer when we explained that visiting hours weren't until two.'

Maddie watched Jake. He was sat next to Petra, his large

palm holding her hand as if it was as delicate as porcelain china.

'I did tell him about the visiting hours, I'm sorry.'

The nurse wiped her concerns away. 'Don't worry, he's been no trouble and, as this is a private room, the rules are a little more flexible. Anyway,' she picked up her clipboard, and made ready to go on her latest round, 'it'll be nice for Miss Reece to have someone with her when she wakes up.'

Maddie nodded. 'I'll go and get him a coffee, then say hello.'

'You his sister?'

'His employer. Friend. And Petra's.' Maddie dug her purse from her bag. 'I'll fetch those coffees.'

By the time she'd found the café, queued for her drinks and got back to Petra's room, official visiting time was half over. She was about to go in, but a sight she never thought she'd see stopped Maddie in her tracks.

Jake was leafing through a book.

Stood in the doorway, she could hear him talking to Petra.

'I know I've already apologised, but I need you to know why I overreacted. No one's put themselves out for me before, you see. Apart from Tony and Maddie of course.' He flapped the slim book towards Petra, giving Maddie a glimpse of the cover. It was a guide to an adult literacy course. 'I hope you don't mind, but I took this out of your bag. I'm gonna try, you know, to learn more. But...' Jake paused, his gaze fixed on Petra's closed eyelids, '...I can't read much of the guide that's supposed to help me.'

The defeat in Jake's voice as he held the volume, his

fingers clearly not comfortable with the foreign object they held, broke Maddie's heart.

As the heat from the Styrofoam cups became too much for her to hold easily, Maddie knocked on the door with her elbow, and went in. 'I got coffee.'

His face pink, not sure if his conversation had been overheard, Jake mumbled, 'Thanks.'

'You okay?'

'Tired.' Jake took a grateful swig from his cup. 'Thanks for letting me stay last night.'

'No problem. You can stay tonight if you can't face going home. The room is there, you might as well use it while Petra's in hospital.'

'Really?' Jake's face lit up.

'Sure. It'll be handy having you on site over the pre-Christmas period if you don't mind pitching in with cooking – and when I say cooking, I mean taking your turn to heat up the beans for beans on toast.'

'I like toast.' Jake tried to smile as he gave an audible gulp, his watery eyes telling Maddie he was struggling not to cry. 'I've been talking to her. The nurse said it might help bring her back.'

'Good idea.' Maddie gestured to the thin book. 'You're reading to her?'

'Hardly.' Jake's response was more a scoff than a word.

'But you're going to learn aren't you.'

'It's probably too late.'

Maddie knelt next to her friend. 'Jake, it is *never* too late to learn things. And Petra will help you. She believes you can do it.'

'I hoped she did.'

'She does, and when she wakes up there will be a long time when all she can do is sit around with nothing to do while her body gets over the shock it's been through. It'll be good if you could help her by letting her help you.'

'You think so?'

'I know so.' Maddie stood up again. 'I'm going to leave you two in peace. I should warn you though, her mother and father are due this evening and they are – well, let's just say they have set ideas about who is allowed to date their child.'

'Petra told me.' Jake grimaced. 'But that's tough, because she's my girlfriend and they're going to have to cope with that.'

26

'What would happen if I was hurt in an accident?'

The fern remained quiet on the matter as Maddie sat at the kitchen table with a round of buttered toast. 'I'm sure that, despite everything, Sabi would be there for me. And Henry would pop in, and maybe Jem would get time off school to visit her aunt, but...'

There'd be no one to hold your hand.

The image of Jake holding Petra's hand in the hospital had stuck with Maddie for the rest of the day. Now, as she tucked into her low-maintenance evening meal, she couldn't help conjuring images of Ed.

'He held onto me as we walked in the dark. It felt good – right, even. We had dinner... but then left me mid-takeaway and hasn't asked to see him again since.'

The fern broke its silence as she munched through a particularly thick crust. 'It's okay to like him. You know he likes you. You didn't imagine the chemistry.'

'I'm not so sure. Maybe I've been having such a rough time lately that I simply *wanted* to feel chemistry, so I did – auto-suggestion, or something.'

Maddie imagined the fern rustling its lime-coloured leaves in a manner that suggested it was unconvinced.

I told him just friends with good reason. I've lost so much lately – if we dated and it didn't work out...

'Then friendship is a good place to start,' the plant stated. 'Why not just go from there? You could call him and just say hi.'

Maddie glanced at the phone next to her as she chewed a crust. 'I'll have to see him again for work soon... better to clear the air first maybe...'

Before she could change her mind, Maddie seized her phone and sent a message.

Hi Ed. Hope you OK. Petra no better, but no worse thank goodness. Would you like to come out for a walk with me after work tomorrow? About 6.30? M x

Reading it back after it had been sent, Maddie wondered if she should have added the kiss or not.

'You should have added two.'

'If you keep giving me advice like that, I'll forget to water you.' Maddie glowered at the fern. 'At least going out for a walk will give me a chance to thank him for all his help.'

Maddie had made up the spare bed for Jake properly, rather than simply throwing him some blankets and an old duvet as she had the night before, when her phone buzzed.

Sorry Maddie. Busy tomorrow night. Ed x

'Well, that's answered that question anyway. I left it too late.'

He put a kiss after his name.

'Makes no difference. He said no.'

Plumping Jake's pillow with extra vigour, Maddie sent a quick reply.

Understood. M

Then she switched off her phone. The urge to cry pricked at her eyes, but she pushed it away.

'You have been on your own for long enough to know you can cope perfectly well solo. You are *not* going to start mooning around like a teenager.' Pep talk delivered, Maddie put her hands on her hips. 'It's time to get on with deciding what to do about The Potting Shed. Being busy is the answer, and there's no lack of things to do.'

Over the past few years, the spare room had been used by Jem whenever she stayed during the school holidays, and before that it had been Sabi's childhood bedroom. The dusty pink paint on the walls had been her sister's choice, picked from a Homebase paint chart when she was sixteen years old; Sabi and Maddie had painted most of the room themselves.

As she stood there, Maddie could see them as they'd used to be – her and Sabi as teenagers, laughing as they'd daubed splodges of emulsion onto the walls. They'd painted funny faces and flowers, rainbows and stars across the room, before finally admitting they needed to paint the walls properly. Walls that were then covered in rows of shelves, pictures and a large pinboard, on which Sabi had stuck posters of her latest obsession, variously ranging from pop crushes to horses, from flowers to literary quotes.

The pinboard and Sabi had gone only two years later, when she'd headed off to university, but the rest of the room remained as it had always been. Lined with bookshelves along one side, there were so many things that had been 'put in the spare room for now' over the past decade, that Maddie suddenly had an overwhelming sense of being boxed in.

'How did we accumulate so much stuff?'

Flicking through the first book on the shelf she came to, Maddie recognised it as one her father had bought Sabi when she'd decided to start growing giant vegetables to win a local 'Biggest Pumpkin' competition when she was twelve.

Maddie recalled how seriously her sister had taken the task. Reading up on the subject, she'd tended her pumpkin seeds, and brought on her fledgling crop, before selecting two likely candidates for her full attention. She had nursed them and cared for them, until the day of the village show came.

Sabi had been gutted at the outcome. Second. Maddie would have been thrilled with second place, but her sister had been sullen for days afterwards. It had been the first time Sabi had shown signs of anything less than first not being good enough.

'We could do with some of that single minded determination now Sabs, but for The Potting Shed, not for BIG.'

Sinking onto the bed she'd just made; Maddie raked a hand through her hair. 'I'll have to hire at least three skips if I'm going to move – and that's if I have the heart to throw anything away.'

Resigning herself to saving cardboard boxes from her deliveries, so she could start packing things up, Maddie groaned. 'Of course I'm going to have to move.'

Standing up, she fought the emotion that was forming a lump in her throat. 'I could have tried to make it work with BIG as a local competitor, but if they want to destroy the nursery and build over it...'

You don't have to sign. You can refuse. Then they will have to use the original site opposite or find somewhere else.

Maddie peered up at the seashell lampshade hanging from the centre of the ceiling. It was a dreadful dust trap and had a habit of singing like a wind chime when the window was open, but her sister had loved it. In itself, it was a tacky piece of kitsch, but Sabi had known it would work in the room, and insisted it was purchased, and – as usual – she was right. Somehow, it suited the room to perfection.

'I bet Sabi'll be in heaven doing up her new house.' Maddie brushed some dust off the lamp. 'Something she won't be able to do if I refuse to sign the nursery land away.'

Suddenly Maddie froze, as a fresh memory, long forgotten, came back to her. It had been in that room, a couple of years before they'd painted it, that Sabi had first mentioned the house in Culmstock.

'You should see it Mads. It looks just like the doll's house Louisa Harriett has got. It's so perfect. Wouldn't it be wonderful to live somewhere like that one day? I only got a glimpse at first, but Dad drove the car back so I could take another look.'

'I'd forgotten about Sabi's obsession with Louisa Harriett.' Maddie picked the pillow off the bed and plumped it into shape. 'You always did need someone to aspire to, Sabs. Shame they're usually people that have a habit of making you feel inferior in the process.' A sense of sorrow for her sister ran through her as she addressed the lampshade.

'Louisa wouldn't let Sabi touch her doll's house – she was only allowed to look. A fact that wasn't a problem until she overheard one of the other girls at school talking about how she'd picked up all the individual pieces of furniture and rearranged them.'

The image of her sister, bewildered by hurt, after the revelation that her best friend at school didn't trust her to touch her prize possession, accompanied Maddie as she headed to the kitchen.

Picking up the particulars for the land in Broadclyst, she blew out a heavy sigh She'd got no further than rereading the dimensions of the first field, when the sound of the front door opening, and Jake's heavy footfall made Maddie stuff the papers under a pile of books, as she called out, 'Hi Jake, how's Petra?'

'Still sleeping like an angel. Her mother, on the other hand, is a total dragon.'

'How's Auntie Maddie, Mum?'

Jemima twirled some noodles around her chopsticks, laughing as they immediately fell off again.

'She misses your grandad.'

Lowering her chopsticks to her bowl, Jemima nodded. 'Me too.'

'We all do.' Henry took his daughter's hand. 'And now a young woman Maddie employs has had an accident. She's in hospital.'

'That's horrid.' Jemima frowned. 'Will she be okay?'

'We think so. It's Petra, you know, my friend Miriam's daughter?'

'Miriam's the snooty one, isn't she?'

'Jemima!' Sabi drew in a sharp breath.

'She is Mum, she's dreadful. Even Miranda Richardson-Smythe's mother isn't as up herself as Miriam.'

Henry hid a snigger behind a mouthful of fried rice. 'Then remind me not to engage in conversation with Miranda's mother!'

'Henry!' Feeling ganged up on, Sabi turned to her daughter. 'This isn't the…'

'…attitude you expect from me?'

'I…' Sabi blanched.

Henry shot his daughter a warning glance, which she noted at once.

'Sorry.' Jemima picked her chopsticks back up. 'I'm not ungrateful. I love school. Now then,' fishing a piece of Kung Po chicken up, Jemima flourished it towards her parents, 'what did you want to talk to me about?'

Wondering at what point her eleven-year-old daughter had metamorphosed into a trainee teenager, Sabi countered, 'What makes you think we had something we wanted to talk to you about?'

'Come on, Mum. How often do you drive up to school to whip me out for a treat in the week? Only when you want something or want me not to do something.'

Discomfited by the ring of truth in Jemima's words, Sabi spoke carefully. 'Okay, I wanted to ask you something. It's Petra's accident – it made me think.'

'*Us* think.' Henry took his wife's hand as he continued. 'Petra's parents have always had very firm ideas about how they saw their daughter's future. A future we've recently discovered Petra wasn't so keen on pursuing. Your mum and I want you to know that we aren't like that. Whatever you decide to do after school, we'll support you. All we want is for you to be happy. Isn't that right, love?'

Sabi smiled. 'Absolutely.'

Abandoning her chopsticks, Jemima ran around the table and gave her parents a hug. 'Thank you! You would not *believe* some of the pressure the other girls are under from their parents!'

'I think we have a fair idea.' Henry shot his wife another sidelong glance.

'I'm only eleven! I don't want to even *think* about my GCSE options yet. Some of my friends' parents are planning what their kids will be doing once they've left university. Scary!'

Sabi put her hand on Henry's leg as she said, 'How about the only decision we ask you to make right now, Jemima, is if you'd like some more prawn crackers?'

27

Sleep had taken ages to arrive, and when it had finally claimed Maddie, it did so in a half-hearted way, sending her into a shallow dream state, where she was packing endless boxes of books, only to be forced to move to a house with no garden. A horror which had woken her with a start.

Gulping down a glass of water, Maddie took some deep breaths. 'This is silly. Why haven't I just got on and done what needs doing? I *must* talk to Sabi, find out all the details of the situation with BIG, and actually make that appointment with the bank, rather than just saying I'm going to.'

Determined to be practical, Maddie swung her legs out of bed and turned her mobile on.

Three texts announced themselves in quick succession as she dragged a brush through her tangle of hair.

Meal with Jemima was lovely. Didn't go quite to plan though. Will explain later. Sabi x

Deciding not to jump to conclusions and wait and see what her niece had said for herself, she read the next text. It was from Jake.

Gonne to see P early to miss her mum. Nurse said it was
OK.

Maddie could well imagine the scene Jake had described
the night before, when Miriam had arrived to find, in her
words, 'an oik', holding her daughter's hand. Jake hadn't hung
around. Behaving with a dignity that Maddie was proud of,
he'd kissed Petra's cheek and left, asked the nurse to keep him
updated, and caught the three buses back to the nursery.

The third text was from Ed.

Sorry for brief reply before. Was in a meeting. Got a few
tricky conveyances at the moment and they are eating
up my time. Walk on Saturday instead? x

Maddie re-read the text. 'So why didn't you text me once
the meeting was over? It was hours ago, and—' Her words
stumbled to a halt as she noted when Ed had sent the text.
It had only been a few minutes after she'd shut down her
phone. 'Okay, so maybe you did text straight away.'

Contrite, Maddie replied.

Would like a walk. Thanks. Perhaps we should make it a
work meeting in the open air?

Sat in the conservatory, making the most of the weak
winter sunshine that shone through the glass roof, Sabi
opened her laptop and braced herself to read her emails.

What with Petra's accident and seeing Jemima, she still

hadn't replied to Leo's request that they meet on Saturday. Nor had she mentioned it to Maddie.

But then Maddie hasn't mentioned it to me either.

She wasn't surprised to see a reminder from BIG waiting for her attention. She scanned it quickly, finding the message to be almost identical to the original, with an additional sentence saying – *Please confirm attendance and your preferred location to meet ASAP.*

Below that sat another email. The sentence in the subject line made her open the email with eager speed.

From Ivan Porter – Farmer's Market.

Having opened the nursery, Maddie had settled herself by The Potting Shed's till to write two different lists.

The first list was for all the things she would have to do if she gave up the nursery; the second contained everything she would have to do to keep it going.

Needing something practical to do straight away whatever happened, both lists had 'have a clear out of Dad's things' and 'streamline the spare room' near their top.

Maddie scanned the moving away list. It was frighteningly long already. Not to mention daunting. 'More daunting still because I don't want to go.'

'What's that dear?'

Maddie looked up to see an old lady shuffling towards her.

'I'm sorry, I was talking to myself. How can I help you, Mrs Jeffries?'

The old lady's face lit up. 'You remember me?'

Maddie smiled. 'You come here every winter for a bunch of holly and a bunch of mistletoe. Although,' Maddie gave a wave of regret, 'I can't oblige with mistletoe this year. Still not a great idea after Covid.'

'Quite right, my dear.' Mrs Jeffries gave an empathetic nod. 'No good encouraging extra snogging and starting it off again!'

Trying not to grin too widely at the incongruous use of the word snogging from the pensioner's lips, Maddie pointed to the bunches of holly Petra had strung up near the back of the shop. 'One bunch as usual?'

'Please.'

As Maddie unhooked two large sprigs for her customer to choose between, Mrs Jefferies looked around the shop approvingly. 'It's good to see you carrying on with your father's work, my dear. My husband, God rest his soul, always had a lot of time for family businesses and made a point of supporting local shops.'

'I remember your husband from when I was a little girl.'

'He was a good man, my Frank, but his time came when it came. Still,' Mrs Jeffries picked the nearest of the holly sprigs Maddie was holding out to her, 'I'm blessed with a family to keep me going. Which reminds me, have you got any packets of cress seed? My grandchildren love growing it. I thought I'd put a packet in each of their stockings. It's less than four weeks until Christmas. Time seems to simply run away these days.'

Maddie was abruptly reminded of the idea she'd had for creating a children's space in the nursery, along with easy how-to guides to encourage children to grow plants.

'Are you alright, my dear?' Mrs Jeffries moved closer to the till. 'You're looking a bit peaky all of a sudden.'

'Fine, I'm fine. Just thinking. I'm afraid I don't have cress seeds, but if you don't mind waiting, I can order some in to collect next week.'

'Please do. Six packets, please.'

Maddie made a note on her order pad. 'Six grandchildren?'

Mrs Jeffries giggled. 'Five, but why should they have all the fun, uh?'

'It was very good of you to come, Mrs Willand-Harris.'

'No trouble at all. And please, call me Sabi.'

'Ivan.' The manager of the Exmoor Drifters gestured to the dog at his feet. 'And this is Sheba. Are you alright with hounds, or would you like me to put her in the house?'

'Oh no, please don't. She's a beauty.' Sabi knelt down to say hello to the black Labrador. 'Aren't you beautiful?'

'You're the second person to tell her that in the last fortnight. It'll go to her head.'

'I'm surprised it doesn't happen on a daily basis.' Sabi gave Sheba another pat and stood up. My sister and I had a dog. Benji. A Border Collie. I still miss him.'

'They're as much part of the family as any human.'

'They are.' Sabi smiled. 'Sometimes they're more human than we are.'

'More humane, certainly.' Ivan nodded. 'So, you would like a run down on how we work the market?'

'Please.' Sabi added quickly, 'I did explain that this is just a theory for a possible extra venue for you at this time?'

'You did. A potential garden centre site near Wellington?'

'I know that's nearer the Blackdown Hills than Exmoor, but...'

'Fear not, Sabi, the Exmoor Drifters will drift to anywhere they are made welcome.'

Jake moved faster than he had in years.

Dashing to the nurse's station, he found he couldn't speak. Relief had rendered him mute as the nurse on duty, understanding the hopeful yet fearful expression on his face, stopped what she was doing and followed Jake back to Petra.

Taking her hand, Jake fixed his eyes on Petra's face. Never had a pair of open eyes looked so attractive. He'd noted how deep a blue they were before, but now he saw they were the deep, rich blue of a peacock's feather. 'Petra, it's me. Jake.'

'Jake?' Her voice cracked from lack of use.

'You're in hospital. You're okay.'

Petra's forehead creased as she blinked against the harsh light after so long in darkness. 'Hospital?'

'There was an accident. You're a bit bruised.'

Petra turned an uncomprehending face to the nurse adjusting the drip that ran into her arm. 'I don't remember. What happened?'

The nurse smiled. 'Perhaps Jake could tell you all about it later. What matters now is that you are awake. We need to get a doctor to examine you. And call your parents, of course.'

Petra closed her eyes again as a wave of exhaustion overtook her.

'Jake,' the nurse dipped her head towards the door, 'perhaps you wouldn't mind letting Petra have some sleep.'

'But she's been asleep for ages.' He held onto Petra's arm. 'Now she's come round, I want to talk to her.'

'I know, but she's been in a very different type of sleep. Her body needs real rest now, plus her parents are bound to come over once I get the receptionist to call them.'

'And they won't be pleased to see me.' Jake groaned. 'The cold way her mother looked at me yesterday spoke volumes.' He looked at Petra. She was already sound asleep, her blonde hair tousled across the pillow. 'I haven't known her long, but she's...'

'Special?' The nurse gave his shoulder a quick tap. 'I shouldn't say anything, but I can see how much you care for her. If you're the one, there'll be nothing Petra's parents can do about it. If you're not, you'll find out anyway, without their interference. Now, why don't you go home and rest. By the look of you, you haven't been getting much sleep either.'

The list of things to do before selling The Potting Shed had been scrunched into a ball and thrown into the bin. Instead, Maddie had placed an order for a whole host of child-focused seed packets with plans to promote them as stocking fillers.

Jotting down a few ideas to add to the children's area she wanted to develop when she converted the house into a flat and garden centre space, Maddie placed a call to her local bank. She'd expected it to be a complicated process, but the appointment with a business advisor had taken less than a minute to set up for half-past-eleven on Monday morning.

'After I've spoken to them,' she told herself sternly, 'I'll call Sabi and tell her my decision – once and for all.'

28

'I can't wait to get out of here, but at the same time, I don't want to go home and become the subject of Mum's fussing. I know she means well, but sometimes it gets a bit much.'

Jake put his arm out, so that Petra could cuddle into his side. 'At least you have a private room. We'd never be allowed to sit on the bed together like this on a normal ward.'

'Advantage of rich parents.'

'And having parents who love you.' Jake examined Petra's face intently. 'Your bruises are starting to fade.'

'So I should hope. I've been here forever.'

Jake searched her expression for any signs of pain or discomfort. 'I'm not gonna be allowed to visit you at home, am I?'

Petra rested her head on his shoulder. 'Maybe not.'

Jake paused before adding, 'I did wonder about asking Maddie if you could stay in her spare room while you got better, but...'

'Aren't you sleeping in her spare room?'

'I am... I just thought...'

Laughing, Petra kissed his cheek. 'As much as I'd love

to share a bed with you, right now I'd probably pass out mid-bonk.'

Bright pink, Jake looked at Petra. 'I meant that you could have the bed. I'd sleep on the sofa downstairs. That way I could see you and...'

'I know. I was joking.'

'Oh.' Jake went quiet.

Kissing his cheek again, Petra whispered in his ear. 'I won't be like this for long. Then, well, I wouldn't want you to sleep on the sofa.'

'Really?' Jake was embarrassed at the sound of hope in his own voice, but Petra either hadn't noticed his tone or had chosen to ignore it.

Petra changed the subject as a yawn overtook her. 'The doctor said I was getting stronger all the time, but my sides and chest were bruised badly on the inside. Everything is so sore.' She was quiet for a moment, before asking, 'Has Maddie said anything to you about the future of the nursery?'

'No, why?'

'Umm.' Petra mumbled, unsure if she should bring the subject up or not. 'Do you know why I'm keen for you to improve your reading?'

'Because you're a lovely person.'

'Thanks, but that's not why.' Petra sat up and adjusted her pillows. 'I'm going to tell you something I shouldn't. Not because I want to betray Maddie, but because I think you need to know, and because she's worried about telling you.'

Twisting around so he could see Petra's face properly, a sense of foreboding crept over Jake. 'Tell me what?'

'You know I was employed by Maddie as a favour, a job

to get my folks off my back while they got used to the idea that I don't want to be a lawyer?'

'Yeah.'

'And that my job at The Potting Shed was always going to be short term?'

Jake rubbed at his arm, 'Til after Christmas. But I'm sure Maddie will keep you now she knows you're good.'

'She won't be keeping me on, Jake. If I tell you why not, then you have to promise not to run off before I've explained everything.'

Jake hung his head. 'I'm sorry I ran off before. I thought you'd stood me up.'

'And you felt humiliated, I know. It's flattering you care that much.'

'Is it?' Convinced he'd never understand women as long as he lived, Jake looked at Petra expectantly.

'The reason I wanted to help your literacy is because the future of the nursery is not certain. In fact, it's highly likely to close.'

'Close?' The word came out as a frightened whisper. 'But it can't close. Maddie loves it. I love it, and…'

'Maddie does love it, and she doesn't want to close, but circumstances have become complicated…' Petra paused. 'If you can read and write a little better, you'll have a much better chance of finding new work.'

'Circumstances?' Jake's face had taken on a deathly pallor.

Taking his hand in hers, Petra asked, 'Have you heard of BIG?'

'Big in Gardens?'

'Uh-huh. Well, they want to open a branch nearby.' Petra

pulled a face. 'They've offered the Willand sisters' money to buy The Potting Shed's land.'

Jake raked a hand over his stubbly hair. 'Why didn't Maddie tell me?'

'Apart from the fact that she is very fond of you, a member of her staff has had a car crash, and she is in danger of losing her home and her business?'

'Yeah, I see. Lots going on for her right now.' Jake sat still, letting everything Petra had said sink in. Then, slowly, he slid off the bed.

'Jake? Are you okay?'

Bending down to the rucksack he habitually carried with him, Jake opened the zip and wrenched out a pile of paperwork.

'I've been waiting for the right time to tell you.' Self-consciously he passed the leaflets and forms to Petra. 'I want to enrol on that course. Will you help me?'

Throwing her arms around Jake, Petra held him close, before wincing as she caught a bruise and had to let him go. 'Of course I will! I'm so proud of you!'

'You are? But you've only known me two minutes.'

'What's that got to do with anything? Being brave enough to change your life is a big deal.' Petra gave another huge yawn. 'I have two conditions though.'

'Go on.'

'You don't tell Maddie I've told you about BIG. She'll tell you when she is ready.'

'Deal. And second?'

'Can we leave the forms until after I've had a nap? I'm knackered.'

Re-reading Maddie's proposal, Sabi drew a line underneath the words *Farmers Market: Invite local farmer's market to use nursery site once a month??*

Not sure what Henry or Maddie would say when she told them she'd been in touch with the Exmoor Drifters to enquire about the logistics of such a market using her family's nursery as a venue to sell from, Sabi read the email that had just dropped into her inbox.

Dear Mrs Willand-Harris,

Thank you again for taking the time to visit. We are always interested in working from new venues, although, as I mentioned, we tend to get booked up for regular markets months in advance. If you are thinking of a one-off market, however, perhaps over the Christmas period, we still have one or two available dates left.

As you will appreciate, not all of the stall holders on our website are always available at the same time, so if there was a specific retailer you had in mind, it would be advisable to let me know.

To reiterate what we discussed:

We have our own insurance, but you would need public liability insurance as well.

As to space, that would be up to you, as would how many stalls you would want on your premises – and for how many days.

The usual arrangement is for the landowner to take 10 per cent of the profits made, rather than for you to charge a fee for the use of the land.

If you are interested in booking the Exmoor Drifters Farmers' Market, then I'd be happy to discuss dates with you.

Best regards,

Ivan Porter.

Sabi muttered to herself, 'So, if the landowner gets 10 per cent of takings, rather than charging a set rental fee, it encourages them to advertise the market well. The more customers, the more sales, and so the bigger the cut for us.'

Scrolling back through the photographs on the Exmoor Drifters website, Sabi's mouth watered as she looked at the pictures of Ivan's cheese and the associated chutneys – many of which she'd sampled when she'd been with him.

Writing a few more points on her notepad connected with ideas for The Potting Shed and the market, Sabi's pen froze mid-sentence as she realised how much she was enjoying herself.

'What the hell am I doing wasting my time like this? The nursery is going to be sold to BIG!' She gave herself a shake. 'I'm getting as bad as Maddie. Clutching at straws. Even if we don't sign, BIG will build nearby and it'd take more than a one-off farmer's market to stop The Potting Shed going under.

'I obviously needed a new project even more than I thought.'

Deciding to call Miriam, enquire about Petra, see if there was any chance of seeing the house again, and ask if there was any news on when she could get a survey organised, Sabi turned the page of her notebook, away from stilton and cheddar choices, and began to write down her ideas for how to decorate her new home.

29

The early morning air was cool, but not cold. A gap of half a metre divided Maddie and Ed as they strolled, side by side, admiring the patterns the overhanging trees' shadows made in the reflection of the canal, as a few hardy mallards paddled across the canal.

If it hadn't been for Jake's insistence that he could cope alone for a few hours, then she would have called off the walk.

Petra's had a good effect on that man, Maddie mused as she stared at the toes of her walking boots. *He'd never have volunteered to interact with customers before Petra came along.*

While sat next to Ed as they'd driven the short distance to the Grand Western Canal's car park, Maddie had felt more nervous than when she'd joined him and a group of strangers on Exmoor.

This is silly. You like Ed's company.

She couldn't stop thinking that, while their limited communication over the past few days hadn't been unfriendly, nor had it offered the relaxed, easy-going conversation of their previous meetings.

Swallowing, she glanced at Ed's feet as he marched along

next to her. *Perhaps I shouldn't have said this should be a work walk?*

The thought nagged at her as they walked along the towpath. Alone but for the occasional dog walker, Maddie glanced at Ed again out of the corner of her eye. He was looking up at the sky as he walked. Unlike when they were on Haddon Hill, his feet were confident of not stumbling down a rabbit hole on the smooth towpath.

He can't be looking for stars. Maybe he's just searching for something to talk about?

Maddie peered into the still green water. Every now and then a subtle splash accompanied a fish leaping or an acorn from the overhanging oaks falling into the water. Beyond hellos, the only conversation they'd had so far was when she'd brought Ed up-to-date on Petra's condition, telling him how pleased Jake was that she was almost well enough to go home, but how disgruntled he was at Miriam's declaration that he was to go nowhere near her daughter. Ed had made all the appropriate noises, saying how glad he was that Petra was recovering, and feeling sorry for Jake when it came to parental expectations. Then their conversation had lapsed into silence, broken only by the occasional quack of a passing duck.

After they'd traversed another half a mile without a word being spoken, Maddie couldn't stand it any longer. 'I'm sorry I haven't been in touch much. What with Petra and Jake not being around to help much, the days have dissolved. And you're so busy now Ronald is handing so much of his workload to you. I didn't like to interrupt.'

Ed kept walking. 'It didn't occur to you that I might *like* to be interrupted by you?'

'I wasn't sure you'd want to hear from me at all. The Dark Skies walk was lovely, but then…' Maddie paused, glad of the distraction of a moorhen crossing their path, '… after you sort of… disappeared mid takeaway…'

'Disappeared?' Ed frowned. 'I had to go… I told you.'

'Yes, but then…' Maddie wasn't sure how to continue. How could she explain she'd felt abandoned? It was ridiculous – she was an adult; she shouldn't feel like a kid who had had the promise of a trip to the fair withdrawn.

'I couldn't tell you what I was doing with Ronald. It was confidential.'

'I didn't expect you to. I just thought, when you didn't call later or the following day… I suppose I assumed that you'd decided against seeing a client outside of work after all.' She wiped her perspiring palms down her jeans as she rambled on. 'I started to worry that had been why your boss wanted to see you, to tell you not to date a client. I wouldn't want you to be seen as unprofessional so…' Maddie shook her head. 'Let's just forget it shall we?'

'Forget it?' Ed's expression clouded. 'I'm not sure that's so easy.'

'I just meant we've both got a lot going on.' She paused as a swan that had been settled on the path ahead got up and, after stretching its wings wide, launched itself regally into the water. 'It doesn't matter. When is the next Dark Skies thing?'

'Wednesday. Do you intend to go?'

'I'd like to. Being with Ivan and Jo made me think how good it would be to have a farmer's market at the nursery. I added it to my new business proposal as a possibility. You know, to host a market once a month or something.

Although I didn't know how pointless that would be at the time.' She took a deep breath, 'Having said that...'

'Having said that, what?'

'I know I'm probably mad, and I know Sabi is going to be gutted, but I'm not going to sell the nursery to BIG. Please don't think me ungrateful for the details you got me. It was really sweet of you to feel sorry for me, and the site at Broadclyst would be perfect, and if my bank manager refuses me a loan, I'll have to change my mind and sell up after all. So, with all that...'

'I know. You have a business to run and a life to get on with. The lack of contact this week made that clear.'

Taken aback by his tone, and surprised Ed hadn't reacted specifically to what she'd said about her decision not to sell if she could help it, Maddie blustered, 'Honestly, it was just that—'

'I know.' Ed cut through her explanation. 'You want us to just be friends. I get it. Although, for the record, I did *not* help you because I felt sorry for you.' Picking up a stone, he threw it into the canal, watching as the resulting ripples stretched out in a series of concentric circles. 'Any word from BIG?'

Knowing she'd accidentally offended him, Maddie mumbled, 'Nothing since I heard they wanted to build over the nursery. To be fair, with Petra and everything, this has felt less important. If BIG aren't hassling me, then they can't be in a hurry to get their garden centre built, which suits me fine.'

Maddie watched as he took up a second stone and threw it in after the first. 'Ed, I didn't mean...'

Not sure if he hadn't heard her, or was choosing not to

return to the subject of their relationship, Ed asked, 'Have you seen the bank manager yet?'

'I've an appointment at eleven-thirty on Monday.'

'Good. I'm glad you're going to stick it out at The Potting Shed.' Ed signalled a hand towards a nearby bench. 'Shall we sit for a while?'

'Okay.' Maddie noticed the preoccupied expression on his face. 'Are you alright? I'm really sorry if I hurt you by being quiet. I honestly thought you were the one being distant.'

Waving away her explanation before it had begun, a furrow formed across Ed's forehead. 'There's something you should know. Something I've been trying to find out for you.'

'For me? Despite me stupidly making you think I don't want... when I probably do, it's just...'

'Stupidly *and* probably do?' Ed gave a weak smile.

'Uh-huh.'

'I'll keep hold of those thoughts for a while, if that's okay.' Ed's expression softened as he watched another moorhen scuttle across the path into the safety of the reeds. 'Do you remember me saying the name Leo Creswell rang bells?'

'The lawyer for BIG?'

'The very same.'

'Have you worked with him in the past?'

'No, but Ronald has, or at least, he knows people who have. That's what the meeting I left you for was about.'

Something in Ed's words made all the hairs on the back of Maddie's neck stand up. 'What is it?'

'It might be nothing, I might be over-reacting.'

'But?'

'According to Ronald, Creswell used to be part of a legal firm in Taunton. A position he gave up when he was headhunted by BIG to be their chief legal advisor.'

'A good job move, I'm sure.'

'Very lucrative.' Ed tilted his face towards Maddie. 'What worries me, is how lucrative. Tell me, what reason did Creswell give for wanting to build over the land instead of near it?'

'He didn't say.'

'I see.'

The fire in the woodburner looked particularly homely as Sabi sank onto the leather sofa, her notebook to hand. Enjoying the way the orange of the flames showed flashes of gold as they licked the end of the disintegrating logs of wood, she looked up as Henry carried in a tray of coffee and Bath Oliver biscuits.

'I thought I'd get a few quotes from curtain designers for the new house this afternoon. I've got all the measurements now.' Sabi gestured to her notebook before picking up the cylindrical tin and taking out a biscuit.

'You were over in Culmstock for so long yesterday, that there can't have been much you didn't measure.' Henry's voice was bright, but Sabi could tell there was something bothering him.

'What is it?'

'I just don't think you should start doing anything for the house until the nursery sale is in writing.'

Sabi laid her biscuit on the tray. 'You think the sale won't go through?'

'I'm sure it'll go through once BIG have all their contracts signed, but Maddie hasn't agreed to anything yet. And nor have we officially for that matter.' Seeing a cloud of disappointment cross his wife's face, Henry added, 'I don't mean to ruin your fun, love, but I've had apparently solid deals disappear into a puff of smoke because promises were made before deals were actually signed.'

Guessing what her husband was leading up to, Sabi sat forward. 'Taunton? The office block?'

'We didn't get the contract.' Henry picked up his coffee. 'The email came through to my phone while I was in the kitchen. It's not a disaster of course, but it was a lot of work for a lot of nothing.'

Sabi's eyes fell on the list of expensive fabrics she'd noted down, with a mind to commissioning both curtains and upholstery for the new house. Bespoking everything, she'd decided, was the way to go. 'Without that contract, are we still…?'

'Able to move?' Henry dunked a biscuit in this drink. 'Yes, but it'll be on a tighter budget as the bonus I would have got from the deal is no longer coming our way. As much as I'd like Maddie to be able to stand firm and carry out your father's wishes, I am beginning to think you're right. She's going to have to give in and sell. And – assuming she does – and you are serious about us having two properties – one to live in and one to rent out, it will be a while before we can afford to make the upgrade and changes to both places you've been planning. Sorry, love.'

Folding the notebook closed, Sabi did her best to hide her disappointment. 'It's not your fault. I can work with what we already have here. It might be fun designing a budget for the new place.'

Henry kissed his wife's cheek. 'Never say die, huh?'

'I'm so looking forward to being busy again, Henry. Sorting out rental bookings, getting the house ready, even doing the change-over cleaning myself doesn't bother me. Does that sound silly?'

'It sounds wonderful. And after a few bookings you'll be able to put some money aside to start on some of those dream upgrades you've got hidden in your notebook.'

'I can see the house in Culmstock so clearly in my mind. Lots of our things from here will go in there nicely, but some simply won't be in keeping, and we'll need furniture left here for our guests of course. I wondered about trying that reclamation place near Exeter. Been ages since I had a rummage through their antiques and shabby chic stuff.'

'Sounds right up your street.' Henry grinned. 'I always thought you'd make a good interior designer.'

'Really?'

'You have excellent taste. Even on a budget, I know you'll do a fabulous job of turning this place into a dream let for folk wanting a week or so in Devon.'

Smiling back at Henry, Sabi was about to tell him about how Miriam intended to promote their let on the Executive Homes website, and how much it was going to cost to do so, when the doorbell rang.

'Did you ask Maddie over?' Henry got up and headed to the door.

'No. I thought I'd call her after work. I have something I want to talk to you both about. To be honest, I'm surprised

Maddie hasn't called me about BIG's latest email. Even with Petra leaving her a pair of hands down she must have had time to check her inbox by now and...' Sabi stopped talking, a hand flying to her mouth, '...Leo Creswell! Oh my God, it might be him?'

'BIG's lawyer? Why would he be here?' A second ring of the doorbell echoed through the house as Henry spoke.

'He asked to meet us and Maddie today. I didn't dream he'd just turn up here without our agreement.'

'Why didn't you tell me?' A cloud passed over Henry's face.

'I wanted to talk to you and Maddie together before agreeing to another meeting. I sent an email to BIG last night, saying that today was no good as Maddie works on a Saturday. I said we'd be in touch once we had a mutually convenient date and time sorted.'

Henry grunted, 'That's sensible at least.'

'It might not be him anyway.' Sabi's palms were sweating as Henry strode to the door. 'It could be Miriam.'

It wasn't Miriam.

'Mr Willand-Harris?' Leo Creswell held out his hand as Henry swung the door open. 'I have an appointment with your wife and her sister.'

30

'What do you mean?' Maddie was giving Ed her full attention.

'Slightly insulting though it was, your suggestion that this should be a business walk is probably a wise one.'

'Ed, I didn't mean to insult you.'

'That doesn't matter now.' He brushed the point away 'If you think about it, all this business with The Potting Shed has happened very fast. Too fast. I got to wondering how long BIG have had their eye on your land.'

Maddie felt nausea writhe in her gut. 'You think they would have approached Dad if he'd still been alive?'

'Possibly, but it's more that it normally takes months to get plans together of the calibre required to be able to progress to the point of arranging road access and so on.'

'Road access?' Maddie frowned. 'I've heard nothing about that side of things.'

'I was afraid you might say that. Do you think Sabi has heard anything more?'

'She'd have said. At least, I think she would. Since Petra's accident she's been a bit more like her old self and bit less Miriam like.'

'I don't know if your sister not knowing either is good or not.'

'Can you tell me what it is you are talking about Ed? You're scaring me.'

'Sorry.' Reaching out a hand, he almost laid it on her leg, but then thought better of it. 'Ronald told me that Leo Creswell has a dodgy reputation. There were rumours of him cutting corners and taking backhanders when he was in Taunton. Nothing was ever proved, but I get the impression that there was a sense of relief all round when he was poached by BIG.'

'You think this Leo is a crook?'

'I think he's too clever to actually break the law. Don't forget, he knows it inside out. And I could be completely wrong. All the rumours could simply be accumulated sour grapes.'

'But you don't think so.'

'Ronald didn't think so. With his help, I've been asking a few questions at the council planning office. That's where I was going when you asked me to go for a walk the other day.'

'You were working on my behalf?' A tiny wing of hope fluttered in her heart.

'I promised to help. I didn't say what I was doing because I didn't want to get your hopes up and then dash them again. Nor did I want to give you something else to worry about.' Ed sighed. 'Apparently, Creswell has been pushing hard to get an access road built to your nursery sooner rather than later. To your land – never the land opposite.'

'What?! So, my land was always the intended site?' Maddie couldn't believe what she was hearing.

'Looks like it.'

'Why would he do that?'

'Softening the blow maybe – make him look good by offering you a decent sum for inconvenience of sale – and then a much larger sum of money when he swoops in to make his intended offer.'

'But for less money than it might be worth! And we would be so pleased at having a rise in the money offered, we – being silly little bits of women – wouldn't notice he was underpaying us?'

'He is that sort of bloke.' Ed shrugged. 'Although I can't say that for sure.'

'Hang on, how can an application for access roads be granted before we've agreed to the sale?'

'Applications are often done early, but they aren't normally authorised so quickly.'

'It's been *authorised*! Permission for a road has already been granted?' Maddie jumped off the bench.

'Not officially, but the rumour is that everything has been put in place and it will be processed quickly once things are signed.'

'Let me guess, Creswell knows all the right people to make sure he gets what he wants fast?'

'That's the impression I got. And there's something else.' Ed reached out a hand and eased her back to his side. 'Ronald did some private digging on my behalf. Bloke he knows at his club. Leo Creswell has shares in BIG.'

Unsure why this was a problem, Maddie asked, 'Don't lots of employers have shares in the companies they work for?'

'They do, but not 48 per cent of them.'

Maddie drew a sharp breath. 'That's not a share, that's virtually half!'

'Which means Creswell has a personal agenda here. He will make a lot of money out of the takeover of The Potting Shed.'

'Surely it isn't legal for him to represent the firm he half owns?'

'He's clever. The shares aren't all in his name. His wife and kids have a portion in their names, but I have no doubt he'll control them.' Ed grimaced. 'So, you see, he's crooked, but not a criminal. No laws are being broken.'

'And there I was worrying about us being unprofessional by going for a walk!'

'No comment.'

'I need to see Sabi.' Maddie rubbed her forehead. 'She can't possibly have known about this.'

Ed hesitated. 'I don't know your sister, but from what you've said, her heart is set on the second house project. Would it make a difference if she knew Leo occasionally crossed the line?'

'*Yes…*' Maddie hesitated, '… at least, I'd like to think it would. We *have* to tell her!' Maddie got back up. 'Either way, the sooner Sabi knows for certain that I'm not going to sign – ever – the better.'

'Why not give her a ring now? Set up a meeting.'

Taking her mobile from her pocket, Maddie said, 'Good idea, then we can try to forget all about it for now and enjoy our walk. A *non*-work one.' Tapping in the number, Maddie listened to the dialling tone. 'How am I going to tell Sabi of your suspicions about Creswell? We can't prove anything, and nothing illegal has happened.'

'You're worried she'll think you're making excuses or exaggerating the situation so she won't sell?'

'If you think about it, it does all sound a bit farfetched. And...' Maddie was cut off by the line connecting. 'Sabi – oh, Henry. How are you?'

Glad they hadn't travelled all the way to the moor for their walk, Maddie hugged her arms around herself as they drove towards Tiverton. Ed's expression was set in determination as he negotiated a sharp bend in the road.

'I can't believe she's done this. *Again.*'

Ed kept his eyes on the road, aware he was dangerously close to edging over the speed limit. 'What did Henry say, exactly?'

'That Leo Creswell had arrived at their home about two minutes before I called, and that they were about to ring me.' Maddie willed the car to go faster. 'Apparently Creswell had been pushing Sabi for a meeting today. She sent him an email saying today wasn't a good time because she hadn't had the chance to talk to me yet.'

'And this meeting, if she had agreed to it, was to be about the terms of the buyout?'

'I suppose so. Sabi thought I had received the same email as it was addressed to us both.'

'And you haven't?'

'No.' Maddie anxiously checked through her emails on her phone. 'Nope, it's not even in SPAM. Henry sounded furious, but whether it was with Creswell for just turning up, or with Sabi for not telling him about BIG wanting a meeting in the first place, I'm not sure.'

'Thank goodness you phoned when you did.' Ed drove onto Park Hill.

'To be fair, I suspect Henry would have called as he claimed. I just wish—'

Ed interrupted, 'Which house is it?'

'Next on the right.' Maddie shivered. 'Why do I have a *really* bad feeling about this?'

'Because lawyers do *not* customarily just arrive on the doorstep when they want to manipulate their clients.' Ed tutted. 'Although it isn't strictly illegal, it's definitely unethical.'

'Dad would have said that was typical of such businesses.'

'Handy you happened to have your solicitor with you this morning, isn't it.' Ed drove into the driveway. 'You okay?'

'Not really.'

'I'm not surprised.'

Maddie sucked in her bottom lip as she tried to apologise. 'Ed, I—'

Interrupting, Ed said, 'If you're about to apologise, then don't.' He threw her a sympathetic smile. 'This is unlikely to be your fault.'

'Thanks Ed.'

Sabi looked flustered as she let them in. 'Maddie, I'm so sorry. I thought you'd got the email too – like the letter – but...'

'I didn't and you forgot to mention you'd had one? Or were you going to talk to me about it later?' Maddie was too worried to raise her voice as she listened to her sister's excuses.

'Both.' Sabi whispered under her breath, 'I got side-tracked looking into—'

'—ways to decorate you second dream home.'

'No, I was…'

Stepping back, Maddie gestured to Ed. 'You met Edward Tate at the office in Exeter I believe?'

'With Mr Lyle, yes. Umm, why is our solicitor here?' Sabi whispered.

'Just be grateful that he is.' Maddie pointed towards the conservatory, where she could hear someone moving around. 'Shall we get this over with?'

Henry stepped forward and shook Ed's hand. 'You were with Maddie when she called?'

'We were strolling along the canal.' Ed turned to Sabi. 'Just so I have the situation straight – this is an unscheduled meeting and no papers have been signed?'

Sabi exchanged glances with Henry. 'I asked him not to come. I'm so sorry. Nothing's been signed.'

Taking strength from Ed's presence, Maddie exhaled. 'Perhaps coffee would be a good idea.'

'Already on it.' Henry gave his sister-in-law a bolstering smile. 'Come on, let's see what he is after.'

Maddie put a hand on Henry's elbow. 'You don't trust him either?'

'I don't trust anyone who pitches up at my home without an appointment expecting my wife and sister-in-law to sign their lives away.'

The large elm table in the conservatory played host to a coffee pot, a small teapot, five cups and saucers, a pot of sugar, jug of milk and three distinct piles of paper and a pen. As Maddie approached, she saw that the paperwork consisted of forms which had clearly marked spaces for signatures.

Only once everyone had gathered around the table and taken a seat could she bring herself to look at BIG's lawyer. Maddie's imagination had painted him as a Scrooge-type character, tall and scrawny, with bony fingers and a hooked nose. In fact, he was a rather squat, overweight man, with a receding hairline and, judging by his mottled complexion, high blood pressure. The suit he wore was expensively cut, and if she'd been able to see his shoes, Maddie would have put money on them being a designer brand.

Leo Creswell rose as she sat down. 'Ah, the elusive Miss Willand, I presume.'

'Not so much elusive, as kept completely in the dark,' Ed answered before Maddie could. 'I shall ignore for now the fact you have arrived at Mr and Mrs Willand-Harris's home without an invitation, and begin by asking why you only emailed one of the two owners of The Potting Shed on BIG's behalf when approaching them about this meeting?'

His eyes narrowing, Leo picked the pen up from the table and tapped it against the table. 'And you are?'

'Edward Tate, Lyle and Tate solicitors. I am The Potting Shed's legal representative.'

'You work with Ronald Lyle?'

'I have that privilege.'

A suggestion of something that could have been unease crossed Leo's face. If Maddie hadn't been watching him so intently, she'd have missed it. She looked at Ed. He was different somehow. His back ramrod straight, his palms folded together on the table before him, he oozed professional confidence.

Creswell's voice was as thick as treacle as he asked Ed, 'How did you know to come here with Miss Willand?'

'Your implication being that you'd rather my clients had no legal representative during this meeting?'

'Not at all.' Leo bristled. 'I was merely surprised one appeared so swiftly. The implication being, that you must have been socialising with Miss Willand when she was informed of my arrival.'

'We were having a walking meeting.'

'A what?'

'A business discussion in the fresh air.' Ed reached into his briefcase for a notepad, pen and Dictaphone. 'I trust you do not object to me recording this meeting?'

'This is just a casual chat. An update of events. No need for recording or legal representation.'

'Then it doesn't matter if we record the meeting or not, so,' Ed hovered his finger over the record button, 'I think I'll take that precaution, providing all other parties here are in agreement.'

Sabi, Henry and Maddie nodded as one.

'Then we shall record it.' Ed placed the device on the table. 'And then, if this turns out to be as informal and insignificant a talk as you suggest, I can give you the pleasure of pressing the delete button, Mr Creswell. Shall we begin?'

31

Maddie kept her eyes fixed on Leo Creswell.

Now he'd been given the chance to speak, his confidence had returned, and his tongue was spinning words that made BIG's plans for The Potting Shed's land sound like a crock of gold.

'So, to conclude, you, Mrs Willand-Harris, and you, Miss Willand, will come out of this with a substantial sum and the region would benefit from a large garden centre, providing plenty of jobs for the locals and a place for them to visit, both socially – a large scale restaurant is planned – as well as a place to come for their garden centre needs.'

That's what I wanted to do. Have a café – eventually – and provide locals with their garden centre needs. Maddie contained a private sigh. *Although I couldn't offer much extra employment, at least to begin with.*

Ed had barely blinked as he'd listened to Creswell. 'Thank you for that recap of everything we already knew. Now, perhaps you could answer my initial question. Why was Miss Willand not contacted personally about this meeting? And, in addition, what is the urgency for these papers to be signed? I am struggling to understand why BIG want The Potting Shed's land so badly.'

'A naive question.' Leo looked as smug as he sounded, 'One I should have expected from a junior partner in a law firm run by Ronald Tate.'

Maddie heard Sabi's intake of breath and saw a flash of dislike cross Henry's face, as her husband countered, 'If you are going to be offensive, Mr Creswell, you can leave. You were not invited here today. In fact, my wife asked for this meeting to be delayed so she had more time to consult with her sister. Please answer Mr Tate's question.'

Leo continued to tap his pen rhythmically against the pile of forms he was hoping would be signed that morning. 'I was unaware you were not expecting me. I thought that sisters talked to each other.'

'What?' Sabi picked up her phone. 'Are you saying you assumed I'd tell Maddie about the email, rather than instructing your office to send her one of her own or copying us both in on the one you sent me?'

'Not an unreasonable assumption.'

Disliking the smarmy tone to Creswell's tone, Sabi went on. 'And are you also telling me that you received a reply from me agreeing to meet today?'

'I concede, I did not. But nor did I get an email saying you would *not* see me at the agreed time of eleven o'clock, and so I came.'

'Without confirmation that the time and place of meeting were acceptable? I understand you offered a choice of two venues for this chat – here or The Potting Shed – and yet here you are. Unannounced.' Ed made a note on his pad. 'Something I would expect from a man with a reputation such as yours.'

'Reputation?' Leo snarled, before speaking with bullet

point precision. 'I did not receive an email saying *not* to come. As to arriving here – it seemed obvious to come here rather than the nursery, which would be open for business.'

Biting back the urge to accuse their unexpected visitor of acting like a petulant child, Henry put out a hand to his wife. 'Perhaps you'd like to show Mr Creswell the email you sent him?'

'Certainly.' Sabi pressed a few buttons on her phone. 'There! Oh…'

'Oh?' Henry followed the direction of his wife's gaze.

'I… Oh God, I'm sorry. I'm sorry Maddie.'

'What have you done?' Maddie felt the colour drain from her face as she stared at her sister.

'It's still in the drafts folder.' Sabi showed the room the email that had been written asking for the meeting to be delayed.

'You forgot to press send.' Maddie rested her head back against the chair and closed her eyes.

'Honestly, Maddie, I thought I'd sent it and I *was* going to call you today. I had this idea and—'

Breaking through Sabi's apologies Ed said, 'It makes no difference, Mrs Willand-Harris. There was still no confirmation of appointment. However, as Mr Creswell is here, let's use this chance to learn a little more about BIG's plans.' Ed locked his eyes onto Leo. 'As you'd expect, I have been doing a little background work on both BIG and yourself so that I may represent my clients better. The financial incentives on offer are impressive, but before I take one of those contracts away to mull over the small print, perhaps you could lay a few of our fears to rest.'

When Leo replied, Maddie got the impression that he was picking his words with caution.

'My employers need these forms signed today, Mr Tate. If you need to mull them over, then perhaps you'd like to read one now?'

'Hold on.' Henry held up a hand. 'No one has agreed to the sale yet, let alone got to the stage of asking to see contracts to sign. What's the rush? I was under the impression that nothing would begin to happen until the New Year. When Mr Tate asked, you said this meeting was a casual chat and an update of events '

'I never—'

'It'll be on the recording.' Henry gestured to the Dictaphone.

Leo gave a grumpy harrumph as Ed crossed his arms over his chest. 'What *is* the rush with all this, Mr Creswell?'

'In a nutshell, Christmas.' Leo picked up his fast-cooling coffee. 'As you will all be aware, most businesses take at least two weeks off at Christmas and over the New Year. BIG would like everything set to go once January 4th arrives.'

Ed leant forward, 'When you say, "set to go" by the 4th of January, do you mean set to start applying for planning permission, or do you mean starting to build?'

Maddie glanced up sharply. So, that's why Ed wanted to record the meeting – to record how Leo replied to the mention of planning permission.

'That is merely the date when we all start working again after the festive break.'

'I see.' Ed scribbled something else into his notebook.

'So, no moves have already been made when it comes to acquiring planning permissions?'

'Obviously questions have been asked, but we'd wait for your clients' permission before proceeding further with applications.'

Maddie looked at Ed. She was impressed by his calm exterior in the face of Creswell's massaging of the truth as he continued.

'I am curious as to why BIG wants to close The Potting Shed down by building storage sheds on it, when there would be plenty of room on the originally proposed build site to have the garden centre and storage units side by side. The Willands' nursery is a small enterprise, dealing with a different, although occasionally overlapping, clientele. What is it that makes them such a danger to your enterprise that your employers want them removed? I'll repeat my earlier question, why do BIG want to take them over so badly?'

Maddie fleetingly looked at Sabi. She hadn't seen her looking so rattled since she was sitting her A levels.

'Standard business practice.' Leo clutched his palms together as he rested his elbows on the table. 'Assess the competition and then, if possible, remove it.'

'But we're tiny by comparison.' Maddie glanced at Ed, who gave her an encouraging dip of the head. 'If you built on the other side of the road as originally planned, I could still operate. But it would be me with the competition worry, not BIG.'

'Well, that isn't an issue now, is it?' Leo was dismissive. 'The proposal has been altered to build BIG *over* your nursery.'

'A move you rather sprung on my clients.' Ed hit Leo

with a cold stare. 'I rather believe that was the intention all along. I'm right, aren't I? It's an old trick – make an offer that's a blow to the recipient – but not fatal – let them adjust to that, while softening it with a cash incentive – before coming in for the kill when they are wondering if it's worth carrying on anyway.'

'I can assure you—'

'Can you, Mr Creswell?' Henry crossed his arms. 'I'm getting a sense that the initial offer was just an introduction. A way to cushion the blow to my family. Take the business first, but not my sister-in-law's home. Then, once Maddie had adjusted to the idea of living there without being able to run her nursery, you'd weigh in with an offer to take the land completely. How long before you change things again and take away the offer for her to be able to keep her house?'

Leo opened his mouth to reply, but Ed cut in.

'Whatever underhand techniques may or may not have been used, there is nothing we can do about them now. What I'm more interested in is BIG's hurried application for permission to build over the nursery and for an extra access road to The Potting Shed site from the motorway. *The Potting Shed* – not the land opposite it. Especially as, when I asked you just now, you denied that any definite plans have been made towards planning permission. An answer I know to be a lie.' Ed's voice rang with authority as he asked, 'How did you get BIG so high up the council's agenda so quickly?'

'Access?' Henry was blunt. 'But that can take…'

'Months.' Ed nodded. 'Quite so Mr Harris. Quite so.'

Leo held out his palms in a placating gesture. 'There is

nothing sinister here. My colleagues were merely fortunate with the timing of the enquiry – an enquiry *not* an application. Very few planning proposals go on during the winter months.'

'If you say so, Mr Creswell. Although I'm less convinced about the claim that nothing sinister has been going on.' Ed laid down his pen. 'One more question — before I suggest we break this meeting and reconvene in a week.'

'A week!' Leo shoved his papers towards Sabi. 'When we met for afternoon tea, I got the impression from Mrs Willand-Harris that signing today was a mere formality.'

'Met for afternoon tea?' Maddie's question came out as a squeak.

Leo gave an almost gleeful smile as he looked at Sabi. 'I'm surprised you didn't tell your sister about our meeting, Mrs Willand-Harris. You were so keen to sign.' He switched his shrew-like stare to Maddie. 'Naturally, I assumed you were too, Miss Willand.'

Ed stood up, his lean frame towering across the table. 'No one is signing anything until I have read the contract. And, as I said, I have one further question before you go.'

'Then ask it.' Leo reluctantly stood up.

'What do you gain *personally* from this sale, Mr Creswell? I can only conclude that the real reason BIG are so determined to remove The Potting Shed rather than just operating in the same area, is so that the shareholders have no threat of lowered income due to local competition – however small. You, I believe, could be considered a *major* shareholder – could you not?'

*

Maddie wanted to tell Ed how grateful she was and how proud she was of him for fighting her family's corner like that, but no words would come out. She felt exhausted and her mind was racing as thoughts bounded around her head in conflicting directions.

Sabi had afternoon tea with Creswell.

Wandering through to her sister's lounge, she sank onto one of the big sofas and tucked her knees under her chin as her head continued to spin.

And where will I live if...

Having steered his similarly stunned wife to a nearby sofa, Henry shook Ed's hand so hard that Maddie feared for his elbow.

'I can't thank you enough, Mr Tate.'

'Ed, please. And it's my pleasure. My job, even. It's just pure luck that I was walking with Maddie this morning.'

'I'm not happy about this at all. That Creswell has such a large sharehold under his control... talk about a conflict of interest.'

'Of self-interest.' Ed followed Henry back into the conservatory. 'I should confirm that BIG have put an offer in for the land opposite the nursery as well – a backup plan I suppose – and so they can look honest if challenged. And I suppose the road planning application might be as simple as he claimed. Sometimes enquiries are made and there are lulls that see things happen with unusual speed.'

'But you doubt it?' Henry was also unconvinced. 'I've been an architect a long time, and only once in all those years has a planning application been completed on time. And they're *never* early.'

*

Maddie wrapped her arms around her knees as she observed her sister on the opposite side of the room. 'You went for posh tea with Leo Creswell.'

'I told you I'd seen him.'

'I assumed here or in an office. Not that he treated you to a pseudo-Claridges' special. Where was it? Taunton?'

Sabi nodded, guilt etched on her face.

'You knew didn't you, about his shares, about his personal gain in all this?' Maddie was surprised by how calm she felt. All her anger at the situation she'd been put in, since Leo had first arrived on the scene, had evaporated now Ed had revealed the man's true colours. She knew it didn't change much, but it might make her sister stop and think.

'I wondered... suspected.' Copying her sister, Sabi tucked her knees under her chin. 'He didn't say much, now I think back. Just that he thought it best to be honest about having shares in the business.'

'Did he imply you'd be doing him a favour as well as yourself one?'

'It wasn't like that! I'm sure he's genuine, just a bit – slippery.'

'Slippery?' Maddie shivered, cold despite the central heating. 'Sabi, were you listening to the same conversation as the rest of us?'

'But surely, if he wasn't honest, he wouldn't have told me upfront that he had a personal interest in BIG?'

'If he was honest, he wouldn't have been so flustered by the idea of recording the meeting.'

'He did let us record it, though.'

'Because it would've looked bad if he didn't.' Maddie echoed what Ed had said when they'd been by the canal. 'I'm not saying he's a crook, I'm saying Leo Creswell is the type of man who cuts corners to get where he wants to be. Look how evasive he was when tackled about planning permission. And I think him owning almost half the company shares is a little more than having an interest in it, don't you? We're nothing to them, but BIG still want to get rid of us. It's pure greed. A greed that looks personal rather than corporate.'

Nodding, Sabi looked miserable as she muttered, 'I don't expect you to believe me, but I was going to call you today.'

Maddie got up. 'I was intending to call you today too. I'm not signing the forms, Sabi. I'm going to do what I said I'd do. I'm going to try and borrow money to buy you out, if you'll let me.'

Seeing the stricken expression on her sister's face, Maddie knelt before her. 'Despite everything, I'd still rather The Potting Shed stayed in the family. If you can't face running it with me, then so be it. It can skip a generation, so it goes to Jem if she wants it when the time comes. Think about it, Sabs. Please.'

32

Maddie and Ed sat side by side in his car in The Potting Shed's car park.

'I am ever so grateful that you swooped into lawyer mode.'

'No problem.' Ed put his hand back on the gear stick. 'I'm assuming you're going back to work now.'

'I have to. I've already left Jake longer than planned.'

'Yet, the place is still standing.'

Maddie could feel a chill in the car that was cooler than the frost outside. 'Have I done something wrong?'

'I've been thinking. Our friendship is all very well, but…' Ed turned the key, igniting the engine. 'I think you were right all along. We should keep things strictly professional now I'm acting as your solicitor.'

'But you were acting as our solicitor before, and you wanted to date me.'

'If Leo Creswell got a whiff of anything improper, he'd use it against us.'

'How?'

'It's not worth the risk of finding out.' Ed sounded brusque as he reached across Maddie in the passenger seat and opened her door, taking care not to accidentally brush her leg. 'Have a good week. I'll meet you at your sister's house on Saturday.'

'Isn't there a Dark Skies walk on Wednesday night?' Confused, Maddie climbed out of Ed's car.

'I won't be able to make it. Pass my apologies to the others please.'

Hating how pathetic she sounded, Maddie mumbled, 'But I can't go if you aren't there.'

'You can. Ivan and Jo will look after you.'

Keeping her hand on the open car door, Maddie bent down so she could speak to Ed. 'Won't you want to know about my meeting with the bank manager on Monday?'

'Email me at work.'

Before she could say anything else, Ed had shut the door and was driving away.

The house had never felt so big or so empty. Even after Jemima had left for boarding school, it hadn't had the sense of a ghostly echo it held now. It was as if a heavy shroud of disquiet clouded every room.

Angry with herself, Henry's parting words flew around Sabi's head.

'You knew, didn't you? Knew Creswell had a vested interest in the company. That's why you didn't tell him the deal was off the moment Ed revealed that he would be one of the biggest earners out of it?'

Henry had left then. Declaring he was going to the golf club to get his thoughts in order. Something he'd never done before.

Henry has a point. *Why didn't I end the meeting there? Why didn't I throw Creswell out of my home before we'd even got to that point?*

Replaying the morning's events in her mind, Sabi cringed. She'd hardly said a word during the meeting, speechless in the face of the implications of what Edward Tate had revealed about Leo Creswell.

She almost wished Maddie had lost her temper with her again. Her sister's sorrowful acceptance of her actions was far worse than her anger.

But she still doesn't intend to lose The Potting Shed. She wants to buy me out.

'Why didn't I tell her that, even though I know she'd never be able to pay as much as BIG can, I'd be okay with that now I've seen Creswell's true colours? I should have told her I've read her proposal too – and that I've seen Ivan?' Sabi sighed. Picking up her notebook, she trailed a fingernail over the patterned cover. It was packed with design ideas for her new home and financial plans for the letting of her current one.

Sabi had an abrupt urge to escape. Without stopping to think, she got up, grabbed her car keys and headed to the door.

'Twice in one week, Mum?' Jemima sank a striped paper straw into her smoothie and took a slurp. 'You are alright, aren't you?'

'I'm fine, love.' Sipping her peppermint tea, Sabi looked around at the hotel's other afternoon clients. Several tables were bedecked with similar afternoon tea stands to the one she'd shared with Leo Creswell. Looking back to Jemima, she mumbled, 'Actually, love, I'm not alright.'

'Mum?'

Seeing the panic forming on her daughter's face, Sabi added hastily. 'I'm not ill. Nothing like that.'

Sitting back with a thump, Jemima glowered at her mother in a manner more suited to a disgruntled parent than an eleven-year-old. 'For a moment I thought...' She paused, bobbing her straw up and down in her passion fruit and mango concoction. 'One of the girls in our dorm. Her mum has cancer.'

Reaching out across the table, Sabi grabbed her daughter's hand. 'I'm sorry, love. And I'm sorry to hear about your friend's mum too.'

'Thanks.' Jem looked around her. 'It's nice here.'

'Isn't it.'

'So, what's up Mum. What did you really want to talk to me about when we went to the Chinese?'

Sabi laughed, 'You are so like your aunt was when she was eleven. Maddie could always see through me.'

'Is she okay? You said that she was missing Grandad. Oh, how's Petra?'

'Very much better. Still in hospital, but not for much longer.' Sabi sliced through the corner of her caramel apple cake with a fork. 'And we're all missing Grandad. But there's something else, something we didn't tell you.'

'Come on Mum, give.'

'Everything your dad and I said about you deciding your own future is true. We meant that. We still do, but something is happening that might affect it – it probably won't – well, not directly...but it might, so...'

Jemima pushed her drink aside. 'This isn't like you, Mum. You're normally straight out with things.'

Taking a deep breath, Sabi launched in. 'BIG – the garden centre people – want to buy The Potting Shed. Maddie doesn't want to sell, but I do, because if we sell, we can buy another house for us to live in. Then I can let out our current house and run it as a small letting business, so you can have a house of your own when you're older. If you want it.'

'Whoa!' Jemima blinked as she took some time to process what her mother had said, before inhaling some more fruit through the straw. 'But Maddie loves The Potting Shed. So did Grandad.'

'I know. But the whole place needs work to keep it from falling to pieces. If we sold, then Maddie could start again somewhere new.'

A crease formed on Jemima's forehead as she continued to work through what she'd heard. 'But, if you don't sell, BIG will build nearby anyway and be harsh competition?'

'I knew you'd understand.'

'Poor Auntie Maddie though.'

'She's quite upset.'

'And you feel bad about wanting to sell.'

'Yes. Especially as the man who is dealing with the sale is unpleasant, to put it mildly.' She took a sip of her tea. 'At the moment, I seem to be doing nothing but upsetting people and then apologising afterwards.'

Taking a mouthful of cake, Jemima chewed thoughtfully. 'Why don't you work at the nursery anymore, Mum? You used to when I was little. You loved it.'

Surprised her daughter had remembered the part-time work she'd put in when she'd been in the early years of primary school, Sabi wondered how to explain that being unpaid labour at a nursery didn't fit in conversationally with the other executive wives.

'Things change. Your dad's business was doing well. I didn't have to work, and I had you to look after. But now you're away…'

'Mum,' Jemima moved her chair closer and gave her mum a hug, 'I do love my school, but that doesn't mean I don't miss you and Dad sometimes. That's why things like this are so lovely.'

Surprised to find herself welling up, Sabi held her daughter tight. 'I love these treats too.'

Jemima's eyes narrowed as she pulled back to regard her mother. 'You're bored without a job or me being around, aren't you?'

Sabi groaned. 'Are you sure you're only eleven?'

'Oh Mum!' She took another slurp of smoothie. 'You know I could just be a weekly boarder at school, don't you? I could come home for weekends. If you wanted me to.'

Sabi took her daughter's hand and squeezed it tight. 'I thought you enjoyed all the weekend activities. And you have lessons on Saturday mornings.'

'I do, but the activities aren't every week, and I could travel in for them, we don't live that far away. I could be home for lunch on Saturday and go back Monday morning after breakfast. I'm happy either way Mum, but if you're lonely…'

Sabi looked at her daughter with a sense of shock. It hadn't crossed her mind that she might be lonely. But now it had been spelt out to her, she knew it was true – she was a bit lost without her only child around. 'You're an amazing little girl, Jemima.'

'Not so little!'

'Sorry.' Sabi grinned. 'If you're sure about weekends, then I'll talk to your dad. Perhaps we can change the arrangement we have with the school from next term.'

'Cool!' Jemima gave her mum's hand another squeeze before retrieving it so she could have some more cake. 'Going back to the house thing, I'm sure I'll be desperate for a house one day, but you shouldn't get another one now just because of me.'

'I'm not. I'm getting one to let out for holidays and earn some extra money for school fees and uni and—'

'*If* I go to uni.'

'Just in case then.'

Jemima plucked the straw from her drink and sucked at its end as she asked, 'So, this new house. Is it for us to move into or is that the one to let out?'

'We'll move into it hopefully. It's the house in Culmstock. The one I've loved since I was little and—'

'Not the one that looks like a doll's house?' Jemima's face lit up.

'I hoped you'd remember it.'

'You used to drive past it all the time. It's beautiful.'

'You wouldn't mind us moving there then?' Sabi's whole body felt light with relief. 'You could pick whichever bedroom you liked.'

'I'd love that! I can just imagine summer there. The gardens are huge!'

'You are okay with us selling our half of the nursery to buy the house?'

Jemima's elation faded as she understood the implications of what her mother was saying. 'Is that the choice then? Either the house or the nursery?'

'Auntie Maddie isn't talking to me.'

'I'm not surprised.' Jemima frowned. 'How about Dad?'

'He's cross about how I've gone about things, but he's all for the house purchase.'

Suddenly suspicious, Jemima asked, 'How *have* you gone about it?'

'Clumsily.' Sabi sighed. 'The thing is, Maddie is determined not to sell, whether BIG are local competition or not. She wants to buy me out. Look...' Digging into her bag, Sabi produced Maddie's proposal. 'I wondered if you'd have a read of this? Your aunt loves you and I am sure she wouldn't mind me showing you her plan for making the nursery work. Even expanding it one day.'

Taking the folder, Jemima nodded to her empty glass. 'Think I might need another one of those. I didn't know I was going to be taking a business studies class on a Saturday afternoon.'

'You know what?' Petra finished reading through the short paragraph Jake had written. 'I don't think we are dealing with dyslexia as such here, I think this is just lack of practice and low confidence. This is good.'

'Is it?' Jake had felt massively self-conscious when he'd handed the piece of unlined A4 paper over to Petra; like a schoolboy doing lines. He'd laboriously written down a short set of sentences after she'd suggested he wrote down why he wanted to improve his reading and writing.

'I'm no expert of course, which is why I'm so thrilled you're going to do the evening classes.'

Jake looked at the pen in his hand. 'I can't remember the last time I did more than write my name or a few short notes.'

'You wrote *my* name.' Petra smiled. 'On my hyacinth pot, remember?'

'So I did.' Jake stared at the paper sceptically. 'Is it really okay?'

'Although there are spelling errors and some guidance is required when it comes to where to place commas and full stops, it makes sense, and I can follow what you have written.'

'Thanks.' Jake paused before adding, 'I wasn't sure I'd be able to think straight. It's been busy at work all day and Maddie was in an odd mood when she got back from her walk. Hardly said a word and she didn't get any work done all afternoon.'

'I thought you said she had a date?'

'I assumed it was a date, with that solicitor bloke. But I'm not so sure now. If it was a date, it didn't go well.'

'That's a shame. Maddie is lovely.'

Jake took Petra's hand. 'Not as lovely as you.'

'Charmer!'

Jake stuck his tongue out before saying, 'I don't want to leave The Potting Shed.'

'Nor do I, but if we have to, then we have to. You never know, it could be fun making plans for the future.'

'Together?'

'Together.' Petra laid her head on Jake's shoulder as he climbed off his armchair and onto the hospital bed next to her. 'So, tell me, what is it you want to be when you grow up?'

33

Maddie had been so desperate not to be late that she had arrived at the bank fifteen minutes early and was now sitting uneasily in the waiting room.

Ever since she'd watched Ed drive away from the nursery car park on Saturday, she'd had the sense that her life was spinning further and further out of her control.

It wasn't that long ago that she'd been a head gardener at Killerton, then she'd given that up to run the family business with her father. Now she'd lost him and was potentially going to lose her home and her business, making Jake redundant in the process. The thought that she'd have a large sum of money to restart her life didn't feel like any sort of compensation.

She stared across the sterile room. The green and brown walls – which she felt carried the bank's corporate image too far – made it rather more oppressive than Maddie suspected the designer had intended.

The business proposal, mark three, sat in a brand-new folder on her lap. Having spent another night working on her ideas for The Potting Shed, Maddie veered between thinking it was a dream business plan and believing the whole thing was a total waste of time and wanting to throw it in the bin. She would have liked to show her expanded plans to Ed, and although she was entitled to, as he was her lawyer, she'd held back from disturbing him. He'd made his feelings perfectly clear about their situation.

I'm just a client.

Telling herself she had far too much to think about without rueing missed relationship opportunities, Maddie checked the time. There were still five minutes until her appointment.

'It's an excellent proposal, Miss Willand. I'm impressed.' Mark Daniels' fingers danced over his keyboard. 'But the amount you'll need to borrow in order to do everything you hope to with your nursery is, at this stage, a little beyond what the bank can loan you. At least, in one go.'

Maddie felt the patina of nervous perspiration that had formed on her palms as she'd talked through her ideas with the bank manager go cold and sticky.

'However, that doesn't mean we can't work out a halfway-house solution.'

'Halfway house?' Maddie took a tissue from her pocket and wiped her hands.

'A loan so you could buy your sister's half of The Potting Shed, pay the first few instalments of Lyle and Tate's fees *and* pay off the inheritance tax.'

'But not the additional money needed get it back on its feet, upgrade the current buildings or convert the house?'

Mark Daniels gave her a kind smile. 'If BIG weren't

proposing to build nearby, then I could push for more on your behalf, but you'd still have to prove yourself able to pay the loan back, and with them as competition....'

Maddie didn't need to hear the rest. 'I understand. I suspected you'd say as much.'

Mark pressed a few buttons on the most high-tech calculator Maddie had ever seen, before saying, 'Of course, if you do reject BIG's offer to buy the nursery, and they relocate their new build further away than the field opposite, then the bank might reconsider if there was no immediate competition.'

Maddie stared at the hands folded in her lap. 'I feel a bit foolish for asking now, but my father and I had lots of plans for the place. I wanted to at least try to carry them out. I'm sorry if I've wasted your time.'

'Not at all!' The business manager swivelled his chair round, switching his attention from the computer screen to his client, looking at her properly for the first time since she'd sat down. 'Your proposal is excellent, and please don't think we're turning your full request down for any other reason than not wanting to saddle you with a debt you might not be able to pay off. You could take the loan to buy out your sister and go from there. I'm just saying that it won't be possible for you to borrow all the money you need at once.'

Maddie reined in her disappointment. 'Practically speaking then, if I took out the first half of the loan now – or after I've spoken to Sabi, that's my sister – then how much of it do I need to pay back before we could think about extending things for the next stage of work? If I tackled my plans in increments?'

Mark smiled. 'That's the spirit! Let's crunch some numbers.'

Even though his office wasn't far away, Henry rarely went home for lunch, or even had a lunch break come to that. Today, however, his concentration was fractured, and he knew he'd get little done until he'd spoken to his wife. His incomprehension of her behaviour lately had swung from annoyance to bemusement, and now he wanted some answers.

Sabi had been quiet ever since Saturday's encounter with Leo Creswell. Experience told Henry she knew she'd dug herself into a hole she didn't know how to get out of. He'd been surprised to learn that she'd taken herself to see Jemima and delighted when he'd heard what their daughter had said to her mother, especially concerning her being a weekly boarder. He missed Jemima being around as much as his wife did. But Sabi had said very little else about anything since he'd crawled back from the golf club bar rather tipsy and morose on Saturday evening.

Sunday had been long and uncommunicative.

One thing he had noticed on Sunday morning was that the notebook with all her ideas for doing up the new house had been dropped into the bin. At least – it had been. Something about it being abandoned there, amongst the paper and cardboard recycling, had made Henry incredibly sad. His wife had put her dreams in that book – and she'd thrown them away.

Now, as he opened the front door, bracing himself for a difficult conversation, Henry was surprised when the scent of homemade bread assailed his nostrils. Sabi had only used her bread maker two or three times before she'd got bored with it. He'd only bought it after she'd waxed lyrical about the one Miriam had.

'Sabi?' He pushed off his shoes and followed the scent of bread.

'Oh.' His wife looked up from where she was slicing a loaf, ready to eat with the soup she was warming on the hob. 'What's happened?'

'Happened?'

'You never come home at lunchtime.' Sabi bent to the cupboard to retrieve a second plate and bowl. 'Soup?'

'Please.' Henry sat down, hating how formal the moment felt. 'It smells amazing.'

'Butternut squash.'

Henry watched his wife slice another piece of bread. 'I wanted to talk to you.'

'Talk to me or shout at me?'

'Talk. Properly. I need to understand – not why you feel awful about BIG and Maddie – that's obvious, but why you've been keeping secrets and acting so oddly?'

'Well I…'

Henry held up his hand as the words which had been revolving around in his head since their encounter with Leo on Saturday tumbled out of his mouth. 'I know you set your heart on having two houses, but *why*? Why can't you be happy with what you've got?' He gestured around them. 'Most people would kill for all this. Why do you have to be seen to be keeping up with the likes of Miriam?'

'I don't! I'm not. I *am* happy. I know how lucky we are.'

Henry picked up his soup spoon and stared at its shine.

'I know I have an executive job, but you know I've never liked the attitudes and assumptions that often go with it. One of the things I loved about you when we met was that you got that. You seemed to understand that I wanted the job – to be an architect designing the future – not a rich man showing off to the world. The money that has come with the job is merely a perk.'

The hush that fell across the kitchen felt as loud as if cymbals were being clashed near Sabi's ears.

Eventually, she ventured a muted, 'Do you really think I'm like Miriam?'

Henry sighed. He'd always found it impossible to stay cross with his wife for long. 'No, not really, and right now I wouldn't want to be in her shoes for anything. I know Petra is fine but…'

'She might not have been.'

'Precisely.' Remembering what his grandfather used to say about kindness working harder than aggression, Henry said, 'When are you going to stop putting yourself in positions that end up with you beating yourself up with guilt?'

Sabi lowered the knife. 'I feel so awful about Maddie.'

'I know.' Getting up, Henry opened his arms wide. 'And I've not been Mr Supportive.'

Flying into his arms, Sabi sobbed into his shoulder. 'Everyone hates me.'

'No, they don't. I admit I've been cross with you – but mostly because I was hurt.'

'Hurt?'

'Whatever I do for you, lately, it never seems enough.'

'What? No.' Sabi was horrified. 'It's not that at all.

Everything you do for us… I am so lucky and…' Sabi scrubbed a hand over her face. 'I've made such a mess of everything.'

Easing her away from him, Henry said, 'Everyone is in a mess about this BIG business. What I'm struggling to understand, is why you've been so one-man-band about the whole thing.'

'At first I just reacted. I didn't think BIG's first letter was serious. When I discovered it was a genuine offer at the same time as the house came on the market, I…' She took a deep breath, '… I got blindsided. Saw a dream I'd always wanted and followed it.'

'Even when you knew it would come at the cost of your sister's dream.'

Sabi mumbled, 'And Dad's.'

'Ahh… I wondered if that was at the heart of it. You've hardly mentioned your father since the funeral.'

'It was when I was with Jemima that I saw how far off the path I'd strayed. She reminded me of all the fun we used to have at the nursery when she was small. Dad running around with her, planting and digging, and helping customers count potatoes into a bag and so on.'

'She's always loved it there.'

'Maddie made me promise to ask what Jemima thought about the sale, but when we went out for the meal, we never got that far in the conversation.'

'So that's why you went to see her again?'

Sabi smiled as she thought of their daughter. 'I've never known a person put away so many smoothies. She must have liquid fruit running in her veins.'

'Not a bad addition to the bloodstream.' Henry served their soup. 'What did Jemima say?'

'That there had to be a way to have both dreams come true. Mine and Maddie's.'

'Ah. Always the optimist,' Henry picked up some bread. 'Sometimes I forget she is only eleven.'

'She talks like an adult and then it slips. I'm glad it does though. I'm not ready for her to be a teenager yet, let alone a grown up.'

'Nor me.' Henry crinkled his nose. 'Can you imagine? I'm definitely not ready to start hating her boyfriends on principle. I'm glad we'll have her at home more. I sent an email to the school about that by the way. We have an appointment with the head next week.'

'Thank you.' Sabi felt her heart lighten at the prospect as she stirred a spoon through the creamy soup. 'I took Maddie's folder with me. I showed it to Jemima.'

Unable to keep the surprise from his voice, Henry asked, 'What did she think?'

'That it was good. That her form tutor would have approved of the layout.'

'And what do you think of it?'

'I think I'd like you to read it and then...' Sabi got up and dug the folder out of her bag, passing it to her husband. 'Then I'm going to tell you about something else I've done without telling anyone.'

34

Maddie followed the estate agent she'd met on the edge of Broadclyst across a stretch of fields that bordered the road that connected the village and Exeter.

She'd forced herself to arrange to view the land after she'd made her appointment with the bank manager, telling herself that, with a bit of luck, she'd be able to cancel it. But the bank's business manager hadn't said yes to her loan – even though he hadn't said no either.

Trudging after her host, watching him gesticulate enthusiastically at buildings that weren't yet there, Maddie did her best to visualise The Potting Shed relocated on the roll of washed-out green fields before her. All she was doing, however, was picturing her own land, and wondering how she could make the best of it so she could take up the offer of half a bank loan and prove the nursery a going concern.

But if the nursery can't hold its own with BIG nearby, then you'll lose the business and have a huge overdraft to pay off.

They'd only gone halfway around the site when Maddie knew she couldn't go on. She wasn't just wasting the young salesman's time; she was giving him false hope of a sale he'd never get from her. It didn't matter that it was a good site with every bit as much potential as Ed had claimed: her heart simply wasn't in it.

Having apologised, taking her leave at speed, Maddie sprayed her hands liberally. Rubbing in the sanitiser, she leapt into her jeep and spoke to the steering wheel. 'This is the situation. One: I am not selling up. Two: that decision could spell financial suicide. Three: I need to find as many additional ways as I can to make The Potting Shed pay its way. Four: I have to talk to Sabi because I'm going to need her onside for this to work.' Maddie paused as she switched on the engine. 'I *want* her onside. She is my sister. Five: I must break the news to Jake and Petra that I intend to fight on.'

As she drove towards the hospital, Maddie squashed down the sixth point – *I need to talk to Ed.*

'Maddie!'

Jake looked self-conscious as he jumped off the bed next to Petra. 'I haven't skived off work, I got a taxi not the buses.'

'I wasn't about to accuse you of neglecting your post, Jake. It's gone five and I said you could lock up at four.' Despite her low mood, Maddie couldn't help being pleased for her friends. 'Anyway, I'm sorry to interrupt your time together. Just wanted to see how you were doing, Petra.'

'Great. The bruises are manageable and I'm eating and drinking fine. I can go home tomorrow.'

Jake wrinkled his nose. 'Which is a good thing *and* a bad thing.'

Maddie grinned. 'Let me guess, Petra, your mum isn't too thrilled at Jake visiting you at home?'

Petra grunted. 'Grade-one snob syndrome. She'll get over it.'

'That's the attitude.'

'She'll accept the fact that I am old enough to make my own decisions eventually.' Petra gave Maddie a quizzical look. 'You're all unsettled. There's something you wanted to tell us, isn't there?'

'There is.' Rather than commenting on how fast Petra had got to know her, Maddie got to the point. 'I'm sorry, but it might be bad news. I don't know yet. I just know it isn't good news.'

Jake fetched a chair for Maddie to sit on. 'This is about BIG, isn't it?'

Sitting down with a thump, Maddie's eyes met Petra's. 'You told Jake?'

'I had to.' Petra looked sheepish. 'It was important, and well, I wanted him to understand why he has to learn to read and write a little better.'

Suddenly rather shaky, Maddie glanced at Jake. 'I know I should have told you earlier. I didn't know how. You've been with us – me – so long. And well, I've been hoping for a miracle.'

'Petra explained. It's okay. I'd never have planned to leave or anything but, if I have to, well…' Jake peered up at his girlfriend, '… then I have to. Sometimes things change.'

'They do.' Maddie would have given Jake a hug if she hadn't known he'd hate it. 'Thank you, Petra.'

'It's okay. I knew you were struggling to find the words.'

'Makes a change from me being the one struggling with words.' Jake grinned.

'The nursery hasn't gone yet, and I'm hoping it won't.' Maddie wished she felt as positive as she sounded. 'But the thing is... whatever happens in the short term, I'm not going to be able to reemploy you both after Christmas, which means I will have to let you go, Petra – even though I don't want to.'

'It's okay. You were upfront about that from the start. Anyway,' Petra glanced at Jake, 'I have an idea now, thanks to you Maddie, of what I want to do with my life, so I won't need a job for a while. Not if all goes to plan anyway.'

'And umm...' Jake's more familiar, slightly defensive, expression returned as he took his girlfriend's hand. 'I won't be available so much either. Not if, as Petra says, things work out.'

'I thought you loved your job?'

'I do, and I owe you and your dad so much.'

'But you're ready to move on?' Maddie felt sad. She'd been so worried about telling Jake, and now it looked as if he'd been planning his exit all along.

Picking up a leaflet, Jake passed it to Maddie. 'What do you think?'

'Adult education classes? Not just a few reading improvement classes?'

'GCSE Maths and English.' Jake sounded unconvinced. 'Petra seems to think I can do it.'

'Of course you can do it.' Maddie scanned the pamphlet. 'I've never doubted you were bright Jake.'

'I know. But *I* doubted it. Was often made to doubt it. If

you're put down long enough...' He smiled at Petra. 'But things are different now.'

'You can say that again.' Maddie asked, 'Will you stay working for me between classes?'

'Yes please. For a while anyway.'

'A while?' Maddie felt as if she was losing her grip on another conversation. Petra passed her another well-thumbed pamphlet. 'It's when this starts. We applied yesterday. We were a bit last minute, so we should hear if we get accepted next week.'

'Horticulture and general gardening apprenticeships?' Maddie felt a hit of pride for them both, especially Jake. 'Good for you. Dare I ask, what happens if one of you gets in and the other doesn't?'

'If I don't get in, then I'll apply to agricultural college.' Jake looked awkward as he quickly added, 'I know I ought to have asked you first, but I've put you down as a referee. Well, Petra did for me.'

'I'd be delighted to do a reference for you Jake – for both of you.' Maddie felt a lump come to her throat. 'And if you aren't lucky with the apprenticeship, Petra?'

'I'll try for voluntary places or jobs with the National Trust or the Royal National Gardens and keep applying for apprenticeships until I get one.'

Maddie grinned. 'Well, if it's the National Trust you want, I can steer you in the right direction.'

'I hoped you'd say that.' Petra gave her a disarming grin. 'But now, I think you should tell us about this miracle you're hoping for, and how we can help keep BIG from knocking on your door.'

'More like, keep them from knocking *down* my door in five days' time.'

'Five days!' Petra clapped a hand over her mouth.

'Well, no. Sorry.' Maddie shook her head. 'Not literally in five days. But this Saturday is the day when I will be refusing to sign away The Potting Shed to BIG, plunging myself into debt and risking Sabi never speaking to me again.'

35

Hi Aunt Maddie,

Sorry this is an email and not a call. I've run out of credit on my mobile.

I spoke to Mum on Saturday. She told me about BIG wanting The Potting Shed. I hope you're OK.

I know Mum wants to sell and you don't.

Please give her a ring or something and sort things out. I can't have my favourite aunt falling out with my mum. It would have made Grandad sad.

Love you lots.

Jem x

P.S. I'll be home for weekends from next term, so I'll be able to help at The Potting Shed.

'Love you too, Jem.' Maddie immediately picked up the phone. It was answered after only two rings. 'Sabi, we really need to talk.'

'We do. I've just heard from Creswell – well, his office anyway – confirming the meeting for this Saturday. Are you okay with eleven again, or shall I ask him to move it, so it is after work hours?'

Picking up on the unease in her sister's voice, Maddie said, 'Let's go with eleven and get it over with. I'm sure Jake will manage for a while.'

'Good.'

Maddie could hear Sabi fidgeting with something at the other end of the phone.

'I don't want to lose you over this, Mads.'

'Me neither.' Maddie felt a tired smile curl up the sides of her lips. 'I've just had an email from Jem. I think she was telling me off for falling out with you. She said it would have made Dad sad.'

Sabi gave a soft moan. 'And she's right. She told me off too. I took her out on Saturday.'

'Saturday?'

'Henry stormed out after you'd gone. He was so angry with me. I needed to talk to someone who didn't hate me.'

'I don't hate you, Sabs. We just want different things.'

'Well, actually…' Sabi hesitated before saying, '… I've had a few thoughts about where we can go with all this – you and me. I tried to say before, but what with one thing and another I never got the chance. I don't like being at odds with you, Maddie. Can we talk after Creswell's gone?'

'We can. Is Jem really going to be home more soon?'

'From next term. We miss her being around.'

'Me too. I'm glad.' Maddie's hand gripped the phone tighter. 'You know I'm not going to change my mind about The Potting Shed though, don't you?'

'I know.'

Four days. That's all there was left until she had to officially tell BIG that she had no intention of signing her father's dreams away. Maddie wondered why she didn't just call Leo Creswell and tell him now, but every time the thought crossed her mind, images crowded into her mind of heavy businessmen with menacing expressions trying to persuade her otherwise until she felt brow beaten enough to sign just for some peace and quiet.

She knew she was being fanciful. Although Ed was convinced Leo wasn't above board, he hadn't said anything to make her think the man was violent or indulged in high-pressure intimidation – yet the notion refused to go away. A persistent, high-pitched beeping took Maddie away from the shop and into the car park. Jake was already striding across to the reversing lorry; its open-topped back heavily laden with Christmas trees.

Normally she loved this part of her job. But today, as Maddie put on her thickest gardening gloves as guards against the prickles, she felt a twinge of sadness. Her father had adored Christmas. *Who will I celebrate with this year if things stay difficult with Sabi?*

The image of Ed flashed through her mind, but she dismissed it. She'd not heard from him since last Saturday.

Seeing the driver of the lorry leap down from his cab,

Maddie put worrying about Christmas day to one side and went to intercept him and sort out the paperwork while Jake unhooked the back of the lorry and began dragging each tree into place.

As they worked, Maddie asked Jake if he'd mind looking after the nursery for an hour on Saturday.

'Sure, but it might be busier than usual. It'll be our first major selling day for this lot.' Jake nudged one of the trees he'd already lined up. 'And I can't ask Petra to come and help.'

'Damn, I forgot about the trees when I spoke to Sabi.'

'I'll be okay,' Jake said, 'as long as you help me get the netting machine in place before you go.'

'No problem.' Maddie patted him on the shoulder. 'It isn't like we'll drown in custom anyway.'

It had been the need for stillness that had finally convinced Maddie she should go to the Dark Skies walk. Hoping that the blanket of sky would comfort her, while the stars' beauty distracted her from all the decisions life was throwing at her – even if only for a little while.

As she'd driven across the county towards Exmoor, she'd turned her radio on, cranking the volume up so that it drowned out the voice in her head telling her it wouldn't be the same without Ed, and that the others might not be so welcoming if she wasn't with their friend.

'Maddie! How wonderful.' Ivan ran a hand over Sheba's back, as the black Labrador enthusiastically wagged her tail with whip-like energy.

'Hi Ivan.' Finding herself returning the older man's smiling greeting, she knelt down to greet Sheba.

'We didn't scare you off last time then?'

'Not at all.' Maddie hoisted her backpack higher onto her shoulder as she stood back up. 'I've got a good torch with me this time too.'

'Excellent.' Ivan glanced past Maddie's shoulder. 'No Ed?'

'He's busy.'

'The price of being a solicitor climbing the ladder.' Ivan spoke without judgement. 'He'll go far that boy. Come on, let's see if Jo's got some coffee on the go this week.'

Even though there were a few wisps of cloud cover hovering above the moor, Orion's belt still shone out across the night sky. As she lay on her folded-up travel rug, the darkness of the moors enveloping her, Maddie tried not to think about how different it was from gazing at the stars with Ed's comforting presence. The view was undoubtedly spectacular, but without his quietly whispered commentary, it wasn't the same. Something was missing.

Listening to the sound of her companions' breathing as they all lay around on the ground, soaking up the therapy of nature and the cosmos, Maddie felt rather small and insignificant. It struck her as odd she hadn't felt that way last time; but she hadn't been alone then.

You're not alone now. You're with Ivan and Jo and the others.

She tried to make out which of the many bright lights in the sky were Venus and Jupiter, but she couldn't remember which of the hundreds of sparkling dots in the sky Ed had said they were.

Maddie had hoped Ed might call her after she'd emailed him about her bank visit as promised, but she'd received no reply – not even in his capacity as a solicitor.

Face it, you hardly know anything about Ed other than that he likes walking and he's a lawyer who used to live in Scotland.

Knowing she needed to speak to a lawyer before Saturday to bring them up to date on her decision to try and buy out Sabi and keep The Potting Shed going, Maddie hadn't been able to put off a call to Lyle and Tate any longer. That afternoon she'd phoned and asked to speak to Ronald Lyle.

It was the right thing to do – and it'll stop Creswell from being able to hurl accusations of unprofessional conduct at Ed.

Now, as the stars above her merged into a dazzling blur against her tired eyes, Maddie tried to take comfort in the reassurances the elderly solicitor had given her, telling her he'd be there on Saturday, and that he was well aware of Mr Creswell's approach to the law. She knew she'd be glad of Ronald's serene, grandfatherly manner, but as a satellite blinked in the sky, thousands of miles above her, Maddie was hit by the certainty that, by talking to his boss, she'd put another obstacle between herself and Ed.

It was a relief when Ivan and Jo switched their torches on at halftime. Maddie was as desperate for a cup of coffee as she was to switch her rambling mind off from reality. 'Coffee?' Jo was already passing a cup in Maddie's direction. 'You like it black without, yes?'

'Perfect. Thank you.' Maddie took the steaming cup. 'You're kind to remember.'

'Taking a mental note of how people have their coffee goes with the job. It happens on automatic pilot now.'

'I'm sure.'

'No Ed?'

'He said he was busy with work.'

Jo rolled his eyes. 'Berk.'

Maddie coughed in surprise as she blew across her coffee to cool it. 'You think?'

'This is his one escape. That's why he started to come in the first place. A time, just once a week for the few months of the year when it's possible to see the stars clearly. A time when he can forget the things that don't matter.'

'Like work, you mean?'

'Work does matter, but the stresses we surround ourselves with often don't. Humans have a habit of making their own crises, often working up a small problem into a big one.'

'You make it sound so straightforward.'

'It could be if we'd let it.' Jo gave Maddie a smile that was almost as warm as their coffee. 'But in this case, I wasn't talking about Ed's work. He's a berk for not being here with you. He obviously likes you and you like him. Why complicate things by pretending otherwise?'

'Ed's just a friend.' Maddie stared into her cup. 'And anyway, it's…'

'Complicated?'

'I was going to say, it's not that straightforward.'

'Same thing.'

'Ed's my lawyer. I'm his client. At the moment, it would be unprofessional to be together.'

'Ed said that didn't he?' Jo took a gulp of coffee. 'It definitely sounds like a direct quote.'

'Sort of.'

'As I said, he's a berk.' Jo knocked back the rest of their drink. 'Want me to spot constellations with you for a bit before we go?'

The forty minutes with Jo talking her through the sky above them flew by, and although Ed crossed her mind on more than one occasion, her worries over BIG and The Potting Shed stayed firmly dormant. Now, walking back towards the car park with her new friends, Maddie found herself keeping stride with Sheba as the dog remained within the projected glow of Ivan's torch.

'Enjoy that again then, Maddie?'

'Very much. Jo is very knowledgeable about the constellations, not to mention relaxing company.'

'That's true enough.' Ivan climbed the stile that took them back into the car park. 'Taught me a great deal when I first came along. That's when I asked Jo to join the market. Intelligence and calm – a rare mix.'

'And after you'd tasted their coffee.'

Ivan laughed, 'I confess if I hadn't liked their beverages, then the employment invitation would not have been forthcoming. That reminds me…' The farmer's market manager called across to where Jo was opening up the back of their van. '… have you got a minute Jo? I've been asked by a new garden centre if we'd like to add them onto The Exmoor Drifters' rota. We have a couple of free weekends over winter, what do you think?'

'Whereabouts?'

Maddie felt her blood chill as she listened, the peace that Jo had instilled in her evaporating into the night.

'Wellington way. It's a new set up, so it's all a bit hypothetical at the moment. But, in principle, it could bring us in a fair bit of trade.'

'Count me in. Just let me know if it pans out and what dates we're talking.'

Slipping off while Jo and Ivan started talking about potential extra Christmas sales, Maddie climbed into her jeep and slammed the door. 'So much for thinking I was having an original idea. Looks like BIG have beaten me to it in inviting a farmer's market on site. How can I take out a bank loan when the only long-play additional income-maker idea has already been pinched by the opposition?'

36

It was almost seven-thirty before Henry parked his BMW on the gravel drive of his home. Friday afternoons had a habit of getting out of control. The pile of emails and small admin jobs that ate up his time often waited until halfway through the last afternoon of the working week to hit his inbox. Henry never wanted to find them waiting for him on a Monday morning, so he tended to stay late and work through them until they were finished. He pictured the gin and tonic that would already be poured, waiting for him to drink, while Sabi served up their supper – a three-course evening meal that had become a ritual since Jemima had first gone off to boarding school. He could almost taste it.

Opening his car door, Henry peered up at his home. Bought for its size, excellent position and views across the Mid-Devon countryside, it had always lacked the external character he knew Sabi craved from a property. Its only concession to English quaintness was a porch over the front door which, in the summer, was covered in a riot of rambling red roses. He couldn't help but think back to when his father-in-law had planted the rose. Henry hadn't been convinced, saying it would make the doorway of the house look like a picture on an old-fashioned chocolate box cover.

Tony had simply smiled, saying, 'Which is exactly how my daughter wants it to look.'

Tony Willand had known his daughters and accepted them for who they were. He'd never tried to change them or make them do things they didn't enjoy or want to do. It occurred to Henry that his father-in-law wouldn't be a bit surprised at how his offspring had reacted to BIG's takeover bid. 'If you'd held on for two more weeks, Tony, your will would have been changed and Maddie would have had sole say over what BIG did or didn't do.'

Henry called out, 'Only me,' as he slipped off his shoes and hung up his Barbour, noting how desperately it needed rewaxing.

'I'm in the kitchen. Your G and T's on the table. Dinner will be ten minutes.'

'Thanks, love.' Hearing the happy lilt to his wife's voice, Henry dashed upstairs to change out of his suit and into his jeans and a cosy jumper. Maybe they'd have a nice quiet evening meal together, without any talk of takeovers or sisters or houses.

Moving around the kitchen, Sabi could feel her heart thudding in her chest. She knew that what she about to suggest to her husband was the right thing to do, but she'd made so many mistakes lately – gone about things in such an upside-down way, that her confidence was shaken.

Henry's words on Wednesday lunchtime had stuck with her, hurting her more than she'd ever let on. *Why can't you ever be happy with what you've got?*

'I *am* happy. I just got lost in the excitement of having

the chance to buy my dream home and on top of that, I'm hurt to discover that Maddie would rather employ someone other than us to upgrade the nursery than me and you, Henry.'

As the sound of her husband's distinctive footfall came along the corridor to the kitchen, Sabi took the dinner plates out of the Aga's warming drawer.

Maddie hadn't been able to stop thinking about Jem's wish for her to make things right with her mother. 'Sabi'll be heartbroken if she can't have her new house. How can I deny Sabi her dream home just so I can move the nursery on?'

'You could say the same in reverse.' The fern on the kitchen windowsill gave Maddie an understanding ruffle of its leaves.

Maddie slunk into the old chair near her plant confidant. 'At least Jake took the news of potential closure well. Sounds like he and Petra—' Maddie scooped up her phone. 'Petra! That is someone I might be able to help at least.'

Listening to the ring of her phone as she waited for the line to be picked up, Maddie knew that, although her former boss at Killerton House was bound to be working late, it could also take him some time to answer his phone. She could picture Dan clearly. He'd be enjoying the quiet of the evening, taking advantage of hardly anyone being around to clear the blown-in leaves from the Bear Hut, and tugging up any random weeds he happened to spot as he pottered his way from the hut to the sheds behind the main house. Everything Dan did was measured and steady, including answering his phone.

'Madeleine! How wonderful to hear from you. How's life in the cut-throat world of bulb sales?'

Having intended to simply ask after work opportunities for Petra, and possibly Jake as well, Maddie was surprised to find herself confiding in her old employer.

'Umm… A sticky problem you've got there, girl.'

Maddie could picture him sitting down, probably on a pile of upturned metal buckets.

'You'll be after your old job back if all goes belly up, will you?'

'I'm sure that position is securely filled. I am after job information though, just not for me.'

'Go on then girl, tell ole Dan all about it.'

Henry put down his cutlery and picked up his wine glass. 'That was delicious. Thank you.'

'My pleasure.' Sabi toasted him with her own glass as she added, 'I suppose it's something I might not be able to do so often in the future. Not if I'm going to be putting every hour I can grab into building up and running a business.'

Henry's eyebrows rose. 'You think that letting out this place will be a full-time job?'

'You're worried that if it was, you wouldn't get your home comforts?' Sabi suddenly felt her hackles rising. 'No gin ready when you get in from work? No three-course Friday night supper? No week-night dinner come to that!'

'You think I would mind doing my bit?' Henry spoke softly, the lack of anger in his voice stopping Sabi's unexpected indignation in its tracks.

'Ignore me.' She took a swig from her wine glass. 'I know you wouldn't. You often cook, it's just…'

'The implication that I expect you to be the little wife tied to the kitchen sink?'

'I suppose so.'

'When have I ever demanded you be a traditional housewife?'

Sabi massaged her temples.

What is wrong with me? Why can't I do or say anything at the moment without talking myself into trouble and then feeling guilty about it?

Henry regarded his wife. 'I have never asked you to adopt that role. You could have had a career, but said you didn't want one. You took on the role of housewife all by yourself.'

'I'm not saying otherwise.'

'Then what *are* you saying?' A frown puckered Henry's brow. 'I know you need a new challenge. That's understandable. You're a clever woman who is capable of doing anything you set your mind to, including running a holiday let, but that's not going to occupy much of your time once it's up and running. If that's what you want, then…'

Sabi cut in quickly. 'It isn't what I want. I've been thinking a lot about the BIG situation and its implications, not just for us, but for Maddie.'

'You told me about the market idea.' Henry felt his chest tighten with incomprehension. 'Have you spoken to Maddie about talking to that Ivan chap yet?'

'No.'

'Come on, love!' Henry couldn't believe it. 'The meeting is tomorrow! If you don't act soon then…'

Sabi gripped her wine glass. 'We've agreed to talk once Creswell's gone on Saturday.'

'Talk about last gasp, Sabi. What if Maddie has changed her mind and has decided to sell up after all? You could be putting yourself through a whole heap of worry for no reason.'

'Henry! She is not going to change her mind, and the more I think about it, the more I think she is right.'

'You do?'

'I've been thinking about Dad.'

Henry tilted his head to one side. 'Funny, I was thinking about him earlier too.'

'Jemima was the one who made me see the obvious. If Dad had changed his will as he intended, then I'd have just accepted the way things were, BIG would have approached Maddie, she'd have turned them down, and that would have been that.'

Reaching his hand out across the table, Henry felt a sense of relief as he said, 'I think you should call Maddie right now. It'll be such a relief for her to know you're happy to let her buy us out.'

'That's not exactly what I meant...'

37

'Thank God you're here!' Maddie called over to Jake as she took payment from the latest customer. 'I'm not sure I could lift that onto a roof rack.'

Jake grinned as he hoisted the netted Christmas tree over his shoulder and headed towards a car that looked far too small to support the eight-foot Norway Spruce.

'When you said it might be busy this weekend, I never dared dream we'd be this busy!'

With no time to think about facing Leo Creswell in an hour's time, Maddie took a swig from a bottle of water. Focussed on the job at hand, she was beginning to wonder if she'd been wise to cut the number of trees she'd ordered this year, as she was hailed by a customer trying to decide between two trees.

Five minutes later, having discussed the pros and cons of choosing a Nordmann Fir, with its low needle drop rate, over a Scots Pine, with its more traditional Christmas tree appearance, Maddie was wishing Petra was there to lend a hand. Years of manual labour meant she was fairly fit, but running back and forth from the car park to the shop each time someone made a purchase was beginning to tire her out, and made her wish she'd had the foresight to invest in a portable card reader.

As the latest customer drove off with a tree in the boot and a back seat covered in holly, Maddie was about to take advantage of a lull in tree trade to make sure there were no customers waiting for her attention in any of the polytunnels, when she saw someone heading purposefully in her direction. Maddie did a double take as a familiar figure in pristine green wellington boots and an oversized Barbour ran up to her.

'Sabi?'

'Isn't this fantastic!' Sabi rubbed her gloved hands together. 'I've not seen The Potting Shed this hectic in years.'

'What are you doing here?'

'If the mountain won't come to Mohammad …'

'Oh.' Maddie sucked in her bottom lip. 'I'm sorry I didn't answer your call last night. I was in the bath. I was going to call you once I'd got out, but…'

'You didn't want another row or another pointless conversation where neither of us changed our minds about what we want.'

'Pretty much.'

'Well, none of that matters right now.'

'When did you get the new sign?' Sabi tried not to sound reproachful as she waved a hand towards the entrance to the car park.

'Petra. She bought it as a thank you present for letting her work here. She didn't think the original one was working.' Maddie watched the sign sway in the morning breeze. 'I hadn't noticed how worn the old wooden one had got. That is so much clearer. And it's working – or at least – it is helping make us more visible.'

'Oh.' Sabi shuffled her feet self-consciously. 'I assumed you'd bought it.'

'With what money? All my spare capital is going into paying for my part of the legal fees and saving to do up this place.' Maddie dug her hands deeper into her pockets as she said. 'Mr Lyle is letting me pay in instalments by the way, which will help considerably.'

Sabi's eyebrows rose. 'Really? That's kind of him.'

'The world is full of kind people.'

'Yes, well...' said Sabi.

Understanding the expression on her sister's face, Maddie put out a hand to her. 'I wasn't meaning to imply you were unkind.'

'I know.' With a deep breath Sabi waved an arm in Jake's direction. 'He called Petra, saying you were drowning, and she called me. So, tell me, how can I help?'

'Petra called you?' Maddie looked suspicious. 'But you said you were coming to see me anyway?'

'No need to be defensive. I *was* coming. Jake called while I was persuading Henry to lend me his coat. Come on.' Sabi gave her sister a shy smile. 'How about I leave explaining myself until we have time later?' She gestured to three new cars that had arrived in the car park. 'For now, let's just shift some trees! Shall I do the till?'

'Till?'

'You know, that thing you put money in.' Sabi calmly took the shop keys from Maddie's hand. 'If we don't hurry up, then we won't be free by eleven.'

'Oh my God! I'd forgotten for a minute!' Giving herself a shake, Maddie said, 'How can I leave Jake alone to deal with all these people?'

'You can't. I'll make a call.' Sabi lifted her mobile from her pocket. 'Creswell can come here. If we're busy he'll just have to wait.'

Laughing, Maddie blinked at her sister. 'Have you had a bang on the head I should know about?'

'If I have, it was long overdue.'

'I'll have to call Ronald Lyle, so he knows to come here too.'

'Not Ed?'

'Umm, no.' Maddie avoided her sister's gaze as she mumbled, 'Ronald Lyle has been our lawyer for so long. It felt right to use him.'

'Because Ronald knew Dad, or because his junior colleague is a good-looking younger man, with similar interests to you, who clearly fancies you?'

Maddie felt caught out as she muttered, 'That is neither here nor there. It's just…'

'I may have been a bit selfish lately, but I've not been blind. You like him too, don't you?'

'Makes no difference.' Maddie brushed some pine needles off her jumper. 'He's our lawyer, it would be unprofessional to date him and, well… I don't think he'd want too anymore anyway.'

Sabi shook her head, 'Of course he does. He'd be a fool not to want to see you, Mads.'

Maddie felt her mouth open and close like a goldfish gasping for air as Sabi nodded towards Jake.

'You can tell me all about Ed later. Right now, we have trees to sell.'

Maddie suddenly found herself wondering if she was having some sort of dream. Was she really tucked up under her duvet, and would she, any minute now, wake up and find that she hadn't just spoken to Sabi, or sold a single tree, or – in fact – had breakfast yet?

Sabi put her hand on her sister's shoulder, proving that she wasn't a figment of her sister's imagination. 'Customers, Maddie.'

'Oh yes, right. Thanks.' Maddie could see Jake directing an elderly couple towards the pre-potted trees on the near side of the fence. 'It's weird. We've always done well with the tree sales, but I thought, with me being late placing our order this year, we might not get good sales.'

'Umm, that might have been me and Petra.' Sabi examined a scarlet fingernail.

'*You* and Petra?'

'I'll tell you later. You go and help that lady with the buggy, and I'll call Leo while I take over manning the till. Still the same sign in code?'

'Yeah. Still the same.' Maddie had taken a few steps towards the woman with the toddler, before she called back to her sister. 'Sab, thanks.'

Jake slid his phone into the back pocket of his jeans before restacking a row of Norway Spruce, spacing then out more now the stock of trees had been so depleted. 'That was Petra. She's ordered ten more of everything except the over six-foot stuff.'

Maddie had a sense of being back in a dream again. 'Petra is supposed to be resting at home.'

'That doesn't stop her using a phone. Anyway, she's bored stiff and happy to help.'

'But how did she know we needed more? I know it's been good today, but once all our regulars have trees, we won't sell many extra.' A trickle of panic ran down Maddie's spine. 'I'm not sure the budget will run to it. Remember what I said about the bank loan. It was a kind thought, but I wish Petra had asked me first.'

'I've sold to four regulars today, including Tim over at the Blackdown Hotel. He bought his usual three trees. Everyone else has been a new face.' A remarkably calm Jake gestured to the depleted line of firs. 'Anyway, it was your sister who sorted it. She and Petra have been texting away like mad about things.'

'They have?' Maddie glanced over her shoulder towards the shop. 'What *things* exactly?'

Ignoring the question, Jake checked his watch as a white van pulled into the car park. 'I can look after these folk, why don't you go and get ready for your visitors?'

Maddie's good humour sank. 'I was enjoying being too busy to worry about BIG.'

'Are you still going to refuse to sign?'

Hunching her shoulders, Maddie groaned. 'I was going to. But the loan involved in doing what Dad wanted is astronomical. Am I going to get into debt and then fail anyway? One minute I want to take the gamble and the next it seems too huge a risk. And now, as if by magic, Sabi is here and being her old self. My big sister, who I love. How can I stop her having her dream home?'

'But I was under the impression that…' Jake's words petered off as a flash of worry crossed his face. 'Sabi's here helping. That must mean she's seen how important this place is to you? That she's changed her mind and won't sign?'

'I'm afraid not, Jake. She simply wants me to get the most out of this place before I say goodbye to it. Sabi told me she had ideas to make extra money before Christmas.' She waved a hand around her, 'I suspect that's what this is, a result of her arranging some advertising for us. It was a kind gesture, but it won't be more than that.'

'But Petra agreed to help Sabi because we thought it might help save the place.' Disappointment rang through Jake's words. 'It didn't occur to me that she could be doing this just so we go out on a high. I don't think Petra did either.'

'Don't worry about it.' Her heart suddenly heavy, Maddie twisted round to face her home. 'Now, I think I'll take you up on that offer of having five minutes to change out of these old clothes before I have to be brave and make a decision, once and for all.'

Maddie had only taken a few steps when Jake caught up with her, pointing back towards the car park.

Two cars had driven in, heading away from the main throng of customers. Maddie's stomach did a nervous somersault as she recognised Henry's BMW. The other car – a sleek black Jaguar – had to belong to Leo Creswell.

'Or maybe I won't be changing first.' Maddie wiped her palms nervously over her old blue jumper. 'It's still quite busy. Will you manage for a while, Jake?'

'I guess, but Sabi said you should make him wait if we had customers.'

'So, she did.' Maddie watched as the two cars came to a standstill. 'Always likes to be in control of a situation, my sister.'

'To be fair, she has been really helpful.' Jake's boots fidgeted against the gravel; defending Sabi was unfamiliar territory.

'When we were teenagers we'd work together here, like this, me doing the heavy work while she did the till, wrapped the pot plants into neat gift wrap, and charmed the customers. That's the sister I want back.'

'Why can't you carry on doing that? This place could survive, even with BIG nearby. I'm sure it could if you worked together.'

'I'd like to, Jake, I really would. But Sabi lives in a world that includes homemade pasta and shuns instant coffee. There's no going back from that for more than an occasional hour or two, once in a while.'

'I'm not so sure. I had begun to wonder if...' Jake paused as the newcomer's car door opened. 'You said Mr Lyle was coming, but that isn't him. That's...'

'Ed.'

38

Seeing Ed in his professional attire felt strange. His slate grey suit and polished shoes were miles away from his dark blue jeans, casual jumper and hiking boots. Even when she'd seen him in his office, he'd been relaxed in his shirt sleeves.

He looks good.

'Maddie?' Jake was looking at her in concern. 'You okay?'

'Not really.' She reined in her pointless thoughts and wrenched her shoulders back. 'But I dare say I will be.'

'Shall I close up and come with you?' Jake looked uneasy, 'I don't want you to face that Leo Creswell on your own.'

'Thanks Jake, but Ed will make sure everything stays civil.' Maddie switched her attention back to the Christmas trees. 'Anyway, I'm the one who ought to stay here with you! How can I leave you to cope on your own when we are selling properly for the first time in ages?'

'I'll be okay.'

'But the till. You hate using it.'

Jake hung his head, as if ashamed. 'I've been hard work over the last few years, haven't I?'

'Of course not. You've always preferred the plants to

people, but frankly,' Maddie shuddered as she saw Leo Creswell, 'I can't blame you for that!'

Jake shrugged. 'I know I could have done more to help around here, that's all.'

'You're a good man.' Maddie patted his shoulder. 'Now then, if you're sure you'll be okay, this shouldn't take long. Let's keep the sales going while we can. I'd better see why Mr Tate has come instead of Mr Lyle.'

'Because he cares about you, obviously.'

Maddie knew she should move, but her feet weren't keen to oblige. Not sure if she should go to the shop and tell Sabi that their guests had arrived, or if she should greet Ed, Henry and Creswell, her thoughts raced in ever-decreasing circles. *I've run out of time. I thought I'd made my decision… but now I'm not so sure.*

Dad wanted me to have this place. He wanted it to develop and grow into a proper garden centre.

Her throat went dry as she saw Leo give Ed's outstretched hand a perfunctory shake.

But Dad didn't know about BIG, nor that the house Sabi fell in love with as a child would come on the market at the same time as we'd be offered a lot of money for the business.

She thought of her niece.

I don't have a family to consider – Sabi does. Maybe I should just cut my losses. I know Jem loves this place, but when she's older she will have her own life to live.

Thinking back to her chat with her former employer, Maddie knew she wouldn't be completely rudderless if she agreed to sign The Potting Shed away. Her old job was happily occupied, but Dan had said he'd take her on as a part-time garden hand if she wanted to go back to Killerton.

As Henry walked in her direction, Maddie saw him weave his way around a family who were excitedly picking their tree.

On the other hand... I love this place... and look how well it's doing today. If I could think of enough things to keep this pace up...

'Is Sabi in the shop?' Henry gave Maddie a hug.

'Yes. She couldn't have come at a better time.' Maddie tilted her head to one side. 'She said she was planning to come and see me before the meeting, even if Jake hadn't issued an SOS via Petra.'

'And you want to know if she was telling the truth?'

'Sorry Henry, but yes.'

'Sabi was halfway through persuading me that my coat would be easier to clean than hers if she was helping out here while you talked, when Petra's call came through.'

Maddie turned to face the shop. 'Good. That's good.'

'It's going to be alright.' Henry put his hands on his sister-in-law's shoulders. 'You and Sabi will get through this.'

Maddie swallowed as she realised she'd known what to do all along. 'We will. We're sisters.'

Leo Creswell peered around him with disdain but said nothing about the kitchen in which he sat. Maddie knew it was a far cry from her sister's designer home. If she'd thought there was even the slightest chance that the meeting would be held in her home, then she would have cleaned the place.

Not quite daring to ask Ed why he was there instead of Ronald, her heart ached to see him as he hovered, his countenance closed and grave, by the same kitchen sink he'd lounged against when they'd laughed their way through a Chinese takeaway – right up until he'd had to leave.

Needing to be busy, Maddie dashed around the house, collecting up enough seats for everyone to be able to sit down. Meanwhile, Henry dragged the table into the middle of the room, heaping all the paperwork and random post and flyers into neat piles and depositing them onto the nearest unoccupied space.

As Sabi filled the kettle, tutting at the absence of anything other than instant coffee and opting to make everyone tea instead, Maddie had no more excuses to keep moving.

'If we could begin?' Leo laid his briefcase on the table and clicked it open. 'I am assuming that, as you've had all week to consider your options and I've had no call to say that the papers will not be signed, then this meeting will be brief.'

'Not necessarily.' Ed sat down. 'There are a few questions I'd like answers to before my clients sign anything.'

Maddie opened her mouth to speak, but Leo got in first.

'There has been more than enough time for questions, Mr Tate. I have willingly disrupted two of my Saturdays to accommodate your clients. Clients who, despite one of them claiming that their father would never sell to BIG *hasn't* turned down the offer, and will do very well out of it, and...' he looked around his surroundings as if he expected a rat to run over his feet at any moment, '... will be able to increase her standard of living quite considerably.'

Ed stared at his fellow lawyer. 'One of the first things that

Mr Lyle taught me when he was kind enough to take me on, was that if a fellow solicitor resorts to personal criticism of a client, then he is either dishonest or frightened. Which are you, Mr Creswell?'

'The sort of solicitor who isn't afraid to sue another for defamation.'

'I'm sure that's true, but in this case, you would be foolish to try it.' Not giving Leo the chance to reply, Ed switched his gaze to Maddie. 'I should explain. Mr Lyle was happy to attend as you were expecting him to, Miss Willand, but as I'd already done some work for you, I requested to attend on the firm's behalf. I hope that's alright?'

'Yes. Yes of course.' Maddie asked her sister. 'Okay with you, Sabi?'

'I'm fine with that, but I would like ten minutes to talk to my sister in private before we proceed. We intended to confer prior to your arrival, but as you will have noticed, the nursery is particularly busy today. There was no time to discuss last minute issues.'

Having assumed a positive response to her request, Sabi was already in the act of standing when Leo said, 'No. I think there has been enough time to discuss things, and now that your legal representative has insulted me, I'd like to cut to the chase and go home.'

'Then, with Miss Willand and Mrs Willand-Harris's permission, I will – as you say – cut to the chase.' Ed gave Sabi a supportive smile. 'I'll say my piece, and then I'm sure Mr Creswell will be more than happy to let you discuss any issues before he leaves.'

Sabi reached out a hand to her husband as she looked at Maddie.

Wishing she had someone's hand to hold, Maddie watched as Ed opened his briefcase and took out a map of the local area.

'My first question to you, Mr Creswell, echoes one I asked at our last meeting. How did you acquire the permissions to build an access road from here to the motorway so quickly?'

'I beg your pardon?'

'It isn't a difficult question for an intelligent man, Mr Creswell.'

'I have been in this job a long time, I have contacts. Not only that, but BIG is a sure bet customer-wise. The new junction would be paid for very quickly. What with that, and the extra employment the place would bring to the area, the relevant parties were happy to comply.'

'With respect, that does not answer my question. Last time you were – shall we say, economical with the truth – a fact I can prove via the recording of the meeting – to which, may I remind you, you freely consented. So, I'll ask again – how come this map…' Ed handed out copies to the other occupants of the kitchen, '… already has the proposed road marked on it? And before you repeat yourself and say that it was a rush job before Christmas, save your breath. It was a rush job because BIG paid a private sweetener to the farmer whose fields would be crossed by the road, and because you have a quid pro quo arrangement in the planning office. Not illegal, but definitely not one hundred per cent above board.'

'You paid the farmer?' Maddie suddenly found her voice, 'before we've signed?'

Ed pointed to the plan, his finger tracing a line from the

nursery's car park to the motorway. 'Enough to ensure that, once the deal is done, he won't back out.'

Leo folded his arms across his chest. 'You make it sound so sinister, but it is not an uncommon business practice. And what's the point of BIG taking this place if there is no access?'

'But the access from the main road is already good.' Maddie frowned.

'It could be better,' Leo countered, rushing on. 'Anyway, that is not your problem. We are here for you to sign the papers.'

Sabi straightened up on her chair. 'I have a question.'

Creswell didn't bother holding back a pained groan. 'Go on.'

'May I ask how you got my address to contact me in the first place?'

Leo picked up his diary and made a play of leafing through the pages, 'I don't know. It was the address I was given.'

Ed nodded. 'That at least is true. With Mr Lyle's help, I've put out a few feelers, asked a few questions. It seems that BIG's interest in The Potting Shed's land goes back rather further than we were led to believe. A theory I put to Miss Willand a few days ago – a theory which, at the time, was just that. Now I know it to be the case.'

'For heaven's sake.' Leo pulled his cooling mug of tea towards him. 'This is turning into an episode of Poirot!

Ignoring Creswell, Henry indicated for Ed to go on.

'It transpires that, during the height of the recent Covid crisis, BIG approached a number of small premises near motorway junctions, on good land, with regular customers. Including a Mr Tony Willand. He was contacted, via the company Facebook page, and answered the query.'

'*Dad* did?' Maddie's jaw dropped as she turned to her sister.

'He did.' Leo rested back in his seat, his expression smug. 'So, you see, the necessary information came from your father himself, Mrs Willand-Harris. Are you still so sure he'd never have sold?'

39

Maddie hadn't understood the meaning of the phrase 'a pregnant pause' until that moment. No one seemed to know what to say.

It was Henry who brought the room out of its stunned stillness. 'Mr Tate, perhaps you could go on with what you were saying?'

'Certainly. But then, after I've spoken, I believe it would be in everyone's interests for us to take a break so that you, Henry, can check that Jake is getting on all right and Mrs Willand-Harris and Miss Willand can talk.'

'Thank you.' It was the first time Maddie had looked at Ed properly since the meeting had begun. 'I would appreciate knowing that Jake is managing.'

Leo waved a hand at Ed, as if to say, 'get on with it', before sitting back in his seat with his mug of tea, as if readying himself to pointlessly sacrifice his time.

'As I was saying, Mr Willand was asked about signing over the nursery to the BIG chain not long before his death, in the months prior to the pandemic.'

'But Dad would never sell up. He loved this place.'

'Precisely, Miss Willand. Your father sent a "thanks, but no thanks" reply informing BIG that he had his own plans for improvements, and that he'd be employing his son-in-law and daughter, Mr and Mrs Willand-Harris, to design, build and provide the interior design of the place when the time came, while his other daughter ran the place. Obviously it wasn't hard for BIG's researchers to know how to contact you once Mr Willand had passed away. You live here Miss Willand, and Mr and Mrs Willand-Harris are in the phone book.

'Then Covid hit and things went on hold – until now.'

'Dad wanted *me* to be the designer? To sort out how the place looked?' Sabi swivelled in her seat and looked at her sister. 'Did you know, Maddie?'

'Of course. It's a family business, Dad wanted you involved, and he knew what made you happy. You're good at all that stuff. I'm not, and nor was Dad.' Maddie rubbed her forehead. 'He died before we had a chance to ask Henry about the structural changes to the house. They're in the proposal, but as you haven't read it then…'

'I *have* read it. We both have, but it doesn't say who'd do the upgrading work.' Sabi's voice was barely more than a whisper. 'Your plans are so good, but they aren't anything to do with me.'

Maddie couldn't believe it. 'Surely it's obvious – at least, I thought it was? Who else would I ask to oversee the upgrade of this place? Or trust to do the job properly, for that matter?'

Gulping, Sabi muttered, 'When Dad died and then BIG pounced… I…' Her voice cracked. 'It never even occurred to me that you'd want me involved.'

Maddie reached out a hand to her sister. 'I think we would like that break now, please E… Mr Tate.'

*

Sabi had left the room at speed, grabbing her bag and making excuses about needing the bathroom, while pulling a folded tissue from her trouser pocket and dabbing her eyes.

Promising Henry that she'd look after his wife, Maddie thanked him as he went to check on Jake. Then, leaving Leo and Ed sat opposite each other at her kitchen table, looking like two stags at bay, Maddie went to find her sister.

Sabi was curled up in a ball on her childhood bed, cradling a cushion in her arms.

'You okay?' Maddie perched herself on the edge of the bed. 'Sorry, stupid question. We haven't done well on the communication front lately, have we?'

'Not so you'd notice.' Sabi sniffed and rolled onto her back. 'Why didn't you or Dad tell me and Henry that we were included in the upgrade plans?'

'Because he died just after we'd made them. The will hadn't been officially changed and then all this happened.'

'I'm sorry, Maddie.'

'I don't blame you for going after your dream. I remembered about Louisa Harriett the other day – it was her doll's house the house reminds you of, wasn't it.'

'It was.' Sabi sniffed sadly. 'I never did get to play with it.'

'You were too good a friend to her. I never liked how she used you.'

'Used me?' Sabi looked up in surprise.

'She may have had parents with money and possessions, but you were a lot prettier and brighter than her. She needed you to make her look good.'

'Oh.' Sabi looked up at her seashell lamp. 'You don't think it's like that with...'

'Miriam?' Maddie gave her sister a kind smile. 'There are similarities, and I can't say I'm keen on her high-handed approach to life – but no. Miriam, for all her faults, always supports you when you need her to.'

'Thanks.' Sabi wiped a hand over her eyes, smearing her supposedly un-smudgeable mascara.

'There's something I need to ask.'

'Go on.'

'The house in Culmstock. Do you want to live there because you love it for *you* – for you, Henry and Jem? Or do you love it because you harbour secret desires to find Louisa Harriett, tell her what you've got, but not let her see inside?'

Sabi gave a rueful chuckle. 'I'd be lying if that thought hadn't crossed my mind, but no. I promise, I am totally in love with the house for my family. Not to show off anything to anyone.'

'Good.' Wrapping an arm around her sister's shoulder, Maddie smiled. 'I've been just as bad as you when it comes to dream-chasing. And anyway, I wouldn't want to stop Jem having a good future. If we do what BIG want then she'll be secure for life, and you'll get your real-life doll's house.'

'But...' Sabi sat up abruptly and blew her nose hard. 'I can't let you sign now! You and Dad wanted *me* to be part of it. I had no idea. If I had, I'd never have considered... and anyway, didn't you hear what that slug of a man said?'

Maddie put out a hand to her sister. 'Hold on... did you think that Dad and I didn't want you here? You felt excluded?'

'Well… yes.' Sabi fiddled with her wedding ring. 'You and Dad were always such a team. I was on the outside looking in. I got in the way.'

'Oh my God! I'm *so* sorry. I've never thought that. And I'm sure Dad didn't either. You liked different things to us; we thought this might be a way to include you in our plans.' Maddie looked stunned. 'The plan had been, once the will was changed, for all of us to have a meeting – including Jem – to talk about taking The Potting Shed from a nursery to a garden centre in small stages. Dad wanted Henry to work out how to swap rooms around so that…'

'This house as a flat with the shop underneath.' Sabi whispered, 'I know. I read the proposal.'

'You really read it?' Maddie was beginning to wish her sister had made coffee; her need for caffeine was growing by the second.

'And if you'd named who you intended to do the upgrades, rather than saying "designer and architect arranged", I might have come to my senses sooner.'

'I thought it was obvious. Who else would I have asked?' Maddie opened her arms and gave her sister a hug. 'I've been a stubborn fool.'

'That makes two of us.' Sabi returned the hug. 'What do we do now? Creswell clearly can't be trusted. Thank goodness Ed has a thing for you. I can't imagine other lawyers going out on a limb like that.'

Maddie sank back. 'Yeah well, I'm not sure he's even a friend. Not now.'

'Oh, Maddie.' Sabi saw the situation at once. 'You really do like him, don't you?'

'Maybe.' She yanked at her tatty jumper. 'But I think I've

blown it. My fault, not his. I'm still wary – you know – men. After Darren.'

'Oh Mads, Darren was years ago. I had no idea you were still suffering from his fall out.'

'Six years ago.'

'You know he was a very specific type of bastard, don't you? If I'd got my hands on him before he'd slunk off.'

Maddie was taken aback by the passion in Sabi's voice. 'What would you have done?'

'I'd have been tempted to engage my knee with his groin, but actually, I'd just have given him a good talking to or reported him to the police.'

'Thanks Sis.' Picturing the unlikely image her sister was creating, Maddie fiddled with the cuffs of her jumper. 'I couldn't have faced the police though – I felt such a fool. The last thing I wanted was them telling me I was an idiot too.'

'I bet Darren banked on that.'

'Possibly.' Maddie grimaced. 'It wasn't just that Darren was with me virtually twenty-four-seven, and then suddenly disappeared without a word…'

'Taking half of your jewellery and the contents of your purse in the process.'

'Quite.' Maddie swallowed. 'It was that he made me feel special, treated me as if I was the most important person in the world – but it was all a lie. A month-long, whirlwind romance – that's all it was. But he made me love him and then he stole from me. All the meals we had, the nights out – every time he made a thing about him paying and not me, but he was taking the money from my purse or "borrowing" my credit card when I wasn't looking. I paid for every single thing we did. If I hadn't checked my credit card bill when I did…'

'I'm so sorry. You'd already fallen for him big time by then hadn't you.'

'Yep. Handsome git.' Maddie gritted her teeth against the sense of humiliation she always felt when she thought of her ex. 'He left me with a sense of worthlessness and gullibility that was only topped by a distrust of any man who seemed both interested in me and a nice person. I can't help thinking – worrying – that they are being nice to hide the fact that they aren't nice at all.' Maddie exhaled sharply as she pulled herself together, 'But it wasn't just the Darren thing this time. I thought I should be distant with Ed because he's our lawyer. Then I changed my mind about that, when I saw that perhaps I could trust him– but I was too late. I'd messed Ed about too much by then, and so he stepped away. I can't blame him.'

'But he's a solicitor! That's a catch and a half. Couldn't you…' Sabi winced as she stopped talking. 'Sorry, that was…'

'A Miriam moment?'

'An excellent name for it.' Laughing at herself, Sabi swung her legs off the bed. 'I would love to see you happy though, Mads. Not every man will let you down.'

'I know. But that's why – before Ed – I've always gone for the Petes of this world. You know, short term, no plans, no dreams – fun but safe. That's when I've even bothered with men at all.'

'It isn't a failure to want someone in your life or fall in love, you know. You can be a strong, independent businesswoman *and* be happy with a partner.'

With a sense that her sister was talking about herself as well as her, Maddie asked, 'And that's what you want? You have the loving husband, but you don't have a business. Hence the house let idea.'

'The thing is, Mads, I'm tired of the life I've foisted on myself. Being seen to be perfect in the eyes of the world is exhausting.'

'Oh Sabi!' Maddie gave her sister another hug. 'Let's go and get this over with.'

'Do you think we should hide the kitchen knives first? I can't imagine Leo reacting well to us refusing to sign.'

'Refusing to sign?' Maddie frowned. 'But if we don't sign, you won't get your new business.'

'Haven't you been listening to what Ed's discovered? That Creswell is as twisted as a corkscrew!'

'But your dream house, and your business plan, and...'

'I'll get my dream house – I'll explain later – as for a business plan, well, I wondered... umm... if you'll still have me, could I share yours?'

'Mine?'

Sabi looked sheepish. 'I showed your plan to Jemima. She loved it. Had a few ideas of her own. She suggested a sandpit for the toddlers. I wondered about a spot between the polytunnels and the shop, so there is somewhere for the children to play while their parents' queue to pay.'

'A sandpit?'

Sabi opened her bag and took out the proposal, opening it on the page about inviting a farmer's marker to the site once a month. 'This is my favourite idea by far.'

'It is?'

'Yes, actually, I wondered,' Sabi's face took on a

self-conscious shade of pink, 'if I could organise that? I've already done some research. Have you come across the Exmoor Drifters' Market?'

Not sure she was hearing what she thought she was hearing, Maddie nodded.

'Well, they are run by a chap called Ivan. He seems very nice. Please don't be cross, I know I should have asked you first, but I wanted to do something to help. I've been to check out his produce and I've arranged another meeting to talk about his market coming here once a month.'

'Ivan Porter?' Maddie's brain caught up with events and a massive smile crossed her face. 'It was *you* he was talking about!'

'Pardon?'

'Ivan – man with a beautiful black Lab called Sheba.'

'How do you know that?'

'On Wednesday night I went for a Dark Skies walk. Ivan was there. I heard him talking to Jo. Jo's the one with an amazing coffee van that's part of the market.'

'The cute orange one?'

'Yes.' Maddie grinned as she saw comprehension dawn on her sister's face. 'On Wednesday Ivan was telling Jo that a garden centre wanted to check the Drifters out. I assumed it was BIG because they said garden centre not nursery, but it must have been you.'

'What was that you were saying about poor communication?' Sabi flicked through the proposal's pages. 'You have some fabulous ideas in here.'

A sharp knock at the door made the sisters sit up straighter as Ed put his head around the door. 'I don't think we can make him wait any longer.'

'It's alright.' Maddie stood up. 'We're ready now.'

Sabi dusted her hands together. 'And we wondered, Ed, as you have done so much work on our behalf, if you'd like to stay after the meeting for a thank you drink.'

40

Leo rested the flat of his palms on the table. Before him, he'd arranged the paperwork ready for signing.

'I think I've been patient enough. You have been offered a good deal of money for this property. And—'

Ed sat down. 'They have, haven't they?'

Leo scowled. 'BIG are not in the habit of undercutting the people they buy land from. Quite the reverse. We like to be generous to ensure a smooth ride – usually.'

'*We?*' Ed challenged. 'Nice of you to remind us of your personal involvement here, Mr Creswell.'

'I meant *we* as in, me representing the company. Please don't try to be clever, Mr Tate.'

Ed held Leo's stare. 'As I said at our last meeting, it came to my attention that BIG *always* intended to tear down The Potting Shed and build over it, despite the original approach to Mrs Willand-Harris being for the nursery to simply stop trading. That was merely a way to ease BIG in.'

'An accusation I did not confirm. You have no proof of that, Mr Tate, and again, I advise you to be careful with your accusations.' Leo tapped his pen against his papers. 'BIG have already spent a considerable sum on surveys of this property and its associated land. If you don't sign, especially after Mrs Willand-Harris made it perfectly clear she had every intention of doing so, I would be forced to advise my employers to sue for breach of promise.'

Sabi was about to protest when Ed held up a hand and turned to Maddie. 'Have you been informed by Mr Creswell of any surveys taking place on your property?'

'No. I have not. Nor have I seen anyone making a survey.'

'Then that was another lie.' Ed folded his arms. 'Or were you saying that the surveyors have been paid, but not actually sent to the site yet?'

'What difference does it make?' Leo blustered, his large palms gathering the papers before him and knocking them into one big pile.

Ed studied his opponent's reactions as he said, 'Mr Creswell, I don't know what assumptions you've made about me, but I should assure you that, just because the ink on my diploma is barely dry compared to yours, I'm not unworldly or easily cowed. The facts are that BIG lied about their intentions in their original contact with Mrs Willand-Harris, they have used personal connections to rush through a planning application, and you claim they have spent money on surveys that haven't happened, in a desperate bid to get the Willand family to let go of their property. It is perhaps not surprising you are pressing so hard for this, considering your own financial investment in the company.' Ed paused as he leant back in his seat. 'Now, while none of this is technically illegal, it *is* highly questionable, but at least I now understand why you so badly want this takeover to work. It was your idea, wasn't it.'

'What if it was?'

'An idea that came at the same time as a vacant position on the board of directors. Securing a site for BIG, just off an existing motorway junction on the main tourist route to Devon and Cornwall, might help you get the position – in fact, you're banking on it.'

'Any plans for my future are nothing to do with you!'

'The information I have is sound. Mr Ronald Lyle is not without connections, and he has used them to find out information on behalf of our clients. Your ambition to join the board of BIG came to light in the course of those investigations.'

Red in the face, Leo blustered, 'I refute the implication that my personal—'

'You can refute as much as you like, Mr Creswell, it is no longer relevant.' Maddie had had enough. 'This meeting is now over. If you wouldn't mind leaving us, Mr Creswell, I'm sure my employee could do with my help outside.'

'Leaving?' The older lawyer's jowls were wobbling in a manner that made Maddie think of a character from Dickens. 'Not until this is signed.'

'We are *not* selling The Potting Shed.' Maddie took her sister's hand as Sabi signalled her agreement.

'Not...' Leo's frown deepened. 'Are you sure your husband would agree to that decision, Mrs Willand-Harris? Shouldn't you speak to him before you throw away the chance to make such a substantial profit?'

'My husband is a good man, Mr Creswell. He does not like underhand behaviour. He also loves me, which makes him both incredible and understanding – in this case, understanding of the fact that this was my father's business, not his.'

'I can't believe he would encourage you to act so foolishly! BIG will *still* build locally. Things have gone too far not to. They'll use the land earmarked for the access road – they'd be on your doorstep. A tin pot place like this will never survive!'

'You underestimate the loyalty of the local shoppers.' Maddie glared at the lawyer.

'You can't be that naive, surely?' Leo countered. 'You don't even have the money to properly decorate your own home, let alone do the work required to get the nursery up to scratch to compete with us. Just look at this place!'

Ed slammed a hand down onto the kitchen table. 'Before you lower yourself once again to the gutter of personal insults, Mr Creswell, I think you'll find it would be in everyone's interests if BIG used a completely different site. In fact,' Ed took some documents from his briefcase and dropped them in front of Leo. 'I've taken the liberty of assisting you. Here is a viable alternative option to present to your employers.'

'I don't think—'

'I, however, *do* think.' Ed's voice oozed authority. 'I think that if I reported your behaviour to the Law Society then you would find yourself with some serious explaining to do. It would not be the first time your name was brought to their attention in connection with self-interest and corner-cutting, would it?'

'Mr Tate,' Leo spoke through gritted teeth, 'Mrs Willand-Harris verbally agreed to sell so—'

'I did no such thing! I agreed to think about it.'

'And I,' Maddie laid a hand on her sister's arm, 'have never agreed to anything.'

Ed pushed the papers closer to Creswell. 'I have saved you some legwork, not because I have any illusions about you seeing me as an ally, but because you are not the sort of man who'd go back to his employers, having failed in his mission, without blaming everyone but himself. I think this family has had quite enough upheaval lately without you making them a scapegoat for your failure.'

'I would never—'

Ed brushed Leo's protest away. 'I have found you a currently unoccupied area, just off a motorway junction, about twenty miles north of here. Close enough to be in the geographical region that BIG wanted, with existing access. You wouldn't have to bribe any farmers as the land is ex-industrial.' He pushed the advantage home. 'Can't you see how forward-thinking you would appear, Mr Creswell, to have this trouble-free site to offer your colleagues – sorry, your *employers*, as a viable, cost-efficient alternative? You never know, it might save your tarnished reputation.'

'How dare you?' Leo picked up his paperwork and threw it into his briefcase. 'My standing with BIG is such that I do not need your help.'

'Help that will save your company thousands in site clearance and perhaps make them overlook the money already wasted on this project?'

Leo swung around to face Maddie and Sabi. 'You are definitely refusing to sign?'

'We are.'

'Well, all I can say is that your behaviour is most unacceptable.' Creswell closed his case with a snap and headed for the door. 'You will be hearing from me. Start saving, ladies, I intend to sue you for wasting my time.'

★

Henry ran into the kitchen, a bunch of holly in one hand, pine needles adorning his jumper. 'I've just seen Creswell marching through the nursery with a face like thunder. What the hell happened?'

Dashing to her husband's side, Sabi threw her arms around him. 'We didn't sign.'

'You didn't?' Henry grinned. 'I knew you'd do the right thing in the end, but what about BIG being next door?'

'I'll explain in a moment. Let's get some fresh air.'

Sabi had ushered her husband out of the door, leaving Maddie and Ed alone.

'You know he has no grounds to sue, don't you?' Ed loosened the knot of his tie.

'He'd be too afraid of you reporting him to the Law Society even if he did.'

'I might do that anyway. I know Ronald would like me to. Leo Creswell is little better than a snake-oil salesman.'

Not knowing where to look, Maddie said, 'You were brilliant. You've done so much for us.'

'I'm sorry I had to lay on the heavy lawyer act. You were right, if Creswell had any idea that I cared for you, then he'd have used it against us if things hadn't worked out so well.'

'Is that why I haven't heard from you all week?' Maddie's murmur was self-conscious.

'And it's why I didn't come on the Dark Skies walk. I needed you to feel distanced from me, so Creswell wouldn't pick up how much I care for you.'

Maddie felt her smile widening. 'Jo said it was because you were a berk.'

'Jo did?' Ed's eyebrows rose. 'Jo never passes comments like that.'

'He wasn't being mean or anything, just thought you worked too hard I think.'

'More likely that he thought I should grab a chance of happiness when it came along.'

Maddie saw the flash in Ed's eyes. 'That's sounds familiar. Sabi has been saying the same to me, but…'

'But?'

'I haven't got anything to offer you but a failing business and a lot of meals based around toast. Plus, it's been so long since I had a serious boyfriend that I can't even remember if I'm a disaster with men or not. And he – Darren – wasn't all he claimed to be. Hurt me. Took me for a fool. The experience made me extra cautious to say the least.'

'Sounds like he was the fool.' Dropping his suit jacket to the back of the chair, Ed came to Maddie's side. 'Well, I don't care what your past was like. You can talk to me about it whenever you like, or you can leave it where it is. I truly don't mind. What's important is that I care about you *now*. And as to having nothing to offer me, if you are referring to material things, I'd hardly have worked to stop you signing your nursery away if I was after your money, would I?'

Embarrassed at her assumptions and mishandling of her emotions, Maddie tried to explain. 'I was scared, that's why I mentioned the professional thing in the first place. Thinking about it now, I suspect it was an excuse to protect myself. It's not just that my last proper boyfriend left me distrustful of potential partners, but I lost my dad, Sabi and I were at odds and this place was in danger. If you and I had got together and then you'd left me too, I think I'd have started doing even crazier things than asking advice from the plants.'

'And puddle splashing?'

'And puddle splashing.'

Ed opened his arms. 'Friendly cuddle?'

Without hesitation, Maddie snuggled into his side, and a long-forgotten sensation of being safe washed over her.

41

'Are you alright, love?' Henry perched next to his wife as she leant against a workbench in the only polytunnel that didn't have customers in it.

Sabi blew out a long breath. 'Dad and Maddie *did* want me. They weren't excluding me.'

'Of course they weren't.' Henry looped an arm around his wife's waist. 'Is that why you've been so private latterly – because you thought your own family were excluding you?'

Sabi nodded as she held him tighter.

'I could have told you that they'd never do that, if you'd shared what your thought was behind all this.'

'It wouldn't have made any difference. I needed to hear it from them. Well, from Maddie now.' She sighed. 'They had no idea I felt left out. I never said because I was ashamed.'

'Ashamed?'

'Of enjoying the easy life we have. Of not having to work – although, I would like to.'

'Even if the likes of Miriam tut as they chink their glasses of Pimm's?'

'They're hypocrites. Miriam has always worked.' Sabi pulled a face. 'I shouldn't be unkind. She *is* a good friend and I know she is worried sick about Petra, but it's one rule

347

for her and one for everyone else. And I'm tired of keeping up. I don't want to play that game anymore.'

Henry kissed the top of his wife's head. 'I'm so proud of you.'

'You are?' Sabi was surprised. 'But I've been such a... I haven't been the easiest person to live with lately.'

'I should have guessed why you were unhappy. Sorry.'

'You've done nothing to be sorry about.' Sabi looked up at her husband as she blurted out, 'I want us to pull out of the house-to-let idea.'

'Seriously?' Henry was amazed. 'While I was helping Jake, I've been mulling over how we might go about organising a loan so you could have your letting business without the sale to BIG.'

'Really?'

'You're my wife. I want you to be happy.' Henry tucked a stray hair behind Sabi's ear. 'You could still have the house in Culmstock.'

'That's lovely, darling, but we'll have bank loans enough for this place to deal with. I'd hate to put us in debt at home too. That isn't the sort of inheritance I want for Jemima.'

Henry smiled, 'My work is good enough for that not to happen, but that isn't what I meant. If you really don't want to do the letting thing anymore, I was suggesting that we sell our place and move to Culmstock. That we *can* afford to do *if* we sell up. And, if we cut down on the expensive lifestyle a bit, we'd be able to afford for you to do it up the way you want to.'

Sabi embraced her husband. 'I don't think I'd spend so much if I was busy. I'm sure the retail therapy was because my brain wasn't occupied.'

'And because you were encouraged by your friends,' Henry added gently.

Sabi laid her head on his shoulder. 'More like coerced. It's high time I led my own life and not the one Miriam and her friends think I ought to be living. Arranging the decor for the new house will keep me busy and so will helping out here.'

Henry was delighted. 'You're going to work here with Maddie?'

'More from home really, I'm going to do the books and organise the farmer's market.'

'The Exmoor Drifters? They said yes to working from The Potting Shed?'

'They are waiting for me to confirm a meeting to discuss options.'

'That's fabulous. You'll do a great job, and you'll be brilliant when it comes to organising the updating of The Potting Shed once you and Maddie have turned this place round. Not to mention redesigning our new home once we've moved in. That notebook of yours is brimming with fabulous ideas.'

'Oh,' Sabi's smile dimmed, 'actually, I threw it away. Having the house when Maddie couldn't have the nursery would have hurt her even more, so...'

'So you let the dream go.' Henry held her close. 'I hooked your notebook out of the recycling and stuck it in your desk drawer.'

'You didn't?!'

'I did.'

Sabi threw her arms back around her husband. 'I love you, Mr. Harris.'

'Just as well, because I love you too.' Henry kissed her before adding, 'I suggest you call Miriam. We're going to need a valuation on our home.'

'I'm ever so sorry, but I must go and help Jake.' Maddie eased herself up from the opposite end of the kitchen table to Ed.

'I totally understand. Could you do with an extra pair of hands?'

'Probably, but after all you've done, I couldn't possibly ask you to help.'

'You didn't ask, I offered.' Ed looked down at his suit. 'I think I'll change first though, or I'll be picking pine needles out of this all week.'

'Surely you don't want to drive all the way home to Exeter, and come back again?'

'No need. I have a change of clothes in the back of the car.'

Her eyebrows rose. 'That's rather convenient.'

'In a pre-planned way, you mean?' Ed laughed. 'Nothing so calculated. I'll leave that sort of behaviour to Leo Creswell.'

Maddie shuddered. 'Ugh. Even the notion!'

Ed retrieved his keys from his jacket pocket. 'I keep a change in the car in case I get caught in a rain burst on the moors.'

'Fair enough.'

Sabi put away her mobile. 'Jemima is delighted.'

Henry wasn't surprised. 'I don't think she'd have wanted us to let this place go. Her childhood memories of this place are still so fresh.'

'Funny, but I feel like that today.' Sabi pointed across to the furthest polytunnels. 'It only seems like yesterday since Maddie and I played hide and seek up there.'

'I can just imagine it.' Henry stroked her hair. 'Both of you in pigtails, stripy jumpers and mud-spattered jeans.'

'Not forgetting the bright yellow wellies,' Sabi laughed. 'That was us.'

'Yellow?'

'Mine had pink flowers on too, while Maddie's had navy dots over the yellow, I think.'

'Purple dots.' Maddie peeped her head around the opening to the polytunnel. 'I loved those wellington boots.'

'You okay, Mads?' Sabi asked nervously. 'I'm sorry I even thought about selling to BIG.'

'I understand why you did. Dad would have as well.' Maddie smiled. 'If it hadn't been handled in such an underhand manner, then perhaps I'd have been tempted to sign in the end too.'

'Really?'

Maddie blew out a puff of air. 'I've no idea actually, but it all stank a bit, didn't it?'

'Just a bit.' Sabi looked over her sister's shoulder. 'No Ed?'

A light flush came to Maddie's cheeks as she motioned towards the house. 'Gone to change into his walking stuff in case he gets muddy.'

'Sensible chap.' Henry, sensing the sisters wanted to be

alone, moved away from the work bench. 'I'll go and check on Jake. He must be desperate for his lunch by now.'

Maddie glanced at her wristwatch. 'It's almost two! I lost all track of time. I bet he's starving. I ought to…'

Henry held up a hand. 'You ought to stay here and talk to Sabi. I'll see how it's going out there. Things were quietening down when I came up earlier.'

'They'll get busy again at three.' Sabi turned to Maddie. 'Well, it always used to at Christmas-tree time.'

'It will. The after-lunch and pre-tea shoppers.'

'Shame we don't have a coffee shop here,' Sabi mused. 'You said in your proposal it was too expensive to consider yet.'

'I did some costings. Going on some info off Google, I discovered it would be a massive expense and we have so much else that needs doing. I thought if I put that on the business plan as an immediate priority the bank's business manager would give me a lecture about not wishing for unicorns.'

'Jemima's always loved unicorns. She would probably tell you to get wishing.'

Maddie dug her hands into her pockets. 'I'm so glad she'll be around more soon. Since Dad died, I've let my trips to school slide.'

'She understands.' Sabi looked about her. 'So, where do we start?'

'We?' Maddie heard the hope in her voice. 'You really will organise the market?'

'If you'll have me, after everything that's happened.'

'Daft woman. Of course I will.'

'In that case.' Sabi fished her phone from her pocket. 'I

ought to make that call to Mr Porter.' She paused. 'Unless you want to, as you know him.'

'Better you do it, that way I'll know he is truly interested in coming to The Potting Shed, rather than because he's a friend of Ed's.'

'When's a good time for me to suggest he comes to visit so he can check the place out?'

'Any time, but the chances of them having a day in their schedule to fit us in before Christmas at this late stage are slim.'

Sabi grinned. 'I'd better use my best persuasive voice then.'

'Oh yeah?' Maddie laughed.

'I learnt it from listening to Miriam talk to clients on the phone. That woman has persuasive skills that would make Machiavelli proud.'

42

Ed crossed to the shop, a tray laden with tea and coffee held out before him. 'Here, I thought you'd be craving caffeine by now.'

Maddie picked up the nearest mug. 'If you were searching for a way to get closer to my heart, you've found it!'

'Is that all it takes? Coffee?'

'It's as easy as that.' Maddie took a tentative sip of the hot liquid. 'Although being a hotshot lawyer and saving my business from the evil clutches of BIG helped.'

Ed passed Maddie a packet of biscuits that had been lodged in his coat pocket. 'And do chocolate digestives swing the balance further in my favour?'

'Oh, they do!' Maddie tugged a biscuit from the proffered packet, before crunching it up quickly. 'Thanks Ed, I was famished.'

'Dinner? Tonight?'

'That would be lovely.' A yawn escaped her. 'Or we could have a takeaway here. I'm shattered, and... Oh, no. We can't.'

'Can't? Or don't want to?' A flash of uncertainty crossed Ed's face.

'Definitely can't. Jake's staying with me at the moment.'

Maddie spoke faster as she twigged what he might have thought she'd been implying by asking Ed to stay. 'I just meant, if we had a takeaway, we'd have to invite him as well. A meal out would be lovely. I'm paying, though. A thank you meal for all you've done.'

'If you insist.' Ed wiggled his phone. 'I'll get a table booked. No point in getting somewhere and finding it full, especially on a Saturday night.'

'Good plan.' Maddie paused. 'Nowhere too fancy, mind. I couldn't face having to worry about what to wear or which fork to use today. Hotshot solicitors probably like silver service when they aren't slumming it with gardeners.'

'Are you teasing me, Miss Willand?'

'Yes.'

Jake wrenched off his gloves as he came into the shop. 'It's been quiet for a while now. Is it okay if I go now, Maddie? I want to tell Petra what's happened.'

'Absolutely. You've been wonderful. I don't know what I'd have done without you. Please thank Petra too. Whatever it was she did to advertise the Christmas trees, it worked. And maybe you could ask her, if she's not too tired, if she'd like to do some more marketing for us soon.'

'Make that very soon.' Sabi appeared around the door. 'Oh, is that tea? May I?'

Ed nodded. 'The mugs at the front of the tray are tea with no sugar. I wasn't sure what people wanted, so I made coffee as well.'

'Perfect.' As she took a chipped mug, Sabi went on. 'I spoke to Ivan. The only free date the market has before

Christmas is next Saturday! They had a cancellation this morning due to a waterlogged site or something. I had to say yes, Mads, but it only gives us a week to get ready.'

'Ivan?' Ed interrupted. 'As in Exmoor Drifters?'

'The very same.' Maddie beamed. 'That is fantastic! Thanks, Sabi!'

'You were lucky!' Ed offered Sabi the packet of biscuits. 'They get snapped up fast. That cancellation wouldn't have remained open for long.'

'That's what Ivan said.' Sabi declined a biscuit as she cradled her tea. 'I only spoke to him a few days ago, and the few spots available then had already gone. The snag is, they want to recce the space here tomorrow, and we don't have time to advertise properly for something in seven days' time – well, almost six days now.'

'Petra can get on it tonight. I'm sure she would. She's bored stiff and her mother is driving her mad. If she had something to do…' Jake's hand flew to his mouth as he registered that he was in the presence of Miriam's friend. 'Oh God, I'm sorry. It's just that Petra's mum doesn't like me. She's giving Petra a bit of a hard time about it.'

'Then it's time I put her right.' Knowing that she was also at fault for seriously misjudging Jake, Sabi added, 'And yes please to the marketing. Petra has already proved how good she is at it. Although don't tell her mother, or she'll be finding her a job in executive marketing instead of pressuring her to be a lawyer!'

Maddie laughed. 'We'll send Petra all the details as soon as we have them. Thanks, Jake. You get off now. Give her our love, won't you?'

'I will if I can get past her parents!'

*

'Basically, it's going to be all hands on deck if we are to be ready for next weekend.'

Maddie closed the gates to the car park's entrance with a sense of relief and hope, as Sabi, Henry and Ed stood by their cars.

'Well, I can't wait until tomorrow!' Sabi beamed. 'I've not felt this energised in ages. Have you seen the posh cheeses Ivan sells? My mouth waters every time I think about them. All organic, of course. And the pastries that come from the coffee van look to die for.'

'They are,' Ed confirmed. 'Jo's van is a haven of deliciousness.'

Sabi was thoughtful for a moment, 'You know Mads, that could be the answer to the café issue.'

'Café issue?' Henry and Ed exchanged glances.

'Well, if BIG do end up on our doorstep – or even if they're twenty miles away – they'll still be our nearest competition, and they'll have an-all singing, all-dancing, coffee shop. I'd like us to be able to offer some refreshments, even if it's just a takeaway machine. But if we had a boutique van like Jo's, that would be so much better.'

'Or even Jo's van itself.' Maddie turned to Ed. 'Does Jo have a regular weekend space to sell from?'

'I don't know, but I wouldn't get your hopes up on that front. I've always got the impression that Jo doesn't like to be tied to long-term commitments.'

'Let's worry about that another time.' Maddie was desperate to kick off her boots and take a shower.

'Good idea, Jo is...' The ring of Ed's mobile broke through their conversation. 'Oh, sorry, I'd better take this.'

As Ed moved away to answer his call, Maddie embraced her sister. 'I'll see you here again tomorrow. What time is Ivan due?'

'Ten o'clock.' Sabi glanced back towards the main body of the nursery. 'Are you sure you don't want us to stay and help you tidy up?'

'I'll be fine, there's not much to do beyond cashing up.'

'In that case,' Sabi opened her car door, 'I'll get home and give Miriam a call.'

'To check on Petra and tell her that you're withdrawing from the house sale?'

'Oh, what with everything else, I never did get back to telling you!' Sabi hooked her bag higher up her shoulder. 'We're selling up. I want Miriam to arrange a valuation for the house. She should give us a good deal selling it via Executive Homes seeing as we are buying from them too.'

'You'll get to live in your doll's house home after all!' Maddie was delighted. 'That's fantastic. I was feeling awful about you missing out on the house you've always wanted.'

'We'll celebrate with a *huge* house-warming when the time comes. In the meantime, you two have a *lovely* evening.'

'No need to say it like that.' Maddie blushed. 'We're only going for dinner. It's not a date.'

'Well, make sure you wear something nice anyway. Men like an effort made for them sometimes, you know.' She looked her sister up and down. 'Maybe some makeup.'

Maddie couldn't help but laugh as Sabi started the engine and drove away. 'Good to know you haven't completely changed, Sabi.'

*

'All week? Are you sure?' Maddie took a mouthful of steak, savouring the subtle flavours of the meat as she chewed.

'Ronald has agreed. That was the call I took while you said goodbye to Sabi and Henry. So, if you want me to, I'd love to help you get ready for Saturday.'

'But you could have a proper holiday. If you come here, you'll spend your days with a broom in your hand or hauling potato sacks about.'

'In your company.'

Maddie smiled. 'And Sabi and Jake's company.'

'Two good people.' Ed picked up a chunky chip. 'Shame Jake is staying at your place.'

'I can hardly chuck him out,' Maddie faltered.

Ed suddenly looked serious, and blurted out, 'I fancy you something rotten, Madeline Willand.'

Spearing a piece of mushroom with her fork, Maddie felt her pulse rate accelerate. 'You do?'

'You know I do.' Ed suddenly looked awkward. 'Sorry, that isn't how I was going to state the obvious, but I couldn't wait any longer. I just had to say it.'

Maddie met Ed's gaze. 'I hoped you did – but it's been a bit mixed signals from both of us and, well, there's still so much going on. I don't even know if this is a date.'

'It isn't. It's an almost date between two good friends.' Ed leaned forward as he added, 'I should warn you, however, I am going to ask you out on a proper date – one of many – after the market.'

'Is that so?' A rush of pleasure ran through Maddie as she laughed. 'Let's see if you still want to once you've spent a whole week seeing me in grungy work clothes and smelling slightly of compost.'

43

'One Portaloo should do it.' Sabi passed an email address she'd written on a piece of paper to Maddie. 'These guys are the most reasonable, and they deliver and collect. I called them earlier. They are just awaiting an email to confirm and then they'll deliver here on Friday.'

Impressed, and a little overwhelmed by how much her sister had done after just two days on site, Maddie started to write the confirmation email. 'We could put the loo at the far side of the car park. Downwind.'

'They'll need a flat surface.'

'Good point.' Maddie heard a crash from outside the shop. 'Sounds like the tables are fighting back.'

Sticking their heads outside, Maddie saw Jake and Ed manhandling a trestle table off a van. Ivan, with Sheba at his feet, was sliding another one out of the vehicle's open back doors.

As soon as the dog saw Maddie she was on her feet.

'Go on then girl, go say hello to your new best friends.' Ivan smiled as Sheba trotted to Maddie.

'I see you are helping the chaps, Sheba.' Maddie ruffled the fur on the Labrador's head. 'I bet you wouldn't drop a table though, would you?'

Sabi joined in. 'Isn't she gorgeous. I miss having a dog about.'

'Me too.' Maddie kept a hand on Sheba, taking comfort in her calm presence. 'How long's it been since we lost Benji?'

Sabi blew out her cheeks as she thought. 'Must be fifteen years. I always wondered why Dad didn't get another dog.'

'He was devastated by his loss. I got the impression he'd have felt as if he was betraying Benji's memory if he replaced him.'

Sabi gave a rueful smile. 'I think of him whenever I see a Border Collie. Best herding dog in the business, Dad said.'

Maddie laughed. 'Except Benji couldn't have herded a snail, he was so daft, bless him.'

'Loyal though.' Sabi let out a long sigh.

'Are you okay?'

'I wasn't here much in the end, was I? Maybe if I'd visited The Potting Shed more, helped out, then maybe Dad wouldn't have been so stressed and perhaps...'

'No.' Maddie shook her head. 'The doctors all said the same thing. Dad was a heart attack waiting to happen. It was nothing to do with what we did or didn't do and everything to do with angina. Dad knew he had it for over a year and didn't tell us. Didn't want to worry us about something we could do nothing about and—'

'He "didn't want to stop living his life because of some stupid heart thing".' Sabi brushed away a tear from the corner of her eyes as she quoted their father. They'd been the last words she'd heard him speak.

Sheba nudged Sabi with her nose.

Maddie smiled. 'She knows you need a cuddle. Go on, Ivan won't mind.'

Swallowing down the lump that had formed in her throat, Sabi knelt and threw her arms around Sheba's sleek black frame.

Leaving her sister to gather herself, Maddie joined Ivan. 'Thanks for bringing her along. Canine therapy was just the thing this morning.'

'Never go anywhere without her.' Ivan lifted the final table from the van. 'She'll be here on Saturday.'

Maddie ran a hand along the edge of the trestle table. 'How long does it take, roughly, to set everything up on the day?'

'About two hours. I've told the stallholders to be here by seven. As I explained when I was here on Sunday, each seller has their own gazebo or cover, and everyone deals with their own public liability insurance. Once the covers are set up, they'll collect one or two of the tables the lads are stacking up.'

'Jake and I will be here to help with that too.'

'Thanks.' Ivan smiled. 'While we're all capable of collecting our own tables, time can run away, and extra hands are always appreciated. And we all help Elspeth with setting up. She is cracking on a bit, and I don't fancy her keeling over on us while dragging a table into place.'

'What does Elspeth sell?' Maddie was trying hard to remember all the names and goods Sabi had reeled off to her in an overexcited planning rush.

'Beeswax candles, soaps and so on. Makes them herself. Very popular.'

'I'm sure.' Maddie was already picturing Sabi buying up

Elspeth's entire stock to kit out her new home. 'And you're sure this space is going to be big enough?'

Ivan grinned. 'Everyone always asks that, but yes, I promise I've got my measurements right. There will be twenty stalls, in two rows of ten at either side of the nursery, with Jo's coffee van parked near the shop.'

'Thank you.' Maddie felt nervous. 'I just hope we can do you proud at such short notice.'

'We've put the event on our website, and Jake's lass... what's her name again?'

'Petra.'

'That's it. She's been blitzing social media. I've seen all the stuff she's tagged us into. There is no reason why it won't work.'

'She's done a heap of posters too.' Sabi and Sheba joined them by the van. 'Henry has been nipping out at lunchtimes to share them with the local shops, and we've told everyone we know.'

'Sounds good.' Ivan closed the van doors as Ed and Jake headed back across the car park. 'I'll leave you guys to get on. See you Saturday.'

Ed supported the last table against his leg as they waved Ivan off. 'I had no idea these brutes were so heavy. And they bite!'

Jake grinned. 'He keeps trapping his fingers between the fold of the legs and the underside of the table when we put them down.'

'Why put your hand in that spot, then?' Maddie tried not to laugh.

'It's the only way I can get a good purchase.' Ed sucked his fingers. 'Seems life in a solicitor's office has softened me up.'

'It's all those sneaky hot chocolates, they've slowed you down.' Maddie gave him a playful shove before forcing herself to be practical. 'Sabi, you and Henry have done a fabulous job alerting the wealthier parts of the area to the market, but with the best will in the world, they aren't going to be The Potting Shed's future regulars. They're far more likely to only visit us if there's a market, and then go online for everything else. Even if we do well enough for Ivan to agree to come back, it's the local community we need to attract. The ordinary people.'

'Are you saying my friends aren't ordinary?'

'You know what I mean, Sab.'

Sabi conceded the point. 'You're saying we need to think in terms of reeling in more of the local community.'

'Any ideas, anyone?' Maddie looked around. 'What will bring in people who'll assume they can't afford anything from the market?'

'Lots of people will come to look and not buy.' Ed massaged the blisters forming on his palms. 'Will the extra Christmas trees be here to sell by Saturday?'

'They should arrive this afternoon.' Maddie turned to Jake. 'Will you be okay running the show on that front again?'

'Yes boss.' Jake dipped his head in the direction of a car that had pulled into the nursery. 'Talking of which, they have a roof rack on, so they probably want a tree. I'll go see.'

Maddie watched him go. 'The change in that boy is remarkable since Petra came along. She told him she believed in him. Sometimes, that's all it takes.'

*

'What's the back polytunnel used for these days?'

'Storage mostly.' Maddie took the toasted sandwich from Sabi. 'Why?'

'Just thinking ahead.' Sabi stepped back, so that Maddie could sell some winter vegetables to a customer who was waxing lyrical about the healthy state of the coriander plant in her hands.

'Perhaps you should expand your herb range?' Sabi suggested once they were alone again. 'You were always good at growing them.'

'I could, but not in the back tunnel. They need more light.'

Sabi mused, 'Would we need a new tunnel then, or a greenhouse? Or could we rearrange what's in the existing tunnels?'

'A smallish greenhouse would work best for herbs.' Maddie pictured the layout of The Potting Shed in her head. 'But it's not a goer yet. Not until we've done up what we've got.'

'Thinking ahead, that's all.' Sabi peered out through the open door. 'Where's Ed?'

'Gone home to tend his blisters.'

'I thought he was staying the week?'

'He's not a hostage, Sab. This is his holiday after all.'

Sabi tilted her head on one side as she asked, 'Has he been staying over?'

'He isn't my boyfriend, Sabi.'

'Well, it's high time he was!'

44

'I've spoken to Petra about doing the social media bit and Jake has been detailed to drop a poster off at every school in Wellington. I'll do the same around Tiverton. Hopefully, it's not too late.'

'And hopefully Maddie will be too busy to look at her computer tonight.' Balancing an umbrella over his head, Henry opened the doors of the shed, indicating for Ed to step back as he did so. 'I haven't been in here for years. The whole lot could fall out.'

Standing in Henry and Sabi's garden, Ed weighed a hammer in one hand and a bag of nails in the other. 'Are you sure about this? The market is tomorrow.'

'Maddie wanted another draw to bring people in, and what better than this?'

Ed couldn't argue. 'Shouldn't we tell Maddie though?'

'Sabi thought it would be a nice surprise.'

'I'm sure it would be, but how are we going to get everything ready without her seeing?'

'Oh, that's easy.' Henry removed several large planks of wood from the shed. 'You're going to take Maddie out tonight.'

'Tonight?' Ed checked his watch. 'It's almost five. She'll

be shattered and wanting nothing more than a bath and to sit and worry about tomorrow. Or she'll be pacing the nursery all evening, tweaking the Christmas decorations and splashing on even more emergency coats of paint wherever she can while praying that it stops raining overnight.'

'Well, we can't fix the weather, but the place is as ready as it can be. The Portaloo is here, the market folk are primed and ready and the advertising has been done. She needs to rest.'

'I know that, but convincing Maddie to leave The Potting Shed this evening won't be easy. Anyway, won't you need my help?' Ed gestured to the growing pile of wood by Henry's feet. 'And what about the rest of it? This isn't just a building job.'

'Jake and Petra are on it. Sabi's doing a bulk shop right now.' Henry patted his friend's shoulder and gave him a knowing look. 'I'm sure you can think of a way to keep Maddie occupied.'

'Maddie and me, it's not like that.'

'Well, it jolly well ought to be.' Henry passed Ed a wide sheet of plywood. 'It's obvious you two like each other, now do something about it before some burly garden enthusiast comes into the nursery and sweeps her off her feet.'

'Are you insane? There's so much to do!'

'No there isn't.' Ed leant against the open back door. 'If you stay here this evening, all you'll do is fret. You need to get away for a little while.'

'Away? The market is tomorrow.'

'Only for a couple of hours.' Ed picked up Maddie's

stripy wellies from the rack by his feet. 'Come on. It's been raining all day. That means puddles. You promised me a welly walk.'

'Ed, I *can't*.' Maddie gestured through the door to the nursery beyond. 'I ought to—'

'You ought to look after yourself this evening, so you aren't too burnt out to enjoy tomorrow.' Ed collected her waterproof coat from the hook by the door. 'Petra and Sabi are doing a last-minute social media promotion and everyone we know has promised to come if they can. The Drifters have been advertising the event as well. It *will* work, and goodness knows there isn't an inch of wood anywhere that hasn't been attacked by your paintbrush this week. The nursery has been tidied and swept to within an inch of its life. But you, Maddie, need a rest. And as there is no way I'd get you to sit still if we stayed here, then I prescribe some puddle therapy.'

'I can't believe you bought brand new wellingtons for this!'

Ed took a large carrier bag from his car boot. 'I only had boring ones. I didn't want to do this half-heartedly.'

Maddie couldn't help but laugh when she saw them. Black, their rubber sides were dotted all over with small white stars. 'You've got stargazer boots!'

'Great, aren't they.' Ed gave a few practise stamps against the gravelled path. 'I'm in your hands.'

Holding her torch out, ready to puddle spot as they walked around the border of the Killerton estate, Maddie breathed deeply. The air, damp and fresh, felt comfortingly familiar, and the guilt she felt about leaving

The Potting Shed for a few hours began to fade. 'This way. The ground is flat but has heaps of potholes. Perfect for puddling.'

'I've never heard anyone so pleased about the presence of potholes before.'

'What can I say? I'm unusual.'

Following Maddie, Ed let his eyes adjust to the gloom of the evening. The earlier heavy rain had diminished to a light drizzle, which pattered against their raincoats as they progressed along a hedge-lined lane. 'You're so lucky to have worked here.'

'It looks better in daylight. The gardens themselves are stunning. I loved working here,' Maddie smiled, 'although I love The Potting Shed too. Shame Dan can't come tomorrow, he's working. He was my boss here. Lovely guy. Something of a mentor.'

'Like Ronald is to me. He's taught me so much.'

Maddie's torch lit up a string of haphazardly shaped puddles. 'Ah, but has he showed you how much fun it is to jump into a puddle?'

'A subject sadly lacking in the law syllabus.'

Maddie grinned as she pointed to the nearest puddle. 'After you.'

'I don't think I've ever eaten out so often.' Maddie ripped a naan bread in half.

'I was starving. You never said puddle jumping would be such hard work.'

Maddie chuckled. 'It's not, unless you go at it as if you're doing a full body splash.'

'I was getting into the spirit of the thing.' Ed wiped at his cheek in case it was still spotted with puddle water.

'You enjoyed it then.'

'Loved it. So freeing.'

'And you didn't feel silly leaping into muddy water like a toddler?'

Ed took a mouthful of mineral water. 'No one to feel silly in front of.'

'Ah, so does that mean I'll only be able to go puddling with you when it's dark?'

'Possibly.' Ed laughed as he leant forward. 'So, are you alright? Are you okay with how it's working out at The Potting Shed?'

Maddie laid down her fork. 'On the whole, yes. I won't pretend I'm not scared stiff about it all going wrong, though. If BIG still build on the doorstep life won't be easy. The amount we've had to borrow from the bank is frightening. And that's just the beginning.'

'The market tomorrow will help. I hear Sabi's already charmed Ivan into coming back in the New Year.'

'Umm…' Maddie broke off some poppadom and nibbled the edge. '… I just hope the novelty doesn't wear off for Sabi. Does that sound unkind?'

'No, it sounds human.'

'The market, even if we have a second one, won't be enough on its own. Jem came up with a sandpit idea for children. I wondered about a small play park.'

'An excellent idea. Although you'd have to check the insurance involved with that.'

Maddie wrinkled her nose. 'Always something, isn't there?'

'Yep, but don't worry, I know a lawyer who'll help you sort all the red tape out at a very reasonable rate.'

As Ed drove into The Potting Shed car park, he said, 'I've just thought of something else you could do. You should start a club. The Puddle Splashers.'

Maddie burst out laughing. 'Come off it!'

'I'm serious. Tonight was so much fun. Therapeutic.'

'It was,' Maddie conceded. 'I do feel an awful lot better for my rainwater stomp, but a club is impractical. It's not like I can guarantee puddles. It could only ever be seasonal and very weather dependent.'

'Like Dark Skies. Only feasible in late autumn and winter when it's dry, unless you want to stay up all night or freeze to death.'

'I hadn't thought of that.' Maddie got out of the car. 'Are you coming in for a cuppa or are you off for your beauty sleep?'

'I'll walk you to the door, then I'll be off. It's almost eleven.'

'Do you turn into a pumpkin at midnight?'

'How did you know?' Ed grinned. 'I've had a lovely evening. And not just because I splashed in some puddles.'

'But that helped, I'm sure.' Maddie suddenly felt shy. They'd had a lovely, relaxed time together, something that she'd never have dreamt possible when she was dashing around earlier, veering between worrying about having enough float money for the till, and then convincing herself she had way too much, and was kidding herself, because no one would come anyway.

Ed took a step closer. 'The company, that's what helped.'

His breath tickled Maddie's shoulder as he reached his arms around her. Inhaling the scent of his thick jumper, she linked her arms and sank into his embrace with a heavy sigh.

Keeping hold of Maddie, Ed leant back so he could see her face, his expression full of concern. 'That was a hell of a sigh.'

Maddie rested her head on his shoulder. 'I was just thinking what an idiot I've been.'

'How so?'

'You offered me a hug on our first walk together. I should have said yes.'

Stroking her hair, Ed whispered, 'We certainly have made a meal of things.'

'Several meals actually,' Maddie chuckled, 'of the takeaway, pub and restaurant variety.'

'I enjoyed them all.'

'Perhaps...' Maddie's pulse thumped in her ears as she hesitantly ventured, '... perhaps you shouldn't wait until after the market to ask me out?'

'You mean it?' Ed felt Maddie as she snuggled against him. She was so strong and yet so vulnerable. He had an urge to tell her he never wanted to let her go. His mouth opened to say the words, when, out of the corner of his eye, he spotted Henry's car tucked into the far corner.

'It's obvious we're supposed to be together and...' Maddie abruptly freed herself from his arms. 'Can you smell fresh paint?'

Thinking fast, Ed said, 'Sure. I don't think there's anything you haven't refreshed since Ivan agreed to run the market from here.'

'I suppose I'd just got used to the smell.' Maddie's voice took on a concerned edge. 'You don't think it'll put people off buying food if they can smell paint, do you?'

'No, and anyway, that's another ten hours away.' Putting his hands on her shoulders, Ed gently marched Maddie to the back door.

'I wish you could stay over.' Maddie cuddled back into his arms.

'As much as I'd like to stay – and believe me, I really want to – you need some sleep, and so do I.'

As Ed stood back, Maddie smiled up at him. 'Thanks for a lovely evening.'

'My pleasure.' He stared into her eyes, his voice husky as he muttered, 'Tomorrow's going to be a big day.'

'No, it's not going to be a *big* day,' Maddie's eyes twinkled, 'it's going to be a Potting Shed day!'

Ed laughed. 'The first of many. I'll see you in the morning.'

'See you in the morning.'

Maddie had her key in the door and Ed had taken three paces back to his car, when he ran back. 'I am going home, really I am. I just wondered… before I go…'

'If you could ask me out now?' Maddie placed her hands on his chest, her heartbeat accelerating as he nodded, his expression intent, his eyes wide.

'Yes.' Ed's arms were around Maddie, his nose less than a centimetre from hers when a loud crash, followed by a line of expletives, crossed the still night air.

'Oh my God!' Maddie spun out of Ed's gentle hold. 'What the hell was that?'

45

'It came from the back of the tunnels.' Panic filled Maddie as she raced across the nursery. A few seconds later she came to an abrupt halt, her heart drumming in her chest for a rather different reason than it had been a moment before. 'Henry!'

As Ed arrived behind her, Maddie took in the scene. A pile of wood lay by the entrance to the furthest polytunnel to the house. A hammer lay next to it, and, judging by the way that Henry was hopping about she guessed he'd just dropped it on his right foot.

'What's going on?' Maddie looked from Ed to Henry and back again, just as her sister and niece, their arms full of wrapped presents, emerged from the nearest tunnel. 'Sabi? Jem?'

Ed picked up the hammer, 'Sorry Henry, it was getting late, I couldn't keep Maddie distracted any longer. I thought you'd be done by now.'

Maddie froze to the spot. 'Keep me distracted?'

Seeing the distress that flashed across her sister's face, Sabi rushed forwards. 'Not like that! We wanted this to be a surprise.'

'It's a Santa's grotto!' Jem held up a handful of

parcels as she stifled a yawn. 'Perfect way to get people to visit so close to Christmas, don't you think, Aunt Maddie?'

Maddie gave her niece a thumbs up, managing to squeak, 'It's a fabulous idea' before spinning around to face Ed. She could hear how brittle her voice was as she said, 'I'll walk you to your car.'

As she marched along, Maddie could feel where Ed's hands had been around her. It had been so good. So right. *It wasn't real. Ed might not have stolen from me, but he is just another deceiver.*

'You took me out so they could surprise me? All of that, the welly walk, the food, the hugs, that was just you distracting me from them.'

Was he really going to ask me out after the market – or was that part of the set up too?

'No!' Ed reached out a hand, but Maddie stepped out of reach. 'Well, partly. But I wanted to be with you.'

Maddie crossed her arms, tugging her jacket around herself. 'It's late. I need to help my family finish up, or we'll never get any sleep tonight.'

'I'll help too.'

'No Ed. You'll leave.' Maddie forced herself to look at him. 'Thank you for all you've done, but your work here is finished. I'll settle the legal bill as soon as you send it through. No need to come tomorrow.'

There were tears in her eyes as she ran back to the part-constructed Santa's Grotto, leaving Ed rooted to the spot behind her.

*

By the time Maddie got back to the polytunnel, the pile of excess wood had been cleared away.

Henry dropped some excess nails into a bag. 'Ed didn't take you out because we forced him to.'

Maddie shrugged. 'Doesn't matter.'

'You didn't need to send him away.' Sabi gestured anxiously towards the tunnel's door. 'Do you want to see what we've done?'

Stepping inside, not allowing herself to consider the sense of loss that was filling her from the toes upwards, Maddie gasped. The far end of the arched space had been transformed. Alternate pieces of wood were lined up to form a fence, behind which an old rocking chair sat, covered in throws and cushions. The chair was sat on a thick green rug, which was also dotted with pillows and cushions.

'I can't believe this. It's amazing.' Maddie put her hand out to Jem, who scuttled to her side. 'I love the chimney.'

Behind the rocking chair, a sheet of wood had been put in place, with a chimney and fireplace painted on it.

'Mum wanted to bring in a real fire or a woodburner, but Dad didn't think you would want the bother of the health and safety forms.'

'He was spot on about that.' Smiling despite herself, Maddie noticed three large sacks, each sewn out of large sheets of red felt and bulging at the seams. 'Did you sew those, Sab?'

'Yup.' Sabi knelt down to retrieve a roll of sticky tape and some wrapping paper. 'I had the felt leftover from that time I did the Christmas decor at Jemima's school.'

'I love them. Thank you.' Maddie ran a hand over the soft red fabric. 'What's inside?'

'Colouring books, jigsaw, crayons. That sort of thing.'

'Perfect.' Maddie began to take in the small details that made up the scene. Sabi had added fake snow around the edges of the fireplace, and the path from the door to Santa's rocking chair had been marked with two rows of screwed-up white crepe paper, which, if you didn't peer too closely, looked like snowballs. The space between the door and the grotto was filled with spaced-out chairs for waiting parents, and an ancient-looking CD player sat on a small table, with a collection of Christmas music ready to be played next to it.

Maddie embraced her niece. 'Thank you. All of you... but, umm... I don't want to sound ungrateful... but...'

Sabi interrupted, 'If you are wondering how people will know it's here, Petra and I have been blitzing social media, and Jake and Henry have sent posters to all the primary and nursery schools.'

'You have? When? We've all been so busy this week.'

'Last night and today.' Sabi lifted a sign up from a pile of posters next to her. 'And we'll put these up tomorrow. We thought three pounds per child.'

'That's fabulous.' Maddie bent to help Henry as he picked up a stray piece of wood. 'But that wasn't what I was going to ask. We have a Santa's Grotto, but no Santa!'

'Of course we have a Santa!' Jemima laughed. 'Dad's gonna do it. He's borrowed a costume from a friend and everything.'

Maddie groaned as her alarm went off in her ear. It was five o'clock in the morning.

Slamming a hand against her clock, she muted the incessant beeping. It had been almost one before she'd got into bed. Maddie was surprised she'd slept at all, assuming she'd lie wakeful, worrying about the day ahead and thinking about Ed.

Sabi had told her at least six times last night, as they'd tidied up the polytunnel, that Ed hadn't taken her out as a favour to Henry, and that she should stop being paranoid. In return Maddie had repeatedly said she didn't want to talk about it.

Finally agreeing to drop the subject, Sabi had accompanied Maddie to the shop, after they'd had a mutual last-minute panic that the nursery itself was looking decidedly un-festive.

By the time they'd left it, the shop smelt like Christmas. Packets of star-shaped ginger biscuits lay next to a basket of cinnamon sticks. Next to these, a trug of locally made Christmas puddings — which Maddie hadn't realised Petra had ordered — waited for their big moment on the festive dinner table. On the opposite side of the shop, an old fire bucket was filled with logs, around which Jake had placed small sacks of firewood to buy.

Mini olive trees, resplendent in silver and gold terracotta pots, lined the far wall, beneath the seed racks – all of which had been restocked – the lowest rung dedicated to seeds for children. A string had been hung across the ceiling, on which were draped individually designed Christmas cards showing every festive scene imaginable, from jolly snowmen to biblical nativities.

'All that's missing are wreaths and garlands.' Sabi linked arms with her sister. 'And I flatly refused to let Petra order any of those. I'd have made some if I had time, but sadly…'

Maddie laughed. 'If you'd managed to knock up some wreaths and garlands as well as a grotto, and sort the market, I'd have started to think some sort of magic was at work here.'

'Well,' Sabi grinned, 'I've never been averse to a Christmas miracle.'

'It might take a miracle to make our money back on this, Sab. I hadn't realised you and Petra had ordered in so much stock.' Maddie rearranged a coil of tinsel that had escaped from its basket by the door.

'It might, or it might be fine.'

With the memory of her sister's optimism echoing in her ears, Maddie decided to head straight to the shop once she was up, in the hope that the festive atmosphere they'd created would bolster her mood for the day ahead.

Opening her curtains, she offered up muttered thanks. The rain had stopped, and a weak sun was highlighting a light frost that hung across the nursery. Maddie shuddered at the drop in the external temperature, wrapping her arms around her pyjamaed chest, and couldn't help but admire the glisten of silver that tipped the Christmas trees and the gravelled paths.

'I suppose Sabi might be right about Ed. He did buy new wellingtons so we could puddle splash. He could have just taken me to the pub or suggested a regular walk if he was just trying to keep me away from this place.'

'Exactly.' The fern on the windowsill ruffled its leaves. 'You shouldn't have told him he couldn't come today. You know how badly you overreacted, don't you?'

Not bothering to reply, knowing she'd made a mistake in a rash of unthinking humiliated fatigue, Maddie forced herself out of bed and ran to the shower. 'Thank goodness I'll be too busy today to think about anything other than this place. Tomorrow I'll wallow in pity over my self-sabotaged love life.'

'Busy or not, you'll miss seeing him around.'

Maddie glared at her houseplant. 'Comments like that are not helpful.'

By eleven o'clock Maddie felt as if she'd walked a hundred miles. As well as making sure Jake was all right selling the trees, she'd circled the nursery, answering questions, and wishing people a Merry Christmas. She'd also visited each market stall a couple of times, checking everyone was happy. In most cases, it took more strength than she had not to buy things, and Maddie had purchased almost all her Christmas presents before ten-thirty.

'Going well, isn't it?' Jo waved in Maddie's direction while restocking some sugar sachets into one of the painted flowerpots on their tables.

'I'm bowled over.' Maddie stood back as a family of four came up to the van. Two young girls, about five and seven years old, held each other's hands as their parents ordered hot chocolates and some chocolate slab cake. Only once they were settled at a little table, the children delighting at the orange-ness of the van, did Maddie go back up to Jo. 'I'd kill for a coffee.'

'Coming right up. Here or takeaway?'

Maddie looked wistfully at the only unoccupied table. 'As much as I'd love to sit and watch the world go by, I'd better have a takeout.'

'No problem.' Jo tugged a biodegradable cup off a stack next to the till.

'How much?'

'On the house.'

'No. This is your livelihood, Jo.'

'And this is yours.' Jo gestured to the steady stream of people meandering along the market stalls and pottering in and out of the polytunnels. 'And I insist.'

'Thank you.' Maddie accepted her coffee meekly.

'You coming to Dark Skies on Wednesday?' Jo opened the top of the coffee machine and poured in some fresh coffee beans.

'I'm not sure.' Maddie held the cup close to her chest.

'Where is Ed anyway?' Jo looked about. 'I was sure he'd be here having seen off that Creswell toad.'

Maddie couldn't contain her surprise. 'You know about that?'

Jo nodded, their expression as calm as ever. 'No need to worry. Confidences have not been broken. I was one of the contacts Ed used to find out what was going on with BIG.' Jo whispered, as if ashamed, 'Don't tell anyone, but I used to work for the council.'

Maddie chuckled, 'You make that sound like drug smuggling.'

Jo made a face. 'Felt like it too.' He tapped the side of his van affectionately. 'We are better off like this, aren't we old gal.'

Knowing there was a story to be told there but remembering how both Ivan and Ed had suggested that Jo was a private person, Maddie said, 'I'd best get on. I want to check on the grotto. Actually, could you do me a couple of cups of tea and a smoothie?'

'For the family?'

'Yes, they're on elf and…' Maddie lowered her voice so the children dipping chocolate slab into their hot chocolate couldn't hear, '…Father Christmas duty.'

Jo grabbed a premade kiwi and mango drink from a mini chiller cabinet. 'Jem was very specific about which of my drinks she wanted to try when she helped me set up earlier.'

Maddie grinned. 'She is more like her mother than she'd care to know.'

'Back again, dear?' Elspeth adjusted the thick handwoven rug that she'd draped over her lap to keep the frost-tinted air at bay.

'I can't keep away.' Maddie cast her eye over the rows of beautifully displayed beeswax candles, bars of soap and pots of lip balm and hand cream. 'You have such an eye for detail, Elspeth.'

Every pot, made from glass the colour of deep purple moor-heather, had a pewter coloured screw cap, on which Elspeth had stuck her own label – *Bee Lucky*. The candles, bound in groups of two or three with purple ribbons, were lined up on sheets of matching purple satin. The whole effect was stunning – and somewhat regal – as if Elspeth was the queen bee proudly selling the efforts of her drones' labours.

'What's this?' Maddie picked up a pleasingly weighty pot.

'Ah, now that's a bit special. I only do those for Christmas as it takes so long to produce. It's Sugar Wax.'

Maddie, who'd already purchased several beeswax candles for Sabi for Christmas, and a pile of soaps to replace the coal tar bars her father had preferred, confessed, 'I'm none the wiser.'

'The best skin cleanser and exfoliator in the world, combined into one vessel.' Elspeth retrieved a pot from a box beneath the table and unscrewed the lid. 'And it smells heavenly.'

Leaning forward, Maddie found herself examining a thick crystallised lotion, the consistency of a whipped mousse, which smelt of expensive honeyed caramel. 'Wow, that is gorgeous.'

'You scoop up enough to cover two fingers, dampen it a little, and then smear it over your skin – arms, legs, belly, anywhere you like. It feels a bit weird – like rubbing sugar over your body. Then you simply shower it straight off again. I promise, your skin will be left glowing, as if it's had an expensive spa treatment. It'll be smooth, light and totally refreshed. Perfect to use before a hot date.'

Immediately thinking of her recent sabotaging of potentially hot dates, Maddie gave a fake smile which she hoped was convincing. 'You are quite the saleswoman, Elspeth.'

'It's the best bit of the job.' The old lady gestured to the flow of customers wandering around the market and the nursery. 'Talking to people, meeting new customers, greeting returning customers.'

'You've certainly had a lot of people visit you today.'

'Over half are folk who've used my stuff before. They saw I was coming here on my website and have popped by for refills.'

Maddie was impressed. 'You have a website?'

'Of course, dear, this is my livelihood.' She winked. 'Plus, once you've tried my hand cream, no other will do.'

'Now, that I can believe.' Maddie looked at the discreetly placed price sticker on the base of the Sugar Wax and carefully placed the pot down. 'Sadly, I'm going to have to pass on this though, gorgeous as it sounds.'

Elspeth smiled in understanding. 'That's why I don't make many. It's not cheap to make and takes time to prepare properly in the correct sterile conditions. I have to sell them at a premium price, as you can see from the price tag, and even then, there's no profit in it.'

On hearing the word 'profit', the optimism she'd begun to feel about the nursery's future stalled. What if this doesn't work? What if none of these people come back after today? BIG could still build over the road.

'You okay, dear?' Elspeth looked concerned. 'I can put a jar aside for you until you've saved up if you like.'

'Bless you, but no, I'm fine. I will save up and get one though. You can bank on that.'

'Just you let me know, and I'll make you one specially. And… oh… Daniel!' Elspeth broke off, pushed the rug from her legs and stood up, both hands already stretching across the stall. 'It's been ages.'

'Dan!' Maddie's forehead creased in a moment of confusion, 'You know Elspeth?'

'I do indeed. I used to keep bees back in the day. Kept this ole gal supplied in wax for years.' Dan took the stallholder's hands and kissed them. 'How are you, lass?'

'Just dandy, Daniel. You?'

'Struggling along since I lost my best gardener to this place. But looking around me I can see it was a good move for her.'

'I thought you were working today?' Maddie felt a brush of fur against her leg and looked down, 'Oh, hello Midge.'

'Making his presence felt, is he? Typical.' Leaning down, Dan ruffled the top of his Collie's head. 'I swapped my shift. One of the perks of being the boss. Total power!'

Maddie grinned. 'I'm glad you came.'

'Me too. I've already had a mooch. Excellent stuff, my gal. Excellent! Although you might want to get some mousetraps outside the polytunnel nearest the car park. Spotted some droppings. Nibblers you do not need!'

'Hell. No, I don't. Thanks Dan.' Maddie crouched down to give Midge a cuddle. 'I've not seen you for ages.'

'He's getting on a bit now. Doesn't come to work with me as often as he used to.'

Distracted by the rumble of her stomach, reminding her she hadn't eaten since half-five that morning, Maddie stood back up. 'If you two don't mind, I ought to check on everything, but do stay afterwards for a drink if you can.'

Sheba got up the second Maddie was in range of Ivan's stall and came to her side, tail wagging.

'Hello gorgeous.' Maddie gave the Labrador a welcome stroke, enjoying her second dose of canine companionship in the last five minutes.

Perhaps that's the answer. Maybe I should get a dog for company. Definitely a safer bet than a boyfriend.

Maddie looked hungrily at Ivan's cheese stall. Row after row of cheddars, stiltons, white cheeses, ewe's cheese, goat's cheese and alcohol- or fruit-infused cheeses sat before her. Each one begged to be tried.

'Cracker and cheese to keep you going?' Ivan flourished a packet of olive oil and poppy seed water biscuits at her.

'That would be wonderful. Perfect with Jo's coffee.' She toasted Ivan with the takeout cup she was holding as she examined the array of cheeses and chutneys on offer. There were noticeably fewer truckles than there had been when she'd passed by just after opening. 'You'll have to help me, there's too much to choose from.'

Ivan regarded his wares before pouncing on the nearest one. 'If you have Jo's coffee on the go, then this is a good one. Double Devonshire cloth-bound cheese. It's a new twist on a traditional Double Gloucester. Mellow with a slight buttery taste. It will complement the caffeine perfectly.'

'Sounds good.' Sabi came up behind her sister. 'Same for me if you can, Ivan. Assuming it goes with tea too?'

'It'll go with anything you wish, Sabi lass.'

'This tea is for you.' Maddie held out the cup carrier in her hands. 'I was on my way to see how you were all doing with the till, and then on to the grotto.'

'Really well. I've sold loads, and I've had a text from Jemima saying we've had so much trade that they're down to one sack.'

'That's wonderful.'

'Henry was in his element when I left them to it. He's always wanted to be Santa apparently. Who knew!?'

46

Relieved that her sister was willing to take over the role of making sure the stallholders and customers milling round the nursery were happy, Maddie checked on her niece and brother-in-law. She delivered their drinks and took several photographs of them in their elf and Santa costumes, before heading to Jake, who'd been manning the till in Sabi's absence.

Maddie had just served some seed packets to a customer who was already laden with paper bags from the market stalls, when she had a feeling she was being watched.

Ed hovered by the door. 'I have news I thought you'd want to hear. I'll go away as soon as I've told you – if you want me to.'

Glad that there were no new customers demanding her attention, Maddie stared at the till's desk separating them. It felt impossibly wide as she stood there, her eyes not quite daring to meet Ed's in case they gave away how pleased she was to see him. 'News?'

'The application for the access road from the motorway, across the fields opposite The Potting Shed, has been withdrawn.'

'Withdrawn?' Maddie's anxious expression lifted as she

grasped what Ed was saying. 'BIG *aren't* going to build over the road?'

'Nope. Creswell has persuaded them to use the site I found near Junction 25.'

'Near Taunton?'

Maddie fought the urge to run into Ed's arms. 'Is this for real? Not just Creswell saying it?'

'A friend of mine with connections at the planning office confirmed it this morning.'

'Not Jo?'

'Jo told you he used to work for the council?' Ed was stunned. 'I got the impression it was privileged information.' Maddie felt touched that Jo had trusted her.

'It is.' Ed tucked his hands into his black jeans pockets and stood awkwardly, as if not quite knowing what to do now his message was delivered. 'In this case it wasn't Jo, but a contact who still works there.'

Maddie was about to apologise for her overreaction the night before, when a customer came in with a heap of bulb pots and a price tag for a Christmas tree that Jake had already heaved onto their car roof.

Once the customer had left the shop, Maddie dived in before Ed had the chance to speak. 'About last night. I don't really think you only took me out to distract me – even though you did.'

'I didn't mean to make it sound as if you were a favour. I could have bitten my tongue out. I was already struggling with my stupid decision to wait until after today to ask you out. We took so long to get to that point and then... Anyway, I'm sorry.'

'Me too.' Maddie patted the stool next to him. 'Fancy keeping me company for a bit?'

'I would.' Ed moved with a speed that made Maddie giggle. ' If you haven't worked it out already, I'm rather rusty at this dating thing.'

Maddie placed a tentative hand in his. 'I'm not so much rusty as seized up.'

Jake closed the car park's gate with a sense of relief and elation. He'd sold fifteen trees and they were completely out of holly. Hooking his phone from his pocket, he tapped in Petra's number as he headed to the shop.

She answered before the first ring had finished sounding. 'How did it go?'

'It was brilliant. Maddie and Sabi are thrilled. The market was dead popular. Your posters and stuff worked big time.'

'I wish I could have been there.'

'Next time. Ivan has confirmed a New Year revisit. He did well with his cheeses.'

'That's wonderful.' Petra sounded wistful. 'Is there a celebration there later?'

'Just a drink, but actually,' Jake paused, 'I wondered, do you fancy meeting up? Are you up to a trip to the pub? I'd far rather be with you.'

'I would love that. I'm sure I'd have been alright to help today, but Mum put her foot down.'

Surprised to find himself agreeing with Miriam, Jake said, 'It was really full on here all day. You'd have been wiped out.'

'Maybe.'

'And anyway, you need to keep your mum sweet before telling her that you've applied for some gardening apprenticeships.'

'True. I wish we didn't have to wait until January before we find out if we've got one.' Petra sighed. 'Sorry for sounding so dismal. I'm going stir crazy here, that's all. I'm glad there's been so much promo stuff to do for The Potting Shed.'

Jake put his head around the shop door, and, seeing it empty, went in and sat on the stool by the till. 'There will be more soon. Sabi is really hot on that side of things.'

'Be good to have something to do while Mum is holding me hostage.' Petra smiled down the phone. 'We can talk about that tonight. Why don't you come here rather than the pub?'

'There? But your parents...'

'Are going out to dinner.'

Jake sat up straight. 'What time shall I arrive?'

Sabi looked sheepishly at Henry as she opened the boot of their car and piled in three cardboard boxes full of purchases from the market.

'Before you say anything, they are full of gifts, food and drink for Christmas.' She paused. 'Well, apart from this.' She took a refillable flask out of the nearest box. It was rainbow striped and made out of recycled cups. 'Here you go, Jemima. For your smoothies, and to say thank you for being such a great elf today.'

'Thanks Mum!' Jemima clasped the coloured flask to her chest. 'It's been great fun. I hope Auntie Maddie enjoyed it too.' She paused as she looked around. 'Where is she anyway?'

'We ought to be helping Ivan and the others clear up.' Maddie could hear the market stall holders behind them packing up their unsold wares.

'We'll help in a minute.' Keeping hold of her hand, Ed led Maddie into the semi-dismantled Santa Grotto and zipped the door closed after them.

Feeling self-conscious, Maddie followed him to the back of the tunnel. 'Won't they notice we've gone?'

'Everyone is busy, and even if they do, so what? You're the boss. You're allowed to inspect your polytunnels whenever you like.' Reaching out, Ed cupped Maddie's chin in his hands. 'And if I have to wait any longer to kiss you there is no way I'll be able to concentrate enough to help out there anyway.'

'Is that so?' Maddie pressed her body against Ed's.

'You'll never know how hard it has been trying not to hold you every day since I met you.'

'And offered me illicit hot chocolate.'

'What can I say? I'm a sucker for a woman who likes to dunk her biscuits.' Ed stared into the depths of Maddie's hazel eyes. 'If I asked to kiss you, would you refuse me?'

'Ask me.'

'Can I kiss you?'

'What a silly question.'

For the next five minutes all the troubles of The Potting Shed were forgotten.

Cuddled up on the rocking chair together, surrounded by piles of unwrapped festive paper and coils of tinsel, Maddie rested her head on Ed's shoulder. 'What are you doing for Christmas this year?'

'Oh, um, nothing much. I'd normally go to my parents, but they are having a winter holiday this year.'

'Fancy a Potting Shed Christmas? All the veg is home grown, although the rest is courtesy of M&S.'

'Do I get to bring you breakfast in bed?'

'Only if it includes kisses between sips of coffee.'

'I think I can guarantee kisses.' Ed immediately proved his point. 'Is that what you meant?'

'That will do for starters.'

47

The trestle tables had been stacked up and most of the stallholders had gone home. Maddie stood, Ed at her side, between the shop and the polytunnels.

'Are you alright?' Ed took hold of her hand.

'It's so quiet.' Maddie examined the gravel floor. It had been churned up by the constant footfall. 'And yet, this is how it's been for months. Quiet.'

'But not anymore.' Ed let go of her hand and looped his arm around her waist. 'The word that The Potting Shed is still here and that it occasionally hosts the best market in the country will spread.'

'It was wonderful.' Maddie looked over at Elspeth who, ably assisted by Jo, was stacking her few unsold items into straw-lined boxes. 'I just hope we can keep the momentum up.'

'You will. You can.' Ed kissed the top of her head.

'I hope you're right. But for now, I think we ought to help.'

'Anyone seen Ivan?'

Henry held a pad out in front of him. 'Jem's starving, so

I thought I'd order in some takeaway. What do you think, Maddie? Up for a celebratory fried rice and a well-earned drink?'

'Brilliant idea.' Maddie looked around. 'We'll never all fit in my kitchen though.'

'Trestle tables in the former Santa's grotto?' Ed pointed back the way they'd come.

'Perfect.' Suddenly incredibly tired and hungry, Maddie was grateful for someone else making decisions for her. 'Who's staying?'

'Me, Sabi and Jem obviously. I assumed Ed?' Henry made no comment on the obvious change in their relationship as he went on, 'Elspeth, Jo and – is that chap's name Dan?'

'Yes. He's my former boss.' Maddie watched as Dan helped Elspeth fold her reams of purple satin table covers. 'I didn't know he was still here, but I'm glad he is.'

'And, if I can find him, I was going to ask Ivan.' Henry added.

'He's probably taken Sheba for a walk.' Maddie looked back towards Jo and Elspeth. 'We'll need nine chairs. I'm not sure I have that many!'

'Don't worry, we'll work something out.' Turning to Henry, Ed said, 'Once you've ordered, can you give me a hand setting the tables up?'

'Sure. And I expect Jemima will... ah, speak of the devil.'

'I'm no devil, Dad!'

'Sure about that are you?' Henry hugged his daughter to his side. 'Fancy helping us out?'

'Only if there's food involved. I'm...'

'Starving.' Henry rolled his eyes. 'You said. And yes, the helping is in aid of food!'

'In that case,' Jem rubbed her rainbow striped gloves together, 'bring it on!'

'We'll never eat all this!' Maddie surveyed the rows of takeaway boxes that Ed and Henry were spreading across the trestle tables. 'Even if Jake hadn't dashed off to spend the evening with Petra, we'd be struggling.'

'I bet we eat every scrap.' Jem posted a serving spoon into each open pot. 'I'm *so* hungry.'

'Me too, actually.' Maddie kicked her boots off as she sat down on a pile of crates that had been stacked and covered with a clean potato sack to act as a chair. Picking up a fork, she admired the mismatch of cloths that had been thrown over the tables. She wondered how Sabi's inner interior designer was coping with the alarming clash of colours. 'Tuck in, everyone!'

Half-listening to the Christmas music that Henry had put on in the background and half-listening to the happy chatter around her, Maddie surveyed her guests.

Elspeth and Dan were deep in conversation about the possibility of developing a new flavour of honey and the various blossoms that might involve. Jem was chatting to Jo about school, while Ed was asking Sabi and Henry about their future home in Culmstock and the nearby public footpaths.

Ivan's chair was still empty, and although he'd sent a text to Jo saying he'd be there, he hadn't yet arrived. His unoccupied chair brought a film of tears to Maddie's eyes.

I wish you were here, Dad.

Wiping the back of a hand over her face, Maddie put her other hand on Ed's leg.

He was about to ask if she was alright, when the flap of the polytunnel was lifted, and Ivan came in.

'Sorry I'm late everyone, but I was on an important mission.'

Elspeth gave a gentle chuckle. 'Trust you to make it sound as if you're working for MI5, Ivan!'

Maddie leant forward, 'Ivan, am I seeing things, or is your jacket moving?'

'Her name's Florrie.' The market's manager opened the flap of his jacket and revealed a tiny puppy.

'Oh my!' Maddie and Sabi exchanged glances as Ivan balanced the small dog in the palms of his hands.

'She's something of a leftover.'

Maddie looked horrified. 'You make her sound like a crust of toast.'

Ivan gave the puppy a tickle under her chin. 'She's homeless-ish. She's a mongrel. Part Border Collie, and part something unknown – possibly spaniel – the owners aren't sure of anything, other than they can't sell her as a pure breed. The rest of the litter have all found owners, but the breeders are relocating and moving day is tomorrow. I offered to look after Florrie here until I could find her a good home.' He looked to Maddie. 'Elspeth was telling me how much you missed having a dog around the place. You two had a Border Collie when you were little didn't you?'

'Benji, yes, but...' Maddie's words tailed off. She'd

been about to say she couldn't possibly take on a dog as well as the running of The Potting Shed, but one look at the puppy's wagging tail as it sat in Ivan's cupped hands stopped her.

'You *have* to have her, Aunt Maddie!' Jem held her hands out. 'Can I have a cuddle please, Ivan?'

'Of course. Be careful though, lass. Florrie's as light as air but as wriggly as a jumping cracker.'

Maddie dug her hands into her pockets. She knew if she had so much as one stroke she'd be lost. She was already in love with the bundle of black fur, dotted with a half stripe of white on her nose and a ginger flash of shaggier fur on her back legs, a feature that presumably made the owners suspect a spaniel father. 'I don't know, Ivan. She's gorgeous and everything, but training a puppy is lots of work, not to mention expensive. Insurance, vet's bills, and stuff. I'm not sure I'm in a position to—'

'We'll pay.' Sabi ruffled Florrie's head, earning herself a licked finger from the pup. 'But she has to live here. Our new house is not really suitable and…' Her cheeks pinkening, Sabi hurriedly added, 'After all, there's room for her to roam here. It'll be like old times. Benji was a firm favourite with the customers when we were kids.'

Jem held her hands out. 'You *have* to give her a cuddle, Aunt Maddie. She is adorable. We can keep her – can't we?'

'Well, I suppose…'

'I'll help walk her when I'm home at the weekends and in the holidays!'

Helpless in the face of Jem's pleading eyes and Florrie's

tiny wagging tail, Maddie tucked the puppy onto her lap. 'Oh, go on then.'

Florrie had fallen asleep, and the takeaway had almost gone. Conversation had meandered from plans for the nursery, places to walk the new puppy, and on to trying to persuade Elspeth and Dan to talk about how they'd first met – a story about which they were both tight lipped, and merely tapped the sides of their noses knowingly.

As Henry poured the last few drops of champagne from bottles he claimed he just happened to have in the car, Maddie got to her feet.

'Before we go to get some much-needed sleep, I'd like to raise a toast to Ivan, Elspeth, Jo and all the Exmoor Drifters for providing us with such a fabulous market today.'

Her friends murmured in agreement as Maddie chinked her glass with her sister's. 'To The Exmoor Drifters!'

'Just a sip of champagne for you, Jemima.' Sabi smiled as she saw her daughter take a gulp from her glass.

'It's lemonade,' Jemima tutted, as she switched her attention to her aunt. 'Today was great. I loved all the running around to help. Especially being an elf and helping Jo tidy up the van afterwards.'

Jo grinned. 'You are an excellent helper.'

'Not as excellent as your coffee, I bet.' Henry became thoughtful. 'If you could get a van like that here all the time, Maddie, you'd have people flocking back.'

'Funny you should say that.' A shadow of insecurity crossed Jo's face. 'I wondered if I could come back tomorrow? I don't have a gig booked and I did well here today.'

'Hell, yes!' Maddie saw Sabi nodding furiously.

'It'll be quieter tomorrow, but you can come back every day as far as we are concerned.'

Jo raised their glass. 'I can't promise that, as I have some bookings in the diary, but if I'm free, I'll come whatever weekends I can – if you're sure.'

'Oh, they're sure!' Jem speared her last piece of chicken with her fork. 'You sell the best smoothies ever!'

'Thank you, Jo.' Maddie felt herself properly relax for the first time in weeks. 'And while I'm doing thank-yous, I have a few more.

'First I'd like to thank Henry, for being a fabulous Father Christmas.'

'My pleasure. I had so much fun!' Henry raised his glass, 'I'll do it again next year if you'll let me.'

'Consider the gig yours.' Maddie turned to her niece. 'And to Jem for being a fabulous elf, gift-wrapper, tinsel-hoister and all-round helper.'

Jem grinned. 'I had another idea for this place. I thought about a grow your own smoothies thing. You know, grow the fruit and veg, and then make the smoothie.'

'That's' brilliant!' Maddie found herself picturing the recipe cards they could make to accompany the rows of plants to sell.

Jemima waved her fork around in front of her. 'I've got heaps more ideas.'

'Your grandad would be so proud of you.' Suddenly choked, Maddie gave a snoozing Florrie a stroke as she said,

'How about you, me, your mum and a notepad get together for an idea-sharing session after closing tomorrow?'

'Deal!'

Maddie looked from her niece to her sister. 'And thank you, Sab.'

'Me?' Sabi lowered her eyes. 'I might have been useful today, but I almost lost you all this. *Us,* all this.'

'But you didn't. Dad would be so pleased to have us working together.' Maddie gave her sister's hand a squeeze. '*And* you get your dream house. I can't wait to see it. Do you think Miriam would let us have the keys to look round?'

'No problem.' Sabi lifted her fork towards her daughter. 'I'm showing Jemima around on Monday night. Why don't you come too? And you Ed, if you like?'

'As long as you're sure I won't be in the way.'

'You wouldn't.' Sabi smiled.

'Then, thank you.'

'Which brings me to you, Ed.' Emotion threatened to overtake Maddie as she mumbled, 'If it hadn't been for you...'

'You'd never have gone welly walking last night?' Ed grinned.

'Nor would we still have The Potting Shed.'

Sabi agreed, 'Maddie's right. If you hadn't dug out the truth about Creswell and BIG, we could have added to the awful man's fortune, and we'd have lost The Potting Shed.'

As the Willand family echoed Maddie's thanks, Ed reached out to Maddie, smiling at his friends, old and new. 'It was my absolute pleasure, although I have to say, I know it has caused heartache along the way, but I can't help being glad that Leo Creswell was such a toad.'

'You are?' Maddie lowered her glass to the table.

'If he'd been an honest man, I'd never have had so many excuses to visit Maddie.'

Jem wrinkled her nose in distaste. 'You two aren't going to go all soppy, are you?'

'As if we would!' Maddie raised her glass again. 'One last toast. Here's to The Potting Shed, may it grow and grow.'

Acknowledgements

My thanks must go to the team at Aria (Head of Zeus), especially Martina, for being so enthusiastic about *Frost Falls at The Potting Shed*, and the series that is to follow.

Also, to my lovely agent Kiran, of Keane Kataria; many thanks for your patience and wisdom – as always.

To the lovely folk who work at all the garden centres and nurseries I frequent (especially those with coffee shops!) – particularly The Old Well in Willand, Devon, where I've been a regular coffee, scone, and toast consumer for over sixteen years. I've watched it grow from a small garden centre into a huge business – which has retained its family feel. It was The Old Well and its staff (especially the girls in the coffee shop) that formed the inspiration behind The Potting Shed series.

Finally, to my family and friends, who support my nonstop passion for writing with understanding, coffee, chocolate, and kind encouragement.

About the Author

JENNY KANE is the bestselling author of many romantic fiction series. These include the Mill Grange series, Abi's Cornwall series, and the Another Cup series. She has had bestsellers in the Amazon Romance, Contemporary Fiction and Women's Fiction charts and multiple bestsellers. If you enjoy Jenny's writing, then why not follow her author page for updates on all of her new releases!